Cary is, among many things, a former trades assistant, soldier, public servant, cab driver, truck driver, game designer, fishmonger, horticulturalist, and university tutor. He has worked for a coroner, worked a forge, and dug up potatoes. He has spent a long time in the Australian bush and even napped stone tools. He now enjoys putting what he has picked up along the way into writing books.

Cary's hobbies include collecting and reading books (the non-fiction are Dewey decimalised), Tasmanian native plants (particularly the edible ones), and medieval re-creation, and gaming. Over the years he has tutored many people on the use of everything from using shortswords, organisational theory, medieval poetry, rocket launchers, and the sociology of recreation.

Cary was born and raised in Sydney. He met his wife at an Science Fiction Convention while cos-playing and they have continued sharing their interests ever since. They moved to a remote part of the Snowy Mountains where they started their family. They then moved one last time to Tasmania in the mid 80's for the warmer winters and are not likely to ever leave it. You will usually find him looking out of the window beside his computer at a sweeping view of Kunanyi, its range, and its ever-changing weather.

The Complete
Warriors of Vhast Series
published by
IFWG Publishing International

Warriors of Vhast Book 8

Fall of the Adversaries

by
Cary J Lenehan

Fall of the Adversaries

Book 8, Warriors of Vhast

All Rights Reserved

ISBN-13: 978-1-923382-15-2

Copyright ©2025 Cary J Lenehan

Printed in Times and LHF Essendine font types.

I respect and acknowledge the Muwinina people, who are the traditional owners of the Nipaluna land where I reside and write my stories. I give thanks to the Tasmanian Aboriginal people and to elders past, present and future. I acknowledge that they never ceded the land where I reside and indeed fought hard in the only declared War inside Australia.

IFWG Publishing International
Gold Coast

www.ifwgpublishing.com

Foreword

In some ways it does not seem to be so long ago that this started out. In other ways it seems like a lifetime. This is the last book of the **Warriors of Vhast** series. The next series, and concurrent in time, is Struggle for Freehold (three books and complete). Whether it sees the light of day is, I suppose, dependent on sales. Three other series are at various stages of completion and there are many stories on Patreon still coming out.

Although I am pleased to say that every Australian State library seems to now have copies of my books, some in hard copy and some as e-books, I realise that there is still a lot more for me to do. It is not just in writing. For a start we are attempting to obtain funding to employ multi-cultural voice actors to translate the stories into audio-books. Stay tuned on this. We also wish to release the Tarot deck used in the books. We have started exploring the options here.

For the first time, in this book, you will see that there is more than just the one continent. Indeed, what has been the site of the tale so far is revealed, in the accompanying map, as being by far the smallest of the continents of Vhast. It is my goal to get every place mapped, along with most of the plants drawn and animals described. Hopefully, one day, these will get collected along with the recipes and other associated things.

I thank you for reading my books and I hope that I continue to entertain you with my stories. If you have enjoyed what you have read, please keep going, share my world with your friends, and (please) post reviews. You would not believe how important these are to a writer, even a short one of a couple of lines. I also am happy to answer questions if you contact me via my website or by my writer page on Facebook.

Cary J. Lenehan
Nipaluna/Hobart

A cast list and glossary of terms used in this novel can be found from page 311. I advise using them when you start in Vhast.

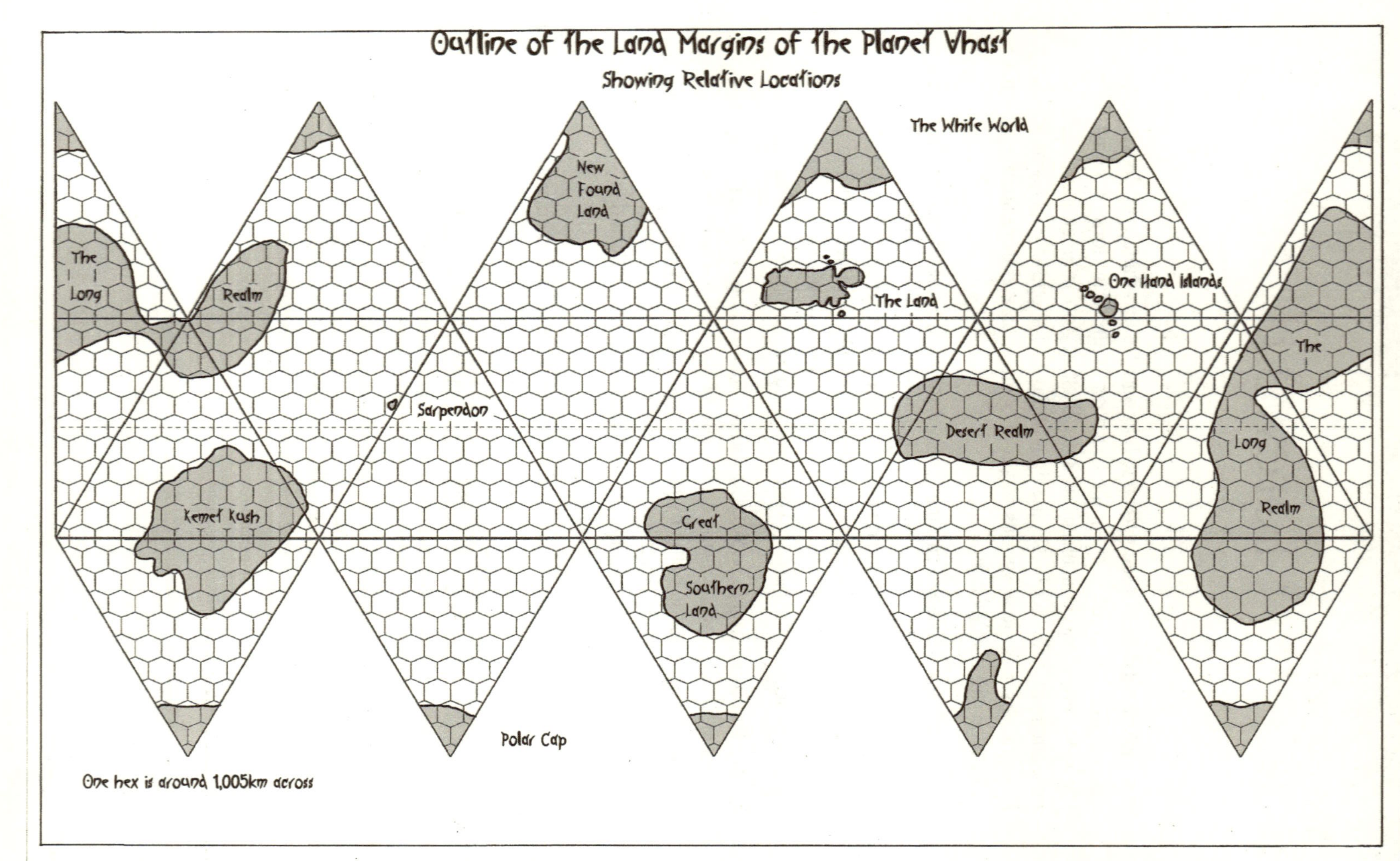

Outline of the Land Margins of the Planet Vhast
Showing Relative Locations
The White World
New Found Land
The Long
Realm
The Land
One Hand Islands
The
Sarpendon
Desert Realm
Long
Kemet Kush
Great
Realm
Southern Land
Polar Cap
One hex is around 1,005km across

How do you fairly thank someone for well over forty years of support and belief? Once again I show gratitude to my wife, Marjorie, for everything. Without her, I am not sure that I would even be here.

Sorry I cannot give much more than this, but at least you get to see the thanks that are due to my friend and beta reader Pip Woodfield for the help that she has also given me over this whole long adventure. She may know some parts of Vhast better than I do (and does not hesitate to remind me of this).

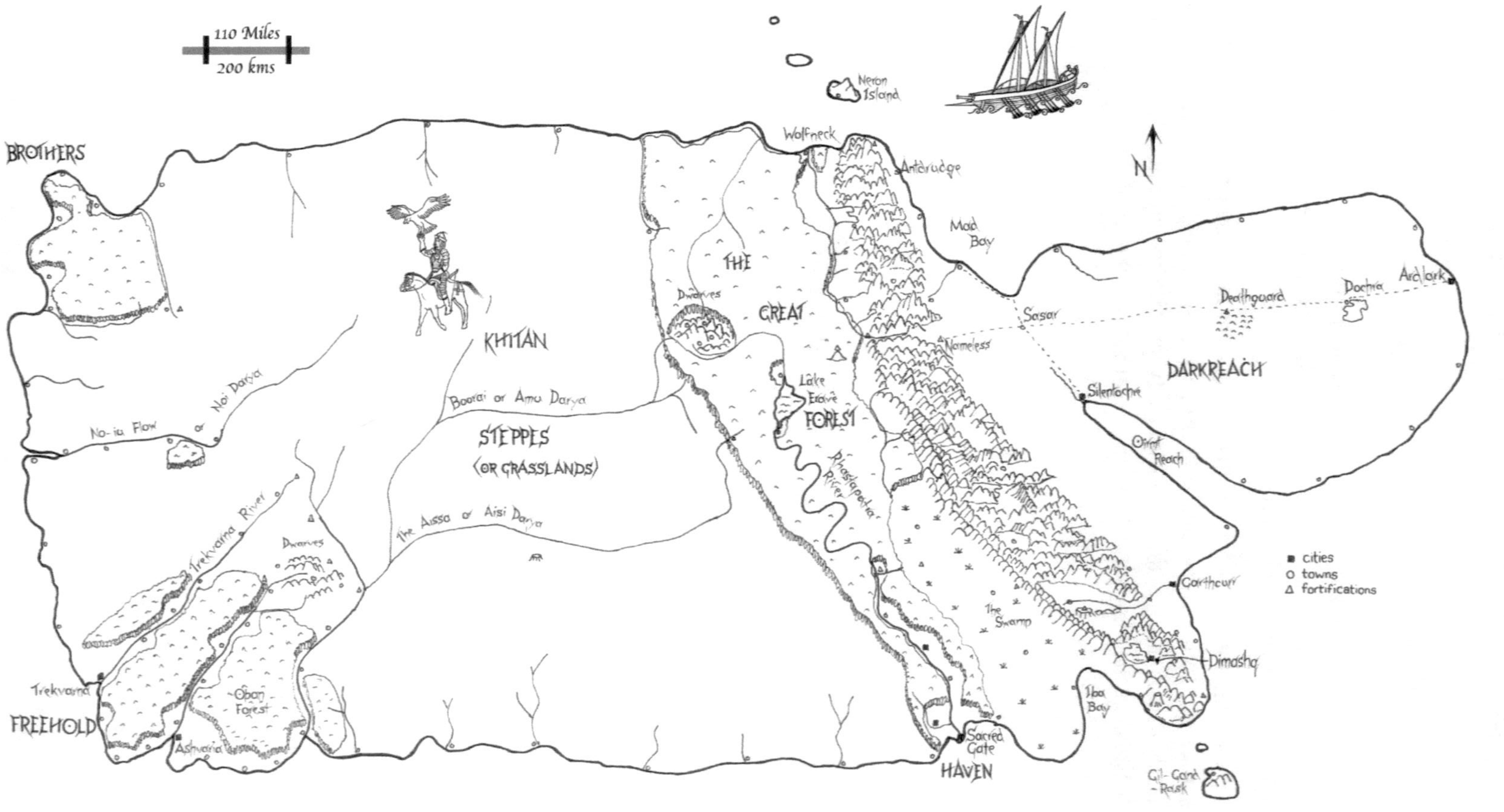

110 Miles
200 kms
N
cities
towns
fortifications
BROTHERS
Neron Island
Wolfneck
Antbridge
Mad Bay
Deathguard
Dochra
Archlark
Sasar
DARKREACH
Silentsight
Orc's Reach
THE GREAT FOREST
Dwarves
KITAN
Nameless
Lake Favre
Boorai or Amu Darya
STEPPES
(OR GRASSLANDS)
No-ia Flow
or Noi Darya
Rhastapetra River
The Aissa or Aisi Darya
Trekvarna River
Dwarves
The Swamp
Corthcurr
Dimashq
Iba Bay
Trekvarna
Oban Forest
FREEHOLD
Ashvaria
Sacred Gate
HAVEN
Gil-Garet - Rausk

From all of the Land they northward come
Called to out to war by sound of drum
Strong Dwarves come out of halls of stone
Mail-clad warriors they are not alone

Men of the coast do eastward stride
Church's horsemen with armour they ride
The Bear-folk of the forest they come out
Stave-like bows and tall axes they tout

The northerners march with shield and spear
Fresh from victory over the Brothers drear
E'en from the east little archers come running
The Empire's green-skins fights not shunning

Ships they gather to carry all on the seas
Some ne'er seen afore with masts like trees
Above the host there be saddles flying high
A tyranny of evil's end it draws on nigh

Armies brought in from lands most remote
After a duel of magic are no longer afloat
Long have dread demon beings held sway
Brought down by allies in a forced affray

*Jottings in quatrains by the Princess Theodora do
Hrothnog done on the way home*

Chapter 1

14th Quinque, the Year of the Water Goat, the Feast Day of Saint Bonaventura

The Mice may have been expecting a nice quiet trip home from the Caliphate, and so it was until they actually arrived back in their valley. Waiting for them there was a visitor with a small but strong escort. Their patience had been wearing thin with the wait. Despite being well looked after by everyone left behind in the village, they were not happy in the slightest with being kept waiting.

Ragnilde, the eldest child of Baron Hrolfr Strongarm of Oldike and the betrothed of Thord, did not like being left to wait in a Human village by the Dwarf who had sought her hand and with no one they regarded as being of suitable status left behind to look after them. At least they and their escort had all found that the beer in Mousehole was good, and Ragnilde was mollified that night as the tale of what had happened in the Caliphate came out.

It was one thing to be kept waiting. It was another thing entirely if the person who had kept you waiting was adding to their legend, and thus to the repute of the family with which you are about to become aligned, by performing heroic deeds that would add additional lustre to the reputation that you are about to share.

Ayesha
15th Quinque, the Feast Day of the Saints Dymphna and Simon

I *have letters from both their Ayatollah and the new Caliph for our captive ghazi, the ones we took prisoner when they were sent to attack our valley, and I am very glad to present them to our prisoners. I was told that in the letters Sayf, Rāfi and Ubāda are told what has happened in the Caliphate and have been ordered to report straight back to Misr al-Mār.*

Ubāda is also given specific instructions to make restitution to Adara for his behaviour, or not even consider returning. He is to contemplate the āyāt on repentance and to put them into effect. I had thought this too lenient until I saw the expressions on the three faces and the looks that they exchanged.

It appears the two older men may already have been expounding on the same theme while they were in the cells, and that Ubāda has come to realise he would not be going back to what he left behind. His life is about to become both much harder and far more ascetic. It may be a while before he is allowed out into the wider world again—that is, if he ever is.

The three quickly agreed and were let out of their cells, and Ubāda was at least man enough to immediately take the first step and go straight away to Adara, who was in the village courtyard, and to apologise to her publicly and very fully. *All can see, from the expression on his face, that this abasement has hurt him, as it was supposed to.* The three had their weapons restored and were sent on their way on foot the next day. *It will be a long walk home for them.*

Astrid the Cat

*W*ithout being aware of what this entailed, Astrid had been flattered to be asked by Thord to act as his closest female relative in the village. She now discovered that one of the duties associated with this was to get the bride-to-be as drunk as she could. She ended up that night with both Ia and Basil holding her hair aside as she emptied herself.

The bride-to-be has an iron constitution and, surprisingly, it is my little Butterfly who was the last girl standing. I lasted well, but she was willing to drink more even when the last of the Dwarves had faded. After all this time of knowing Thord, I should have realised that drinking is a very competitive matter among that race.

I still think Ragnilde looks just like any other young Dwarf, but now we are in the sauna and recovering—that is, if drinking shots in a cloud of steam in the very early morning can count as getting over a drunk—I can see that, despite the hair that almost completely covers her, and the total lack of any apparent breasts, she is very definitely female, as are her entire escort.

Whatever the gift that Ragnilde brought her fiancée was, no one is saying, but the two have announced themselves to be happy and are now to be considered as being officially betrothed. In fact, once this announcement had been made, Ragnilde moved from a good room in the Hall of Mice to Thord's bed in the barracks. He still doesn't have a house of his own. We need to correct that straight away.

Tomorrow the two of them will set out for a visit to Dwarvenholme as Thord again shows off his status to his fiancé. The escort will get to stay behind as they would have to travel by road, but Thord is just able to take Ragnilde on his saddle. We will look over the houses and see what we can do while they are away.

Ariadne

I cautiously experimented with the small oval objects that came from the Adversary's store when we were in Ta'if. As it was, I was not cautious enough and was very nearly killed. The only thing that I could see to set them off, seeing they give no indication of magic, is a small ring on the top that looks like it is meant to be used to pull a pin out of a lever.

I used a rope to pull out the pin, having distanced myself a lot further than I would have needed for setting off a molotail. When I tugged on the rope, something flew away from it—the lever, which I found later. Nothing then seemed to happen for a while.

I waited a bit, before starting to rise to check why nothing was happening, when the whole thing exploded like the head of a war rocket. It did not belch flame, but pieces of metal flew all around; I was blown off my feet and had to quickly drink some potion, and ended up having to get Lakshmi to pick several small pieces of metal out of my skin.

I then tried another one, from a greater distance this time, and counted slowly to five before it blew up. I think I like these things. You want to be a long way from them when they go off, but they would be good to drop from my saddle. They are also small enough that I could carry the whole box safely with me in pouches and in my saddle bags. Now, how do I get more of them?

I need to arrange for Stefan to make me some—I think four—special pouches to fit on my belt, each holding just one. I can carry them, along with my Thunderer and its little boxes of projectiles, all the time, just as others carry a sword or a bow. I have even thought of a few ways to make them into a trap, just as Astrid did with the molotail in the Swamp. It is a pity that I only have fifty of them...well, forty-eight of them now.

While Stefan is making me new pouches, I will see if I can get my Princess to turn my Thunderer around itself. I want it to fit into my left hand, and I want to be able to use it more easily, without having to use my right to reach the little lever that makes it discharge and the button that lets me change the little metal box holding the projectiles.

Theodora

*A*yesha *is dealing with the ghazi, so the problem waiting for me is the other captive, Virginia, and her nurse, Ursula. Despite what her mistress wants, Ursula still insists on trying to be of help around the village. It seems Virginia is the exact opposite in every conceivable way.*

Several times the spoilt chit has attempted escape, and apparently she even attacked poor Lamentations and tried to steal the gate release from her when she was on guard on the roof one day. Lamentations has great potential as a mage and she is learning to use a bow, but she is neither large nor strong. What is more, she is not yet skilled in any arms at all, and it was only the surprise arrival of her sister-wife with Kaf that enabled the two of them to overcome Virginia.

Her punishment has been held in abeyance for our return. Once I heard the tale, I inadvertently looked at Astrid before I spoke to pronounce a sentence. The girl suddenly realised what was about to happen to her and she tried to run. It did her no good, particularly in that stupid dress she wears. We do wear long puddle dresses in Darkreach, but only for formal events. No one moves at more than a slow walk in those, nor is anyone able to.

Astrid quickly caught her and carried her over to the veranda of the hall under one arm. There, she was immediately put across a knee and spanked while Astrid loudly told everyone that she was not an evil person, nor even really an adult, she was only a very naughty child who would be treated as such every time she misbehaved. She was then locked in the now vacant cells to think about her behaviour.

The indignity of her treatment, as if she were merely a naughty infant who knew no better, I have decided will be more of a punishment than the actual spanking. Despite Ursula's request, I have not allowed her to be locked in with her charge and she was forbidden to stay with, or even visit, the spoilt young girl except with a meal. Despite, or perhaps because of this ban, even I can see that Ursula is almost immediately happier.

Now I sit in my house, in my study, thinking. Why cannot Virginia be more like Guy? They both come from the same set of nobles and yet they are very different from each other as people. She has no control and no purpose, and will suddenly give way to the impulse of the moment. Virginia is only a wilful and stubborn child.

She was mulling over this when she realised something and was appalled. *The girl is behaving just as I did for two hands of years after my twentieth birthday, except that no one in the Palace spanked me, or even tried to take me in hand. There was no Astrid for me. That was when I was chasing in the Ludos after the criminals in the Arena to take them to bed. It was when I was refusing to learn anything at all. I was the one who was the spoilt child then.* Her cheeks began to burn at the memory.

For many years my nurse and the servants had to endure the same treatment that Ursula is enduring now. My behaviour has slowly changed, but it was really not until I left Darkreach that I have gotten over this time in my life. Even my decision, taken on an impulse, to first make love to my Rani was a part of it.

It has taken me a hundred years to grow up. In memory of this her cheeks burned even hotter with shame, even though she had been born over a century before when The Burning was still happening.

Rani came into the room. "Why are you all red? What is wrong?"

Theodora just shook her head and looked away.

"Nothing, it is just an embarrassing memory." *I am not going to admit a single bit of the thought that has occurred to me, not even to my husband. I think that, for my soul and to purge it from my system, my Confessor must hear, but he is the only person who will. I am mortified by what I have just realised. At least I understand Virginia better. For far too long, I was her.*

Astrid the Cat
16th Quinque, the First day of Easter

As soon as Thord and Ragnilde had left the village, the Mice swung into a frenzy of activity on his behalf. *There are still plenty of houses left vacant and we have decided that it was not suitable for a soon-to-be-married couple to live in the austerity of the barracks. For a start, even for Dwarves, the beds are regarded as being too small and too hard to be truly comfortable.*

Her escort have agreed and are helping, even if most of them prefer to work with metal and stone rather than wood. Almost all of the Mice are also helping in one way or another as one of the spare houses is being made liveable and furnished as well as we can on such short notice. It is the one directly beside the village wall, and it has a good cliff above it. It even has room to expand back into the cliff behind it if they wish.

Goditha had so much help with the stonework from Dwarves, who were fascinated by her magical tools, that the building ended up as the most solidly repaired of all the structures in the village. By the time the two had returned the work was complete and their clothes and possessions had been moved across.

Yabaribaykus ogulin Tatlikayisia

It has been easy to settle into this village. I am fascinated with this world that is so different to mine. Back in ugrakden çok kabilu, at least in our tribal area, we Gulyabani are still largely hunted and killed by the Duvaryuz and our lands are taken. I have not been able to visit them, but apparently the tribes hold hard to their land here.

In this Mousehole I have found several different races living together and a church that does not seem to distinguish by race at all. I have even been for a visit to Dhargev to talk to some of the Hobs in their valley. Now that I am back, I am applying myself to learn as much as I can before heading back to my homeland when next the River Dragon *goes that way.*

I am continuing to work with this Latin, and now also Greek, but I am also keen to learn how to smelt and work metal. It is a skill that we Gulyabani entirely lack and, unless we steal them, all of our tools and weapons are made of stone, bone or wood. This leaves us at a big disadvantage in the continued contest over our homeland.

I am determined to change this imbalance. I must spend as much time as I can in this forge *place doing all of the learning that I can. I must admit that I may be pushing myself too hard at times. Last night was not the first time I had to be woken after falling asleep after my meal and so sent to this* bed *place to sleep.*

Rani Rai
17th Quinque, the Feast of Anastasi, the second day of Easter

*S*itting in her study and looking down the valley towards the gate, Rani lost herself in thought. *The question now arises of what to do next. There is still at least one of the so-called Masters around somewhere and five of the*

Adversaries. Will they be as powerful as they once were when they are missing one of their number? Do they even realise he is gone yet?

What was that word Dobun used to describe something shamen do to add their power together when they are communing with each other? Gestalt, that was it. Would their gestalt be weakened? After Easter is over we will have to sit down and consult our various oracles. I am sure we gain much in wisdom by adding together what we each see.

Now, with the addition of Ia and her crystal ball, we will be seeking four readings from different media. It should make for far greater accuracy of prediction and is a chance that few decision makers have available to them. It seems that we also need to look at our library. Ruth has been going through the books while we were away and she says there are things that she wants to discuss with others.

Rani sighed. *I am still avoiding direct contact with Sharan… Or they are avoiding contact with us… It is not quite the same thing. As well, we still have the mystery of the Bear People. What role do they play in all of this? They openly said that there was a prophecy connecting them and us, but they did not seem eager to either bring it around or even to say what it is.*

It must be nice to be as simple and uncluttered as Astrid. Beyond food and drink, sex and killing, there is not a lot that seems to concern the woman. I have not seen either her or Ia from my window today and so they are probably still in their shared bed. I wish that I was. Theodear got up early and has disappeared into her study again. It seems that she has something on her mind.

Astrid

As she lay in bed and thought about the slain Adversary, Astrid looked from the plastered ceiling to the warm body beside her. Lying there was Ia, still asleep. She slept naked, and was only partially covered by the furs. One of her was hanging over the side of the bed. The other had crept across the sheets to rest between Astrid's legs.

She does the same when it is Basil who is beside her. It is as if her body is constantly seeking some sort of a reassurance at the most basic level. When she wakes up at night with the sort of dreams that Parminder has, she needs the same manner of soothing from one or the other of us.

Astrid idly stroked her hair and looked at her pretty face as she lay there. *I still don't love my little Butterfly, at least not in the same way that I love Basil, but she is good to be with and certainly makes delicious loving. She really does know how to please a girl. I am at least fond of her as a warm friend and am more than happy to allow Ia to show her passion.*

*The young girl's life has not been a good one until recently and she is owed some happiness, and it is easy and—*Astrid smiled at the thought*—indeed a pleasure for me and Basil to provide it. Olympias was right. My husband has adapted to his having two wives very quickly, even if being properly attentive to both of us is hard work for him sometimes.*

Ia had been up early to greet the dawn and had come back into their bed with cold feet to be warmed up. *Mousehole in autumn is a lot cooler than Rising Mud was. Maeve is lying curled up asleep on the foot of the bed and from the outer rooms I can hear Sin with her work cut out looking after the children.*

Georgiou and the Kitten are over two years old now and are experimenting with using words, and far too many of them are variants, in various of the many languages that we use in the village, on the word "no". What we would do without the girl in the house I do not know. She is far more patient with the children than I am, and I am their mother.

On returning to the bed Ia had tried to use Basil to warm her cold feet. *Basil refused that idea. He always has. He took it for a hint that it was time to get out of bed. He has already had his breakfast and gone to get ready to take some classes. We have elected to just be lazy until I have to get out of bed myself to take my first class.*

She had gestured at her body when she said that to Basil. *I asked what was the point of spoiling my fair skin collecting this many scars if I do not earn a reward with them, even such a slight reward as being able to lazily lie in bed occasionally.* Empty Kaf cups stood on a small table beside the bed and Sin had fetched some pastries from Nathanael, but now they were all gone as well.

Reluctantly, Astrid dragged her mind from the happy and domestic back to her previous thoughts of the past and future. *Theodora agrees with me as to why Maarshtrin died so easily. But I have not mentioned to her the one thing that I seem to be the only one to notice. I think that Maarshtrin may very well have been what Hrothnog once was and is no longer. At least I hope that he is no longer like that. As much as I dread the idea, I need to ask him.*

He has, apparently, done a lot more to himself than just change his name to something that sounds very different, even if the spelling is very similar in some tongues. He said that he had chosen to take a different path. There were no tales I can find about hordes of missing girls in Ardlark, and I even found out all about Theodora's ancestor, the once-Empress and now Saint Kassiopeia, from over three thousand years ago. It has to be the case that he has not lied to me.

Perhaps it was that change that has prompted him to become a stronger mage than Maarshtrin, or it may be that it was the other way around. I have heard tales, and indeed Butterfly has confirmed them, of evil Wiccans who use human sacrifice as a part of their attempts to boost their power. Perhaps the other Adversaries were even weaker once and he was already the strongest of them.

It seems that I am already learning some of the things he refused to tell me in Ardlark. He said I might discover some of them myself. I am not sure why he refused, but I have a good reason for not telling Basil everything. It is quite likely he has a good reason for not being as open as I want with me, as well.

Astrid sighed. *For the present my job is just to kill the Adversaries so that our family's children will be safe. I can let the Princesses worry about the details. Enough of this thinking, though. I want to enjoy the rest of the morning.* She rolled over and, leaning on an elbow, gently took a nipple of the sleeping girl beside her in her mouth. *I think that I know one good way to do that.* Her other hand went down under the blanket.

Rani

Ruth *has us Princesses, and, for some reason, Astrid and her little witch girl, all here now. It seems there are more things in the books to learn from.* "According to what Simon of Richfield wrote," said Ruth "the island north of Skrice was called Ovington." Rani and Theodora looked at each other. *So? We found that out for ourselves. What is special about it? My wife raises her eyebrow at me. She must think the same.*

"It is, according to Simon and the people of Wolfneck and of Skrice, uninhabited." *Now she is looking at Astrid.*

"Of course it is," Astrid said. "It is far too close to Arnflorst and it is also windswept and bare. No one can grow anything much there and there are almost no animals living on it…although no one knows why… Apart from the seabirds, a few wild sheep and goats are all that are ever seen. If there were any people there we would all know about them, unless they were powerful enough to hide from everyone, and how likely is that?"

"What did you say when you last came back here from visiting Darkreach and its Emperor?" asked Ruth archly. "Even Hrothnog, the most powerful mage that we know of, is saying that there are many areas on Vhast that he cannot see into with all of his spells."

Ganesh, come and softly whisper words of wisdom and advice in my ear. "You mean that this island is where the Adversaries are?" asked Rani. "It isn't Arnflorst?"

Ruth shook her head. "Let me read you something," she said. "This is from a book, but I do not know the author and I do not know how old it is. It was one of the many part-books that we brought back from Dwarvenholme. We only really have a few pages of it and most of the words cannot be made out. Now listen…"

She has put on the wire-and-glass device she got from somewhere in Ardlark that covers her eyes when she reads. She says that she finds it much easier to read when she wears it and she no longer gets headaches. She then pulled out a tattered and very faded volume with a thin slip of leather marking a place between the pages. She opened the book and took out a scrap of paper.

"The original is in Old Speech, but in the characters that Astrid's people use, and I tried to do what she does and use the sounds of the letters to make the words, rather than what we use them for. I then tried different languages to see what the sounds might correspond to. I have been doing this with several of our old written things, but this is the only one that it has worked on so far as it is a very slow job and I have been busy.

"It may be my pronunciation that is the problem and I will get Astrid to check, but this is what I think it says." She looked down at her piece of paper, which had several rows of different script on it, one written under the other. "It says: 'Living on the island north of there, and south of the island we do not name, are the clan of shape-changers that are called *merrow*'."

She interrupted herself by looking up: "I had never heard that word before, but that is what it looks like." She then looked down again and continued reading. "'They are by reputation powerful wielders of magic who hide themselves and their people away from the evil that lives beside them. According to…' and the next few lines are lost and then it says: 'so you must have a shapeshifter of the mother with you to talk to them.'

"There are only a few more words here and there that I can make out. One is 'key' and another phrase is 'end of cycle' and a little later 'found'." She handed the original and her notes to Astrid as she pointed at the page. "I have no idea if these last words have any importance."

"I might disagree on how a few parts of the words sound, but you have translated them down fairly well. If the sounds mean that in Old Speech, then it is close enough," Astrid said.

Ruth looked at the Princesses. "I think we need to talk to these people before we fight the Adversaries on their island…and we need help to do so." She turned to Ia now. "I presume that saying 'of the mother' means that the skin-changer must be a Wiccan. That means the important question, then, is: are you a shapeshifter?" Ia shook her head. "Do you know of any who live in the Swamp?" she asked, a plaintive tone in her voice.

Ia thought for a while. "Not among the Free," she said. Ruth's face fell. "But that does not matter," she said. "There are many more around that are not among the Free. Just ask among the Bear People. Some of their priests are druids but, more importantly for us, most of their priests and priestesses are Wiccan.

"They could send many skin-changers along," she continued. "That is if you could talk them into coming, but how you will get them to leave their forest I do not know. They almost never leave it under any circumstances, and when they do it is only to come to our area or, at the most, I believe that some will sometimes travel to the shores of Lake Erave."

"They will leave their land for this," said Rani. *Now I know the answer. Thank you, Ganesh.* "We have not made it widely known, but they have told us there is a prophecy among their people that their isolation would come to an end and that we would be the ones who would end it for them." *The other three are looking at me and still waiting for more.*

"They have told us little more than that," she said. "We were told we were the prophesied ones who would end their hiding away from the rest of the world, but that is all they have said about our role. We have puzzled over how, and even why, we would end their time apart. Now it seems that we know."

"It seems very important that we take at least some of their priests or priestesses with us when we go north. I suppose we need to do it before we attack, but how far ahead I do not know. I think we should add that to what we seek when we consider the path ahead of us later on."

Basil Akritas
18th Quinque, it is the Feast of Kyriaki tou Pascha

Carausius has again missed Guk, but it is good to see him, Candidas, and the rest of them back safely with the three carts and the horses he promised. He is happy with the experiment of using carts. The road proved to be hard, but good enough, and so the packhorses will be staying with us. We will agist them here until Guk next comes through and pays for them.

Apparently Karas and Festus have tools on the carts and had to repair some of the bad spots on the road as they went along. They are grumbling over having to do such menial work instead of being guards but Carausius has chided them, in return, about how much hard fighting they'd had to do each trip to get him here safely. The two are grinning at each other as soon as his back is turned, of course. They know how right he is and, after all, they are still getting paid as guards and not as trail workers.

Rani

*O*ur trader's load is made up of a lot of metal as well as a full load of roofing slate and things that people had ordered through him from the makers in Ardlark, and things that Guk wanted for his other customers, the Dwarves, the Hobs and the Bear People. At least this time he has come with orders for things from us as well.*

For a start our shipment of Gasparin had found favour in Dochra and the man there wants more, as much as they can give him. He has even sent some of his hot hopper salamis for us to taste. I will never get used to salami, but my wife thinks that they are good and apparently the markets in Ardlark think so as well.

To the delight of the unmarried girls and to show that the unique circumstances of our valley are not forgotten, he has also brought another three men from Ardlark with him. The first two men are Libanius Monomakhos and Dionysios Kydones. They are both younger sons of farmers and neither from an especially poor background. However, both come from large families. Like Stefan and Arthur, they say that they are unlikely to ever be able to afford to marry.

It seems that the legend of Mousehole and its women is proving to still have the power to pull some men out of their accustomed path. The two were handed over to the rest of the growing farming and herding community of the valley to discover what skills they had and where they would best fit in.

The third man seems very familiar to Basil. He is not all that old but he calls himself Marianus Gerontas, or Marianus the Old. "My name, it is a joke," the man said in a resigned fashion. "I am less than forty years old. Marianus the Young had joined our Corps the year after me, but it is a joke that I have been stuck with since I was sixteen.

"I have been in the Antikataskopeía all of my life," he said to the Princesses. "Most recently I have served under Procopia Ampelina, who Basil used to also serve under, and who his sister now knows very well." *All eyes are looking at Olympias at that stage, and there are a few raised eyebrows around the room.*

I guess that not everyone knew before now. "I have never been posted in one place long enough to find a woman for more than a temporary relationship. I rose to being a Starşiyrang, but I am not likely to be able to rise any higher. Now I want to settle down somewhere and find a woman who wants children and a stable man.

"I am not very romantic, but there may be someone here who will accept me. Apart from the skills that I learnt in the Antikataskopeía, I am afraid that I have little else to commend me. It is not what I have done before, but I am willing to learn to herd sheep if that is what you need." *I think that a shepherd is the last thing we need at present, if what I have been told is right.*

"We need you as you are," said Rani. "In fact, I wish there were two or three of you. We have a factory in Sharan, Haven, and Basil has told us that it needs someone like you to be there all the time. We have a ship that lacks someone with your background as well. The ship may be the more important job at present, but I am not sure of that. Our supercargo tries, but she is too busy doing her real job…so if Olympias agrees…"—*Olympias is already nodding eagerly. I thought that she would be pleased, she has already spoken to us about looking for someone to take on that role.* "And lest you think that you will be away from all the women, there are six unmarried girls on board and no unmarried men. We will make no guarantees to you, but one of them may be agreeable."

"In that case, if you do not mind and do need more people," said Marianus, "I know of a couple of other men and women who are like me. In fact"—he turned to Basil—"Aella Sgoura and Elias…you remember them…they have been married for years but they wanted to stop being posted all over Darkreach, sometimes apart, and to settle down and start a family." He turned back to the Princesses. "With your connections, and those of the Tribune, it should be easy to get them transferred. They are both originally from Garthcurr, if I remember rightly, and should like the heat of Haven. I will write, if I may, and the Tribune might countersign my letter. It should help them get free of other duties."

Rani and Theodora quickly looked at Basil who, after a brief moment of thought, was nodding, and agreed. *It is obvious that having a settled and experienced couple to take charge of our site security could be exactly what we need in Sharan. Once they are sure of our building they can begin a serious clean up, even if they have to recruit locals and train them to help.*

Lakshmi Pitt

The midwife smiled in satisfaction. *It matters not how much conflict occurs and to what extent the Mice may be involved in the great events of The Land, the normal things of life still keep happening. Now Kalliope has given birth to her twin daughters, Berenike and Iris.*

Kalliope was terrified and had her sisters-in-law holding each of her hands, but Fear again has proved her worth and alerted everyone that one of the girls was around the wrong way. Iris needed to be turned around. This time, seeing how far she has come with her skill since she first revealed it, Danelis was brought in to see if she could use just her mind to turn the baby in the womb. I hear that is what they do in Darkreach, after all.

While Fear listened and everyone watched fascinated, Danelis moved her hands slowly over Kalliope's stomach and, under them, the bump that was Iris followed her hands around, for all the world just like a kitten under a blanket, until the girl and the woman pronounced themselves both to be happy and the birth could proceed. Danelis has already learnt how to use her mind to close off any bleeding that she could see; now it seems that she has yet another tool in her learning of physiking.

Chapter II

Theodora
19th Quinque

Our return to a more normal life is almost complete. I have been "asked" by Ruth to come to the school and to show an interest in what the children are learning. It seems that we are expecting some more children from around the lake at the school already and perhaps, on her next trip there, Shilpa thinks some will come up from the south coast as well. Now Ruth wants me to see how far her first class has come.

It seems that Guk has agreed to bringing another of Zumruud's sisters along to join her…and Zumruud herself, to her delight it seems, will be staying at least until she is twelve and perhaps until a marriage is arranged for her. Guk had apparently refused to say any more when he came while we were away, but it appears that his senior wife is already engaged in negotiations on that point, even if such an event is still a year or more off. He apparently was looking very smug over the matter.

Astrid must have heard the same. She wondered to me if Zumruud might be in line to be the first wife to Nacibdamiir. After all, the chief is still a young man and not only is not yet married, but still even had his youth name. I think that Guk could also have a priest in mind. He could be for the second daughter, though. Time will tell, I suppose.

It seems that Guk is very pleased with his daughter. The bride price that she would attract would be very large and is growing each time that she pays a visit home and shows off what she has learnt. Whoever marries her will be gaining an asset who will be able to help them run anything they are involved in.

Theodora got to spend most of the day watching the children recite and show off their skills. For her, the most memorable part of the day was watching the

Freehold noble, Guy, attempting to teach the near-naked Hob girl, Zumruud, how to perform a proper curtsey.

Such activity is new to all of them. They receive training in languages and sciences, arts and arms, in fitness and in trades, so Guy has decided that all of the children need to be able to handle themselves with the manners and graces of a courtier as well. Ruth approves of this. She would, seeing that she wants her students to be rulers themselves, and matters such as courtesy and social skills are now a part of their regular lessons.

It takes me back to my first deportment lessons in Ardlark. However, the children here are far better behaved than my cohort and I were. We were easily bored and misbehaved most of the time. I will be doing penance over that Confession for a long time to come. At least this lot get to play—after all, Ruth insists on it—but the children do work hard. It seems that they often get to go to sleep fairly late.

Theodora

Carausius has left to return to Ardlark with a load, not only of the produce of Mousehole, but also turquoise and garnets from Dhargev, other gems from Dwarvenholme and mead, spilk, fine wool and cheese from the Bear People. There are even herbs and potions from both areas that Guk has left here for him to sell on.

Most is on consignment and it is a valuable load that he is returning with from our area, goods whose like, and indeed volume, will not have been openly seen in Darkreach for quite some time. Although they all made light of the matter earlier, his guards were on a state of high alert when they left, and they had made sure to spend a lot of their time in the village practising with some of the people who could teach them more.

The picks and shovels are put away until the next trip out and their shields are on their backs and their bows are in their hands and strung. Candidas and Theodora Ligo, driving the carts, have weapons at hand as well. I am sure that they will be at their most alert on the way back. At least it should be obvious from the road they are on that they are from here, and surely word about us is spreading.

We all regard it as very unlikely that any raiders or bandits, even the Wild Tribes of Goblins or the northern Hobs, would dare to interfere with something coming from Mousehole, but you never know. For extra protection I have directed that our saddles keep a watch around him until they are at Mouthguard anyway.

Tonight, though, we forget about our visitors. We have put the time aside to look at the omens that point to what lies ahead. I am sure, with the death of one Adversary already, that we are possibly entering the final stages of our battle, but you never can be sure.

The main question for us is to be: is there anything else to do first or do we just launch an attack on the place that we have presumed is the base for the Adversaries, the Shunned Isle of Arnflorst? We are fairly sure that this is the place we seek, but for all we know the place we end up attacking may be Zim Island, or yet another island somewhere else on the seas. Tonight we should find the answer to that.

Chapter III

Basil
the night of 19ᵗʰ Quinque

It seems that we started our adventure with prophesies. Will tonight end them? We shall see, now that we have eaten and all the prayers and services have been held. We are all gathering in the hall. We even have Virginia, with Puss beside her to keep her quiet and still, out of her cell. It is so different to that night under the tavern in Evilhalt.

Around the seated people, sleeping on the floor, are small bundles of young children in baskets or lying on heaped blankets. Other infants are being breastfed. No one wants to stay with the children in the houses and perhaps miss what is revealed. It is a sign of how the village has changed that this formerly childless and unhappy place now has nearly as many children of different ages present as there are adults.

This might be the last time that as momentous a set of auguries is sought in Mousehole. Those who had not seen such before have been told what will happen, and Ragnilde and her escort, in particular, are riveted. They have realised that they are about to see a part of the ongoing legend unfurl in front of them. This will be something for them to talk about all their lives, hopefully.

Rani stood and told everyone what they knew and what they suspected. She laid out all of the options she had thought of. "However," she said, "we cannot be sure that this is all there is. There are still so many things we do not know. For instance, we know that there was a contact for the Masters among the clans of the Northern Waste. Do we perhaps need to go there first?

"We also know that Baron Toppuddle was one of their people. Are there more of them in Freehold we have to deal with first, as we had to before we could get into the Caliphate?" *Astrid is having to silence Virginia's attempt to interject there with a glare and a finger to the lips. Rani has noticed and now stares directly at Virginia.*

"Do we need to look towards the Newfoundland first? Do we need to crush the Adversaries' people there?" *Virginia is now looking quite alarmed at that question. She has an odd look on her face. Does she know more about what is happening there than she has let on?* Rani looked further around the room and continued. "Are there other areas outside The Land that we must investigate?

"Accordingly, we have decided to do what we normally do and to consult our various means of divination. I will seek my information first and Bianca will shuffle for me. Then Bishop Christopher will lead the Christians in prayer and go on to consult their holy book. Ia has already prepared herself, so she will then look into her ball." *Our little witch has been very nervous about that part.*

"Lastly," Rani continued, "Dobun has said I can tell you he will be going, along with the rest of the Horse, to light a fire and walk in the Spirit World. He will tell us tomorrow what he discovers there that can be told. That means we will have four prophesies, four different people to seek the truth for us, all of whom have shown themselves to have power in this regard."

She looked around again. "Let us start," she said, and she handed her deck of cards to Bianca, who stood near a small table in the middle of the room and began to shuffle and cut them. Rani looked around the room again. "I would like everyone to concentrate on what I have said and to keep your minds open as to outcomes," she said.

Bianca took her time, but eventually she handed the cards to Rani and went to where her husband had a seat held for her.

Rani slowly laid out four cards and then, after a pause during which the tension in the room was so high it was doubtful anyone drew breath, she began to turn them over. The first card was the card of the Major Arcana that is called 'Justice'. *We have seen that one before in our readings. It shows a robed and blindfolded woman who holds in one hand a jeweller's scale and in the other a sword with an owl flying above.* "Justice," intoned Rani, as if they were seeing it for the first time. *Her voice is very different to her normal one whenever she does this.*

The second card we have seen just recently. It is the reversed card of the Five of Talents. It shows two coins on each side of the card with a fifth sitting in the base. In between there is a depiction of the Hindu goddess Lakshmi as a four-armed woman dressed in a sari and wearing a crown as she stands under a leafless tree with bare roots. As usual, there is writing in each corner. "The Five of Talents reversed," announced Rani portentously.

Interesting. We have also seen the third before and in this position. It is the Six of Swords, a sheaf of six swords and above them is an armsman striding out set for war, with his weapons, and travelling with a backpack. Again there are words written in the four corners of the card. "The six of Swords," she said in the same voice.

The fourth card is new. I am not the only one to realise this, from the murmurs around us. He looked carefully at it. *It shows seven armoured people, I think four men and three women, and each has a sword in their hand pointing to the top centre of the card where there are two dice; one shows three pips uppermost and the other four. Once again there are words in the corners.* "The Seven of Swords," said Rani.

She paused and held her hands above the cards for a while before speaking again. "Justice, called the eighth card of the Major Arcana, but actually the ninth, as we know, tells us that right will prevail over wrong and evil will be vanquished and feel retribution. If in the position of the Enquirer, as it is, it means that the enquirer, in this case us, is the chosen tool of Justice. We know we are that tool, and I would have been almost surprised not to have seen this card here."

She paused as she moved to look down at the next card. "We last saw the Five of Talents in the position of being our result. Now it stands as our history. It is normally unusual to see this happen with a reading, but when it does it gives great certainty to what you see in front of you. We now know that our recent forays have enabled us to reverse a difficult situation, and that we have seen a gradual improvement and have had encouraging news as a result of this."

She is taking her time over the next. "One difficulty of using only four cards is that there is not a lot of precision in the reading. I hope that our other seers will add that precision as this reading does not give it.

"The Six of Swords and its words of 'courage' and 'travel' have the obvious meanings of long and often difficult travel associated with warfare coming at the end of it, and perhaps even before. Of course, we'd already predicted that, and unfortunately, the card gives us no guidance as to either direction or target.

"What we do know," she said, pointing at the last card, "is that it is not our last set of battles. The Seven of Swords has in the top corners the words 'fiþmelçmtõ' and 'tralçti cĩarĩn'. These mean 'fortitude' and 'hope' in Old Speech. This card talks of a favourable and perhaps lucky turn of events that will lend hope for future success. It tells us that we need to show strength, but still be vigilant.

"What we have is not a card of final resolution. It tells us, instead, that what we do now will lead to yet another battle. Even though I have no grounds for it, I feel it will be the final one. However, this battle, and the events that lead up to it, are not covered by what this set of cards indicates to us. I have a feeling, but only a feeling, that this may be the penultimate reading that we will see before our geas is finished."

She stopped and sighed and looked around before speaking again. "While the omens are good from these cards, they are very imprecise in their guidance… If we do not achieve more clarity with the rest of our prognostications, then I think that I will need to look at trying to perform another and more detailed reading tomorrow night."

Now we all shuffle around and it is our Bishop's turn. Christopher first led the Christians in prayer and then asked for guidance in what they found. Then, with his eyes closed, he allowed Bianca's Bible to open flat. Slowly he put his finger down onto a page. Only then did he open his eyes and look down and consider what he had found.

"I am reading from the Book of Micah, Chapter Five and Verse Nine. It says: 'Thine hand shall be lifted up upon thy adversaries and all thine enemies shall be cut off.' Amen." He raised his head and addressed everyone.

"Once again, we lack a specific direction. What we have here is an instruction to act and we are even directed specifically against the Adversaries." He paused and thought "It is almost as if we are being told to act as we are inclined…but I do note that it said…"—and he sought the verse again— "'thine enemies shall be cut off.'"

He paused and stroked his growing beard. "I have a thought that I will talk about after we have heard from Ia and what she sees in her ball… Come up, dear… Do not be nervous…" *Our little Butterfly is obviously very anxious about what she is about to do in front of all these people and she has nearly dropped her ball. Astrid is helping her up and has nodded at me. I think that means I need to move to sit beside Virginia.*

Christopher patted the seat he had vacated and Ia took the seat and glanced around. *Over fifty people have only one place to look and, unlike Puss, the Butterfly is not comfortable being the centre of attention. She still thinks that she should only look at these things privately. Her pupils have expanded to take up the whole iris of her eyes. How much extra hashish has she taken to be sure in what she sees?*

She is fumbling as she sets her ball up, looking nervously back at the eyes watching her. Astrid has changed places with Bianca now and has pulled the chair up to be right beside Ia. She laid one of her hands gently on the witch's thigh and lightly caressed it.

"Close your pretty violet eyes and pretend that the others are not there," she said softly into her sister-wife's ear, and then lightly kissed the tip of it. "It is just you and I who are here in a silent room, and you are going to look deep into your new ball to tell me what you see about our future. You will say what you see about our going out."

Good girl. Despite her attempt to seem independent and strong, our little

Ia needs to be treated very gently and made to believe in herself when she does not. Ia nodded and closed her eyes. *The silence lies heavy on the room. You cannot even hear the sound of breathing from the adults. Even all of the babies seem to have gone quiet.*

A few minutes passed and Ia opened her eyes. She began to stare into the ball as she ran her hands around it. They were held just over the surface. Finally she was holding them still as if she were holding the ball on each side, even though she was not touching it. Suddenly she gave a slight start and peered closer at the ball.

Damn, the clear crystal ball is clouded, and it is easy to see that with this new ball. How did that happen? Are we all hallucinating with her? From the drugs that she has taken, her voice sounds as if she is speaking from far, far away. It is as if she is speaking to us from out of a dream. It is quite impressive.

"I see us on the ship," she said "and going down the river… It rides high in the water… We stop at the city, but we are not there to trade…and once we leave we sail straight out to sea… We turn right and circle The Land but far, far away, riding deep in the ocean and long out of sight of the shore… We will fight…once…perhaps twice or more…at least two very different ships… strong and wicked ships… We will meet…" She broke off and then resumed with a note of surprise in her voice "There are three ships that are similar to ours but I think that the two are bigger… The smallest is in the lead and they sail together… They go to a place that is bare and empty-looking and to another island that has a mountain and also to a third place that has tall trees on a river and all of the buildings are timber instead of stone… It feels like my home…but I have never been there or seen it before… No… It is us and we do it around the other way… We do go to the place with trees first and then the other two."

She sounds confused. "My sight ends there and people are waiting for us in the town on the river… It is just like home… We are on one of the ships…and it is about to turn spring." She fell silent and then spoke up again as she turned to Astrid with a dreamy smile on her face "And you are pregnant again… You have yet another set of twins and so am I and so…oh…I think that I am hungered…very hungered."

She is looking at Astrid sitting beside her and she has a silly smile on her face. "We are all having children… All of us." *Somehow I am sure that last part was not supposed to be said publicly.* "Did I just say all of that out loud?" she asked, and her pale skin blushed red as her last comment broke the tension that people felt. *It wasn't. It seems I have to get used to even more children running around the house.*

Puss is trying hard to keep a straight face and failing as she begins to pack the ball up for her. "Yes dear, you did. Hush now," she said as she patted Ia's leg again. She turned to the crowd. "If I can explain what I think is some of what my sister-wife has said, I think that we have to circle around and cut the Adversaries off from their supporters," she said.

"One ship, I am sure, will be the fire dromond that was stolen from Darkreach… The second I have no idea. The ships that we sail with… Most of you do not know of the Sea Nomads, our books sometimes call them the Kanaka, but they use ships like the *River Dragon*, and these rarely touch land." She paused.

"As for the land… I am sure that one will be an island called Ovington and the other is Skrice and we will end Ia's vision in my home village of Wolfneck, but go there first. Because it is my home village and Ia and I are… joined…it feels like home to her." She turned to the Bishop. "What do you think? Does that fit in with your idea?"

"Very much so," he replied. "If our enemies are to be cut off we need to find anyone who would otherwise support them and destroy them. That would mean the two ships, and one should be the dromond and the other… It could be one that the dromond has captured or it could be one from Freehold itself or from the Newfoundland. In my mind it will be the Newfoundland."

"We suspect, from what we saw with the Goldentide and from Father Simeon and from what Yabaribaykus has said that there is something happening in that land. It may have an effect on what we are going to do." *Virginia is getting restless again. I am sure that there is something that she knows about and that she will not tell us.*

"Either way," Christopher continued, "we need to go west. From what I understand of your northern waters, we do not want to sail them in winter, do we?"

Astrid shook her head definitely in answer to that and then the two stopped and both looked at Rani.

She looked around her. "Then, if no one else has anything to add, we will now wait until tomorrow when Dobun will tell us what he sees and any advice he gets from anyone or anything else he meets in the Spirit World."

She looked around the room. "I have some interesting things to think about… I wish you all a good sleep tonight, my people." She smiled. "Mind you, I believe that I may have too much to think about to do that myself." *I suspect that we do as well. How many children will end up in our house? I am also left wondering if there is more in store for our family that Ia did not say aloud.*

Basil

*A*strid *is carrying Ia in her arms as she, in turn, clutches the ball. I get to help Sin bring the babies home. Ia has her arms around Puss' neck.* "I am having a baby... You have two..." *She does have more to add, then. She is looking at me now.* "You made us all pregnant, you did... All of us." *She is giggling a little. She is still very much under the drugs. She probably will still be that way tomorrow. She is tiny, they affect her a lot.*

Astrid turned with Ia still in her arms and looked at Basil. "It didn't affect her like this last time... I am not sure how much of the hashish she had...but it was probably too much."

"Six biscuits," said Sin primly. "She said that it was important and that she wanted to be sure in her sight. It sounds as if she was."

They went inside the house and closed the door. Astrid went to lay Ia on the bed and take her boots off and put a blanket over her. She came out, closing the door behind her and back through the hole in the wall that led to the second house and was at present only covered by a leather curtain. She went to where the others were putting the children into their cots.

Once Astrid had joined them, Sin paused in what she was doing and looked from one to the other. "Seeing that we now know that you are going to be having more children...probably many more children..." *She is speaking in a very composed voice. I think that she has been considering her words for a while. I am beginning to worry a little.*

Puss is looking at me with alarm... I know what she is thinking. We have just gotten the girl to help us; are we now going to lose her? "I am telling you now that the time is coming when I will want a child of my own... I mean that I love yours and I am sure that I will love Ia's, but I am starting to want one of my own."

I am not sure where this conversation is going but, now with the children tucked in and already back asleep, we can all move back out to the kitchen. As they moved, a realisation hit him. *From the sinking feeling in the pit of my stomach, I have a bad feeling about what is about to be said, even if Puss still looks blank.*

"If we were still in the Brotherhood then it would not be a problem... That is, it would not be if I was still alive." She flashed a brief and humourless smile at that thought and turned to Basil. "You would already have made me pregnant at least once by now without me mentioning it and whether I wanted it or no," she said. "Instead, if I do not have a husband of my own—and to be truly honest I don't really want one—I am going to ask you to give me my own child. It is your duty one way or another."

Puss has already started fussing around our stove to make Kaf. Damn her. She has started to grin. She is using making Kaf for us as an excuse to not say anything. I can feel myself turning red and have no idea what to say. Sin, however, is not yet finished. She is looking at me and waiting to see if I will say something. I think I will just stay quiet and hope I am wrong.

After a little while Sin spoke again into the silence. "I don't want to marry you as I do not want to make love to another woman as your wives do. That does not interest me at all," she said primly. "I mean you no disrespect, Mistress," she turned and said to Astrid, "but that is your way, and the way of several other women here, but it is not mine.

"I know why you made your choices... This house is too small for me not to have overheard you all talk...and I respect you for what you have done for Ia and to keep her alive...but I do not have to make the same choice. I have a different path to walk, one that is my own."

Now she is turning back to me. "I will want a solution and I will want to be with child before you all leave on this next trip. Remember that Ia said we will all be pregnant. I think she meant me as well. She could have said that you both will be pregnant...but she said 'all'." *She did, didn't she? Damn it.*

"What you are doing will be very dangerous and while you are all three far more deadly and stronger than I am, there is still a chance that none of you will return to us." She stopped and added in a very matter-of-fact tone: "That means I will have to be your heir so that I can properly look after the children anyway."

Astrid

The ibrik foamed up and filled the house with its strong, sweet smell. Astrid served them all Kaf in the tiny cups. *No one is saying anything. Basil has just picked his up and sipped at it without waiting. He is so distracted that he almost scalded himself, but Sin is perfectly composed.* She thanked Astrid as if she had not just said all that she had.

Basil went to bed first without giving a definite answer and Astrid lingered as Sin cleaned up. "Don't worry," Astrid finally said. "I don't know what we will do, but you put it in terms of his duty and that will always work with him. There will be a solution."

"I know," said Sin with a grin. "It is the solution with both of you...and I suspect it will be with your sister-wife as well. You are all very fierce and so different, but also so much alike. That is yet another reason I cannot see me being married to you. I am not like that at all. I am not a warrior woman. I like houses and children."

She paused. "I am willing to learn to use a bow in case it is needed, and I apply myself with that and, when Harnermêŝ is up here he is teaching several of us his way with hands and feet, and that is even sort of fun, but I am not interested in fighting battles. I saw enough of that at One Tree Hill and the terror and the blood and fear is not for me. I want a different fate. I want a quiet and simple life in a safe place with a home and lots of children that I love around me all of the time. I want a life that is made up of making bread, and cooking soups, and of sewing."

Astrid grinned. "Then we will see what we can do between us. As you probably realise, I like making children, and I love them very much when they arrive, but I am not good with looking after them in the fashion that you are. In the meantime, goodnight, Sin."

"Goodnight, Mistress."

To make Ia burn off the drugs and also to take their mind off the questions Sin had posed, the three made love until late that night. When not doing that Ia was half awake and half asleep in a drugged dream world of her own. *When she is awake she keeps talking about her baby daughter in her dreamy voice. She even talks about Sin's baby as well, and she should not have been able to hear that conversation at all. It seems that Sin was right: Ia really has also seen that as a part of her vision.*

That night a fire glowed on the small, flat rise to the right of the entry to the mine where the Khitan had started to put together a small pile of rocks as the start of an *ovoo*, a shrine to the spirits, and the next morning, after morning prayers in their several faiths were finished, the Mice all gathered together in the hall.

Rani
20th Quinque

I need to get everyone quiet. He is still not used to saying these sorts of things to people outside his clan. "Go ahead, Dobun. Let us know what you feel that you can share with those not of the Tribes. Only say what you are comfortable saying." *He is still looking nervous, but he looks at Hulagu, who nods, and then he clears his throat.*

"Firstly," he said "I flew over the Caliphate and did not feel what I felt before. No one acts there now to hold your spirit back. The other shamen that

I spoke to in the real world say the same about that place. It is clear of the fog now and free to be felt. It just the same there now as it is in any other place that is not under the sway of evil.

"They do not need to say it, but the others are well pleased with our work, as we have taken firm control of the mountains that will be our home and made them truly ours. I then went into the future and I agree with what Ia proposed. It is still hard to see, and it becomes harder the further north and forward that you go." *He is saying more than I thought he might.*

"There are friends and dangers to the west that we will find…but there are also areas that I cannot see into. Some have a sense of evil about them and others do not. I dared not go too far north as there are things there that try to reach out and trap your soul… They never sleep and they are cold…" *He is hesitating, but I think it is uncertainty, not reluctance.*

"Ariadne spoke to me about her ideas," Dobun continued, "before I went to the Real World last night, and I agree with what she said. She said that what is trapping and blocking and holding is not really living; it is a machine, and that is why it feels so strange and it never varies. It is not really alive… although it can act as if it were. It is if someone has made a golem in the Real World as a trap for our souls."

You had to be watching close, but I think that I saw a faint shudder in him when he said that. "It is so very wrong and unnatural. If I were stronger, having realised that, I might use that against it but I did tell others about what we thought. I leave it to those who are stronger than I am to act on this if they can, as I cannot do so yet. I have done all that I could… Oh, and I only had to go forward to spring to see what I saw…and what is more, I could only go forward to spring as well as if what is beyond that is not yet determined."

He pauses again, as if unsure of what exactly to say. "The Horse are to be people of the mountains and the sky. I decided to no longer confine my senses to the land, but also to seek answers for my questions in the wind and air. Usually none look there as there is nothing to see for the most part. I saw nothing to tell me who—but perhaps I was looking in the wrong places—but I have a feeling that there are those who watch us." *I think that he means more than the Adversaries.*

"There are more than one set of watchers, and they are somewhere in the sky and perhaps some of them travel in the sky as well. I do not know whether they are good or whether they are ill or even if they are just there, but I am sure within myself that they are there trying to see us. I had a faint feeling of frustration…but I know not if that was from them or from me." He finished and gave a faint smile after his last comment. *We need to think about this.*

Thord
21ˢᵗ Quinque

Now we leave and the Crown-Finder gets to show off his bride-to-be to the rest of the Dwarves. Although Ia had been able to ride one of the new saddles once she married Basil, a betrothal, it seems, is not sufficient and my little rock-delver cannot yet take one up in the air. She must ride behind me and hold on. It is such a trial.

At least we now have a good timeframe to work with and can give firm invitations to all of the people who should attend. It will take them some time to assemble from all over The Land. If they *wish to be at our wedding, that is.* He grinned to himself, baring his teeth to the wind as they flew. *That had better be anyone who gets an invitation.*

Olympias

The Princesses say that that we can keep travelling and trading around the south with the River Dragon. *In the time that we have we can easily fit in at least two more trips covering the whole southern coast from Saltbeach, east to Rainjig. It will make our ship seem to be more a part of the normal life of the south for it to just appear as a trader.*

What is more, I want to have a look at the rivers leading up to Dolbarden, if I can, and to look at buying potions, herbs and some of the jewellery that have been remodelled there and that will suit Havenite tastes. Shilpa wants us to carry a small supply of jewellery at all times so we have something suitable to sell for weddings or gifts wherever we dock. Such items will weigh very little, and there is a constant demand for them anywhere.

If we can buy things from the source, I have been told that we get a far larger margin as we cut out the middlemen…even if the ones whose trade we take do not like us. We have several advantages over other merchants, however. Most travelling merchants have difficulty carrying a large amount of jewellery around with them, and it makes them a target for thieves. Seeing that we are operating from a ship, we can just carry a strongbox in one of the concealed lockers without much risk.

What is more, Shilpa says that most do not have the capital to tie up in a speculation that may not sell for years. We must prepare and do this right.

Astrid

After the readings, the Princesses want to go see the Bear Folk. It was just supposed to be them and our family, but it seems that Ruth has other ideas here. She has announced that another school trip is going to take place. We will be overrun with children to look after all of the way there and we will probably end up returning with more. At least Sin can take care of mine.

Ruth wants to take Guy. I suppose they will both need to be there to keep an eye on them and she wants to take her husband as well. That will give them one adult to keep an eye on each of the local children and, wherever they are, the rest are likely to be near them. That makes sense.

At least, although we have nineteen children, we now have two carpets, as well as the saddles, and many of the children are still small enough to ride behind someone. Our new carpet is slower in the air than the old one, so it will take us a full day to get there, but it will be worthwhile. In the usual trade-off of magic, although it is slower, the carpet can also carry more people on it.

While we were away, apparently the children of the school have already been down for visits to Evilhalt and to Erave Town. Listening to them chatter, Tiffany and Stefano seem to be very much enjoying the new status that comes to them when they go home through their association with our valley. She kept listening as they flew.

It seems, because of that, the three children from the Bear folk, all of them still too young to know if they will come into their skin-changing or not, are eager to show their school friends around their home. For now we have to just fly low and slow along the escarpment road.

Much as Goditha has worked on the bridge over our river, from this height it is easy to see where Guk and Haytor and Guk's children have been working on the old road as they move along it. The few saplings that managed to grow through the paving have been cut down. Some have even had all trace of their presence erased. In a few places you can see where washed-out sections are beginning to be repaired.

The work that they do as they travel must be adding a couple of days to each circuit of trade, but essentially they are working on what is, for the moment at least, their own private road. Their track up the ridge to reach the Dwarves is getting to more and more resemble a real and well-travelled path as well. They obviously do a little bit of work to it each trip.

Astrid went up the path a little way and found they had already started work building their own campsites, with rough wooden fences for the animals and supplies of cut timber in cleared areas under makeshift shelters drying for use as firewood.

The only part of the paths they have not worked on, and it will be deliberate, are the turn-off to Birchdingle and the actual turn-off to their path to the Dwarves. The first is still almost invisible unless you know what to look for among the bushes and the second is just not marked in any way, and care has been taken to make sure that a casual passerby, if there were any, could easily mistake it for a game trail.

They flew into Birchdingle in the late afternoon without any of the children falling off the carpets, although Ruth was glad that they had roped them together as they constantly threatened to tumble in their restlessness. A full day of sitting like that in the chill, clear autumn air, in close proximity, except for short stops when they were needed, had been tiring for them and for their supervisors.

The children had not expected their lessons to continue as they went, but Ruth was not going to miss a chance and was running through the plants, birds and animals of the southern forests and mountains with them and showing the children how the forests changed both with altitude and with a move more to the south.

One or another of the three of us seems to be constantly in motion to one side or another. We bring things up to the carpets to show to the children, so that they do not have to slow down to look at them. Leaves, fungi and even leaf litter from under the trees are all fair game. My prize was one of the little rounded hoppers that I caught by swooping down on it.

Too big to be prey for most of the sky-based predators in the thick bush, it had not noticed me coming from above it. It turned out to have a baby in its pouch. This led Ruth off on another set of explanations before she allowed the little pouched thing, and its baby, back on the ground to escape.

As soon as we land, the children erupt off the carpets and those from elsewhere are soon introduced to family and to familiars and the other numerous animals that roam at will through the village. Ruth herself has been dragged off to meet various parents and be interviewed by them over the school. It seems that Ruth was expecting that. The children all end up being brought together and showing off. It seems that the show for Theodora was a practice for an audience of parents and prospective parents.

Our oldest child is Gurinder. She is well and truly old enough to be starting to develop as a young woman, and is now also training as a mage, to the delight of her adopted parents Parminder and Goditha. It seems that she is going to be a Fire mage. In what she is wearing she may still pass as a child, but she can also proudly light a fire, at least.

Astrid
22ⁿᵈ Quinque

Now we are returning and the Princesses have a commitment, not only for priests and priestesses to go with the River Dragon *when it sails, but also for a force of fifty or more to travel north by land to Wolfneck to meet the ship when it arrives and to sail with them to the north to fight alongside us. It was interesting to sit in on that conversation.*

"What you have asked for," said Cathal "is far too modest. If we are supposed to come out of our isolation it must be that more than a hand of us is going to be needed. Most of us going will travel north by land and we will gather others of your people from Erave Town and even further north as we go. Our people who go by land will meet with those of us who travel with you by sea in Wolfneck in the spring."

As they went back to Mousehole, they also had with them three more children for the school, two girls and a boy. The second class in the valley will be looking at taking much younger children than the first. Ruth is looking at taking them from as young as five to only seven and these are the first children for that class to start with. I suspect that the valley is going to get even noisier.

Just before they left, a surprised Astrid had also been presented with a just-weaned bundle of fur, whose teeth were already looking like her own. *It is a cute little creature, but it is a young female hill-cat, a medium-size hunter of the mountains which is, apparently, very suitable for a life lived on a flying saddle. From what they tell me, my saddle will be very full by the time it is grown up.*

Apparently hill-cats can climb better than goats on cliffs, even if they lack hooves, and can fall long distances safely, landing happily on their feet even if they fall from a filled hand of paces up. They freely jump from ledge to ledge on cliffs and are very active hunters. Maeve has already taken to expressing her dominance over the young and fluffy kitten. She is showing her who is the boss. I think she wants to stay alive when it grows.

"I think that they have given her to you as a test," admitted Ia. "I am sure that it is to see if you are just playing at being a Cat or if you are a real one and so a suitable partner for me." She held up her hand to forestall anything Astrid, whose mouth was already open, might say. "It is not my idea, but I am very flattered by it. It is the sort of thing a mother might do for her daughter. You may take the meaning of your gift up with Cathal if you wish to, but that is how I see it."

Astrid held the bundle up in front of her to look over it as they were flying. *Just as we do with Maeve, I have her fastened on to the saddle with leather straps for the present.* "So, furball," she said as the kitten swatted at her nose with claws retracted, "you are to join our family as well, are you? We will name you properly when we find out a little more about you, perhaps from Parminder. Now, you settle down here and learn to behave."

The young cat, on being put back down on the saddle, promptly curled up in front of Astrid, began to purr and then went to sleep in between her legs and the saddle pommel. Except for a brief, unconcerned glance over the edge of the saddle, it entirely ignored the large expanse of sky beneath it. *I will admit that is a good start.*

Astrid

I see now why Theodora was so impatient to be back. She rushed straight off to complete her enchantment and bring it out. It does not appear to be much, just a small lead triangle set onto another triangle of cedar and drilled in the centre so that it can be fixed onto something. In fact there are eight of them. She is obviously proud, though.

Theodora shrugged, "It is not my element anyway and the extra mana to go from making two to eight is nothing compared to the effort of the rest of it. Besides, Ia said we would have other vessels working with us. I thought that I would make enough for however many we use.

"They are for big ships," she continued, "and each will protect the ship from as great a spell as Rani's hardest Fire spell or my largest Air blast. If these Adversaries have a spell larger than that, we will not win anyway as they will be as strong as Granther. From what we have seen, I do not think that this is the case. There are many other things that they can do to us, but this should stop any direct attack on our ships by magical blasts of any element."

She is pausing for murmurs of admiration, isn't she? The mages can do that for her. "They will only work perhaps eight times a day, but that should be more than enough. I do not think that our opponents are as strong as we fear them to be..."—*or as strong as Hrothnog, their Renegade, has become.*

"I think that they have succeeded so far because they use strong machines in place of their own weak magic." *It seems that they have all taken up Ariadne's idea. I admit that it does make sense.* "They have not been conquered before because they hide their presence and work from the shadows, and they are skilled at being able to subvert the greedy and the naïve...and there are a lot of those sorts of people all over, in every land, for them to work on."

"They only need to control enough of them who are strong enough to be useful." She started to put the new protections away. "This has taken me a while to work out. Now it is finally done I can go back to the accustomed tasks of making saddles and the magical shields to protect you all in the combat to come."

She stopped and then noticed someone who looked as though he was about to speak. "Yes Ariadne, I will try and do your Thunderer as well. I do think that I have an idea about how to do that."

Christopher

I should stop being surprised by these visits, but usually the women are here as well. He looked at Basil. *He may hope to be given a straightforward answer that will help him avoid what he has outlined, but having gone down this path there really is only one answer that, in the end, I can give. He will be disappointed.* "How do you feel about this?" Christopher asked him.

Basil looks dejected. I am sure that life was far simpler for him before he came west. "My sister, when I married Ia, unkindly said that I would adapt… that any man would very quickly get used to having more than one woman as his… Unfortunately, I think she is completely right. I still do not love Ia as I love Astrid. As you know, we married her because we felt it was the only way to keep her alive, but now I have the feeling that, given time, I will eventually grow to love her in her own way."

He stopped and thought for a moment. "Sin does not even ask for love or marriage from me. She doesn't even seem to want either of these. She simply wants to have children. I look at Robin and Parminder and I see an analogy there. But he stands for his sister there and so it is different. Even the Princess, when she got pregnant, used Rani's brother as a substitute."

I wonder if he realises how deep that sigh was. "This is so completely different. Sin is a pretty girl, and so it will not be hard for me to perform but I will be breaking my vows. My wives would be excluded from their own marriage bed when I am with Sin; Sin was clear on that. I don't know… She says it is my duty as her master to provide for her in this way, and I have said that she is free and that I am not her master, and she didn't even reply. It is as if I said nothing."

Now he gets to sound put upon. I heard exactly the same tone from Norbert when we first arrived here and I was first faced with this issue. He is continuing. "She only stood there and gave me exactly the same sort of look that I get from the other two when they think that I am not only wrong, but stupidly so."

Christopher nodded in thought. *I have thought and prayed over this dilemma. I had an idea that it could arise.* "Bring all of your women to see me and we will hear what they have to say," he said. "It is not just your decision that is important here as your wives have as much at stake as you do. You are not faced with an easy decision and I do not have an immediate or easy answer."

"I know that there are some analogies in the Old Testament—indeed from Abraham himself among others—but, while I often use them, I also think that it might not be good to rely too much on some of the older books for guidance on our morals; otherwise, you would be stoned for shaving, Aziz for his new tattoo, and none of us could eat oysters, and having found out about oysters, I find that that I like them. Jesus himself regarded the old commands as often being out of date as he brought new commandments of love."

Christopher

*B*asil *has not taken long to return. I think that the three women must have realised where he went and been waiting for him.* Christopher took them into his office and sat them all down, and Bianca brought them all refreshments before taking a seat herself as if she had a perfect right to be there as well. "Sin," the bishop said, "Basil tells me that you want him to give you a child. Is that right?"

"Yes, Bishop," she said.

"You do not want to marry him, though?"

"No, Bishop... With respect, Mistresses," she said, turning to Astrid and Ia, "I do not wish to join the Mistresses in their marriage bed. I just want a baby of my own...or even perhaps more than one."

"Basil," said Christopher.

"I cannot make a child with her outside marriage," said Basil. "It is wrong... I know that it is common in Freehold"—*my wife is nodding at that*—"but it isn't in Darkreach. People will have sex...and sometimes even children... all without being married. They may not want ties to bind them to another. However, once you are married...well...marriage is about a commitment to another, and I have made that commitment. Now I have made it twice over. In my mind, that does not halve my promises—it doubles them."

In an unusually tactful fashion, Astrid has silently raised her hand like a child waiting to be recognised in class. "Can we speak?" she asked when I nodded at her.

"Certainly," said Christopher. "You have as much at stake here as anyone."

"Good...then...after Sin mentioned it...Ia and I were talking. We thought that neither of them would compromise very much—Sin dear, we don't want to lose you—and we understand you not wanting to get in bed or make love with us but…well, you know why it has all fallen out as it has…but if you marry Basil, then we realise that you do not have to share our bed."

It is the turn of the girl to look surprised. "You and Basil can make babies in your own bed… You can even make love to him just for the fun of it without the babies…even if we will have to get you a bigger bed. You can make love to us in our bed if you later change your mind and decide that you want to. The choice on that will be yours and it will be yours alone." *She has a more serious look on her face than she usually does.*

"As long as Basil does not ignore us because of you, then I am sure that we can share him with you." *Now she is talking to me.* "We do know that it will happen. Ia saw Sin as being pregnant at the same time as she saw me and herself with children. In fact she has seen it twice now in her ball, but had forgotten the first time until she saw it again. She didn't see any other male at the time, so it has to be through Basil that we are connected." *Basil does not like that comment.*

Astrid turns now to Sin. "However, we have a condition that you do not close your bed to us. If we want to sleep in there with you we can… The idea may be hard to accept," she said with a grin, "but one of us may want to make love with Basil and the other may just want to go sleep and so the one that wants to sleep will come to your bed… We understand that it is just to have company when we sleep…nothing else."

Sin purses her lips in thought, but only for a moment. I am sure that she was actually used to sharing a bed with at least one more girl: it was sleeping on her own that would be unusual. Astrid turns back to me. "That is it, then… My husband will now have a third wife…and I just want to say that when I left Wolfneck for the first time this entire conversation would have been the last thing that I would ever have thought I would have."

"You do not mind if I do not make love to you?" Sin said to the pair.

"If you decide to, then I am sure that the bed is big enough," said Astrid. "but if you do not want to, then we would never ever try to force you to. Marriage is about love and respect. Basil and I respect Ia, and lust over her as well, but we are still working on the love. I guess we need to work on that with you as well now. I suppose the point that we are making is that we are willing to share our husband with you if you want us to."

"Do I get any say in this?" asked Basil, almost indignantly.

"No," said his wives together, and with Sin only a little way behind them.

"Perhaps a little bit," added Astrid. "You—and to be honest, I did as well—adapted quickly to having Ia in the bed. I am sure that it will take just as long to adapt to having Sin married to us as well. She is pretty and she is very different to either of us so you will have more variety than most men see in their entire lives without having to pay a penalty…except in lack of sleep.

"If we want Sin to stay working with us"—a thought struck Astrid and she turned to Sin— "that is right. If you marry him Sin, then you no longer get paid… You do realise that?" Sin nodded and Astrid turned back to Basil, "And if marrying you is the only way that we can keep her to look after our house and our children, then you will marry her and get to like it quickly."

I think that Basil just received instructions there. "I admit that I was very worried about our decision when you married Ia, but you seem to have enough love in your heart for both of us and you do not seem to love me any less now that you have two wives, so I trust you and I am sure there will be enough in your heart for the three of us."

"And, although you have not seen her fully naked, we have. I tell you that you will like what you see very quickly," said Ia, moving her hands as if outlining an hourglass. *And there goes the seriousness.* Sin blushed red. *She is one of the more modest girls and, while she will wear a kilt, she also always wears a short chemise on her top as well, at least when she is in front of men.*

Ia now turned to Sin and spoke: "Darling, he is going to be your husband. He is the man that you will be naked in front of. I will take none of this silly business, of which I have heard from the west, of people making love with their clothes on. It is wrong, very wrong. You may not believe in the Mother, but I do and the Mother did not intend you to hide yourself away from your husband."

Chapter IV

Shilpa
22nd Quinque

After trading down to Haven and along the coast in the River Dragon *we are now back at our home. It seems that the size of her holds opens up new possibilities along the coast, to the disadvantage of Haven, whose merchants largely ignore the sea and keep to the land or their river. We can even out-compete the far smaller ships from Freehold.*

We met one of these, and while we bought goods from each other, I saw that they were not keen to toast the success of the venture from Mousehole. At least I was able to find no rumours that the River Dragon *is connected with anything ill. The traders were also very happy to hear that we would not be venturing west as far as Ashvaria and Trekvarna.*

We even carried passengers and cargo for others from the villages further along the coast. While it may not have been their most profitable trip so far, Shilpa was very happy and she had even brought back a copy of the first set of accounts from Rakhi. *I gave them a good look over before passing them on to Kalliope.*

She and Zeenat, as our factors, have been very busy and they need more money. They are busy loaning it out at a rate that undercuts what the Brahmin moneylenders usually charge. Our money is becoming very attractive to those who want capital. From the number who want our money they can pick and choose who to lend money to.

They are attracting the best ventures, those that are most likely to be profitable, rather than just attracting people who are desperate or who want to finance a wedding or some sort of spectacle. They have even had some people in businesses that would be profitable, if it were not for interest, borrow from them to pay out their existing loans.

Some of the loans being paid out have existed from their parents' time and could never be paid back normally as the family got itself deeper in debt and was forced closer and closer to real servitude to those who held the loans. We will get a high-level profit from the borrowers for several cycles of years to come, but at least the loans that are being taken out now will be capable of being paid back eventually.

The second reason for needing more money is the rebuilding of Anta Dvīpa. They have a church to build, or at least a building to be modified into being one, and, when Imam Iyād sends his next man across, the start of a mosque to think about as well.

There was even another building being turned into a tavern and now they were shipping to it a real dark northern beer from Evilhalt, the paler southern beer from Jewvanda and spirits from Erave Town, and some of those taken from a consignment from Southpoint, and food from all of these areas.

I should have read all the notes earlier, but we were busy trading and sailing. It seems that foreign guards and handlers who work on the caravans did not take long to start finding their way across the islands to this enclave away from home. They are quickly becoming an increasing part of our revenue as they spend their wages with us.

She smiled. *I thought that this could happen. Many of the decreasing number of land-bound traders, unless they have a regular local buyer with whom they are happy, are even starting to trek their caravans across the islands to the growing factory of the Mice. Those that arrive on the island can sell their entire stock to us instead of having to look for buyers for each single item.*

This increased traffic means that the girls need to be able to repair buildings and make them into stables and to have provision for grain and hay stores as well as to make secure their increasingly large warehouses. They are even making sure that traders can buy goods in the factory for the return trip. I must tell the Princesses that we need more people there as well.

At the current rate of sale of its products, Rainjig might even need to increase its production of salt. It is proving to be a good seller for them and the normal merchants who bought their produce must already be regretting the lack of their trade. Good quality salt is always in demand, even if, with increased supply, the sale price has dropped.

Theodora
about the same time

The aerial sentries have told me that the River Dragon *has come home from its first short trip. My husband wanted Olympias to come back between the two trips as, before we set off again, she feels that we have to at least give the Maharajah a chance to let Haven take part in the whole affair. Admittedly, the last time they involved themselves in the affairs of the outside world they lost the entirety of their armies, but that was when they invaded Darkreach over three thousand years ago.*

She is sad that, beyond the Kingdom just sending her out on her way, there has not even been anything since she first came north years ago. It is as if nothing has happened at all. She is sad that she seems to have just disappeared from Haven and her report has vanished. It is as if a small pebble has been dropped into the middle of the Rhastaputra. She has vanished for them without a trace and with not a single ripple reaching a bank.

There has not been a single word of reaction from Haven, not even when war had seemed most likely. Nothing has come back to either Erave Town or Evilhalt and no more troops or patrols of any sort are being seen than before. We have seen their traders, but that is all. As for the Mice, we are still greeted warmly at Garthang as allies, but then we are almost totally ignored at Pavitra Phāṭaka.

Christopher

The first people up from the ship, arriving on saddles even before I thought it was to be docked, are Simeon and Marianus. Looking out I can see that Marianus isn't even first trying to report to Basil or the Princesses, who are in the Hall, as they arrive. I can see out of my window that the two men are heading straight up the village towards where I am sitting. This could be serious.

Glad soon ushered them into the room that Christopher used as an office and seated them. Simeon got straight to the point. "I am sure you know by now how the Brotherhood girls tend to do things together in groups or at least in pairs." Christopher nodded. "I think it is because of how they were brought up. They often lose their real family, or sometimes do not even know it and so those people that they find themselves living with turn into their family and, because these families were so casually broken up by their owners, now that they are free they cling tighter to them."

Christopher nodded again. *I know that well with with Pass and Lamentations. They are far closer than most sisters are.* "On the ship, the six girls call themselves the Saints from the names they have taken now and they are very close." He thought for a moment before adding: "That is to say, not close as the Princesses or the cousins are, just as sisters."

He stopped again, choosing his words carefully before continuing. "They do not want to be parted even in marriage. Marianus was honest with them and told them of his life and how he came west looking for a new life and to find a wife, and asked if any of them might favour him. I will let him speak now."

Christopher turned to the former Darkreach man. "I have a career that was built on dishonesty," he said, "both in catching it and using it to get what we wanted. I wanted to be fully honest with these women from the start. I told them that they were all astonishingly beautiful and hard-working, and that any man would be lucky to have one of them for a wife, especially a man who had as little to commend him as I do."

His words come out in a rush. "I said I did not care a fig for their past—that was behind them—if they did not care about mine. I fully explained my situation and said I was sure that, if one of them wanted to marry an older man who was also starting a new life, then we could perhaps come to love each other in time."

He may have just managed a deeper sigh than even Basil can produce. "Mary—she is the leader of the six… I don't know if you realise, but she named herself after the former prostitute and not the Mother of God, you know—she told me to wait patiently and that they would talk and discuss the matter among themselves." *A sound idea.*

"I suppose I should have started to get worried then, and again later as they sat around at the prow of the ship talking and looking at me and then fell silent if someone else came near them, but it was not until the next day that they revealed their decision to me. They even slept on it. Mary said that they were not averse to the idea of marriage but had already had to face a lot of sex… It had not been a happy time for them and they didn't know if they necessarily wanted to have sex constantly, and they saw that as being a part of any marriage vows that they took.

"They had decided they were happy to marry me…but I need to stress the word 'they'." He paused. *That is almost a look of despair that is passing over his face.* "Because they wanted to stay together and face everything as a group, they had decided that I could either have all of them, or I could have none.

"They say that you have allowed Christian men to marry two women and that there is no difference between two and six, and they point to Solomon. I have said that I am not as wise as Solomon, but they scorn that as an answer and say it is as *no* moment. What do I do?" *He said the last words with more than a hint of desperation in his voice.*

Christopher sat thinking. *In principle, Mary is right. However, even the Prophet of the Muslims only allowed a man four wives as a matter of practicality. I do not want to mention my decision to allow Basil to have three wives already. That might be a matter be for that particular family to announce publicly.*

Eventually he spoke up. "It is, outside this village, rare for a Christian man to have two wives, although there is not a word that directly goes against it in the Bible. If my memory is correct, then Genesis says that Lamech had two wives as did David, and Jacob had more than one wife as did Esau, and God thought well of them." *They are both looking at me and waiting still.*

"Judges says that Gideon had many wives," Christopher continued, "and Chronicles tells us that a man called Abijah had fourteen, and he was reckoned a great and holy man. Solomon probably had too many, for some of them turned him towards false gods, but we are not talking Solomon's numbers here…" He trailed off and stopped again in thought.

He went silent as the two in front of him shifted around, and it was quite some time before he spoke up again. The other two sat silent and sipped on Kaf and nibbled on biscuits while they waited. *They both already look a lot less worried. They have shuffled this off to their Bishop now and just need to wait on my decision on the matter. It is now out of their hands. That is nice for them, if not for me.*

"I have to say that I am not happy with what I am about to say, as there will be ones who take it wrongly but…given the circumstances…and I stress this and will also stress the unique circumstances in my writing down of this decision…for all such decisions are written down and kept and shared among the rulers of the Church."

I am not making sense. "If you are right in their opinion"—*Simeon, their Confessor, is nodding at this*—"then I will not need to talk to the women before I give you an answer. I think that I am going to rule that you can marry these women as it is their express wish for it to be this way and you are not forcing the choice upon any of them."

He stopped and gave his blessing. *I think that perhaps he needs more than that and more than I can give.* "Before you go back and tell your women the news, I suggest that you gather Basil, Stefan, Denny and Norbert and perhaps even Hulagu, although his situation is…very different… and talk with them." *They are both just looking at me again.*

"I will not ask their confessor. I suspect that your wives will be in a different position to either Stefan's or Basil's women, but they will all have much to tell you. If you choose to go ahead in this, I suspect you are going to have to work far harder at being a husband—and I do not just mean the trivial time that will be spent in the marriage bed—than any of us."

"I want you to think on whether you want that ahead of you before you think of having your own gynaeceum." He thought for a moment before sighing and continuing. *I don't want it to be made fully public, but perhaps it is as well for it to be known in this particular case.* "I want you to pay particular attention to what Basil says. It is not common knowledge, so I charge you to say nothing to anyone else, but he is about to take a third wife and the choice in that matter is not entirely his own, either."

Marianus Gerontas

I will leave Simeon talking to the Bishop about Basil and go and find the man himself. It being Krondag, Marianus easily found Basil at the practice area outside the village wall. He was showing some of the Brotherhood women how to use two shortswords. Most of them felt that a shield was too heavy for them and they were not likely to be in a full-sized battle anyway. If they fought they would be fighting to protect their homes in the valley or the village.

Basil, Ayesha and Guy were trying to show the women different alternatives: Basil with shortswords, Ayesha with knives and Guy with a rapier and main-gauche, which he used very stylishly and with extravagant flourishes whenever he could get away with it. Astrid and Ia were watching on with their weapons at hand, although Ia, as she often did, stood tucked comfortably within Astrid's arm with her arms around the larger woman's waist.

Marianus waited, and while he waited he looked at them and thought about their situation. *By reputation, Astrid is a woman who stands in high favour with the Emperor and she is a dour fighter. She is dressed only in a kilt and laced leather vest for this practice. Her muscles stand out on her arms, legs, and stomach. I can see some scars showing on her body even from here. She has no difficulty with having another woman in her life.*

I need to talk to Basil. Marianus waited until he was free and went over to where he stood with his wives. Astrid had handed Basil a jug of cool water which he drank from while Marianus explained his problem quietly to the three of them. To make it more uncomfortable for him, the two women not only approved of the decision of the women, but they thought that it was a good joke and sent their best wishes on to the six.

"I pity you. Two wives make for hard work," Basil said with a smile.

"Even though these two are ideal partners whom I would not lightly trade for…" His smaller wife stopped him by throwing a towel at him so that he had to dodge it. "I will gather the others up and you can meet us in the Hall and ask us what you will. Are you sure you want this?"

Marianus shook his head. *The one thing that I am truly sure of is that I am really not sure as to the wisdom of the decision at all. While on the face of it the situation is ideal for any man, one man who should know best seems to be counselling me against it. At least I will not go into it without having thought hard on the matter.*

By the time he left to return to the ship, at least he had some questions to put to the women so that they might, in return, think about exactly why they wanted to embark upon this course and how it would all work.

Theodora
25th Quinque, the Feast Day of Saint Aldhelm

Virginia has been in the cells on her own for three weeks. Her only company, except at mealtimes, has been a copy of all of the interrogations that we have done. Given that we have added to the book several of those done at Misr al-Mãr, this is sadly getting to be a sizeable volume of confessions, and the tale that they tell is largely one of horror, of cruelty and of death.

She started off with a two-week sentence, but on the first day she tore several pages out of the book in a tantrum. I assigned her a second and even more solid, public spanking for that behaviour that left her weeping and unable to sit comfortably in her cell, apparently for well over a day. I also added an extra week on to her confinement for her tantrum.

At least I am learning more about spells; it was a simple change to make to the repair spell and I was able to give the intact book back to Virginia at her next meal. I was told that, having spent the day with nothing to do, except staring at a wall when she could only stand and not even comfortably sit, she was almost glad to have it back and actually began to read it.

By the third day of confinement I have been told that she was asking questions during her meals and, by the time she was let out, although no one trusts her to behave herself, she appears to be remarkably chastened. I saw her actually seek out several of the women who were named in the confessions. Bianca tells me that she got them to tell their tales directly to her.

Guy Rossignol

The second class at the school, my own class, is starting to take some shape with ten children arriving within the last couple of weeks and the last on the ship. I only had Guk's sister and three children from among the Bear Folk to start with. Now two unexpected children have come from Dolbarden in the Swamp on board the River Dragon.

One is the daughter of two mages, and so she is very likely to develop that way herself, and the other is the daughter of a mage and a priestess. She would most likely follow one parent or the other. There is also a boy each from Erave Town and Evilhalt, come up the road with riders to deliver them. The first was the son, the eldest child, of the two Wiccan religious. The child from Evilhalt is the son of the man who is apparently the best at distilling the attar of roses and he wants more for his youngest child than would normally be on offer for him.

Coming up with them, even the village of Glengate is represented by two children. One of the Orthodox priests has sent his twins, one boy and one girl, to the school. Given the number of Wiccan children, not only will I be busy teaching, but Ia will be busy with her spiritual duties when she is home.

Theodora

Arriving along with the children from the Swamp are some more women. It has taken a while, but my speculation about some of the girls from Rising Mud seeking to find a new life is bearing fruit. Two more girls, both known to Ia, both orphans, and who used to work in the brothel there, have also come north with the ship. It seems we are now a haven for former prostitutes to aspire to. I need to make sure that they know of my ancestor, Saint Kassiopeia.

They are sick of their old life and want to start it all over again in a new place. My husband is dismissive of the place and I tend to agree with her. There is little to appeal there, particularly for a woman. As it is, they have few skills that go beyond the bedroom, but at least they seem keen to learn others. She sighed. *That is, once they work out what they are to be.*

We have conditionally allowed them to stay, but they will have to prove themselves as capable of being useful to the village. They almost ran to find the kitchen after my husband said that to them. They have scarce emerged from there since then. I suppose that is a good start. We can always use spinners as well, and they may end up liking a more physical trade yet. Who knows? We will find out more when we return from the south.

Chapter V

Rani
28ᵗʰ Quinque

*D*eciding to go back to Sharan and actually getting something positive from the visit may be two very different things. As the *River Dragon* travelled further down the Rhastaputra she became less and less sure about why she was here and what she wanted from the stop. *I do not even know how I want to conduct the visit.*

The Maharajah has had plenty of time to make up his mind about the events that are surrounding Sharan and to actually do something positive about them. Of all the rulers in the land, except those who fight, or did fight, on the other side, the rulers of Sharan have received the earliest notice that something important was happening. However, apart from me being sent on my way, there has been nothing heard from the Maharajah at all.

My letter has not been taken away from me or retracted, and the garrison at Garthang still treat me with the same respect and co-operation, but that is all. There has not been even the slightest sign of Sharan moving out beyond its borders to join the fight or of the Kingdom attempting to help in the conflict in any way.

They passed swiftly down past Garthang Keep, with nothing much to declare at that post, and with no messages waiting for them. *I had been forlornly hoping that, with the seers available to the Maharajah, there might be something waiting there for me. We are a well-known vessel now and few craft come out from the villages and settlements to try and sell us anything. The* River Dragon *speeds down the river into the increasing warmth of the south.*

It is taking less and less time to make it down the river with each trip. Although we still send the saddles out to take soundings and look for obstacles on the upper river, each voyage we make increases the assurance with which

Olympias navigates. Even the stretch between Erave Town and Garthang, while it has some treacherous parts with many hidden dangers, apparently changes only slowly. Apparently, our captain is getting to learn the pattern of the changes.

Astrid
29ᵗʰ Quinque

*T*he start of the trip south is marked by a marriage. Marianus is marrying Mary first. Last night, our first spent travelling, the ship's crew, as well as those passengers who were on board, had their pre-wedding celebrations. Ia and I sat down with the cousins and a few others with the six women and went over things with them.*

Bianca stayed with us listening and several times turned scarlet at what she heard, which amused all of us. The Princesses fled to their cabin early on. In these conversations they are getting far too much information about us for them to be able to handle. Despite the original novelty of their marriage, the two are both somewhat prim in regard to the world in general and, it seems, much more conventional in their bed than we may be.

Marianus would keep marrying one girl on each day until Anne, Cecilia, Catherine, Winifred and Bridget were all taken. The girls had even determined the order and, apart from having secured the relative seclusion of the near empty rear hold, a made-up bed on the floor and some privacy for the next six nights, Marianus was given very little choice about the matter.

The girls were not much fussed with fine wedding dresses and had chosen, and already had delivered, seven nearly identical rings for themselves and their husband. They preferred to marry on the ship with the rest of the crew around them and with their own chaplain. "With all due respect, Bishop," as Mary said to Christopher, "he is our priest, not you."

It appeared, from the muffled sounds occasionally coming from below deck at night, that at least some of the girls may have underestimated their reaction to a careful and gentle man from their time as slaves, and it appeared that Marianus was going to be quite busy for some time. When he appeared, which was usually only to marry the next woman or to answer a call of nature, he looked stunned.

Food was even taken down below by his women and they seemed to be enjoying their unique situation even if Marianus did complain to Basil, with a smile, that he felt like he was their toy sometimes. "And you should be glad we have decided that we want to play with you," said Anne as she pulled him away with a grin.

Rani
30th Quinque

*O*ur arrival in Pavitra Phāṭaka is by now commonplace. Even as a paradēśī vessel we are almost ignored, apart from a cursory few questions and a small bribe. She shook her head in disgust. *The* River Dragon *will be loading here from our stocks and then going on to trade, first to the east and then to the west, while I try to establish a communication with the Maharajah.*

In case it turns out badly while the ship is away trading, enough saddles are to be left behind to evacuate us all out of the city and, with the people of the three triple marriages as well as Thord and Ragnilde, we should be able to physically fight our way out of most tight spots that we may find ourselves in.

She looked at what was happening on the shore. *The raccoon and the kitten seem very glad to reach land. Their mistresses restrained them on the ship as they were worried, what with the number of crocodiles and other predators in the river, of what would happen if they fell into the water from a mishap while they played.*

Now, at last on shore, they have resumed their climbing activities with the kitten displaying its ability to run straight up a smooth wall as if it were a gecko instead of a cat and the raccoon using her hands to find purchase in the gaps between the bricks to accomplish very much the same sort of feats at a pace that is not much slower.

Now Basil and Marianus can confer with Zeenat on what has been heard in the way of rumours in the city. I have decided that the first move tomorrow morning will be to go and talk to my family instead of going to see the Maharajah. It is a cautious move and although I do not regard my parents highly, if anyone knows the gossip and the feeling among the upper castes of Haven, it is sure to be my grandmother.

Everything is in hand now. She looked around. *In the meantime, I need to talk to my wife.* She walked over to where Theodora had been talking to some local men she did not know, both of them with swords. "If I take you to visit my parents' house," she said when she could draw her away, "are you going to try and get pregnant again?" she asked.

She is pursing her lips. I may not get a straight answer here. "I presume, from what you have let slip, that you do not want to do the same with one of my many brothers or countless cousins," said Theodora.

Rani shook her head distastefully. *I have given thought on that and have come to realise that I am really quite happy to stay a virgin as far as a man is concerned.*

"In that case, if I am to have a sister for Fear and Aikaterine without us using a spell—and I have not given up hope on that front—it would be best if it were done before the exact nature of our relationship is fully understood by your family. Do you agree?" Reluctantly, Rani had to signal assent. *I know my parents too well.* Theodora tried to console her husband and put her arm around her.

"I do prefer making love to you, but I have had sex with a man many times before. It does not disgust me, even if I have never felt the same with one of them as I feel about you, and I will not really enjoy it now. Pleasure is not the point here, however, and I realise now that I never did really like having sex with a man, nor did I ever reach the heights with them that I have with you."

I suppose that is a consolation of sorts.

"It seems that I was waiting for you all of my life," she continued. "If I can, I will seduce one of your brothers again and, while I have not taken any special preparations, I am at the right time and, if a chance comes about, I will take it. I will not be obvious, and will not disgrace you, my love. I promise you that. I will have Ayesha with me as a servant as well, to cover for me, just as you will be taking Lakshmi." *I am taking Lakshmi?*

"Ayesha has been training her and all her knives will be out of sight. We will also have two young men. Both of them are Kshatyas, whom Vishal knows and trusts from his childhood and they have been checked by the priests. I think that our factors may be sounding them out either as lovers or as husbands. I have not asked them which it is. It seems we have finally convinced them that caste is not important and I was told that Vishal has talked to the men on that subject as well." *What else is going on around me that I do not know about?*

Theodora looked at the expression on her face. "My love, we have sent them here away from the valley and have not provided them with husbands. If they act for themselves it is to the best. Although they both seemed to be a little scared of me, they seem to be nice boys from the short time that I have had with them." *That must be the ones she was just talking to.*

"If they are to be kept permanently by the girls, then there will be time enough to bring them to the valley and make sure they realise what they are getting into, but I do not think they are even lovers yet…but I have not asked. Stop looking surprised. You are really their Prince and their war leader and so I get to be their Princess and their mother. They are the roles that, it seems, we are best at."

Really? When was all of this arranged? "All of the girls…even Astrid… tell me things they do not think to tell you. Now Zeenat has already arranged for a boat for us in the morning. She has already made prior arrangements with the boatman we used last time to be available to us when he is wanted."

I suppose that, just as I tend to start ordering people around in battles and such situations—even those who are not our own—my wife tends to do the same on the domestic front and roll over everything that is in her way as if she were the Juggernaut unleashed. It is best if I just give in and prepare to go and approve the work that is being done here on Anta.

Fathers Hilarion and Eustathius had been waiting to show them what was happening on the island from the moment they docked. Their church had not yet been properly consecrated, and Metropolitan Cosmas had taken passage with the boat from Erave Town with a small retinue for this purpose and to look over this part of his new flock.

He has been interested in some of the events that have happened so far on the trip, and some of his people have been more than a little shocked by what is going on around them. He and Christopher have discussed the matters, and he understands the background. He seems relieved that now it is his turn to act instead of just being a spectator.

He will have a new church to consecrate. Earlier he made it through to Rising Mud to fully consecrate the new Saint Mark's, so he will have the rare privilege of officiating at the establishment of two new Churches and, with the sending of more priests into the Swamp, he has also admitted that he has high hopes of extending his See by consecrating several more.

Theodora and Rani went with the Metropolitan and the Bishop to look at the efforts of their people and saw the houses being repaired for rent and the kitchen still serving its cheap food. *It is now even larger than it was. I suppose that, especially here, food is a good way to start talking to the poor at least.*

They looked over the stables, the grain stores, the warehouse and other constructions, such as a building close to the bridge to Vyāpārī Dvīpa, which was being set up as a barracks in a position where its occupants could keep a good eye on anyone who crossed the bridge. *My wife says that it will be a base for our own experienced Antikataskopeía, when they arrive from Darkreach.*

As well as the six original guardsmen and the two young men who will go with us to visit Rani's family, all of whom are already a visible presence on the island, Zeenat apparently also has two women, whom she knows from her past, and who wanted to leave the bedroom part of their life behind to work with them as peacekeepers for "their" island in return for security.

They are already trying to act in the role in a little way, although they have to stay clear of the City Guard as they were only recently reformed and perhaps still are a little too well known to them for their past. I wonder what magic we can make that will help our people. I wish I had not said that in front of my wife. Now I am leading her around as her mind wanders.

Astrid and Ia seem delighted to discover that the young children they had held, once almost skeletal and close to death, are now running around the area and are delighted to play with the two familiars. I hope that it is safe.

The two children have been warned to be careful, and the hill-cat has been instructed in how to behave by Parminder, who is here without her husband, but it is still only very young and, after all, it is basically a wild animal.

Basil
that evening

*T*he Consecration of Saint Paul's took place as a part of the Hesperinos service and Cosmas is delighted to discover that his priests have already gathered a more than reasonable-sized flock for the occasion, including traders and their guards, Mice, and local converts. The local priests have not thought it worthwhile, or perhaps have forgotten to tell him, that food and free drinks have been promised in the tavern for all attendees.

It took a quick trip over the islands to organise their presence, but I am gratified at the result. The only problem—and it took a while to sort out—was in getting the Khitan guards to understand that the offer applied only for the Christians, and while they were welcome in the tavern, they could not have the free drinks.

Now Hulagu has ruined all of the work we put in there by establishing his own slate for them behind the bar. It seems that it will be free drinks all-round. At least everyone has acknowledged that it was a good service, and a merry evening seems to be being enjoyed by all of the attendees.

Chapter VI

Basil
the morning of 31ˢᵗ Quinque

It is a more elaborate, and indeed much more formal, preparation to go across to Hāthī Dvīpa than we made on our last visit. For a start, there will be a larger visible group going across, with the Princesses, two guards and two servants. They even have with them a number of gifts of incense as well as spilk and sh-hone for saris.

What neither of the Princesses realise is that I, along with Ayesha and Zeenat, have made a few additional arrangements for this visit. The boat is also accompanied by Puss and me on saddles, and I have Ia mounted with me. We move invisibly and so close that seemingly, to one who used a scrying, we are a magical component of the boat.

The boat has its own magic, a common propulsion enchantment and, since the Princesses are not looking for anything else and are seated far enough away towards the front, where they cannot see through the shade screen at where the enchantments are, neither of the mages has noticed the extra spells at the stern where we will stay unless we are needed.

Theodora

Warning was sent that we would be coming, and Rani's parents are waiting, but we received a slightly chillier reception than on our last visit. Initially the entire family was lined up. It is obvious that Rani's parents want to say more to her but do not want to do so in front of the paradēśī. I have even made a point of sitting a little apart from my husband, and I can see that she is nervous.

Theodora, having caught the eye of Rani's brother, soon stood.

"I think that I am getting in the way of what you want to say to your daughter. I am sure that you will all speak more freely to each other if I am not here," she said, turning to Rani's parents, "so, if you do not mind, I will take myself off to view your beautiful gardens. I am minded to sit and think for a while in that fine arbour that I found on our last visit."

She bowed and moved away, scarcely acknowledged by the family as she did so.

Theodora found her way to the bower, the scent of flowers hanging heavy in the air, the sound of songbirds ringing from their hidden cages. *It is very pleasant to sit here and it reminds me of the similar nooks on the roof of the Palace in Ardlark.* It was not long before she was found by her silent shadow, Ayesha.

This time she had not taken any special precautions so, to give her body the greatest possible chance of conceiving, it was quite some time before she returned to the reception area. Despite her chosen donor's wishes for it to be otherwise, all of his seed was placed where it would do the most good.

Rani

*O*ne by one Rani's brothers and sisters and their families left as well on *their own business.*

"I am glad she is gone," said Tanushri, Rani's mother, once they were alone with her grandmother. "Why you have to rule alongside a paradeśī, a foreigner, one who is without caste, I do not know. She seems to be sensible and have an awareness of when she is not welcome, but you should not need her. Are you not a Kshatya and a battle mage? Can you not rule alone?"

Rani sighed and glanced briefly at her grandmother. She continued to sit there, impassive and silent, and Rani returned to face her parents. "Mother, you do know who her grandfather is, don't you? Does that not make her effectively the same caste as me, if not even higher? As for her magic, she is far stronger than I am and possibly stronger than anyone I know—except for her ancestor, that is."

All I am getting are impassive looks from them. "Since I have known her I have grown greatly in my power, and I still am nowhere near as strong as she was when I first met her, and now I could destroy our entire house and gardens with but a single spell and I could cast that spell from the shore on Anta." *They frustrate me with their obstinacy.*

"You do realise that there is no caste outside Haven, don't you? Even the traders who leave here have to ignore it while they are away from here. We are going to go from here soon to a battle that could decide the fate of everyone in The Land, and we want the Maharajah to send people with us to fight. You should forget caste, it is but a temporary thing of this world and of just this cycle of our existence. What is important at present is the battle that we are fighting." *Even that has no effect.*

"There will always be caste, regardless of where we are, and that is why we should not leave here or ever send people outside," said her father, Eshwardutt. "From what you have told us you are nearly done with what is fated for you, and so you are nearly finished what you were sent away to do as our representative. When it is finished you will doubtless be coming home to marry and settle down. You will finally be leaving the paradēśī behind and will have no more to do with them." *He speaks with finality, as if that were a certain thing.*

Tanushri interjected: "I have been asking around among my acquaintances and I think there are several possible husbands who we had not considered before, who come from other towns rather than just from Pavitra Phāṭaka, who will be suitable as husbands for you. We have a very good dowry still set aside, and these are good boys of the right family and not too different in age. Soon you will be too old for children, and such a mage as you are should have many children to raise and care for."

I so much want to tell them about Theodora and Fear and Aikaterine and, seeing who has headed into the gardens after Theodora, possibly another child as well. She opened her mouth to see her grandmother, still silent and seated behind her parents, shake her head. *I think that she realises what I am going to say and she counsels against it.*

Rani changed tack. "Mother, in my valley I—or rather we—rule and we are strong. I am not saying that we are strong enough on our own to beat Sharan, but after all, it was Theodora and I who led the armies that destroyed the Brothers and eliminated their evil. Us, your daughter and my…other Princess." *I have to be careful. I almost slipped there.*

"Between us we brought together a coalition of forces that could have beaten Sharan easily. It was one that could probably have destroyed any one Kingdom in The Land except Darkreach. We have even started making raids across the oceans towards another land. We may be a small valley—we do not yet have two hundred people in it—but we are strong beyond our numbers. I have a woman among my forces, one woman, not even a man, who has killed over fifty men face to face in each of two battles with hardly a scratch to herself. Is she not worthy to be considered Kshatya?"

"If she is that virtuous, then she may be reborn as one," said her father primly. "The Maharajah has sent you out, but he will send no one else. We have talked with him after your last visit and he has made that clear. You can keep playing on your little island with the paradēśī and he has said that he will ignore what you do there."

"Many were upset that you were allowed to buy the land, but the names on the deed, although not Brahmin, are all of suitable station. It is noted that some, who the papers say were born outside Haven, have parents unknown to any here, but that happens and it is good that they are back. Apart from your people, only harijani and paradēśī live on Anta Dvīpa anyway. What you do with them, none care about."

"Has he told you to say that to me?" asked Rani. "I intend going to see him for my next visit when I have finished talking with you."

My parents are looking at each other as if deciding which one of them will speak the words. Predictably, it is my father who has lost the contest. "Yes, we have talked to him," said Eshwardutt. "You have been out among the paradēśī. You have admitted that you live as one of them in your barbarian valley." *He has a look of distaste on his face that he does not try to hide, hasn't he?*

"Do you even have a single priest there to lead you in the right rituals? Have you been to the Ghāts to purify yourself even once in all of your visits here? Have you been to a temple? You are polluted, and because of you your entire family is now polluted to some extent and we will have to be purified as soon as you leave here. How could you even think of polluting the Maharajah in exactly the same way? He will not see you, no matter how you ask, and you should not even try to do so." *Well that is direct.*

"So, if you must do it, then go away again and kill these creatures and then return here soon," said her mother. "I do not know why you bother with what you are doing. These creatures would not be able to do anything to us here in our strength. Not even Hrothnog could do anything to us when he invaded us in the last Age."

And now I know that this is not even remotely the truth. Indeed, it is the opposite of what actually happened, despite what we have been taught all of our lives. Unlike the vague comments and fanciful histories that we have here, those of Darkreach name names, they give dates, and places, and I have seen the battle banners and relics that were left behind back then.

"Anything outside of here is, in the long run, not important. So what if we lose trade? It is not essential. Everything that we really need we have here in Sharan already. However, if you have done what you have said, then it will not be hard for you to finish this whole thing off quickly and return to us to be purified. You can then be married suitably. I want to live to see my many grandchildren become mages."

I wonder if I should tell her mother that, from everything I have I learned, it is obvious that what she believes of history is wrong. The Maharajah

Balashankar was under the influence of the evil I fight now when he died attacking Nameless so long ago. No, that…that will only upset them. She tried another tack: "What if I find a partner from outside Sharan and marry them and give you children that way?"

"Then," said her mother, "I would have to say that you would be lost to us forever, and so would the children be as well. They would not even exist as far as we are concerned." *My father is nodding in agreement. A thought has occurred to my mother from the look of horror on her face.* "Is there a man outside whom you have not told us about? You have been gone so long away from us… Have you already born children to…to…a paradēśī?" *She speaks the word with distaste.*

"No, mother," said Rani, choosing her words carefully, "I have met no such man, and I think it is safe for me to say that I am not likely to. What is more, I can tell you honestly that I am still a virgin, and that I fully intend to remain that way." *My grandmother is smiling at that. She is jerking her head as if she wants to go aside and talk more freely.*

I cannot get away, but it is not needed. The conversation with my parents has petered out to an awkward silence. If I say anything else I am far too likely to explode in reaction to what they say and reveal everything. They sat for a while in silence. *We have grown so far apart that there is nothing else for us to say to each other.* Finally it was her parents who took their leave and went away to leave her alone with her grandmother.

My parents have just left us sitting here, out in the garden, where we talked. They have not invited me further into the house. No doubt they hope to lessen my polluting presence, and the amount of the house that will have to be purified once we have left. Rani could feel a sense of loss. Perhaps even tears were not too far away.

"Do not be angry with them," said her grandmother. "Your mother has always been…*conventional*…in her ways. She once had the promise of becoming a strong Water mage, but she refused to learn how and I am sure has since lost any chance of doing so. Like a muscle, if you refuse to use it, the ability decays.

"She made her choice. If she was not going to be a Battle Mage, then she would concentrate on raising mages, and so she married my son and took on a new duty. You will note that all of your birthdays lie within summer, and yet you are the only one with the gift to become a mage. It was a heavy blow to her that her only success was her daughter.

"However," she continued, "they are right in a way. You will do what you must, but you will get no more help from Sharan. The Maharajah was, indeed, very clear about that. The most that you will get from him is that he will offer you no hindrance in what you do. Someone, and I know not who, has prevailed on him to do that much. Do what you want on Anta. If you do not own all of it yet, then you should buy the rest before any of the authorities notice that you have done so. I do not think that you will be stopped.

"They will ignore you," she went on, "hoping in that way to ignore what you are doing outside and what is happening around them. In the long run it will be at their cost. I am sure that they realise this, but they chose to ignore it and pretend that it cannot be seen ahead in all of the futures. I have seen this in my scrying. Now, do I have great-grandchildren?" she asked in a swift change of subject. "My readings seem to tell me that I do,".

"You do, grandmother, but I did not lie: I am still a virgin." Her grandmother cocked an eyebrow. "You will notice that my wife... I told you about her briefly when I was last here and about the prophecy and how it came true. I am so glad to finally call her that in this house... My wife has left us and the first to leave of all the others was Kundan." *Realisation has dawned.*

"He thinks that he is the one who is seducing a Darkreach Princess; instead she treats him as we would treat a prized bull elephant and uses him to breed the child she wants. It aches for me that he takes her when I want to give her a child myself, but he has already given me one daughter called Aikaterine and hopefully he will now give me another." *She is smiling at that.*

"We also have an adopted daughter called Fear, and I am sure that she will not only be a strong mage, but she has other talents, and we have so many others with us who are talented. We have even found girls who were born among the harijani who are very strong mages. What does the whole of Haven lose from not having them and their talents?"

Rani had calmed down a little, but now her frustration showed again in her voice. "There is one girl we have who is even a mage of the Spirit realm and she was a vēśyā, a common whore, before the slavers took her. Her sister will be a Battle Mage, as I am, and shows promise to be as strong as I am one day, although she has only just come into her time as a woman."

"I have started training her, seven full years before I would be allowed to do any work with a Kshatya girl here. How much stronger will she be growing up learning how to cast Battle magic instead of just learning how to arrange flowers in order to keep a man happy? If a man wants her—I am very sure that one will eventually marry her as she shows no interest in women and will probably be as beautiful as her sister is—then he will want her for what she is in herself, not for how she was born."

The talk went off into other matters until her husband returned to them some time later. Theodora looked at Rani's grandmother as she took a seat.

"Usha knows now all about you and where you have been," said Rani sadly.

"We will make up for it when we get back to our ship, my love" said Theodora. She looked at the older woman. "I wish to be open with you. I love your granddaughter. I never thought that I would love a woman, but I do. I will make her as happy as I can for as long as she lives. She has servants and she has bodyguards and attendants and she is wealthy and she is loved."

Usha looked shrewdly at Theodora. "Do you love her just because she is firm and ripe with breasts like mangoes, or will you love her when she is old and wrinkled like I am?"

Rani felt herself blushing.

"I am working to try and find a way to make her live as long as I will," Theodora said. *Is she? This is something that we have not discussed.* "I have not found it yet, but it is always in my mind. I want to have another five hundred years with her, making love and watching our children and our grandchildren grow and prosper. My Granther made his Empress Kassiopeia, my ancestor as well, live for much longer than her allotted span. I will ask him how if I have to."

"What is more"—*Theodear is not even looking at my reaction*—"I somehow think that it is likely that my ancestor is looking for a better casting to use for his new wife and he may share what he finds with me. For my part, if I have to give her half my lifespan or more to do this, then I will. If we are to wrinkle as we age, then we will either find a way to stop it or we will not. It does not matter as long as we are together. Do you understand?"

Usha is nodding. "I do," she said, and paused. "Rani, you can either close your ears if you wish, or else you can go away so that you will not be shocked ..." Rani sat still. *My grandmother has secrets about her love life?* After a brief while, as Rani made it clear that she was not moving, Usha continued.

"I also loved another girl when I was young, and to make it even worse, she is from another caste. We both knew how our families would react, and we lacked your courage, and so we did as we were expected to and married men and had children... Close your mouth, child, you will catch a gnat" *That is directed at me. I did not even realise that I was gaping.*

"I did grow to love your grandfather and she grew to love her husband, but both of our men are dead now and my lover and I still see each other every day and make love when we can, and I would have her forever if I could—she is one of our servants, and no, I will not say who it is." *I really was not going to ask who, and I certainly cannot guess.*

"We accept what we have and are glad of having it in our twilight years, but I envy you both for your freedom to have it all your life. You have my blessing, and I ask you to look after my granddaughter...or, rather, grandchildren." She looked at Lakshmi and Ayesha standing silent behind them near the entrance. "You, girl, the one from Sharan... Come closer."

Lakshmi looked at Ayesha, who nodded. "You are not a servant," Usha stated and then reached out and patted Lakshmi, to her surprise, "but, despite carrying blades, you are not a thug." She looked at Ayesha. "She looked at you, Caliphate girl, as one would look at their śikṣaka, an instructor. You are one of their holy warriors, are you not?" Ayesha looked at Theodora, who nodded.

"I am," said Ayesha.

I would bet she wonders where this is going.

"That is good. She needs protection. I do not think that we can trust the Maharajah at all once your business is over. He may decide it that it will be tidier if you, as a problem, were to disappear. You will need to be wary of the Guard, or it may be someone who can be denied. Is there more than you?" Ayesha nodded.

"Good… Now, the other girl pretending to be a servant… My granddaughter has never paid enough attention to religion. There are many chhand, verses, in the Karma Sutra that will apply to her and her…wife. Get her a copy. I will also give you some of the names of shopkeepers who you will go to for her, and you will ask to see what they have. You will be able to find them on Vyāpārī, will you not?" Lakshmi nodded. "You may tell them a name that I use and they will know what you want, and they have been getting some interesting new toys as well lately."

Usha turned back to Rani. "See, I love you and I am doing something for you that I never did for any of my daughters or the wives of my sons…to their cost. I ask only one thing in return: can you bring the little ones from your valley to Anta that I might come to visit and see them on one of your trips here? If this is impossible, you will send a boat and I will come to you."

Rani was stunned. "Yes, Grandmother," said Theodora, and patted her stomach. "If this one takes and is a girl, she will be born in summer and I will call her Usha after you. If she does not take…I will be back and I am sure I will be able to get serviced again." She grinned and looked at Rani. *Is there no way to be more subtle about this in front of my grandmother?*

"What Lakshmi said some time ago is very right," said Theodora. "Your men seem very concerned with caste, but only until their liṅgam starts making ethical judgements for them, and firm breasts and a hungry yōnī are very persuasive arguments against any moral code." The tension was broken as all three women shared a laugh, and even Lakshmi and Ayesha smiled.

They talked for a little more before the pair gathered together their servants and the guards, those who had been left standing back near the entrance, and headed back to the wharf without seeking to say goodbye to Rani's parents.

They could not have avoided noticing us leaving their estate, but I am not going out of my way to look for them, and they, in their turn, have not come out of the main house to see us leave. Of all my family it is only my grandmother who waves us off. She has tears in her eyes, but also a faint smile on her face.

Chapter VII

Lakshmi
the afternoon of 31st Quinque

I may have been shopping for the Princesses but, from what I remember, I thought that it might be a good idea if I also take the cousins as well as Astrid and Ia, and I was right. Parminder wanted to come along when she heard as well. The woman who runs the shop we went to may have been surprised to see the paradēśī women there, but she was certainly not going to ignore their custom.

She had to explain what many of the items of carved ivory and ebony and other material that she was showing off were for, but one or another of the girls is interested in most of them and we only left after several hours and each of them was carrying a bag or a box or had things in their pouches.

To the surprise of most of the Mice, until they read it, the shopkeeper even had copies of the named holy book for sale, some even in other languages, and that in fact was how her store advertised itself—as a religious supply shop. Both Basil and Stefan may have thought that their wives had no more surprises in store for them. They will soon find out that they are very wrong.

Christopher

They have returned, but Rani went straight to their room. Theodora has had a few words to our factors before quickly following her husband. I suspect that the visit did not go as well as it could have. Now it is Hesperinos and they have just emerged. It is obvious, from the redness and puffiness of her eyes, that Rani has been in tears.

When the service was finished, Rani went straight up to Christopher and addressed him. "My family have rejected me and have made it clear that my people in Mousehole are not good enough for them to accept. It seems that unless I return to Sharan permanently, I am now lost to them. We will get nothing from here that we do not take, and so I think that it is time that I made a final break from my past and took the religion of my wife."

Christopher looked astonished.

"She does not mean all of her family, Bishop," Theodora said. "We have the blessing of her grandmother, who is a lovely and gracious lady, and she has not rejected us at all, and I am quite good enough for her. She may be shocked by this decision on religion…but that is all, and I suspect, after what I have heard from her, that perhaps even this will not make her dislike us."

Rani continued. "I cannot be bothered with all of this nonsense about caste anymore." *She is pointing at the man and woman who now look after the cleanliness of the church and the warehouse. They are the same people who had been quietly starving to death in this very building when we first arrived.*

"See these people… They walk around me as, even though they are Christian, they know that I am not and they do not want to pollute me." She walked in front of the two of them at their work and looked at the woman. "You were born harijan?"

The woman nodded. "I am becoming Christian and so I will have no caste. You already are Christian and have no caste."

She took the surprised woman in her arms and hugged her and gave her a kiss as a sister might. "I may be your ruler, but you did not pollute me when I did that. We are both free of that whole idea now." Still holding the woman, she looked at Christopher. "I am right, am I not, Bishop?"

"You are, my daughter," said Christopher. "In the sight of God all are equal. Now, before we can go ahead… I am sure that you have been listening to what I have said over the years, but I need to see that you know your catechism first and then we will arrange for the formalities of your conversion." *I have to admit that I am having difficulty stopping myself from doing a dance of happiness and excitement. I have been praying for this day for many years.*

Rani
the evening of the 1ˢᵗ of Sixtus

"You have told us," Astrid said, "that this is almost our island to do with as we want. I know that you have set out to buy the rest of it to make this fully so. Is that right?" Rani agreed. "In that case, once we own it all, the people that live here will be almost Mice." *I am slower to agree this time. Where is this going? I have learned to not trust Astrid when she starts off by asking questions that sound so innocent. They can lead us anywhere.*

"You will notice that"—*she is just ploughing ahead*—"the children here have no school. Our cleaner's children—and they are the first we should worry about—are the right age for Ruth's new class. They should come back with us. Eventually they should all come up for school and only come back home once or twice a year to see their parents."

I have not thought about that. Although they are not from Sharan, if you think of them in terms of here, almost all of the children already at the school so far are really either Brahmin or Kshatya. Only a couple of the children are even Sudra by birth. I have accepted that almost as if it were natural.

I embraced the cleaning woman as casteless when I decided to convert, but I did not think of her children as being worthy for the school. I am glad that I can now talk about these things with Bishop Christopher. In fact, I have a very long backlog of such questions that I want to address. I have been silent for a long while, haven't I? Astrid is standing there with the patience of a cat watching my face.

"You are right," said Rani. "I will speak with them."

Astrid now grinned broadly and held up her hand. "No, I don't think that you should do that. You scared her enough when you gave her a hug. I thought that her heart would fail from shock. Ia and I will talk to her instead. After all, we are the ones who nursed her children back to life when we met them and they were dying. She will obey whatever you tell her to do, but she will accept what we say, and she will do it gladly."

Rani
16th Sixtus

Little by little, we are acquiring more of Anta, and the workers who are actually ours, the guards, the people working in the store, and so on, are benefiting from the training that they are getting. The rest of the island also benefits. I am told that other people are beginning to move onto the island to live now that it is becoming a safer part of the city.

It seems that the priests spend a lot of time checking all of these new people, and a few of them are being discouraged from settling. However, there has been little else happening. It has almost been a holiday here with my wife.

Our lawyers are finding it easier and easier to buy up the rest of the island. As people leave behind their old abodes and shops and move to places that we own, the revenue dries up for the absent landlords and, while they still want us to pay as if the buildings are both very profitable and tenanted, they are at least happy to sell. They wish to wring out a final profit from the land.

I have done as my parents said and made no move to contact the Maharajah and, in return, no one has contacted us. Basil tells me that there have been some curious people who have been asking many questions, but that is all. They offer no interference.

However, I am well and truly glad to have the River Dragon *back in port. The Metropolitan left several weeks ago on the first available river trader. He took as many of his people as could fit on board and the others who came with him followed behind on the next boat that was going up the river.*

We will leave tomorrow with the two young men that Zaanat and Rahki are interested in on board and with the new children for the school. The young men will come to see Mousehole for a few days. They can return back here on the next trip down the river. The children will stay.

Chapter VIII

Astrid
22nd Sixtus

As they entered the house, Basil asked Sin if she was still minded to get married. She confirmed that she was, but she was more than a little indignant that he might think she would change her mind.

"He was just making sure, dear," said Ia. "Don't get upset with him. It is better that he gets in the habit of first asking your wishes than have it the other way around."

I am sure that Sin has been thinking of a quiet and simple ceremony. She has not even talked about getting a new dress made. Unless she did it while we were away, she has not mentioned the wedding to anyone in the village at all. That will change. "No woman will become my sister-wife without being dressed spectacularly," said Astrid.

"But I married you two lying in bed and all of us naked," said Ia, objecting.

"Exactly," replied Astrid, with the smug expression on her face of a person who has unexpectedly trumped an opponent's ace. "You were spectacular." She spoilt it by sticking her tongue out and then grinning.

Now Sin is embarrassed when we take her with a hand each, setting off to see Eleanor and Fortunata. She can get used to it. Basil, Maeve and Fluff-Ball can look after the children while we attend to this. Between them they should be able to cope. Bianca already knows of the marriage but, since she is nearby as we head out, she can now be told to let everyone else know as well.

Olympias
23rd Sixtus

Guy and Maximilian look serious. "Unlike the ladies," Max said to her, "it is obvious that we cannot have children however we work it, and while Guy teaches those of everyone else, he also wants our own child to raise. Can we ask you, while you travel the world, to look for an orphan…or even for more than one…one who has no relatives to properly love them."

His husband is nodding. "We don't care where they are from… We just want a child to love and to raise up as our own." *I suppose that I can keep an eye out. It should not be too hard. Although it is rare to see unwanted children in the villages that lie along the coast, I have seen far too many lost ones in the shadows on the streets and hiding out and barely surviving in the wreck of old buildings in Haven, for a start.*

Naeve Milker
24th Sixtus, the Feast of the Holy Trinity

Guk has arrived and pronounced himself very happy with his horses and their gear, even if he did grumble a bit over having to pay not only for them, but also for their agistment. His growing herd of animals will now give him the freedom to allow some to rest from travel and will also let him breed from them.

He now has bloodlines from outside the valley to add to and invigorate his herd. It seems that now all he needs is to encourage people to make more goods that he can travel around with to sell. He says that some, mainly among the Dwarves, complain that he does not pay them well enough and that he charges too much for what he brings. He said that now he can take their items on consignment at the prices that they set.

He was chuckling at that. He thought he had been generous with his prices and what he bought and was gleefully waiting to see what happened when something he took to sell for them didn't sell and he still charged cartage on the item as it went around the circuit. If they didn't like that, they could set up in trade themselves. He thought that this was funny. It is, but he is still paying for us to fatten his animals up on our pastures.

Christopher
29th Sixtus, the Feast of Saint John the Baptist

It is a momentous day in many respects, not only in itself, but also as the third anniversary of the freeing of Mousehole. To top it off we have the Confession and Baptism of the Princess Rani by myself as the Bishop of the Mountains. Her confession was nearly as long, with her unresolved questions accumulated over three years, as Lakshmi's was.

More importantly, although the building is still not even close to being finished, with well over half of the roof being incomplete and even most of the walls around and over the entry only low fences, the basics of the Basilica have been put in place and we could arrange to all stay dry at the altar end even if it rained.

I was able to consecrate the incomplete building to Saint George before the baptism and to also install the triptych. Using the carpets and saddles, all of the priests of my flock, even those from Dhargev, are able to attend. They will all have late services to perform when they return home, but now they can at least talk of the magnificence of the new building, and of its music, to their people.

Only one of its windows has any glass in it yet and, with some of the walls and most of its roof missing, the building is unavoidably draughty and chilly, despite Rani's best efforts. The rest of the windows have painted oilskin on them, but Hand, one of Goditha's assistants, is trying to teach herself to use the stained glass we have been given to make panels to fill the gaps.

So far she has only completed one very small window, just three hands across and six high, to a quality she thought good enough for her to allow it to be put up, but it is a start. She is now working on others of the same size that will go around what will one day be a large round window, one that is currently covered in stitched-together hides. We do not even have a design in mind for that one yet.

Astrid

It seems that Kalliope has added to her list of duties by taking the role of organist as well as linen maker and accountant. Organ is another thing that, apparently, a future wife of a Brotherhood priest is supposed to learn. Astrid looked at her sister-in-law. *She already has Erika in her office, but I wonder if that will be enough in the long run.*

At the moment she seems to be thriving on it, but she is doing so much. Luckily I was able to hint to my brother that Kalliope needs more help around the house, and he has quickly taken the hint. One of the former prostitutes from the Swamp is now happily installed as their housekeeper.

As a part of the Consecration, the gargoyle Azrael had to be moved from the Hall of Mice to the Basilica. It is a sign of how much she has grown in her role that, where once Christopher was able to carry her easily when she was a baby, it now takes me to move her, and even I found her weighty. Much more growing and we will need a litter to shift her around, and it will become a full ceremony for us to do it. At least she let us do it. I am not sure that I would like to fight her.

She moved around the outside of the building a little, seeking the right place for her perch, before settling down happily on a bare eave facing away from the gate where she would still catch much of the sun. Her only visitors now on her chosen high perch will be Maeve and Fluff-Ball, who often seek that same patch of warmth.

Astrid
35th Sixtus, the Feast Day of Saint Magnus

*S*in *was not consulted on the subject, but I think that today is quite an auspicious time for her wedding. She wanted a quiet marriage, with just those affected being present. Now it will be the first marriage to take place in Saint George's. I like that idea.*

For a while it looked as if she might back out of the affair, but I would not let her. Sin walked down the aisle with her green Freehold-style dress and her flaming red hair and pale, freckled skin contrasting against her escorting maids, a large blonde in red and an equally small and pale raven-haired girl in black. Basil chose Stefan and Hulagu to accompany him.

That night, Astrid and Ia cuddled up and slept in Sin's bed with some of their purchases from Haven and only got out to look after the children when it was needed, and it was their turn to bring breakfast into the bedroom like a pair of excited schoolgirls and embarrass their naked sister-wife and husband with questions about how they had enjoyed themselves.

Sin scrabbled to try and futilely cover herself with a blanket. *She will get over this silly modesty, at least in our own house.* The newly married pair, lying in their marriage bed, were only rescued by Maeve coming to fetch the two other women to attend to toddlers who had taken the opportunity of being unattended to make an attempt to escape from their own cots.

Chapter IX

Guy
27th September

The River Dragon returned two weeks ago and left behind it two of the many orphans of Sacred Gate for us. The poor things are so young. They were so fragile when they arrived, clutching each other tight in fear at the strangeness that is all around them. It is cold here for them, possibly for the first time ever, as winter arrives.

We are trying hard with them, but they cannot act in any way like the other children, and going outside the house to play is too hard. They grab any food that they are offered and then run and hide under a bed to eat it. They stay hidden there until they are hungry again or until they have to use a pot. The normal toilets of Mousehole are well beyond their learning at this stage.

Although they are probably at least three and four years old they have only a few words between them, and they know nothing about where they came from. They would have had someone early on to help them, but they must have been surviving and scavenging on the streets for a year or even more when Olympias found them, caught them, and brought them to us.

I arranged for an endless parade of other children to go through the room playing with toys on the floor and eventually it is this play that slowly coaxed them out from where they had hidden themselves. It is very slow work and the children do not even know their own original names. Eventually we have given up and baptised them as Lazarus and Anastasia. The names seemed to be appropriate for them.

Astrid
29th September

*D*warves from all around The Land are arriving to celebrate the marriage *of the Crown-finder. I see that Thord's parents are still surprised that their son is now reckoned to be the most important Dwarf in all The Land, at least until the King is revealed. A Druid had been brought down from Dwarvenholme to see the facilities and he advised Goditha on what needed doing.*

He has given her plans, and the underground storage area in the ridge has been *extended especially for this purpose. While this was being done, the rock has been taken out to be used for the building of Saint George's. The carrying straps we have made ensure that this is a reasonably easy operation, but it is slow and the air is full of dust there.*

Although it is nowhere near as grand as such an event would be in a Dwarven town, for a wedding held in a Human town visitors reckoned it to be the first time that a proper Dwarven chapel has been provided. That the room is otherwise to be used to store treasure and magic when it is not being used for its new purpose only adds to its appeal as far as they are concerned, particularly when many of the more decorative objects of treasure are put on display in niches in the walls when it is to be used as a temple.

Entertaining the Dwarves had been hard work for Harald and me. Many who arrived from distant parts have been shipped up to Dwarvenholme temporarily to keep them busy there. It is easier to do that and bring them back in time for the wedding than try and provide for them in the valley. Others amuse themselves on the cliffs and some help in the mine or in building.

For many Dwarves mining is not so much a job as a vocation, and the opportunity to work in such a unique mine is for them an opportunity not to be missed. The buildings outside the valley, the farms and the tannery, in particular, benefit as well. This was especially the case when we ran a contest of dry-stone walling.

There are scarce any leftover piles of stone after that, and a goodly part of the cleared fields are now fenced in. They await only a priest to bless them and add to their fertility and a mage to charm them into being proof against the cursed possums and hoppers that are starting to find our fields attractive, and against the birds and insect pests as well.

Thord's sheep, Hillstrider, has had more work to do than he has for a long time as visitors take him for a ride up to the top meadows and go to look at various local sites. Some of our other features, such as spas and the sauna, are well patronised. Crossbow competitions, often shooting against the local archers, are popular, as have been a series of lectures that Ariadne has given on artillery and the art of siege mining using her new knowledge.

Theodora

*F*irst Ruhayma, and then Roxanna, the adopted daughters of Sajāh, Norbert and Fortunata, took the first steps towards womanhood and both also show signs of being capable of becoming mages alongside the slightly older Gurinder. To the delight of their father, they are both showing that they favour Earth as their element.*

Seeing that the Earth signs are those that are most favourable for enchanting magical items, he now insists that his daughters also have to start learning how to work metal themselves. A mage who can make their own weapons, chanting the spells in as they are forged, is very rare and in great demand everywhere if they ever want to travel. Even if the girls decide that they do not to want travel anywhere beyond the valley, people will one day come to where they are to buy their work.

Rani
30ᵗʰ September

*C*arausius has delivered Aella and Elias, the new Antikataskopeía recruits for our factory, as well as Mullah Sharīk ibn Ishāq and his wife Faatina. They are all destined to live in Haven, and Faatina has the additional advantage of having experience with books of account. She can help Rakhi with the books and with taking rents, although not with the money lending.*

Sharīk is only a fairly recent graduate and has not yet obtained a posting and, seeing that they both come from the south, they are keen to return to the warmth as the other alternative they had been offered was Cold Keep, on the sea south of Skrice. Each has just as small a flock for him to care for, but at least this one has a better chance of growing, and they will be warm.

Astrid
1st October, the Feast Day of Saint Teresa of the Roses

Panic is two-thirds full, but the fact that Terror is new makes last night the darkest of the month. Even though the wedding was held underground, for some reason this is significant. Except for those caring for children, or on watch, almost the entire village crowded in and, with all of the visitors, it was very crowded. We all assembled in our best martial array.

Even Christopher and the village priests left their vestments at home and wore their war-harness. It was a splendidly soldierly gathering with the marriage being performed by the head druid of Dwarvenholme. It was reckoned to be a good omen for the marriage when it was announced that the bride is already pregnant. Thord's parents look especially proud.

The Mice used the feast to show off the skills and the resources of their village. The dishes were largely Dwarven, but food dishes from all over the land, from rollmops to pilaf, were being served.

Many local foods were used and those living at Dwarvenholme, which is still a couple of years away from being a place of plenty, despite the best efforts of Guk and lesser traders, made sure that they went away from the event well fed. The last of the Dragon sausage was even served as a special item.

I was in charge of getting the Dwarves drunk and between local beer, the rough Evilhalt arrack, the local brandy and wine, the whisky from the Newfoundland, and the smoother Southpoint rum, I think I succeeded. I made the night memorable for some and forgettable, or even totally forgotten, for others.

The Dwarves have now started leaving. As they leave for their homes the guests are pronouncing themselves well content with the event, and are even more gratified when we show the old Dwarven custom of the hosts giving gifts to the guests, with each person receiving a small pouch of ancient gold to help them on their way.

Christopher
4th October, very late in the night, but still the Feast Day of Saint Francis

*T*hat night, as most of the village lay sleeping, there was a terrific commotion in the roadway down from the valley path and the mine. People began running out of their houses, weapons and wands in hand, expecting an attack. Some of them wore clothes, but others did not. *It is as well that all of our guests have left by now.*

As they emerged from their homes they discovered that the watch had already unveiled Rani's newest spell, a device that, when triggered, brought lights into operation that banished the night from the entire lower valley. When they arrived at the scene of the commotion they then discovered that two other things had happened.

It appears that, firstly, we now have two gargoyles, and secondly, that it is just as well. Each of them is on the ground and feasting on a pig-demon. Someone—probably the Adversaries, and perhaps triggered by all of the recent Dwarven traffic—is wondering what is happening, or is about to happen. They have dispatched something, and something strong, to find out things and to wreak what havoc they can.

Where the other gargoyle appeared from will probably forever remain a mystery. That he is male is indisputable, and I tried calling him different names. When the name Chamuel was used he at least looked up briefly from his eating. I hope that this signifies agreement or at least acceptance with that name.

In the morning the demons were entirely gone and the two round and growing gargoyles were now sitting beside each other on the high wall basking in the sun. *It is possible that we could soon start to have our own flock of the beasts up there. This, and I will make sure that everyone knows my thoughts on it, is a sure sign of divine favour.*

Olympias
12th October

*W*e are back and need to be ready to set out again on the nineteenth. It does not give us much time, but at least we can be slipped and have our copper bottom checked and scrubbed clean of any growths. Then we need to stock our ship as full as we can with food and water. I want her to be able to *travel as quickly as it is possible for her to do with the load that we will have.*

We have a very long way to go on this voyage, the furthest of any of our trips by a long way, and we are also sure that the trip is going to involve battles on the sea as we go. Everything is important in a battle, and the speed and manoeuvrability of the River Dragon *have to make up for her lack of size against the fire dromond and the other craft that were seen in the prophecies.*

We are taking a far longer path around the land to Wolfneck, heading south and then sunwise to the west. We plan on going across the ocean and north along the coast of the Newfoundland as well before heading east. Rani has allowed us two months to make this trip. There is a lot can happen to a vessel in that time.

Chapter X

Theodora
19th October

The celebration of the feast of Saint Luke was performed yesterday in our partly built Saint George's Basilica, with a pale and chill late winter sky behind us. It will be the last service at home for some time for those who will be leaving to go out of the valley on what might be our last major campaign. At least it is the last that we know of at this time.

Unlike our first trips out of the valley several years ago, this time we leave behind us a strong place. It is one that is well able to defend itself and its children. Those going out are leaving a valley that is nearly fully equipped with saddles and also with enough people to run the valley in our absence, at least at a basic level.

All of our people can use a bow from horseback or saddle to effect and there are even several mages left behind. None of them are strong, but they do have a supply of wands and devices to aid them if the valley is attacked. We have been busy, and there is also a good supply of saddles on board the River Dragon, *stacked in a hold ready to be used in battle, or even just to help the ship find its way.*

Everyone going has said goodbye to those staying behind. Now we sail out of Evilhalt on what might be the final campaign. It will be dangerous. From what we have discovered it seems likely that the creatures…or people…or demi-demons…or whatever they are that we oppose, if I remember right what I scarce listened to in class as a child—ended the last Age over three thousand years ago when Darkreach was invaded.

I now wish I had paid more attention in school, but I am sure they were responsible for destroying the cities of Zim-Gand, Gil-Gand and Arnflorst, or at least polluting them with so much of their evil that they destroyed themselves. If I am right, the Adversaries are responsible for most of the bad things that have happened to The Land for the last many millennia or more.

I wish that I could get the Granther to talk more about these matters, but he waved me off when I asked. To make it worse, I have a feeling, from what she has let drop, that he has talked more with Astrid about some of these things than he has with me. It is hard to talk about them with others. The written histories dealing with those times disagree with each other and struggle to be accurate for even a small fraction of that time.

Now our small shipload of Mice is setting out from our home to either kill these Adversaries or to die in the attempt. At least all are well conscious of this from what Bishop Christopher talked about in what could be his last home sermon. It made the goodbyes harder for those who are setting out. We hope to find allies as we sail, but even without them, the die is cast.

Most of us who were going left behind children, but Basil has left a wife as well. His is one of those marriages that will be sundered by the trip. I believe that Astrid and Ia gave the pair privacy for the night. Sin has hugged her sister-wives and wished them all well when we left. All three had tears in their eyes as they said goodbye.

Atã, Tāriq, Asticus, Neon and Menas, the others setting out who have left wives behind, were also seen off nervously by their women. Goditha and Parminder are both coming along and have secured a place for their sister-daughter Gurinder. She will be our youngest mage on the trip. However, the pair of women are leaving their children, Melissa and Daniel, behind with carers.

Thord is taking Ragnilde, who can now ride a saddle. Gurinder is not the youngest person on board however, as the crew all have their children still on board and they refuse to be parted from them. My husband and I have to take Virginia and Ursula with us, as well as Yabaribaykus. On a trip like this the girl and the woman will find it hard to escape, and a solution to the problem of what to do with them might be found.

Yabaribaykus is looking forward to perhaps going home. The Goblin has managed to earn tools, a spear, a dagger, a bow and two full quivers of iron-headed arrows with his work while he was in Mousehole. Add these to his new grasp of languages and his new skills of finding and working with iron and he will be going home to be an important, and indeed a wealthy, man.

He has been talking with us and with Ruth and he has definite ideas about how he wants the relations to change between his people and the Humans who are moving into his people's realm and taking up such large parts of the most arable land. Virginia has still not worked out how to treat him, even if she has learnt a little of his tongue.

From what I have been told, for all of her life she has been taught that, because he is not a Human he is not a person but, given what she has seen in Mousehole, that whole idea of there being only one special race is getting harder and harder for her to accept. Unbeknownst to her, Ursula has been much more assiduous in talking to the small green man and she is almost fluent in his tongue.

It seems that her family has lost too many young men and women in fighting the Goblins and she is sure that she wants to see an end to war. Whatever the nobles want, she is certain that the people like her just want to stay alive in peace. She said she could happily live with a small green neighbour, or even, if what he says is true, tribes of more distant large green ones, if that is what it takes.

She looked back. *We have left Evilhalt now. This trip will be our longest away from land. We have plenty of fresh food and barrels of water on board, and something new, an enchanted box to keep some of the food fresh when it would otherwise have been inedible. However, Gundardasc is already pressuring Olympias to actually stop in the Newfoundland to re-provision. He does not fancy having to deal with being up to two months at sea with just dry and preserved food to hand.*

Our first leg will only be going across the lake. Before we sail down to Haven we have to call at Erave Town to pick up the Bear Folk who will travel with us into the north, as Changers of the Mother, to fulfil their own prophecy and their ancient writings. It seems that these stem from a time when our world was new. They are reluctant to discuss them beyond saying that these were written down by the woman who was the very first to Change and that they have been preserved by magic.

Saddle-riders have already confirmed that, to the wonder of the people who live there, a small contingent of the Bear Folk is already waiting for us to arrive. They bring word that others have already started journeying in a leisurely fashion towards the north to join up with us eventually in Wolfneck.

While sometimes one of them is seen in the town, never before had so many of them left their forest fastnesses and they have never left them when they were so obviously armed for war. I am already told that tongues are wagging and others are asking themselves whether they should be taking part as well.

The second stop will be at Sacred Gate, to drop off the Mullah and his wife and our own Antikataskopeía for the factory. All four of the people from Darkreach, although they are still a bit nervous about talking to me, are looking forward to leaving the chill snow of our mountain valley and returning to what they regard as the more welcome constant warmth of the south. They will be working in a new and very different land, but at least the work will be familiar.

Rani
24th October, the Feast Day of All Souls

Garthang Keep just waved us through, not even coming on board, but just accepting that we carry nothing for trade. Pavitra Phāṭaka again showed no sign of acknowledging our presence, beyond the cursory, when we arrived. The customs official did not even blink at us being so obviously armed and when he was informed that there were no trade goods on board, only supplies.

There could be no doubt in his mind that our ship is going to war, but no questions were asked and the garrison in the lighthouse, one of the few real parts of Sharan that is still on the island, shows no more interest in our movements this time than they have shown on any other visit. To the Maharajah, the bulk of the River Dragon, *tied up at the wharf on Anta and flying its flag, with its four ballistae now openly displayed and manned, may as well have been invisible.*

The passengers disembarked and were greeted by the residents of Anta, more money was left with the factors and more deeds were shown. *Zeenat and Rakhi have taken note of what I relayed from my grandmother and have already bought out two more landlords. They are buying vacant properties now. No one wants to pay the price demanded for unprotected and higher rent property when that belonging to the Mice has more security and is generally cheaper to rent.*

It seems that we now own the entirety of the dock-frontage property and are working on the rest of the waterfront. The girls are confident that they can pick up the remainder of the island over time but we now own over half of it. I am sure that we must be the largest landholders in Pavitra Phāṭaka already.

The girls are even about to lodge claims on several pieces of land that have no registered owners, or at least none that have survived the Burning. A small matter of a few years' back taxes and a gift to the right person are all that would be required there. None has wanted to spend so much on derelict land and buildings before. That will bring us to near seven-eighths of the land. The rest may follow in time.

What is more important, their business dealings are reaching the point that soon they will be self-sustaining. It is only the pace of our purchases and the making of loans that are stopping us from showing a goodly profit already. People are starting to make the payments on loans and we are getting a good income, even if the money rarely stays in our coffers for long.

They spent the day transacting business. The supplies of food on board were added to. Rani sent a note quietly to her grandmother expressing her thanks and love to the older woman and letting her know what was happening. The Mullah was shown the warehouse next to the church that had been cleaned and repaired and would be his mosque, and food stores were replenished and extended.

Gundardasc brought three goats on board and placed them into a pen that his wife had put there. They would give milk for the trip and, if needed, meat. Most of the people on board were prepared to sleep the night on the dry land and many took advantage of the last privacy that they would have for some time.

Basil

I have introduced our experienced people to their local recruits, and the more openly visible guards. We have a booth already in place near the bridge in front of our barracks building. In the long run it will increase security for the whole island. This would now have at least one person sitting in it around the clock. They will be there to look at suspicious individuals as they cross near the bridge and the Sthānēy Ghāt—I still struggle over saying that name—beside it.

To help them, they can detect any magic coming near their post with a glowing gem. Of course, unless one person at a time approaches it, they cannot pin down exactly where the magic is and many people carry magic with them. However, at least the occupants of the booth can tell how much magic is coming near by how bright the gem glows.

The booth has its own protection amulets in place. They also have talkers for whoever is on watch and, to encourage the people of Sacred Gate to regard the booth as an innocent addition to the facilities of the island, I have gotten our builders to paint the word "Information" in several languages on a sign that is above its open front flap.

In Darkreach this is the normal sign placed on a similarly open Antikataskopeía post and the word is well understood there as one that will work both ways. Now it is time for the people of Haven to learn of the same double meaning. They can ask here where something is, but most of the time it is those who are based here who will be finding things out.

Apparently the few Havenite peacekeepers who come over to the island from elsewhere, and do not go straight to the Entry Fort, wander bewildered through a new island. They are always greeted warmly and then ignored. They go through streets that are starting to be cleared of rubbish for the first time in many years.

Goods are now displayed in shops, and small traders and tradesmen are setting up in certain streets. Now we have temples available for foreigners. They are the only ones in all of Sacred Gate that are operating openly and, as yet, there are none for Havenites, apart from those at the Foreskin, of course.

Caravans come all of the way across the bridges to end their trip here now, local merchants throng here, finding markets of their own, and the traditional businesses who have been so poorly serving the traders for centuries over on the Eastern Shore languish instead of taking advantage of them.

My people smile when they say this, but if their City Guards try to practice any of the petty extortions that are almost expected in the rest of the city, then one of our landowners and an armed guard or two seem to be on the scene within moments. It is almost as if they are being watched in what they do but, however they look, they can see no one.

Our first two local girls are both experienced thieves and quite good, but there are only two of them as of yet. Just wait until we can recruit a few more like them and get everyone properly trained. The so-called Guard really will not know what has happened to them then.

Olympias
25th October, the Feast Day of Saint Anne

*I*t is a nice early start for us, leaving straight after Orthros. The day is still mild, and the air clear. Most were at the mosque, or the church, with Stefan giving special thanks there to Saint Anne for his resurrection at Misr al-Mãr. I had not realised it, but apparently the person who has been most affected by the patronage of the Saint in question, if there is one, takes the reading from the hagiography to mark the day.

Actually being raised from the dead sure counts there. I saw that his wives were even more vocal than their husband in the singing, and they lit a whole battery of candles between them when the service was over. I noticed that Ayesha quietly came in and lit a candle there as well, even if she took no other part in the actual ceremony and she made her own prayers next door.

We were seen off to sea by most of our people, and those people who work for us in Sacred Gate, although the rest of the city showed little sign of being awake yet. As they emerged into open waters, the upper edge of the sun was just rising over the rim of the world. A pallid band of light quickly circled around them from the horizon, and above them the light-coloured winter day soon drove the stars from the sky. *This far south it does not take long for the day to grow warm.*

As they left the river behind them, the green-light box suddenly showed a shoreline expanding behind them instead of the garbled images it had shown when they were in port. As the day went by and they sailed due south, the line of the coast receded further and further behind them and their ship's wind, ignoring the faint natural breeze coming steady from the west, drove them away from the land.

The ship swayed gently in the low swell that was coming in from the starboard beam as it headed south. Eventually, once they were out of sight of land and any fishing vessels, the saddles took to the sky to scout ahead of them. They were also given talkers so that they would not have to come back to the *River Dragon* to say what they had discovered.

Adding talkers to the available equipment should make the saddles even more useful as scouts than they were before. They can report what they see immediately instead of having to return to the ship. From now on I think that we will keep several saddles in the air all of the time, day and night. They will be built into our watch roster.

Midwinter is still near two weeks off and spring is nearly nine weeks away, but the long trip into the far north has to start out by us first sailing far to the south. She looked towards the horizon. *It seems that there is someone that we have to find there, and we have no idea where they are and are only guessing as to who they are. The best clue to their direction is that my sister has once, probably, seen one of their craft riding well to the south of Gil-Gand-Rask.*

Olympias
26th October

Since she woke this morning, Theodora has been sitting in a corner behind the wheel. She is sitting in one of our folding chairs with a slate on her lap. She is ignoring all that is happening around her and only eats or drinks in an absent-minded fashion if something is almost forced upon her. She has obviously had something occur to her and her mind is off again in one of its wanderings. I guess that we will just have to work the ship around her.

As we sail, we settle into our routine of travel with the crew looking after the ship; Hulagu and his people are up in the sky and the others are variously using what space they can for drills and practice or just staying out of the way, sometimes catching strange fish such as many of them have not seen before.

Some of the fish take the lines with them instead of being caught and the fishers are soon only using the strongest lines on rods, rather than hand-reels that might easily be lost. A more-than-usually careful watch will need to be kept the whole time now. On this trip we know that we will encounter some unfriendly craft at some stage.

As well we face the dangerous beasts of the open ocean, the dragon turtles, the great whales and the creatures that they prey on and that prey on them in turn. Olympias ordered that the light throwers be brought up from below and mounted in place of the two forward arbalests. They were covered with a cloth in case someone did penetrate the magic that hid the *River Dragon*, but that cover was easily cast aside for a battle.

Ariadne took the opportunity to bring out one of the small light throwers she had found at Ta'if. "They do not throw as far as your big ones," she said. "But they will be a nasty surprise for anything that tries to come on board." With that she slung it over her shoulder on a sling. *She already has her Thunderer on her belt and some other strange pouches, but otherwise she only carries an eating knife.*

Olympias
28th October

*W*e are well out into the ocean now. There is little chance of an accidental sighting by a fishing craft having a try at deep-sailing, not that we have talked to any from Haven that go too far out of sight of land. Olympias put the helm over and took a course to the west. *The air is hotter here than I have felt before. Not Haven, nor even Gil-Gand-Rask, was this hot.*

We have saddles out so far in all directions that they are only dots on the edge of the green-light box. Flying this high patrol proves to be a popular duty. The air is so much cooler up high, but even then people have to wear hats and long sleeves or otherwise cover themselves with a cream of Frozkintz brought from Darkreach, as the sun soon burns people's unprotected skins.

The priests and physicians soon had to help several people with that and with unguents of Froljarn, also brought from the desert lands of the east where the people are well familiar with this problem. How it becomes cool, and then actually cold, as you go further south, as some of the books we have found insist, I cannot understand.

All around us is a clear horizon. We have seen no sails for days and the only thing to break the view is the occasional leaping fish or the head of one of the long-necked sea lizards, the Uaumi, as they search the waters around them or come up to breathe. The line on the green-light box shows nothing as it sweeps around except an occasional flicker from a wheeling bird.

Now we are well below The Land and we will sail over these hot and limpid seas, breasting the faint swell for some time, until I think we are somewhere to the south of this New Found Land. When it feels right I will turn her around and sail towards the north again. Hopefully, somewhere in that trip, we will find what we seek. If not, then we will go around the circuit again.

No matter how well I keep a very close watch on the log and use what I found as we came south, I am only guessing the speed of the current we are nosing into. I can really only hope that I have made the correct calculations for when I want to turn. I am too reliant on charts and known bearings and having the details of currents on my maps.

Although our latitude is easy enough to establish, I have no accurate way of estimating how far east or west we are. If I knew more about astronomy then I guess I could discover this from the Immobile Stars, but while I know that they exist, that is about it. It is frustrating having to guess these things in unfamiliar waters. It goes against my nature to do so. I need to find out more on these things, it seems.

Olympias
29th October

*W*e have run into a shoal of fast-moving giant fish, some weighing as much as a person and with steaks on them like a land animal. They travel with us for quite a while, before our ship is outpaced by the faster-moving fish. In that time we have stocked the steaks of several into an empty water barrel which Gundardasc has happily filled with clean salt water.

Another has been put in the enchanted locker for fresh food. Gundardasc has not caught one before but he is familiar with seeing them occasionally when they are brought in by fishermen in Southpoint. He grinned when they were caught and refused to say why. Tonight we have been served raw fish and rice wrapped in sheets of seaweed, brought from Haven "just in case".

Some would not eat it, but my sister ate hers and then asked him if we had enough onions and pickling herbs on the ship with us so that, when we get to the north and, if she was able to catch the right fish, she could make rollmops for everyone. I am not sure what we just ate and I am even less sure what a rollmop is.

Theodora
32ⁿᵈ October

Now that we are headed west on a steady and even course with plenty of spare time and unlikely to be interfered with, it is time to work the spell that I have been considering. I think that I have an elegant solution for a difficult issue. Now we need to ban the use of all magic for a while until the enchantments are completed. We should only take an hour or so.

After we visited her parents we were able to confirm that Goditha is not only an Earth mage, but also one born under the sign of the Spider. This makes her best suited of all of the mages that we have on board at creating the matrix needed to enchant items. Today she will be casting a major spell that will overdraw her completely and also drain everything that she has stored up.

Despite Parminder's concern, I have decided that the casting should be fairly safe to perform under these conditions. We need to do everything to maximise the chances of success. My husband wants Goditha to stretch herself more and more in order to grow further into her role as an Earth mage. Ia is all the proof we need to do more of that stretching when we can.

Once Goditha creates the matrix, she will stand aside, and I will then cast the spell to go inside it and complete the enchantment. We have discussed this—after all, she needs to know—but what the enchantment is can be a surprise to the others. We have quite an audience today. The Bear Folk are fascinated by it. Apparently, just as it is in most cultures, much of the casting done by their people is kept secret and away from others.

In almost all places, mages jealously guard all aspects of their craft; my husband and I think this is another reason why there are so few of us. This is another thing that my husband wants to change. As far as she is concerned in her new view of magic, if nearly everyone can cast at least the simple cantrips that are needed in their daily lives, then life will be a lot better for everyone.

As the preparations were going ahead Theodora looked at the Bear Folk and the interest that they were showing in the doings of the Mice. *Perhaps, if this expedition succeeds and we all return safe, we can expect to see a rush of children from that area for the school. Ruth will be pleased and so will my husband. We may need more teachers.*

They stopped the movement of the ship with its own wind and then Goditha drew on her stored mana as well as that of her wife. The completion of the spell was marked by her starting to stagger as if she were drunk or very tired. "I am fine," she said. "It were as if I doest a full day's work and doest it all at once." After her pulse and her response to questions had been checked, she was quickly fed sweet food and drinks and soon regained her normal composure

Theodora then took her place in the charged pattern on the hatch-top. *I can feel, in that part of my mind that can sense magic, that the matrix has been well-established, it feels nice and firm, and it is eagerly waiting to be filled up. I hope no one even opens the food storage box at present. That avidity of a matrix to grasp something to fill it is always a problem when casting onto an object that already exists.*

It is far easier if the item were just being made as the casting is performed. As well, sometimes an already made object has a resistance to having new things being added to it. This is particularly the case if it already has enchantments as a part of its fabric, as the River Dragon *already does. At least I do not have to overdraw my strength for this.* She kept marshalling her thoughts and looking at her notes.

If it had been a spell capable of being cast on any ship it would have been nearly twice as expensive as this one. This spell has been made specific to the River Dragon *and anything that comes with it. If we need to change it to cast on another ship, that will take far more power than we use today.*

Theodora made sure that she was centred in the pattern, nodded at her husband, who was holding her spell book open, and began her chant. Using High Speech she completed her active component to go into Goditha's matrix. With a final twist of her fingers and a last piece of mana she locked the casting and then felt around the resulting enchantment with her mind's eye.

It feels successful to me…but the only way to find out is to test it. She went over to Olympias, who was standing there waiting and watching like everyone else. *I have not even told her what I proposed to do and Olympias is nervous of what is going to happen next to what she considers "her" ship.*

She looks surprised at what I whispered in her ear but has given the order to furl all of the sails. As they were taken in, the speed of the ship decreased until it was just slowly gliding forward down a long swell under its own momentum. Theodora kept giving her instructions while this was done. Then she again looked curiously at Theodora.

Theodora nodded and Olympias gave an order *"River Dragon…move forward."* To everyone's surprise, and with no sails up, the ship began to gather way, although it was only moving along very slowly. Olympias looked at Theodora again, and again she nodded. "Faster…faster." Gradually, and with the log being cast to check, she brought the speed up to seventeen knots.

"It seems that our casting has worked," she said. "Our ship is now fully independent both of the winds, and even of the condition of the masts." The water creamed away under her forefoot as if she were travelling under full sail and with a very strong breeze directly behind the ship. "This gives us another option for moving our craft and one that could prove quite a surprise if needed."

"When we are near others we should probably use our sails," said Theodora. "That will be just to keep our capability secret. However, we can now go into a battle with our sails stowed away. It means we will be far harder to see and, more importantly, harder to set on fire. It also means that the loss of a mast—if we can cast it loose quickly—will not even slow us down.

"I got the idea in Sacred Gate. Even the riverboat we use there to get around has something cast on it to make it move. When it is used for the ferries, the spell makes them travel a lot slower than this, but anyone who can afford it seems to have a similar spell cast on their vessel. It is far easier if the craft is light.

"One or more of their senior mages must make a lot of money off this casting. We will, over the next few weeks, add this spell to our two small craft so they need not be rowed at all, and then they can travel along at the same speed if we want them to." She paused and thought for a moment before continuing. "Actually, because they are so much smaller, perhaps I can make them go even faster."

Olympias
34th October

All of the time we have been headed west, nothing has been seen either on the green-light box, or by the saddles except marine life, patches of drifting seaweed, sometimes quite large, and sometimes a rare piece of wood covered in barnacles. The marine life is varied and we have quickly learnt to keep the small children either below decks or near the centre-line of the ship.

One morning one of the giant long-necked lizards of the sea stuck its head over the side to see what it could make away with and one of our goats was taken quickly from its pen. It gave a despairing bleat as it went and was still struggling as it was pulled under the waves.

Bloody Uaumi. I suppose that I should have thought of that. Ariadne was too slow to react as well. Perhaps she or her husband should be in the top all of the time for just such a situation. They both have those light throwers. We should use them.

After that, a person in the tops was charged to ignore anything far away and to just keep watch, wand in hand, for shadows in the water. One of the people who could operate the small light throwers was also kept up there. *Several times they have had to be used to discourage the enquiring heads of the great sea-lizards. Some of them are very persistent.*

It turns out that the light throwers are best for this job as they sometimes leave a beast thrashing in the water, blood spilling from a severed head or a missing limb, to distract predators that might otherwise attack our ship. The water boils in the feeding frenzy behind us as the weakened beast is attacked by other marine predators, and we sail on.

Olympias
8th November, it is called Sixth Tagma Day in Darkreach

*M*id-winter was a non-event. It seemed wrong to celebrate mid-winter under a cobalt-blue sky with nary a cloud above and most of our people wearing very little in the way of clothing. I had to even order the setting of the staysails simply to provide more shade on the deck. The timbers there have had to be wet down regularly to keep the planks from opening up from the heat.

My sister and the cousins have complained bitterly that their skin is not meant for these latitudes. We are running low on Frolkintz cream and people, despite the heat, have to wear broad-brimmed straw hats and shirts lest their skin turn bright red and peel. Nothing has really happened the whole way west.

Today I have ordered the helm put over and we are now headed north. This brings our battles closer to us and it seemed appropriate that we do this today, of all days. Our battle is yet to come and we have to hope that our sacrifice will not be as great as those we remember. Of course, those of us from Darkreach have spent the morning explaining to the others why the day is important. I do wish that they taught proper history among the varvady.

Theodora

*W*e draw closer to what may be the end of our journey, and also closer to what could even be the end of us if we fail, or perhaps even if we succeed. Only those of us who are from Darkreach understand Sixth Tagma Day. No one else has the same sort of idea. It does not mark a Holy Day or one of festival. It is a time to just sit down and think about sacrifice.

I cannot wear a poppy, but I have been thinking nonetheless about what it means. My great-grandmother Veronike died in those battles, another great-grandmother, Kassiopeia, fought in them and became Empress, and we won them. I have just realised that now I am doing exactly as Veronike did.

Would Veronike be proud of me? I think she would. She led a Tagma into battle, I help lead a little village. However, what we do we do for others, not for ourselves. If we save people because of what we do, they may not even know it. Even if they know it, they may not know who did it for them.

Somehow, I think that the Granther will be pleased with what I have just worked out. I think he allowed me to leave the Empire in the first place to see if I could grow or if I would wither when I met the horrible world that the varvady live in. He, I think, deliberately—although I don't know why—stays inside the bounds of his Empire, but now it is up to me, and the others that do come outside, to act to make this outside a better place for all.

Chapter XI

Olympias
12ᵗʰ November, the Feast Day of Our Lady

"I can see an island through my telescope." *It is Anahita on a far-speaker. She has the forward scouting position in the sky at present.* "It is away on the far horizon and I can make out that it has ships near it, and some other dots that could be smaller boats." *That is a surprise.*

I have collected all that is known from Darkreach and from the maps that the Mice have collected. My master chart now has on it everything that I have been able to find out or even guess as to what lies out in the sea. It shows no detail, just the outlines of land, or at least the outlines of places where there might be land. Mind you, it does all lie on a map that is more notable for its vagueness than its accuracy.

I have one small group of islands marked as existing somewhere to the east of The Land, but that is the only unknown island in the open seas that we know about. We have no precise location for it, but everything I have says that it is not located anywhere nearby in this sea anyway. What is more, we should now be sailing away from the landmass that is called the Great Southern Land.

I know little of that place, except that it is now probably somewhere directly to our south. What we know of that land comes in contradictory accounts; all we are sure of is that it is the place the Eldar fled to when they were expelled for their treachery. Most importantly, nothing is indicated in this area at all.

"I will bet that it is flat," said Astrid, "so flat that it looks as if a big wave would wash over it, and the only things standing on it are buildings." Olympias just looked at her sister-in-law.

Olympias picked up her far-speaker. "Is it very flat with just buildings on it?" she asked.

All those around Olympias could hear the reply: "How did you know?" *The faces around me echo my question.*

"Because it is not an island, it is a town of the Sea Nomads," Astrid replied to those around her. "Everyone keeps forgetting about them. Remember what I said about Ia's vision? As well, I am sure that it was one of their towns that I saw when we were on the top of Tor Karoso on Gil-Gand-Rask. Harnermêŝ has some of their tongue, I think. He can talk to them." She bent down to the talker held in Olympias' hand. "Are the ships like ours?"

There was silence from the other end. "I can see more as we get closer… One is like the *River Dragon* but with another mast… It is sailing off to the east… There are two others…like the ones on the lake… I suppose that they are fishing boats… There may be another like ours, but bigger, tied up against the island…the town…but it is hard to see it against the buildings and there may be other small ones… The dots… I am not sure."

Harnermêŝ had come down from above in the mast by now. "Remember," he said, "that when you came to the reef, and brought me Jahnifer, we thought you were a Sea Nomad ship when you first arrived. All of their ships that we saw are like this one or bigger, some much bigger. The towns never come too close to the island. It is too dangerous for them as they do not steer well.

"Do I get to go there?" he asked eagerly. "Hardly anyone of our people ever gets to actually land on their floating islands. They deal with us most of the time from their ships and they come to our island to do it." *Everyone is looking at Rani.*

Rani thought for a while. "We will send the air group up and Theodora and I will go with them. We will stay well clear of the island unless we are needed. Harnermêŝ can go with Astrid and make contact with the people that are on it. Two people should not seem like a threat to them. Just be careful and take all of your magic with you." People began to move.

"I want you to take no risks at all," Rani hurriedly added, "and I want you to be polite. Remember that we are supposed to find ships to sail with us as well as against us…according to the vision that Ia had. It would be nice if they came complete with crews and people to fight for us instead of just a hull that we have to somehow crew."

"I want to go with them," said Ia suddenly.

"Why?" asked Rani.

"I don't know… I just feel…for some reason…that I have to," replied Ia. "It is my vision that we are following here after all. Besides, neither of them can cast a spell or sense magic in any way or even knows when to use a wand or not. My beloved sister-wife can protect us all physically, but I want to be there as well."

Calgacus interrupted. The chief priest of the Bear Folk and the rest of his people that were on board had said little so far on the trip beyond the usual pleasantries of people confined together in the same small space. While it was being revealed what could be seen, they had been talking in a huddle and now joined the general conversation.

"My wife, Bebin"—his voice dropped with the habitual reticence of the Bear People to speak openly about their business as he said the next part—"who, as you know is also a priestess of our faith, believes that you should go with them as well.

"We have many legends and tales and prophecies about the beginning and the end. Some of those concerning the beginning of all things use words to the effect that, after some of the other gods argued with the Mother and disobeyed her, they fled to sea to avoid the consequences and so disappeared. Some, it is said, stayed on the island and hid. These may be among the ones who went to sea. I do not know, but perhaps this is the case."

Rani thought about that only briefly. "Go then," she said, handing Ia a talker. "Perhaps you will be able to stay a little clear of the others and relay back to us all that happens."

After kissing their spouses, the three moved towards their saddles to make ready to take off.

Astrid

When Astrid arrived at her saddle, Fluff-Ball was already sitting on it waiting. She looked at Ia's saddle. *Maeve is sitting on it in an identical fashion.* "Are you two talking to each other?" she asked her cat, and turned. "Parminder, does my cat know that we are going over all this water?"

Parminder looked at Fluff-Ball. "She knows. I think that the other one told her, but I cannot be sure as I cannot talk to her. Your cat is not as easy to read as the house cats in the valley are and I am still learning the shape of her mind…but she knows. I think that she thinks she has to be with you all of the time in case you are in danger."

Me in danger. Astrid grinned and tousled the cat's furry head and then, with her laughter ringing in the ears of the people on the ship, they took off. *Behind us the rest of those who will be following and staying clear, unless there is a problem, can take more time to mount their saddles and take off. I am away before someone realises something I don't want them to realise.*

Olympias

The *River Dragon* turned its prow directly towards their destination and Olympias kept a close eye on the green-light box. *I am keeping one saddle well to the rear of the ship. It is maintaining an eye out there in case of any surprises coming up on us from that direction.*

A cluster of dots on the screen indicated the forward air group, all now well out of sight. They had joined their scouts and they were now all moving forward. Ahead of them were the smaller group of three, now merging together into one dot as they moved further away and out of sight. Others rose into the air to keep looking to the flanks. Soon most of the saddles were in the air.

The first flyers, now all one dot, are nearly at their destination and the green-light box finally picks up the first sign of a dot from the Sea Nomads. It would be from the supposed barquentine heading east rather than the town. It is further away from the River Dragon *than the island-town, but the billowing sails on its four tall masts make it stand out more easily than the lower structure.*

Astrid

Fluff-Ball has refused to be tied onto the saddle. The strange grip that lets her hang on to a sheer rock wall seems to work just as well on the saddle, although, as her fur streams back in the wind of passage, at this speed she is also using her claws. I really will need to do something to reinforce the leather on the saddle or it will end up in shreds eventually.

Astrid glanced sideways. *Ia has ended up looping some leather around the fittings of the saddle and Maeve uses her rear claws to hang on and adds the use of her hands to steady herself, just as an inexperienced human might use their knees but also hold onto the reins of a horse. The smaller animal also seems to be enjoying herself. The animals sometimes glance at each other.*

It took a long time before Astrid came up to Anahita. The scout waved her telescope to point them ahead at a dot on the horizon. *Well, they won't be seeing us easily from there. Even I can barely see them.* Anahita quickly fell behind as she waited, stationary, for the rest of the flyers to catch her. Astrid, Ia and Harnermês drew together to talk as they flew.

"Do we stay high or go low?" Astrid asked. "Either way could be seen as an attack."

"I think that, when we think they should have seen us, we drop to a hundred or so paces up and, when we get to a long ballista range we should slow right down," said Harnermês. "However, perhaps, seeing I speak their language, I should take the lead then and you two should hang back a little and not land until we see how they greet me."

"I am useless floating around in the air like a hummingbird if something happens," said Astrid. "I should land at the same time as you... Ia is our cover and I have the bracelet anyway." Harnermês thought for a moment and nodded, and they flew on as Ia reported back to the ship what they had decided to do.

Astrid

*T*hey drew closer, gradually dropping down as they did so. *It took quite some time, but it is obvious when we are finally seen by a lookout. There are four structures around the edge like huts on tall legs, with bracing to keep them stable, and they are roughly equally spaced around the village. In the one that is closest to us a person is ringing a bell and pointing in our direction.*

He must not have been looking up into the sky until now, or else he had thought us to be birds. His actions are clearly visible to us. Harnermês began to drop lower to their agreed height, and slowed. Astrid joined him, staying about thirty paces to his left. *We should stay out of the range of one normal bursting spell.* She looked around. *Ia is about the same distance behind us and in the centre. The talker is up to her lips.*

"Here we go," Astrid shouted across the distance between them.

Harnermês turned to her and grinned. "I have never heard of them being unfriendly," he said cheerfully. However, he spoiled it by adding in the same tone: "But then, I have never heard of anyone coming and landing on one of their rafts before without an invitation."

"Just remember that I will not understand a word of what you say," said Astrid. "I didn't point it out to the Princesses, and they didn't think of it, but you will notice that we have to speak in Darkspeech. You've read a book and learnt it. For both Ia and me, though, our Hindi is...ahhh... strongly accented, and your Greek is as bad as mine is. I don't have any of what they speak here, and have no High Speech at all."

"But..." Harnermês looked surprised.

"Yeah... You thought that I would mention something like that, didn't you? There is no chance of that happening. Theodora is the next best after me at close combat and she also speaks High Speech well enough, but I would cop hell from my husband if I let her come. Just don't be obvious: pull your left earlobe if you are worried and scratch your head if you are *really* worried and your right ear lobe if all is going well." She grinned widely.

"Don't worry," she said, "What could possibly go wrong? You can be a friendly islander and look all innocent and unarmed to them, and I will look like the dumb armsman who is there to back you up if need be… I am very good at that." She grinned again.

They drew closer. *The structure looks like almost any other village, particularly one of the island villages of the Swamp. There are only a few details about it that are wrong, like the fields covering it that are between and even under the houses, the masts that are around the edge of the platform, and the fact that it is in the middle of an ocean.*

Each of the masts is nearly the size of the mainmast on the River Dragon *and they carry a mix of sails on them. I can see, however, that the course they are steering has nothing to do with the real wind. They are headed towards the north, apparently with a following wind, despite the gentle westerly that is actually blowing.*

"They have their own wind pushing them," she said to the others. "It does not move them as fast as our ship can go, but there is a lot of island for the wind to have to move."

Although I can see lower ledges around the edge in several places, the actual platform of the raft is far higher out of the water than the deck of the River Dragon *is. It also has a fence around it, placed some way from the edge and one that a person could only just see over.*

It looks like they have come upon a simple system that will help them to avoid having the same problems with the different types of long-necked swimming lizards that we have encountered. Perhaps the need to gain the extra freeboard is why their barquentines are so much larger than ours. It is unlikely that they have light throwers to help drive the beasts off.

The side of the village that they were approaching, facing the rear as it sailed north, had a huge gated dock let into it. The gates on it, seemingly made of very thick stalks of bamboo, were currently open. The dock jutted deep into the island, opening up into a huge square of seemingly open water. *It even has finger wharfs coming out into their artificial bay.*

It will take far larger craft than the River Dragon *and one of them is moored there now. It has four masts and is tied up to the centre wharf. Three smaller craft are at the sides of the dock. Well back from the water, leaving enough room in front of it for a ship to load and unload, is another smaller fence.*

"Head for the dock?" asked Harnermês.

"I guess that it is where they would expect visitors to enter," replied Astrid. "Perhaps, for once, we should do the expected thing," she said, and they began steering that way.

Covering the huge raft are houses, all of them built on stilts to save space and allow things to grow or be stored under them. Most of the surface is hidden under crops of different sorts in raised beds. There are even vines, and palm and fruit trees, even if it is obvious that many of these are growing in huge pots and supported against the winds by having ropes attached to them.

A small patch of the thick-stemmed bamboo can be seen and it looks like they cut the smaller stalks to make their fences and the larger ones to make legs for the houses, as well as the gates and pots. Paths run all around. The houses are grouped in the centre around an open square. "I think that they have a well in the square," said Harnermês. "Do they drink salt water?"

"You are the one who knows them, not me… It looks like their archers are ready for us if we look too hostile and they have arbalests on some of those platforms as well. I wish they were not following us with them… Now smile and try to look friendly. We are getting close and some of them are using glasses on us."

Astrid was guiding her saddle with her knees now as she scratched behind Fluff-Ball's ears, ready to hang on to her if she needed to. *She is already far bigger than most house cats, although not ours in Wolfneck, even if she is still only young. I can see a few animals that look like cats now we are lower. It may not be very good if a fight starts between the animals.*

As they flew in and looked down it was apparent through the clear water that the whole side of the raft seemed to be a mass of woven vines. *I can even see vines trailing out into the water around the sides. Without getting a close look, it seems like some of the patches of weed that we have seen floating out in the open sea. Here they are all woven into a mass that stands high out of the ocean.*

Harnermês

I *think we will land at the end of one of the docks. It seems like a good idea to be as far from anything as is possible and to even get the benefit of cover of the docked ship from the ballistae on the walls and many of the archers.* He climbed off his saddle and waited, standing meekly beside it until someone came near.

Astrid has done the same beside me, although one of her hands remains resting on her fluffy cat. "Good luck," she said. *I am not sure if I like the sound of that. I would prefer not to need it.* He held his right hand up with the palm facing the people approaching and made sure that his left hand was visibly away from his belt. He had a dagger there, but his bow and javelins stayed on the saddle.

I am unarmed and dressed only in my kilt. At least I still look exactly like the islander that I was. I am glad that Astrid decided not to put her mail on before leaving and is only wearing a short kilt and a shirt tied at the front under her breasts in the same fashion as the girl sailors do. I am guessing she didn't forget, she just went for comfort.

Even with her huge weapon she doesn't look all that threatening as she even has bare legs and feet, just as most of the Mice are doing on the ship. The people that are coming towards us have their weapons in hand as well and theirs are at the ready. All of them look to be far more aggressive than she does.

"Greetings" said Harnermêŝ loudly, so that all might hear him, in his highly accented Sea Nomad tongue.

"You speak our language?" one of the people coming towards him said, an expression of surprise on his face. He stopped about four paces away and looked at the visitors in front of them. *We are just returning his gaze. They have even darker skin than I do, but they are generally all like that from what I have seen before.*

They all have black hair, some held back from their faces, but most have their hair brushed so that it is almost a globe around their head. Their hair has combs and decorations stuck in it and some of the faces ahead of us are heavily tattooed in a dark ink. They wear little in the way of clothing—just a skirt.

They are generally big people; even most of the women are as tall as or taller than Astrid and far broader. Some seem fat, but from the breadth of their shoulders it is probably fat that is underlain with huge slabs of muscle. They would not run fast, but I think that I would not do well in a wrestling match with them.

"I have a little of it and I have talked with some of your people before when they came to our island," said Harnermêŝ. "I was born on Gil-Gand, but I was not thrown off it and I am free to return if I wish. My name is Harnermêŝ. This is Astrid." He waved in her direction. "She is from the north and does not speak your tongue, and neither does Ia, who flies along behind us. We come to visit you in peace and want to talk with you."

"If you are from Gil-Gand, and she is from the north, why do you fly to us from our south? You cannot travel for many days on those things. Where is your ship?" *I may have been open and introduced us, but none of the people ahead of us have yet given me a name or welcomed us.* He paused and pulled on his left ear. *Astrid has stood more upright and let go of the cat.*

"It is some way behind us, but it will be on us in a few hours," he replied. "If your watchers look into the sky from where we came they will see that there are others on saddles like ours." He turned, pointed to where they were visible as dots in the sky. *I suppose that they are easily mistaken for birds, when you look from here.*

The person that he was talking to barked something that was too quick for him to follow and another ran off towards the nearest watchtower. Harnermês continued: "They wait to see if they will be allowed to approach. We did not wish to seem threatening, so only three of us came ahead."

"Three of you threaten us? One ship and some flyers threaten us?" *At least the man seems to be amused by the concept instead of angry. I wonder how much I should say.* He glanced around. *Astrid is looking over the people ahead of her speculatively.*

I wasn't with her when she took on so many enemies in battle, but those ahead of us look to have no armour or shields and very little in the way of weapons, apart from various swords and light spears. Some of their weapons even seem to be made of a polished green stone. What is more, being on this wharf they can only come ahead at us four or five at a time.

I think that they might receive a rude shock. He tossed it up in his mind. *Let us be honest: if we are going to be in trouble we can see how good these charms that we wear are. Their bows are mainly behind the fences and that should be far enough to give us an edge.*

"The lady standing beside me led an assault on the home of the ghazi, those that most of us call assassins, in the middle of the Caliphate. I was not there, but I believe that she, on her own, killed over fifty of them. She is not our only warrior, nor is this the first time that she has killed so many in one battle."

He spoke modestly but he could see their attention begin to shift towards Astrid. *She has obviously noticed the same as she smiles at them. That could have a variety of effects. I think that they have finally noted her teeth from their muttered comments and a general drawing back.*

Harnermês continued: "But we are not here to challenge you. We are part of a challenge to the evil that afflicts the world. So far, the people with me and on our ship have brought down the Brotherhood in their corrupt malevolence and have slain many other fell creatures. Ia, the girl who flies behind us… She is a priestess of the Mother and she had a vision that our ship would encounter other ships that are like it to aid us in our Quest."

As he spoke he indicated the ship tied up beside him with one waving hand and continued. "We have been embarked on a Quest, some of us have been on this journey for many years, and as a part of this we seek to find and destroy a stolen fire ship from Darkreach as well as another large ship of our enemies that would prey on the helpless. Once this is done we will seek to find the source of most of the evil of the world to crush it for the final time."

"What do you mean *a fire ship?*" asked the man abruptly.

"It is a great vessel, with a hull the size of one of your vessels. It is covered in metal and it can use either oars or sails, although, like your island, it has its own wind behind it. It has…huge exploding arrows that leave fire behind them as they fly and that can travel further than any thrower…and, when it comes close the ship is able to breathe fire like a dragon and this fire cannot be put out by water, but only by special magic. It will burn all that it touches. This craft was stolen from Darkreach by the evil that we seek and we are charged to sink it as soon as we can. Ia tells us that, if we come this way, we will find it."

Harnermês looked at the consternation ahead of him. *I am not sure what it is, or why, but there are very few of the islanders bothering to watch us now. They are only half looking at us and are mostly paying attention to each other as quiet discussions and arguments break out among them. We are almost being ignored by the people ahead of us.*

Even the one who had been doing the talking is now consulting behind his hand with the two men on either side of him. His eyes are entirely on the people beside him and not on the Mice at all, he is turning his back on me. I could probably walk up and slap them without anyone noticing what I did before they were hit.

"What did you just say?" asked Astrid "They certainly seem to be excited by it." Harnermês filled her in on what had taken place. He was talking loud enough that Ia could hear what he said and relay it all back to the others.

Eventually the attention of the man came back to him. "Get her to land," said the man, pointing at Ia. "We would speak to her about her vision."

"I have already said that she cannot speak to you," said Harnermês.

"You will translate for me."

Harnermês turned around to Ia. "It looks like you were right to come with us. They want to speak with you through me." She nodded and reported what was happening and then brought her saddle down.

Maeve is sitting up and looking relaxed. She is chattering at the cat. It is sitting on the back of the saddle like a panther on a tree branch. The tip of her tail is just barely moving.

Ia hopped off her saddle and came forward to where the man stood. She took a place directly in front of him and less than a pace away as she looked him up and down. He looked down at her. *She has her hands resting on the pommels of her sword and main-gauche and is dressed the same as Astrid, except for the open pouches of wands and the two single wands that are strapped to her arms. She is not taking any shit from him, and he will know it.*

The man in front is far darker than me. His nose is broader, although fitting with the breadth of his face, as are all of the ones ahead of us, on both men and women. In their hair, as if they were crests, around their necks as necklaces and even through piercings in their noses and ears are a variety of bones, shells, rough-cut gems, bright coloured birds' feathers and even polished wood.

With Ia standing there in front of him it is even more emphasised that these islanders are all tall people and broad with it. All of them wear a kilt made of a material I have only seen on them. Ia smiles sweetly up at the man but says nothing.

Eventually the silence of mutual inspection was broken. "Tell this child to describe exactly what she saw," the man said.

Harnermêŝ turned to Ia. "He is being quite rude about this, but he wants you to say exactly what you saw."

Ia shrugged. She spoke a few words and then paused for the translation. "I can do that easily. I saw the *River Dragon*…our ship…leading two larger ships as they sailed north. They were travelling together and were not fighting each other. Having now seen this one"—she pointed at the barquentine beside her—"this was one of the ships I saw in my vision and the other was like her."

She stopped to see the reaction to her words as Harnermêŝ finished his translation. What he said caused more discussion and she waited for it to die down before she continued.

"It is hard to say if it was before that or after, but the *River Dragon* fought two or more ships. One was the dromond with its great lateen sails and its metal-covered hull. The other could have been one of the great ships of Freehold or it could have been another barquentine. I am not sure, but I think it was a Freehold ship. It was not one of the two that were with the *River Dragon*." Piecemeal, Harnermêŝ translated that and again there was a round of discussion among the people in front of them.

"They are speaking fast," he said, "and I am only catching bits of what they are saying. They have had some sort of loss, and I think the dromond may have been involved in it, or at least some of them now think that it might. That is what they are arguing about. They seem to be like the Khitan and to not allow interference in their affairs, but my use of this language is very poor and I have to think to translate, and they are speaking so fast that I am missing a lot when I think about a word. I guess that we may not find out unless they tell us."

"I think that they seem ready to hear the next bit," said Ia, and she continued: "I do not know if we will sail with the two ships before or after we fight the dromond and the other. I do not know if we will fight the others separately or together. All I know is that we will fight the other two with our ship. Now end by asking if they are with us and wish to fight against evil or if they wish to fight against us and be on the side of evil."

"Are you sure that you want to be so blunt in what you say?" asked Harnermêŝ with a hint of worry in his voice.

Ia shrugged. "They certainly are," she said. He reluctantly translated as Ia smiled up at the man again. *That is provoking even more discussion. Ia is taking advantage of the lack of attention to report back to those behind them on the talker.*

"What is she doing?" asked the man.

"She tells our people to the south that we are safe and what is happening here. If you led a vessel, would you not want to know what was happening to your people if they were on someone else's ship?" Harnermês replied innocently.

"Why should we not think that you are going to attack us? Why should we not just kill you all now and take your weapons and magic from you? Why should we believe you?"

Harnermês scratched his head as if in puzzlement. "Firstly, you will not be able to use most of our magic. You can try and fly my…sky-boat…if you wish." He stood clear of the saddle and waved towards it.

"Second, the talker will only talk to another like it, and they are all in the sky and on the ship. Thirdly: although we come in peace, we are prepared for war and, if you try to kill us, you may succeed with your entire village against just us three, or you may not, but in the end we will kill you and destroy your village. Our people do that to any who serve evil and if you attack us you will be serving evil."

I am trying to look confident. I am learning the games of cards that are now being played to while away the spare time on the ship, and I have my best card-playing face on. I am hoping that it works at least a little better here than it does when I am on the ship and losing money.

The man who stood in front of Ia has several of the others in the crowd rebuking him for his attitude. This includes a big, bare-breasted woman who has pushed her way through the crowd of men and is now berating him as her stupid husband and as a man who doesn't have the sense to get out of the water when a pack of…and I don't know what that word means…are approaching him.

The woman turned to Ia and took her hands in her own and looked at Harnermês. "Tell the little ghost girl that my name is Wiki and this is my stupid and rude husband Taine, and that the women of Tabuaeran welcome the women of your ship to ours." She leant down and rubbed the nose of the surprised girl with her own. Harnermês did as he was told, pulling on his right ear the whole time. *The man before me looks deflated.*

"They seem to have men's and women's councils like our island," Harnermês added.

When he had finished, the woman looked at him and glanced a little more dubiously at Astrid. "The girl with teeth is also welcome. Is she from the same land as little ghost girl?"

"She is the sister-wife of little...of Ia, and they share a husband," said Harnermês.

"It is not you?" Harnermês shook his head. "He is not here with them? Does he not love them?" said Wiki.

"He has duty to keep him beside one of those in the sky," said. "He is a"—he struggled for a word—"a captain-guard."

The woman seemed to understand, grunted, and gestured behind her. Another, much younger and smaller woman came out. "He might have more sense of what is right than some other men." Her husband looked indignant and there were several snickers from the others nearby. "You tell girls that we will let them on island and that this is my sister-wife Hopo... Ghost girl speak anything but that tongue you are all using between you?"

"They both speak some Hindi," said Harnermês. "Ia also speaks the tongue of my land and Astrid...I think...speaks the tongue of the people of the far north in the ice. I do not think that you will know any others that they have."

"Then you can wait for my idiot husband to make up his mind as to what the men will do. We will get the girls to come with me into the island." She turned to Ia and was about to speak when Taine finally got a word in edgewise against the torrent that was his wife.

"Their people in the sky may land and then we will welcome them all into the village. Until then we will wait here." *Wiki seems satisfied with that and she has moved to where Ia is and gathered her up and gone to Astrid.*

Astrid

Leaning forward, Astrid rubbed noses with the woman. *At least I expected that. It seems to be what they use like a hug or a handshake here. The Inuit do the same and I am used to their habits. It seems that these people are a lot like them.*

Wiki began speaking in a mix of High Speech and very broken Hindi and asking the two about themselves. *She seems to be almost a force of nature in her personality. She even silences me a little with her flow. No wonder she is the leader of the women. She would be a leader anywhere. I wonder if her husband owes his position to her and if he really is as stupid as he has been made to sound. Perhaps he is the hard voice and she is the soft one.*

She turned. *Butterfly has used the talker to call the others and they are now coming into the island village as she talks to the big woman. The younger and thinner one has come to rub noses and is trying to talk to me now, but her*

Hindi is almost non-existent. I have to concentrate to make out a single word of what she says.

Astrid

Eventually the Mice from the sky landed and a few introductions were made. *It seems that many of these Sea Nomads speak at least a little High Speech and that some have a little Hindi.* Each one as they approached another person for the first time rubbed noses with the person that they wanted to talk to.

Only one woman had approached Astrid and, after rubbing noses, had tried out her Inuit on her. *It is as bad as mine, and between our accents we each have to repeat everything several times and we are both laughing. These people laugh out loud and slap their thighs when they think something is funny. They slap their thighs a lot.*

I like these people. They seem to find it easy to laugh. I don't know what all of the laughter is about, but everything seems to strike them as funny about their visitors, from our hair to our clothes, both of which they finger openly and without asking permission about once they are introduced. Astrid did the same to their hair and the odd cloth. *They don't object. The cloth does not seem woven. It seems to be almost like a soft and very thick vegetable leather and the patterns on it are painted on rather than woven in.*

When everyone had been introduced they were led inside the wall to where three rows of men were drawn up. *Their faces are painted and several have tattoos on them that cover most of their faces. They are armed as if for war and most have spears, although several of the weapons seem to be of the green stone rather than a metal. They all have skirts that seem to be made of grass, with strips of the strange cloth down the front and the back.*

"It is a welcome ceremony…I think," Harnermêŝ said.

The lines of men began chanting and stamping their feet and twisting their faces into wild expressions as they shouted and hit weapons and spun them around in the air. *They move in unison in what looks like a dance of war, but still it is a well-choreographed performance. They poke their tongues out and open their eyes wide, they slap their thighs and their arm muscles with their hands and run towards us and stop and then back away while still calling their chant.*

It is obvious that they are showing off their muscles and their power in what seems to perhaps be some sort of challenge. It seems they are all chanting the same words, just as monks do. Eventually they all gave a great shout and laid their weapons down beside them.

Rani started to speak, but Astrid interrupted her reply. *Whatever she is saying in High Speech will not be right. Rani can give me a dirty look if she wants, but I am sure that I am right about this.*

"Tell them that I will dance them a dance in return," she said to Harnermês as she handed Ia her bardiche and stripped off her shirt, leaving her upper body and limbs as bare as that of the local women except for the golden torques and the bracers on her arms. *I have bigger and firmer breasts than most of the women on the island and my muscles really stand out now.*

Astrid took her weapon back and strode out in front of the men and began to improvise around one of her exercise routines that, among other moves, had her rotating her huge blade like a quarterstaff. She broke out of that and made the great blade swung through the air, missing the nose of one of the men by a few fingers as his eyes opened wide.

He has been watching my breasts swinging in the air and not at the dance. He rapidly changed focus after the blade going so close made him pull back. *From some of the cries and laughter and thigh slapping from them, I think that the local women noticed where his eyes were focussed as well.*

I just shout and cry out random words in Darkspeech and thump the ground, or whatever it is that the raft has. It seems to be made of dirt, but it has a faint bounce to it when I land. Eventually she performed a manoeuvre designed to clear a low blow and leapt high into the air, tucking one of her legs up beneath her and kicking the other out in front, as if she were going to kick a man in the head.

She jumped so high that she was nearly two paces up, before coming down softly and landing on one knee with one knuckle on the ground and the other laying her bardiche down as she stared at the man in front of her with her teeth exposed in a big grin. The Sea Nomad women erupted in applause and were gradually followed by the men. It seemed that her display, so different to theirs and yet obviously meant in the same way, found favour with them.

A girl the size of Ia but so young as to have breasts that are only little black buds comes over with a jug of water and hands it to me. At least it seems to be good and fresh water. As Astrid was drinking, the girl looked to see if anyone was close to them and then whispered in fluent Hindi: "Ask them where Moorea is now."

She is looking grimly at me. "Moorea. Remember the name," she repeated and then, taking the jug, went away. Astrid rolled the word over in her mind. *I have never heard it before.* Standing up, she went over and regained her shirt, but did not put it back on, just throwing it over her shoulder. *It is cooler without it.* Her husband and sister-wife came over and kissed her.

Astrid looked around. *None of the Sea Nomads are near us at present.* "You will be in the party that talks to them," she said to Ia. "I was just told to ask where Moorea is now… I don't know what that is, but I am willing to bet it is a village or a boat that has gone missing, from the expression on the face of the girl who told me that. I have a feeling that the question may not go down well with everyone, but the answer may be very important to us. Be near that Wiki woman when you ask. She seems to like you."

Astrid

The Mice were brought into the centre of the village, to where there was a large, open area. *We have our animals trotting alongside us. As we go, various cats, all of them slender with startling blue eyes, all of them a dark cream in colour and with dark brown tips to their feet, tail and ears, look at our two and promptly disappear.*

Fluff-Ball ignores them regally and stalks in with her tail held high in the air and fluffed up like a possum's. The open area we are headed to seems to be, apart from the space just inside the docks, the only open space on the island that is not covered with something else like plants or buildings. Large mats are spread on the ground and we are being invited to take a seat.

Once they were seated opposite each other, Taine stood and, using High Speech, welcomed them to the island of Tabuaeran. After he had finished, Wiki stood and made a shorter speech. *Now they are looking at our mat and at Butterfly.* She stood and thanked them in High Speech and made fuller introductions of the Mice to the whole village.

Theodora has already spoken, so she then hands the speaking role to the Princess. While Ayesha is a far better storyteller, Theodora, with her experience in Court and in the upper society of Darkreach, has a lot more skill in persuasion. It seems plain that the task here is not so much to entertain as to convince the islanders to take part in what is about to happen.

Theodora tried to keep the story short, but the islanders did not want that. Like any community that never actually touched solid ground, they'd heard so little of *The Land*—or, indeed, of any land—that it was all fabulous to them. They wanted more and more and more from her. Food was brought out and served to everyone.

As he sometimes had to do for Ayesha, Christopher had to dispense mild healing potions to stop Theodora from losing her voice and others took over while she ate. They soon found that the islanders particularly liked it if people acted out the story as it went or when some of the songs that had been written about their adventures were sung as interludes.

They don't even seem to care if the songs cannot be understood, as long as someone translates what they are about without drowning out the singer. The fact that we have singers and storytellers is to them a marvel. Their island has only one bard and his apprentice, but having the same entertainer over and over, no matter how good they are, palls eventually.

They later found out that the islanders had been looking for another island to swap bards with for this reason. *Bards rarely stay on any one island for more than a year and will probably see all of the islands of the* Kanaka; *it seems that our books are accurate as to what the Sea Nomads call themselves, during their lifetime.*

In time the afternoon of stories and songs was interrupted, but only briefly, by the arrival of the *River Dragon* and its docking opposite the larger vessel on the centre wharf. The doors to the sea swung open and Olympias brought the *River Dragon* in. She discovered that, far under them at four fathoms, this dock had a floor and it was not open to the sea.

Except for those prudently kept aboard, and those kept on watch in the sky, the rest of the Mice joined them in the village and added their quotient of entertainment. The Bear Folk were also introduced and it was emphasised that they were a different people to the Mice. More food was provided and it was very late at night that the tale reached its climax.

Theodora concluded by asking for their help. *She draws on what I said in Wolfneck. Ia has to repeat her vision for them and then the men and the women of Tabuaeran draw apart in separate groups, apparently each reaching their own decision. They then join into one group and discus these briefly as we are left waiting. It does not take them long.*

"We have decided that we will join you in this quest of yours and that we will send our ships to gather others to us," said Taine. "Can you use one of those flying craft to take one of us with a message to the *Ofu*, the ship that is headed east?" Rani agreed that they could do this and all seemed ready to retire for the night.

Ia had been translating what was being said for her partners, but Astrid now nudged her and, reluctantly, she stood. "There is just one thing," Ia said nervously. Everyone looked at her. "It would be best…perhaps…if you are going to join with us…that you told us everything that has happened." She looked around.

Our people may look puzzled at Ia, but the faces of the islanders are far more interesting. I would say that at least some of them realise exactly what she is about to say. "I want you to tell us what you know about what has happened to Moorea." Ia sat down again.

Taine and Wiki looked at each other. "I told you that she would find out," said Wiki to her husband. "It is another island," she said. "We were supposed to meet it near here but we have searched for it and it no longer appears to exist. We have tried to find it in…other ways than the physical as well. All that we have found in our search are some charred vines and fragments that may have come from the island floating in the sea." She paused and shook her head.

"Fire will not normally destroy a whole island, it is too big. That is why we were so interested when you said about a *fire ship*." She looked at her husband again. "When we saw you, some of us at first thought that you might have been responsible for this, for we seek to find out what has happened to it. The *Ofu* is off now to spread the search." She pointed.

"The island of Ulithi is east of us and the *Rongo*"—she next pointed to the big barquentine still in the dock behind them—"would have been leaving this afternoon to go to Tupai to our west. We will be sending it tomorrow now as it spreads the news of your quest, but you can send messengers with it if you wish. They are closer, as they sail towards us, and we will gather people, from here and perhaps from there to go with you."

She stopped speaking and looked around the faces of the women present as if she were silently counting their opinions. As if in mitigation of what had been left unsaid, she continued: "The people of our islands usually stand alone from those who are bound to the still lands, and we do not lightly tell others what our business is."

Theodora
13ᵗʰ November, early on the Feast Day of Saint Homobonus and of Saint John Chrysostum

*D*obun *is here with Hulagu. I suppose that one day he will get used to speaking of what he sees, but today is not going to be that day.* "You know," he said, "that there are areas that cannot be seen into." *My husband and I nod. He looks at Hulagu, who indicates that he should keep talking.* "Last night I was in the real world and was told that I was speaking from inside one of them." *Now* that *is interesting*.

"My words and image were a blur to those I talked to, even though I saw them as is normal. So at least one of the areas that cannot be seen into is this Sea Nomad village. Perhaps some of the others are as well. I am told that it is as it was on the plains when Dharmal was first being sought. They had to stop looking out for him and instead look for the areas in the plains where nothing could be seen."

He is warming up a bit now and perhaps forgetting who he speaks to. "To find a Sea Nomad village you do not look for it… You look for places where you cannot see anything. It is slow, but it can be done." *He is thinking a bit.*

"It is just as it is with Mousehole: everyone can now find it easily, simply because you cannot see into it. I think that there is another such area north of us now, but I am not used to this yet and cannot tell how far away it may be. It seems that, seeing the Horse travels on the fields of the sea, as well as in the sky and mountains, it is our problem to deal with what we find here."

Soon we have some of our saddles and a carpet flying on the way east bearing messengers and messages, while others are moving to where the Rongo *is getting ready to depart. Other saddles are already in the air keeping a watch out beyond the limit of the green-light box. Olympias tells me it is mostly blocked. All it sees are reflections from all of the masts and buildings.*

Now we are sure there is something in the area that is dangerous, we do not want to take any chances; after all, Astrid and Ayesha managed to easily evade being seen by the green-light box when they attacked those who used it to watch for us on East Zarah.

Astrid

*A*fter talking with Theodora about hiding magic, I think that it does not matter how well the fire-dromond is hidden; unless it is actually flying or has access to immensely powerful magic, it will have to leave a wake of some sort in the water, and that is what I now have all of the sentries watching for. Concealing the wakes is why the Princess used an illusion of fog to hide what had happened, instead of just making the ship disappear when we sank the* Goldentide.

Now, with the Rongo *dispatched, and Mice on saddles and with other messengers sent from this island to its ship the* Ofu, *the rest of us can settle into the village as we begin to learn about each other. It could even be a couple of weeks more before we have word of volunteers coming back to help us.*

The young girl, Ele'ele, who had told me about the village of Moorea, is the apprentice of the bard and she originally came from the lost village. In fact, it seems that many of the people from here originally come from somewhere else. She asked questions. *When a man marries, or is first married at least, he comes to live in the village of his wife.*

It seems that the women run things more here than they usually do on the land. "It is obvious to me," she said to her family, "that we need a Women's Circle to be set up at home. So long as Mary stays always on the *River Dragon*, then I will be the senior woman of Mousehole." She grinned.

"You mean that we need a Men's Circle," her husband replied. "Women already run everything at home. It seems that we are just there to take care of the spiders and such tasks." Astrid poked her tongue out and went off with Ele'ele to look around the island.

It is built on a huge raft of a type of floating seaweed. It naturally grows in clumps; some time in the distant past the islanders learnt to cultivate it and its bladders of air, and they learnt how to make it grow tighter and higher. I am sure our people who have an interest in plants will be fascinated by this.

The well in the centre of the village taps into a central part of the plant that only starts to grow when the clump is large enough. It is a sort of bladder that produces pure water in almost unlimited amounts. Going to the actual bladder you can even scrape salt off its outside surface, but how the plant does this none knows.

The fresh water is not only used for drinking but allows them to cultivate their own plants and vegetables, like taro, and the village waste is broken down in special beds filled with worms, turning it into new soil. In addition, each time a person goes to the still lands, as they call the islands that they visit, they always bring back at least a pouch of soil.

One of the palms that they grow produces the cloth that nearly everyone wears, but it takes a long while to grow and so they always have far less cloth than they want at any time. They weave the leaves and pound them and wash the green out, and then pound them again. It is a slow process, but the villagers have little else to do. They live a good life.

Sometimes they grow sh-hone around the edge of their village as well, or harvest sea grasses for their skirts. In addition they grow hemp, but only for its leaves or to make rope. They use a lot of rope. Otherwise, their gardens are fruitful and the fish plentiful.

The green stone that they use for some of their weapons they gain from an island to the east. I am told it is a type of jade. Like the stone, they gain their timber from the land and heat all of their food with magic, usually on large, flat stones or by putting hot rocks into containers until they boil.

The fences mark the current growth of their village. A new independent island will only have a fence with one hut inside it, everyone on the island living in the one hut and barely enough land to feed them, unless they catch lots of fish. For their first generation at least, they would need to stay near an established island-village until they have enough land to farm, and they will be often poor and hungry for another generation or even two after that. The new island would not move away and become independent from its parent village until the plant can make its own water. Still, many of the young people look forward to going to an island-village of their own.

They grow bamboo, too, which is used for building huts and for new raised beds, and this adds to the space they have for food production. They grow hemp around the edge outside the fence for their rope, and that is all. Being very careful of the beasts around them, people dive into the ocean water and plait the new growth of the weed together into the shape that they want and, eventually, when it is firm and stable enough, and they have enough dirt to pound into the woven base, the fence is moved out just a little bit more and the process is begun again with a second hut being added.

They tell us that a new island may take many generations before its families have a hut each and its people can produce everything that they want in abundance. Until then they eat lots of fish and seaweed and learn to like it.

If the island-village of Moorea is truly gone, a group of volunteers from different islands will start to grow a new one, taking the old name as their own to help remember the people who lived there and their history and their stories.

Unless an island is driven by storm onto land, then there is little to threaten them once they are established. Once an island is mature, even the great Dragon-turtles cannot harm them much. No island-village has been lost for many generations. They suffered during the Burning, as did everyone else, but even then, none had been fully lost.

Olympias

*I*t *seems that over their life, a person might circle the globe very many times, and I was keen to talk to the navigator of the island-village, who apparently holds the title and name of* Puleleiite, *which we have been told means "ruler who can tell the future".*

Now that I have done so, I have discovered that my maps are inadequate in very many ways. Although they have all of the lands listed, I apparently have many in the wrong spots and the distances between them are far too short. With the measurements I was taking, I was starting to suspect that the world was larger than I had thought. Now I am very sure of that.

The Puleleiite does not use maps as I do, although he understands them, and so I could not look at what the Nomads use. I just have to make notes based on what I am told about places and who lives there and what he indicated to me on my maps.

He said he would not usually admit it, but conceded I have the best maps of any of the land-dwellers he has seen. I am willing to share the knowledge of the land that he lacks, and to explain what is happening with the Newfoundland.

His people call it the Wild Realm, but they have noted with concern the sailings to and fro between it and The Land.

They now avoid the area as some of their small ships have been lost there and they are becoming cautious. Due in particular to their lack of metals, not many of their ships are well equipped to fight back if someone attacks them. They have learnt over time that the best way to deal with conflict against the land-dwellers is simply to run from it.

The Puleleiite was very pleased to have heard, on the first night, of the taking and sinking of the Goldentide. *Olympias went back on board the* River Dragon *and brought Virginia out. The girl has been sulking on board since she discovered that the islanders have no intention at all of helping her get back to her land. She is, however, bored with the trip so far and is almost glad, in her own petulant way, to answer the questions that the Puleleiite asked of her through interpreters.*

Ia

*N*ow *Astrid and I are introducing Basil to Wiki. We had to. She has just looked at him up and down and turned to the girl, Ele'ele, who is translating for us.* "She asks if you do not love him enough? He is small and thin. You need to fatten him up and make him happy so that he gives you lots of children."

"I am with child already," said Ia, patting her stomach, "and we already have four children, or rather Astrid does, and she is pregnant again. She has two sets of twins already." The message went back and the reply came.

"She asks where they are, then. We have seen children, but they are all for the crew of the ship except the older girl, who belongs to the two other girls."

I have gone this far in explaining things so… "We have left our children with our other sister-wife. She is also pregnant and she stays in our village to look after our house and to raise the children by herself if we do not manage to return."

"He keeps three wives happy, does he? He has all of three of you pregnant as well?" *I think that Wiki is now speaking with a much more approving tone in her voice.* "It seems that there is more to him than there looks to be. Two sets of twins you say?" *She is now looking at Basil in a new light.*

"Now," said Astrid, "she looks Basil up and down as I would if I were the village matchmaker. She is like a mother with too many girls at her disposal. Is she thinking about his possible suitability as a prospective husband for a daughter or a niece who wants to travel?" She nudged her husband. "I am waiting for her to open your mouth and look at your teeth."

"You tell her," said Basil to the young translator, "that three wives are quite enough for any man and I have no desire to look for or take another wife." This was translated and the island woman burst into laughter and slapped her thighs.

"Wiki says only that we shall see what comes to be," said Ele'ele, without bothering to hide the grin on her own face.

Chapter XII

Astrid
19th November

It is a lovely morning and I could try and do things on my own, but I think that any more and someone will get upset with me. It is time to report in. She raised the talker to her lips. "Can someone wake up Rani please and get her to the talker?" While she was waiting she looked down at the view below her position as the northern watcher again.

"How do you know that she is not awake?" asked her sister-wife, who was out of sight on another saddle far to the east.

"She has nothing that she has to do and so does not need to be up, so she keeps Princesses' hours." She was proven to be right as it was another five minutes or more before a sleepy-sounding Rani answered her.

"What is so important?" she asked.

"Remember what we are looking for out here?" asked Astrid. "Well, I have found it. I saw the wake, as I said we would. I put on my ring and went down and came up from behind it." *I can hear the spluttering starting.* "Don't worry. I was careful. I kept low to lessen the risk of them feeling my magic and I felt all over it on the outside as I could see and hear nothing."

Now it is just silence from the other end. "It is a big vessel and covered in metal as we are, but it is much, much, bigger. At the front there are two big hatches and there are hatches for oars all down the sides, but they are all closed as well. The ones that I saw in Ardlark and Antdrudge had around sixty oars on each side. So does this.

"The hatches at the front are closed as well, so I could not see or feel into them, but I am sure that I could smell old fire around their edges. It will have the advantage, in that we cannot see it directly and it will be able to see us. If its magic is anything like mine, the green-light box will not see it, either." *I will bet that went over well.*

"I have an idea for this, though, and need to think it through. I am heading back to a high position to keep an eye on it and Tabuaeran is not yet visible. Once I have its exact course I am coming back for some supplies. You have time to work out what you want the ship to do, but Ariadne will be firing her light thrower at something that she will not be able to see unless I can outline it."

Rani

A riadne, for the last couple of days, has been working on something with Galla and I, apparently, have to climb up to her instead of her coming down to me. Rani found her in the main top. *She has a grin on her face and something with a cloth draped over it.* Ariadne whipped off the cloth. *One of the light throwers is now mounted on the main top of the mast. It looks like there is a mounting on either side.*

"As long as I do not cut a stay of ours," Ariadne said, "I can now fire down onto a deck instead of just across it. It is improved as I now have a much better chance to cut something open near the water and we can put a couple of the smaller weapons in the top of our second mast as well if we need to."

"Good," said Rani, as if it all made perfect sense to her. *Despite my confident exterior, I am still not sure about everything that the woman says. She speaks far too much about machines and what they can do. I do not trust machines beyond the simplest ones, like a boat, where nothing much can go wrong.*

Magic is far more predictable and dependable, and if it stops working you know why, and it is almost always because someone has disenchanted it or the magic has grown old and not been properly renewed and maintained. "Now come down and talk to Astrid," Rani eventually continued. "You have an invisible ship to fight."

"Really?" Ariadne replied in an excited voice as she grabbed hold of a stay with her calloused hands and slid down it to the deck. Rani looked down from where she was, high in the air. *I am climbing down, slowly. My wife may gallivant all over the rigging, but I will not. At least the Mice who are on the island are starting to come back and others are being woken up.*

I can hear Taine loudly insisting to Theodear that his warriors had to come along to provide us with more power in a battle. "A mage… Can you send a mage? Or a priest?" she was saying back. *Yes, something useful.* "We cannot even see their ship. It is likely that no one of us will fight hand to hand, unless Astrid attacks their ship on her own."

Taine looked around and brought a man out of those nearby. "This is Mele, he will come with us; the Puleleiite cannot leave Tabuaeran, of course. Mele is a Water mage."

"The rest of you can come along as well if you want," said Theodora, "but you will most likely be bored. Mele, what spells can you bring to this battle?"

Astrid

A strid arrived back at the *River Dragon* after a long flight. She had been at the very limit of the green-light box being able to see her when she had said to the watch that she was going further out to check on something.

"You have at least until lunch before it will reach here. It will be a while before you will even be able to see them." She turned to Olympias. "Sister, I would not tell you how to fight your ship, but I have this idea…" She outlined it and then went to see Parminder to make sure that Fluff-Ball knew what was going to happen.

It was not long before she left to take up her part in the battle with a very full baby-quiver for the cat to peer out of and an even fuller saddlebag hanging off the other side.

Rani
an hour later

W e leave from the island's dock, and as we leave the other vessels are being made ready to flee the island with as many as they can carry of the villagers in case the battle goes against the Mice. The islanders hope it does not come to this, but they think they should be able to fit everyone on board if their island has to be abandoned.

If Astrid's plan comes off, we should have a good chance of winning, but you never know. There will be no room for anyone to make mistakes in this fight. If we do, then it is likely that the island-village of Tabuaeran will follow Moorea into flaming destruction. At least this time the people will have a chance to be saved.

The *River Dragon* went out from the dock with bare masts. *The islanders all seem surprised by this. We approached them under sail, against the wind, but still under sail, and they are used to that, but a self-propelled boat they are not used to. The mage, Mele, says that he cannot perform a casting of this magnitude on his own, but he still wants the details of how I did it.*

He and Theodear are soon intent on calculating whether, if the enchantment is cast on the new Moorea, when it is established, it would grow with the raft. An enchantment that grows is an interesting idea anyway and it seems, from what my wife and I have seen with some of the other spells of the Mice that, if the spell is worded properly, this is just what they do.

There are ramifications to this, as it implies that magic is itself a living thing if it can grow and change. The University in Sharan has never considered this to the best of my knowledge. Moreover, if the spell is able to grow, it will be far easier to cast when the island is far smaller. The idea of having an island-village that can ignore the wind entirely is far too good an idea to resist for the Kanaka mage.

It means they will not need to use their scarce supply of timber for masts and spars, and so can build more ships if they wish. It is something mages could join together to do, and one island after the other would no longer have to stay away from land unless they want to. If the enchantment works for them, then they will no longer risk being stranded against rocky shores.

As the two mages conferred and planned, Olympias was already taking the *River Dragon* wide out in the ocean and far away from the island. *She will be trying to pass unnoticed by the intruder and so be able to come at it from behind and out of the arc of its rockets.*

According to what Astrid saw from its wake, unless it is deliberately travelling slower than it needs to, the River Dragon *is much faster through the water than the dromond. From what we saw and heard in Darkreach, they are all wide vessels, considering their length. They are thus quite manoeuvrable but built more with an eye on their capacity and power in a battle than just speed.*

Olympias
two hours later

*A*strid *is reporting that she should be coming up to the port of the invisible ship. She can see both the* River Dragon *and its wake from where she is, hanging in the air behind the target. She paused and waited.*

"I think that I can see it," called Harnermês, at the top of the mast. "I can see a wake. It is heading roughly towards where Tabuaeran wallows." The island-village was now quite close, a fat and inviting target.

He is pointing to where we need to steer. Olympias adjusted her course.

Neither Astrid nor Harnermês indicates that they are changing their course, so I am still hoping that our approach from the port quarter is completely undetected. I hope that their attention is so fixed on the inviting target ahead of them that they do not notice the bare masts behind.

Astrid began her attack while Ariadne stood in the maintop, Denizkartal had the other light thrower and Krukurb manned a ballista and was ready to change position to another weapon if it was needed. "Dropping now." Olympias heard the words from Astrid and relayed them.

I need not have bothered. Astrid has been accurate in her throw and the molotail burst and briefly outlined in flame the shape of a huge ship. Ariadne seems to be the only one both sighted and ready. She has fired. The others must be placed wrongly.

The beam stabbed across the distance…and again… *Now she is aiming into the flame spreading on the water and then ahead of it. Finally, Denizkartal has joined in with his lower-placed light thrower, aiming at what is hopefully the deck or the masts. He sweeps his weapon from side to side as his beam stabs out and dies, while Olympias moves hers up and down, firing in bursts.*

The River Dragon *is still going forward, but it is too far away from the target for anything else to join in yet. We made the first attack at what should be long range for the dromond's rockets for a good reason. Denizkartal cannot hit the hull from here, but hopefully he can take some of the crew or the masts with his fire.*

Now, however, to do more damage we have to close and hopefully our enemy is unable to fire its war rockets. They are usually on a rack that is aimed forward and cannot turn far from side to side. Some can turn fully as they are mounted on a timber plate, fixed in the centre. I hope that this is not one of them.

If we have made a mistake…well, a single one of those rockets, if it hit, would nearly destroy the River Dragon. *Hopefully, we are going to stay too far away for the onager on board the fire-ship at its rear to engage us. Another molotail explodes. This time, from the shape revealed, it is clearly at the bow of the vessel.*

Ariadne has changed her point of aim. A beam of light stabbed out as she swung, and then another and another. *Astrid's second molotail has obviously hit something vital. It is probably the rack of rockets. They have begun to fire wildly into the sky in all directions, and explode in the sky or after they hit water.*

"People are jumping into the water," Harnermês reported from his lookout position. "Some of them are on fire. I can see them as they leave the enchantment."

Ariadne and Denizkartal are still firing into the flame. Despite everything, the dromond is still coming towards us. Now, even from my deck I can see it is leaving a trail of flaming drops of hugron pir on the water. They are invisible while they are clinging to the ship, but become visible when they drop off it.

Another molotail hit a mast and exploded in the air. Briefly, the full outline of the ship could be seen as the hugron pir exploded in all directions and formed a red and visible backdrop before it contacted the ship or fell to the water. *One mast is down.*

There was a blast. Debris rained around the ship. *That must have been some rockets on deck, stacked ready to use. Now there is a burning mass floating away, separated from the rest of the ship. It must be the bow that has been lost, as forward movement seems to have stopped. Screams can be heard and the sound of explosions and roaring flame.*

Regardless of the onager, we are now getting close enough for Krukurb to join in. He has fired near where the bow had appeared. Unlike the fire from the molotail, which will only affect things on the outside of the metal cladding, and the light thrower, which cuts clean and true, Krukurb is using exploding rocks. They will send fragments of stone in all directions to tear open everything, and anyone, they touch.

His second shot hit something important. Suddenly a massive explosion rolled across the water and the wreckage of the dromond became fully and permanently visible as it was wreathed in flames at the base of a growing column of roiling black smoke. *He must have fractured the metal tank where the hugron pir is held under pressure.*

Quickly these flames expanded out over the water. One by one the screams in the water were silenced by the swiftly spreading pool of flame as black smoke climbed skyward in a mushroom-shaped funeral pyre. As an aftermath, pieces of timber and other items began to pepper the water almost all of the way to the *River Dragon* as they fell out of the sky.

"Astrid!" cried Ia.

Mice leapt into the air on saddles and began searching. No survivors came out of the growing flames and the column of smoke that marked the grave of the stolen ship, and there was no sign of Astrid. The Mice spread out on the saddles but, with her wearing her ring, there was little chance of seeing her until she was able to take it off.

There she is. A dot had suddenly appeared on the green-light box. Ia looked out in the distance and called and pointed at a dot that was just visible. Saddles flew in its direction as it moved towards them.

"I was just stunned for a little while," said Astrid when she returned. "The blast must have turned me around and I seem to have just kept on flying. We have both had some potion now and I am just a little singed." With that she dismounted and then promptly fell over onto the deck. By stripping her magic off her, Ia had Verily confirm that her contingency spell was no longer in place. *It has been another close moment for my sister.* Fluff-Ball was a little worse for wear but, from the look of things, had been largely shielded from the bulk of the blast.

Chapter XIII

Goditha

Now we have found where Astrid put the talker and the telescope, I can take over the northern position as sentry. Even from where I am, a faint mark shows that something is still on fire there. As she flew out she went back down to the level of the sea. *At least the smoke is harder to make out from down here and it could perhaps be mistaken for a thundercloud—at least, I probably could make that mistake.*

Once she had found that out and reported it to the *River Dragon* she went back to a high position where she would seem to be just the speck of a high bird by anyone who saw her from the water.

The eastern horizon had begun to darken into the short twilight of these latitudes when she realised that there was a spot now on her horizon...more than just a spot...it was a ship, and this one was fully visible. Quickly she reported in and headed north.

I am staying high, but even I can clearly make out that it looks to be very similar to the ship from the New Found Land that we have already destroyed. At any rate, it has the same high stern, the same design on its sails and it flies the same flag. It is perhaps not quite as large, but it would not be too far off it.

She tried to work out its speed. *Astrid has no difficulty doing that without thinking, but I am very fully and quickly aware that I am a mason, not a sailor. I cannot even realistically guess whether it will arrive at the village during the night or tomorrow after dawn. I think that I need to hand this over to someone who knows these things.* She explained this to the ship.

Olympias

I am not a good flyer, but I will not be doing anything fancy and I really need to see this for myself. Quickly she headed north. *I hope to see what I can before the light utterly fails and the ship is hidden from sight in the dark.*

She drew closer and allowed Goditha to return to the *River Dragon. I need not have bothered hurrying. Whoever is in charge of this vessel is confident, very confident. They are either innocent or else they are expecting the sea ahead of them to have been cleared of anything that may trouble them.*

The deck of the vessel was ablaze with light and the ship stood out clearly on the sea, even when that was lit by the moons. It was the night after full for Terror, and Panic was nearly half full as well. She had her husband read off the range from the green-light box. *The ship has just become visible on it, apparently.*

The night is brightly lit as the reflected light of the moons dances on the sea. That removes some of the advantage that the green-light box gives to us. However, the ship below seems not to have any major enchantments that conceal it or a green-light box of their own and they are now fully visible.

How do we take her? She is no fast barquentine and Taine, listening on the River Dragon, *has confirmed it is not one of theirs. The Nomads have no fat galleons with their huge capacity. They do not need that as they only trade with the land for timber and rarely exchange anything except locally made specialities with the islands.*

The question is whether it is an innocent ship or not. If it is innocent it should not be sunk, even if Ia has seen us fighting it. If it is a ship of the Adversaries and we allow it to get too close it could be dangerous. It is a hard decision.

Keeping on the far side of the ship to the moons, and staying high, she used her glass. *It seems that there are many Freeholders on the ship, but that is to be expected. From the sails it is one of their ships after all. Being from Freehold doesn't necessarily mean that they are evil. My ship's chaplain came from there, as has Bianca and, well, several others among the Mice.*

What I need is to see something that will give them away as an enemy or at least neutral, one way or the other. In the meantime, I have gotten the island village steering west, beating as much into the strengthening wind as it can go with its own breeze behind it, while the River Dragon *begins again circling around to gain the rear of the approaching vessel.*

My ship is now so close that I can see her behind where I fly. Even though she does not have her lights lit, from this height she shows clearly against the sparkling bright sea, lit up as it is by the moons. Soon I will have no choice.

I can see no rockets and no light throwers on our opponent but that means nothing. I can see some ballista, the same size as our own. They are mounted on the stern, in the bow, and there are even several on each side of the main deck. It is a powerful vessel and would be able to sink any normal craft even without any magical aid.

The ship is heading south under its own wind and is about the same size as the Goldentide had been. It is huge next to the River Dragon. *It can carry more soldiers on board than the entire crew of my craft and eight of my people are now away from us with their saddles looking for islands and ships.*

Finally, just as she was about to give up she saw a Kharl, an Isci-kharl, come on deck from below to go and relieve himself at the jakes. *In these seas surely only our enemies would have a Kharl on board without us having heard about it from Darkreach. That is going to be the best indication that I will receive. Now, how to take the ship?*

"Is Astrid able to do anything yet?" she asked.

There was a delay. *I am betting that my brother and Ia are saying no and that my sister-in-law disagrees with them.* Despite the situation she smiled and waited in the warm summer night. Eventually Astrid came on. "I am well enough," she said. "What do you need?"

"Can you do what you did last time and destroy its rudder?" asked Olympias. "Only this time I want you to do it quietly. I want you to ask Goditha if her chisel will cut only rock or if it would cut metal as well."

Through the talker she could hear the muted but indignant reply. *Goditha must have been close.* "Metals are rocks… It is just that they are refined."

"Did you hear that?" asked Astrid.

"Yes," said Olympias, the strange idea of a "refined rock" running briefly through her head. "In that case, get someone to fly you out and you can use it to cut the metal that holds it. Out you come and I will come back. Let me know once it cannot steer." Olympias went high again and out towards where her ship lay and outlined the rest of her plan to the Princesses as she went.

On the way she passed Ia flying Astrid out. *For once their animals are not with them.* She drew near to talk. *Astrid is naked except for her torques, a knife strapped to each arm, a rope slung over her shoulder and tied around her and the stone carver, which is also tied to her.* "Why are you not invisible? Why have you no clothes on?"

"My magic will only do for one and Ayesha may need hers," said Astrid. "Ia will wear my magic and drop back when I am left there. I will tie myself to the ship as I will have to dive below the water to cut the metal and I do not want to be left behind if I let go. I also do not want my clothes to weigh me down. Besides which," she grinned, "if one of them sees me they may think of me as a mermaid."

Astrid

A *gain we come from the rear and fly low towards the ship. Our approach to the craft is more dangerous this time. There is no invisibility for protection and no battle going on to distract anyone who is actually alert. Luckily, people usually only see what they are looking for, and something skimming over the waves in the open ocean is something that few would expect.*

Even a casual glance could possibly mistake us for a giant seabird. As well, the stern on the ship is raked so high that I can see nothing at all on the deck. What is more, between the rake of the stern and the huge lateen sail on the mast on the quarterdeck, I cannot even see the main top or the lookouts. That means they cannot see us.

The rear windows have drawn curtains, and two boats hang from davits near the rear windows ready to be launched. They will further block the view from above. As they grew closer, she could see that there was a top deck in that rear mast as well. *No one mans it at present. It is probably only occupied during a battle.*

If they had been fully alert, the ship is set up to see anyone making an approach such as we are now making. The ship is even lit at the rear by a great lantern with an enchantment bathing the area in light. I will be working directly under that if anyone comes out onto that rear walkway and looks down.

When I last did this sort of thing I just used brute force to chop away at the timber and break the wood and rope where it entered the ship from the rudder. What with the excitement and explosions I did not need to keep quiet. Now, without the cover of battle, I will have to work at my task quietly.

She got Ia to move closer and looked. *This ship is made slightly differently to the other. For a start it is not only smaller, but it must be older as well. Instead of a rudder this one has a tiller, presumably leading to a whipstaff up on the deck to steer the ship with. The tiller is attached to the sternpost with hinges, two above water and I do not know how many more below. I will need to be diving deep into the water.*

She tied her rope to the stern gallery. *Hopefully it will not be seen; at least there is some shadow here.* "Take me down and hold steady," she whispered in Ia's ear. Quietly they moved to beside the top hinge and Astrid applied the chisel to the metal. *It is not as easy as the time when I helped Goditha and cut some stone for her.*

Goditha said that even hardness of the stone varied. Limestone is easy to carve, and basalt is harder. Before we left the River Dragon, *Goditha said to remember that iron is a lot harder than basalt, so it will be challenging to cut and more difficult still.* Gradually she pushed and pushed and finally the huge hinge gave way.

She squeezed Ia and got her to move down. Now they sat on the saddle with their feet in the water and Astrid started on the second hinge. *It is even harder work now. This time I have had to lean down to push against a hinge that is four hands long, made of iron and over a finger thick.* Eventually it broke free. *Between the tiller up top and the hinges still in place it seems to have no effect. I suppose that, with the ship travelling straight ahead, it is not likely to have much anyway. Now comes the time.* "Now let me off," she whispered in Ia's ear.

"No," said Ia and rose. "Untie the rope from the walkway and tie it to the saddle," she replied, also in a whisper.

"But we agreed…"

"I thought that it was a lousy plan at the time," said Ia, "and now I am sure that it will not work. I have been watching how hard it is for you. You will be made too tired and will be left behind if you lose your grip, and you cannot really swim very well at all, so then you will be dragged behind the ship to drown. There are three of us, and the children, to mourn that now. If we do it my way I can stay with you and bring you back to the ship when you lose your grip and drift away, and you can rest if you need to."

"But you will be seen."

"I doubt it. I can stay below the stern gallery. I will be less visible there than where the rope is tied now. Go on. Untie it." Astrid thought about it for a moment and then did as she had been told. *If I am honest, except for the chance of the saddle being detected, it does seem to be a much better idea.*

They went down to the water again and Astrid gave Ia a kiss and slipped off to lower herself into the warm water of the south. She took as big a breath as she could and then lowered herself down with her fingers in the gap between tiller and sternpost and went to the lowest hinge first. *It is best to get the hardest part of the job done first.*

I hope that they do not put their steering over hard though. If they do I will lose my fingers. She could only work briefly on the hinge before she had to come up for air. Again she took a big breath and pulled herself below the surface. *Later I will tell Butterfly about how I have unconsciously trained for this task of holding my breath.* She had to try hard to avoid laughing.

Time and time again she went down into the water. More than once she lost her grip and had to be rescued and brought back by Ia. "You were right," she said as she gave her sister-wife a kiss. "I could not have done this alone." She was able to break the bottom hinge free of the ship on the next dive.

After that it was a little easier, but she still had three more to do. Despite her strength, she was quickly tiring and she had lost her grip several times. She had the chisel tied to her wrist, and that was also just as well as she had already dropped it several times while descending. *This is very hard work, even for me. I really need to marshal everything that I have in the way of reserves.*

At least the water here is warm. She set to work on the second last hinge. *It will not be enough to just cut it all free. We will have to tear it out of the ship as well.* She connected a rope from the saddle to the rudder to do this, looping it so that it would be easy to pull the rope free of the rudder once it had done its job. She then dived back into the water.

As she was taking breaths and preparing to go under again, someone came out onto the gallery above them and Ia, seeing the door to the balcony start to open, quickly brought the saddle close under the stern. They could look up through the lattice floor of the gallery and see the bottom of the man's boots.

He lit a pipe and smoked it as they huddled together under the balcony, hoping that he would not look down and see them. The wake of the ship curled around them as it cleaved its way through the water. Looking up they could see that one of his hands rested lightly just where the rope had once been tied. *If we had tried to stick with the original plan I would surely have been caught, even if I had somehow survived until now.*

He knocked out the pipe on the rail and Astrid had to stifle a yell as some hot ash landed on her bare shoulder and more on her hand. He was still standing there and they wondered how long he would stay when a stream of piss arced over their heads to splash into the water. Ia inched the saddle a little further away from him as the women smothered giggles behind their hands. Eventually he went inside and they could resume their task.

The last hinge is the easiest so far. Astrid could see that, as she was cutting the last pieces, the metal was already trying to tear itself free with the strain that was being placed on it. She abandoned what she was doing and quickly surfaced and grabbed hold of the saddle.

"Quick…go," she said, and Ia flew a few paces away from the ship until the rope was taut as Astrid clambered inelegantly onto the saddle and slumped against her. The rudder was now hanging loose and the last hinge must have finished tearing itself apart.

She urged her sister-wife to pull hard and, with a creak, and then a cracking sound like a large branch falling and splintering, the whipstaff wrenched free from its mounts. *It must have leapt out of the hands of the steersman and maybe even injured him.* First gradually, and then quickly, the tiller began to come out of the ship.

Shouts of consternation could be heard as Ia reported success. Once the assembly was free and a little way from the ship they loosened one end of their rope and fled quickly, staying low and dodging between waves as the end of the rope went back towards the ship and then trailed behind them on the water. Astrid was pulling the rope in as they flew directly away to the rear.

It did not take long before people had appeared on the narrow top of the quarterdeck and more were appearing on the stern gallery and at windows. *They are looking down at the rudder as it floats away from them. It seems, from their lack of reaction, that none of the people on the ship have thought to look any further away than the rudder floating behind them. None of them have noticed us fleeing.*

Their consternation is directed at what seems to be an accident, a very unlikely one, but still an accident. On the ship, cries in Latin marked the taking in of sail as the huge ship slowed to a halt in the water. *Our raid has been a success.* Soon they were far enough away that, even if the women were seen, it was unlikely that anything could have been done about them.

Olympias

I have been nervously juggling my speed. It is taking the two women a long time to do what I sent them to do and Harnermêś can now clearly see the topsails of the larger ship from where he clings as lookout at our highest top. I am keeping Ariadne in the maintop just out of sight of the other ship, but it is getting progressively harder.

Parminder, on watch from above on a saddle, can clearly see both ships and the village. It will not be long at all before the watch on our target ship picks up one or another of its opponents. On the deck of the River Dragon *everyone waits nervously for something to happen.*

Olympias saw Virginia on the deck, looking out. *The stupid girl will probably call out if she can, or do something else to upset things.* Quickly she ordered her to be searched and tied up below. *From the girl's reaction, which included bursting into tears, I was right. She had a flint and steel, a small flask of strong rum and some tinder. She was preparing to signal the other craft.*

It seemed forever before Ia breathlessly reported success and Olympias gasped a sigh of relief and allowed the *River Dragon* to spring forward. *The waves and wind are from the west. The captain of the other ship will probably set a sea anchor now while he attempts to recover his rudder. We are to his east. I am gambling that he will pay little attention in this direction.*

She wondered at the power of his mages. *Will the crew be able to fix the rudder back in place in time? I doubt it, but it will be quite some time before we are up with the other vessel. Now it cannot run nor even manoeuvre into a more favourable position. It has to just drift, unless it has some spell of propulsion, and no one on a saddle is mentioning that.*

Ariadne called down that she could see sails, but Harnermês soon added that they were being taken in. *Soon the masts on the other ship will be as bare as ours are. It isn't going anywhere now. If it had kept the sails up it would have had a limited chance to manoeuvre using just them—not very well, but it would have been better than nothing. Now even that is gone.*

It sits dead in the water until it can get something up to move it again. "I can see small boats being launched," Harnermês called. *It will not be long before they reach the rudder. How long will it take before they look at the brackets and realise that it was not all an accident, that the rudder had been cut free of the ship?*

There was a brief flurry on the *River Dragon* as a moving dot was seen and reported, but almost at the same time Ia reported that she had just seen the ship and stated that they were on the way in. Exhausted after performing that long task on top of the effects of healing, a sleepy Astrid was taken to a bed below while Basil and Ia dried her and poured Kaf into her and fed her some sweets.

Ia

*O*ur *Puss has recovered enough to grab us both and kiss us heartily and has then fallen back on the Princesses' bed without even bothering to dress.* "Wake me if I need to repel boarders," she said. "Otherwise I am sleeping here until they need this bed. I have decided that I hate hammocks." She hugged the bed.

"I might think that a hammock is far better than sleeping on a deck, but beds are much better. You cannot have sex in a hammock safely, so…" Her words had been getting drowsier and she did not complete the sentence. Ia and Basil threw a nearby cloak over her before going back on deck. "You two look after her," Ia said to Maeve. The two animals jumped up on the bed as well and curled up on the sleeping woman.

Rani

*I*t *looks we have lost our bed, but at least Astrid is not underfoot. Basil and Ia are back up on the deck and Olympias has yet to give the order to attack. I would say that is still some way off.* Swiftly the *River Dragon* flew across the moonlit sea towards their wallowing target. *I can see the enemy ship, its stern* *towards us, now with boats in the water clustered around it.*

It seems like forever before Olympias gives the order to attack. When she did so the two light throwers stabbed out as one. *Denizkartal may have taken out some stays, but at that range I think he has missed the masts themselves.*

Ariadne is more accurate. From where she was in the maintop she had a far larger target to aim at. The very top of the quarterdeck, and the people leaning over its rail, or at least the top of them, fell away into the sea. They fired again. More of the elaborate stern-castle was shorn away and this time the masts were affected and much of their height started toppling.

There is panic on the crowded stern gallery and that seems to be Ariadne's next target. Even at this range they could see that the beam had cut deep into the ship and the people there had little chance to do anything, although one, or maybe more, had leapt clear into the sea. *By now Denizkartal has all of the masts down with sweeps of his light thrower.*

He is learning how to better aim his weapon and to time its bursts to better effect. Steam began to go up from where he hit the water as he next started aiming at the far harder targets being presented by the boats floating behind the ship as they frantically tried to scatter and get free.

The enemy has at least one strong Air mage or priest on board. It is too far from the stricken ship to the River Dragon *for a mage to cast most spells directly, unless they are ready and strongly favoured. However, now, above us all, a cloud is slowly beginning to coalesce over the battle. I am ready. Should I cast at him? Olympias has not asked me to.*

The cloud will take a while to form as the night is clear, but in these latitudes a thunderstorm is always possible, so it will not be an impossible task to shape it. If the storm is left unchecked there will soon be lightning bolts stabbing down at us. That would be an ideal spell under normal circumstances, but we have the light throwers. I will wait.

Rani ordered Stefan to take the saddles out to their opponent and told Basil that they wanted prisoners. The saddles flew out, staying well clear of the direct path. "But take no chances," she called after them as they departed.

It would have to be someone who can see us who is trying to cast the lightning and, with the way the ship lies, and the loss of the stern part, that can only leave them standing on the fo'c'sle of the enemy vessel. Rani yelled instructions up to Ariadne. She abandoned the hull of the ship and began trying to hit anyone in that area who was standing still.

It was harder to hit a single person than a ship, but she kept trying, and that part of the vessel was soon falling to pieces. Lightning began to flicker in the cloud, but it played only briefly in the sky, making a few rumbling sounds high aloft, and did not have a chance to strike out at the *River Dragon* before the cloud, as quickly as it had formed, began to dissipate.

She must have found her target. One of the people she has hit must have been the mage casting the lightning spell. The saddles are now in place all around the hull of the great ship, waiting for the order to go in. Resistance seemed to have died out when the remains of the fo'c'sle slid into the sea.

After conferring with Olympias, Rani used the talkers to order the riders on the saddles to form a circle and keep their positions until the *River Dragon* arrived. "Tell everyone," Rani said, "to use arrows or wands on any on the ship who show resistance, but to leave alone any who do not look as if they are trying to strike out at us."

Chapter XIV

Basil
the dawn is breaking on the 30th November

It has not taken us long to get here. In the east the light is growing and in that light you can see that we have left the galleon as a mere hulk. Under the threat of the two large and two small light throwers, and with a ballista standing by, the remaining crew gathered on the main deck and Basil took Shilpa, Ia, Christopher and Aziz across to the other vessel.

There are ten survivors, and a miserable lot they look to be. Stefan can look after getting them back while we look for anything interesting before the remains sink. A stream of wealth began to appear. *It is all plate and boxes of coin from the main cabin. Strangely, the rapidly filling cargo hold is almost empty apart from some food, four large cages, and a lot of points to tie things down.*

A banging noise was coming from a small room at one end. Basil cautiously opened it, to be greeted by a barely clad girl who threw herself at him with hate etched into her features. She stopped herself with her nails almost on his face and one of his blades stopped just short of her.

"You are not one of them," she said as she slumped.

"Probably not," said Basil. Without taking his eyes off her he called Ia over and gave the girl into her charge. He looked into the room. *It is bare apart from an already floating chamber pot. From the mark of the light thrower in the ship's timbers, the girl must have been lying on the floor when the beam cut through the hull above her.*

There is a pair of dead men outside. They must have been standing near her room. They have both lost the lower parts of their legs, one of which still stands upright in its boot beside its owner's body. Blood is lacking on the timbers and the wounds have been clearly sealed shut by the beam of light.

The men seem to have died from the shock more than anything else. One was hit a second time. That would have sealed his fate.

It is clearly of no use trying to go down into the steerage deck. It is already full of water. Basil returned to the main deck and began looking for charts. *Theodora has the mage-apprentices organised to search for anything of interest and a small pile of weapons and other items is growing on the deck. Around them are bodies, or parts of them, and the other debris of battle.*

In the captain's cabin he found what he was looking for. *There is a charred, brass-bound box that has lost a corner from a light thrower. It probably was enchanted to hide itself—perhaps it could become invisible, like the fire ship—when threatened, but was caught too suddenly by the weapon's blast.* He opened it. *We have a set of rolled-up charts, each in a leather tube with a stopper on either end.* He grinned.

My sister will be very pleased with this find. From the look of it, most of the world is laid out on these and they are all written in Latin script. Mind you, I wonder who the Chin, *who live in Ērānshahr and Kemet-Kush, might be, and who the* Sslan'ssisswani *are.* Bryony came into the cabin.

"Better come on," she said. "It doesn't have long to go before it goes down." She called out to her cousin and the two quickly went through some of the clothes, looking at their sizes. *They seem to like what they see.* The two women ended up dragging a sea-chest out of the room. "Stefan…we think that the captain was your size," she called.

The girl is still there waiting with Ia. "Wait for a bit," Ia said. "There should be some women's clothes somewhere here," and she went into a storage room under the remains of the quarterdeck, which now had no ceiling. It didn't take her long. "Found them… Give me a hand," and Basil nodded at the girl. *She has hurried inside, relieved to be away from me.*

The two came out carrying another chest. Quickly they put ropes around it and attached it to a saddle. *The girl has a scared look in her eyes; she flinches away from me, and I presume she has a general fear of men.* Ia mounted the girl behind her on the saddle and took her back to the *River Dragon. The girl clings to her as if she were drowning.* Basil was left standing on the deck as the water lapped higher.

I am the last Mouse left on board. Is there anything we have missed? He'd stuck the maps into his saddlebag and turned for a last look around before he left when he sensed movement and quickly ducked behind the stump of the mainmast. *A hand has appeared on the rail. Then another appears there. Well, well.*

Silently, Basil moved over to the rail, staying low and removing a shackle from its pouch. *I can only see the ends of fingers as I crouch behind the rail. I will bet that the owner of them is peering carefully over the edge to see if anyone is still on board.* Patiently he waited. *The man must have stayed overboard in the sea deliberately until the sound of movement on board died away.*

There was a grunt, and a foot swung over the rail above him and was lowered onto the deck. *Good. The man's back is going to be towards me.* The other foot was put down as Basil struck out with his sap, a leather pouch containing lead. The man fell flat on his face and Basil pounced quickly on to him with a knee in his back. He shackled the man's hands, one after the other, before removing another set of manacles and putting them on his feet and stripping him of several rings. *He has a wand pouch on his belt, but it is empty and the top flap hangs open.* Basil patted him down. *Apart from a wand and a dagger on each forearm, he has nothing of interest.*

Basil peered over the gunwale and checked the water for any others hiding there. *All there is to see are several floating bodies, a number of timber fragments, and a drifting tangle of fallen rigging. This flotsam is now nearly up to the level of my feet as the ship sinks lower and lower into the water. Already I can see the corpses are being nibbled on by fish. Soon the large creatures will come and the small creatures will leave.*

Before the man recovered, he was out over the water, slung face down under the saddle. It was easy to tell from his struggles, which rocked the saddle, and his inventive use of Latin invective, when he regained consciousness. Basil reached down and hit him again. *He is a mage. He probably should have tried to cast something instead of swearing at me. Too bad.*

Basil
it is now full light

Now that is interesting. Just seeing him terrifies the freed girl. He nearly put the saddle down on his prisoner as her reaction distracted him. "Someone get me a gag, please," said Basil. Shilpa had seen him coming and already had one to hand and, despite the man squirming, resisting and making muffled complaints as he came to again, Basil put it on him. "This one is a mage," he said.

He looked around. *From the fearful reaction of the other captives, all of whom look, and are dressed, like simple sailors, this captive will probably prove to be the one that we will get information from. The men are afraid of him and the girl is near petrified with terror. She clings to Butterfly.*

Christopher came up to Basil as he was going over to his wife Ia and the girl. "The girl is neither good nor bad," he said, "and I would say that the men generally have just the normal levels of sin that weak men have, although none of them are particularly nice." He stopped and looked at the mage, who was already being pinioned ready for questioning.

"That one may be only young, but he is nasty…really and truly steeped in evil. He makes my flesh crawl as I go past him. Did he have any rings?" Basil opened his pouch and removed them. "Put them on the tips of his fingers… One at a time, please—but be ready to take them off quickly if he casts." Basil did so. "Stop," Christopher said at the third, a gold seal ring with a Gryphon etched into it. "That is the one… Once you know about them… You can tell the feel of them when they are being worn."

Basil continued over to where Ia waited with the girl. *Ia is stroking her hair as if she were calming a scared horse. The girl looks more scared when I approach.* "Stay clear," his wife said. "I have sent Maeve to wake Astrid and bring her up here. I know that she is good at this. This one has been abused and her mind is…wandering." *Is she mad, then?*

"Her name is Jillian and she and two other girls were hired for the officers of the ship as companions for the voyage. The other two are dead and this one…" *She is turning over the girl's arm to show a series of scratches on it. The first is only a faint line, so it must be couple of weeks old. The most recent has freshly bled. None seem to be healing properly. They all seem to be festering a little as if, although only tiny, something unclean lives within them.*

"I think that they used one of those knives on her. That one"—she nodded towards the mage—"is called Clarence. I think he may be some sort of a noble from their new land. I believe that it is time for us to bring little Virginia out again to see what that reveals to us." Basil nodded and hurried off to see his sister and get the girl brought up.

Virginia appeared and looked to where the last standing mast of the sinking ship was still just above the water and gave a cry of despair. Ursula, her nurse, ran over to her. "They have your cousin Clarence Garlin as a prisoner," she blurted out. Basil had been alert and noticed her reaction. *He may be a cousin, but Virginia just shuddered and her face shows an expression of distaste.*

He quickly came over to her. "What is wrong with your cousin?" he asked.

Virginia gives every appearance of being reluctant to answer, even if she does have a look of intense dislike on her face. Loyalty to family wins over her feelings. She stays silent. Ursula looked at her. "He is not what I would call a nice man at all," said the nurse firmly. "I am sure that he tried to rape Virginia when she was twelve." *Not nice at all.*

"It was at her older sister's birthday party," she continued, "and he had been plying her with drink and managed to get her alone, away from the others and away from the servants in a quiet part of the house. I believe that he told her he had a surprise for her. I found them and interrupted what was going on.

Her bodice was unlaced and her breasts were exposed. One hand held her neck and the other was fumbling between her legs."

"We were both drunk and it was a misunderstanding," said Virginia. She speaks loyally, but her voice lacks any conviction. "He swore that this was so, and I accept that as he is my noble cousin…but often his hands do accidentally go in the wrong place…if we dance or sometimes at other times…and his hands are always sweaty when they touch you.

"I really cannot stand him. He makes me shudder inside the way he looks at me. I think that my mother suspected I don't like him. So, despite him being a mage and her nephew and otherwise a good prospect for me, I think that is one reason why I was sent away to find a husband and you were able to kidnap me."

"He was not drunk," hissed Ursula. "If I had not walked in… He is a snake." She turned to Basil. "Now that I am away from there and may not get to go back home, I will tell you. He has a bad reputation all over. He has not been back to his home for some time. Wherever he is, he ruins far too many young girls, mainly servants and peasant's daughters.

"Sometimes they may agree to what he wants but sometimes they just find themselves whisked away and end up waking in his bed or that of one of his friends. Often they come back bruised and sore and mishandled. It is rumoured among the servants that some girls just disappear completely, and his friends are as bad as he is or worse."

"You are wrong," said Virginia. "It was all a mistake and a misunderstanding, I tell you… My mother has often told me that the servants are just jealous of us. She has said that they will do anything to try and get their hooks into a noble by getting a child by them so they will be supported all of their life without having to work, just like the bitch who stuck to my father like a leech was trying to do, until she ran away with Mother's jewels.

"Clarence cannot be like that at all. He is the heir of Epibati, and anyone can see that he is a noble knight at tourneys, and his mother and mine are first cousins. He just gets…overly familiar… I didn't like it but the servant sluts seem to, and they will always play up to it, and they lie back and open their legs wide for any noble."

Ursula turned on her indignantly. "That is wrong and you are wrong," she said firmly and with evident emotion in her voice. "If they make a complaint to anyone they will lose their jobs and sometimes even their parents will lose their jobs as well, and then they cannot get another…so instead they lose their virginity or else they flee," she said crossly. "If they protest, they disappear. Here I can tell you exactly what I could not say at home, lest I lose my job. Here it does not matter. For once I can be honest."

"You can still lose your job," said Virginia threateningly.

Ursula turned immediately to Basil. "You have three wives and they are all pregnant. It is obvious that you need a nurse to help your wives with the children, don't you? I think it is about time this one learned how to dress and mend and look after herself." *Virginia's face shows that she is completely horrified with the idea.*

"Let us hear what your cousin has to say," said Basil, quickly changing the subject. *I have more than enough women in my life and do not need another one, even as just a servant.* He quickly went over to Rani and told her what he had discovered. Next he checked that Bianca was free. *She will need to do the recording. My wives are already busy.*

Are we ready to start? Puss, who has at least donned a kilt, is sitting near the quarterdeck with the girl in her arms. The girl is clutching her as a small child who has been hurt holds their mother. Her eyes are wide open and there is a look of horror etched on her face. Ia is trying to feed her something, probably poppy.

Astrid is rocking back and forward and I can hear her singing her "calming song" that sometimes helps to calm Ia when she has her nightmares. The girl is hanging tight onto Fluff-Ball as a child holds on to a stuffed toy for reassurance, and the cat has a resigned expression on her face. Ia is now trying to use a brush on the girl's tangled hair. Maeve just sits there and chatters.

Rani stood in her pattern as the pinioned man glared at her and fought to get free. *He has just noticed Virginia. His eyes open wide in surprise. I would say she is possibly the last person he expected to see. More interestingly, when he sees Ursula, there is pure hatred in his eyes. I know how I will start the questioning.*

Rani finished and nodded at Basil to allow Clarence to speak while she got him to drain his mana into storage devices. When that was done, Basil drew up a stool in front of the young man and then sat down. He angled himself so that he could see Virginia and the other prisoners from the ship. *I want to gauge their reactions, as well as seeing and hearing the reactions of Clarence.*

"Hello Clarence," he said in his heavily accented Latin. "I am called Basil, and I will be asking you many questions and you will be answering them, and when it is all over we will see whether you are going to live or whether you are so evil that you have to die. I think we will start with what should be a very easy question for you to answer. Did you try and rape Virginia at her sister's party?"

"No," was the reply. "I knew that she wanted me to take her... They all do... All she needed was a few drinks to get her to open her legs up. I took her older sister exactly the same way the year before at her own party and she never said anything either. Once you have had them they are usually grateful, unless they get hysterical. Then you just have to slap them a bit and they stop that sort of nonsense.

"Noblewomen realise that they cannot make a fuss beyond a few tears, or they are finished and will never get married. They may as well go off and become nuns. Her sister ran a long way away. If they are servants and they persist, you can get rid of them so that they do not annoy you." Basil looked at Virginia. *There is a look of horror on her face.*

"So if, say, a servant girl complains, you kill her?"

"No... Well, only a couple of times... Most of the time as a part of our ceremonies... Usually cousin Leo has a place where he can send them if you ask him to... I don't know where it is... I think that it is a nunnery or something."

"Who is Cousin Leo?" asked Basil.

"Leo is my father's brother's second son. He is also the Abbot of the Benedictine Monastery at Sweetwater. He is the one who arranged for the old Abbot to so conveniently die. Several of us came together then and, with the help of the Ancient Ones and a pretty servant girl, we cast some spells we had been given and that arranged his election. It is good to have an Abbot on your side." *He sounds smug.*

"Leo is really the head of the Church in the New Found Land. We used potions and the Archbishop's mind is fading and, although they may object, the Bishops all have to do what he tells them to do. I think that they have been told to obey by the Abbott."

Simeon was suddenly at Basil's side. "I thought that his death was suspicious," he said. "The Abbot was a good and holy man." He turned to Basil. "His death and the elevation of Leo is why I first had to set out on my journey," he said.

"I remember you," said Clarence. "Leo pointed you out to me. You are the skin-changer. You were like the Abbot Franciscus and you were supposed to die as well. If we had caught you, we were going to sacrifice you to the Ancient Ones. Doing that would have let us cast some powerful magic." *Simeon seems to forget his vows for a moment. It looks as though he comes very close to hitting this Clarence.*

"Being holy was why Franciscus had to die, the sanctimonious fool, he tried to stick his nose into our business, and he tried to convince the Duke that we were evil and he always tried to make us take off the pledge rings of our brotherhood."

"These rings?" asked Basil, holding up the Gryphon seal ring.

Clarence nodded in agreement. "We all are given one of those when we pledge to the Order. We are the Brothers and Sisters of the Gryphon. One of the things that we are sworn to do is to never remove our rings."

Virginia fainted. She hit the deck hard. For once, several have rushed to help her as everyone stops what they are doing and looks in her direction. After a moment, when she had checked the girl, Ursula looked up at Basil from where she knelt beside her charge. "Her mother has one," she said. "She is a Gryphon."

"Is Virginia's mother one of you?" asked Basil.

"Yes, she is," Clarence replied, "but she may lose her place as our head when I report her to the others. She was supposed to give us the girl in Trekvarna, not to send her away to you."

"What would have happened to her once she got to Trekvarna?"

"She thought that she was going to find a husband. Instead she was going to die. We needed to establish some sort of big pattern that we could all draw upon. The Ancient Ones said that these tap directly into the Cosmic All. The higher the rank of the one that you kill, and the greater her sense of self, then the greater her fall is as she dies." *He seems to believe this rubbish.*

"We have sacrificed enough trulls and servants and it is time to move on. We were told that, if we wanted to have real power over the All, we had to start killing people of noble birth. We lost the Queen's youngest sister. This one was supposed to be taken and kept alive and made to feel safe as her replacement sacrifice." *Lovely people.*

"When we were ready, seeing that I was her cousin, I was going to be one who got to take her first, once she had been cut. I could take her in any way that I wanted to and then we would have killed her. I was promised that after she arrived I would be brought in to do this, but she disappeared and we looked and looked and could not find out what had happened. Then this trip came up and we were busy again."

"Ah yes," said Basil. "Tell me about this trip."

"It was going to be our second like this," replied Clarence with a look of hate in his eyes. *He cannot resist answering, but he realises that he has already signed his own death warrant.* "Our other ship, the *Dragon of the Seas*, destroyed a floating village and between us we carted most of the villagers away." A howl went up from the islanders of Tabuaeran. "The *Meander Rose*, our ship, was going to get another load of slaves when the *Dragon* destroyed the next raft. All of those we can get we take to the northern seas."

"To Arnflorst?" asked Basil.

"To Arnflorst," agreed Clarence. "They are now slaves there and the good-looking girls are a pool of sacrifices. We will kill all of them eventually, but it is much more fun doing it with the young girls and most of them break better." *The Mice are having to holding back the Sea Nomad men from the other prisoners.*

Clarence continued speaking in his conversational tone. *It sounds as if he is discussing how to arrange a ball. This tone lends a certain horror to his words. As they come out they mark the banality of his evil.*

"It seems it will be the *Dragon* that will find you now and it will have to destroy your ship and use your crew instead of the slaves that we should have taken off a village. At least there are a lot of girls who seem to be pretty. It is a shame that you may be able to kill me and I may not get to take some." He licked his lips.

That explains why the hold of the ship is empty. "No it won't," said Basil. "We destroyed it yesterday." *What else do we need from him?* "Was there a Master on your ship?"

"No," said Clarence, "he was on the fire-ship. They are creepy, but he was the last one and no longer needed as they are far too weak. Our Order is taking over their role. The Ancient Ones rarely leave the island and they want servants out among the world to rule it in their name. I am going to be the next ruler of Freehold after the idiot Toppuddle got himself accidentally killed by some witches and others trying to strike at us." *We did well there, it seems.*

"The Queen dies when we can arrive back there." It seems that he does have more to give. "Hopefully we can sacrifice her as well. She is the most noble of all and her death should give us lots of power. She is an older woman and she has a girl lover. I have wanted to take them both for a long time, but have had to wait."

"Now, if I am still alive I can get to take my tight little cousin there after all, just like I know that she wants me to, and then I will kill her when I think that she is properly broken and will do anything that I want her to. I will make her beg me to do it. I have done this to other girls, but it will be more fun with her. I have already worked out what I want to do to her." *I had better stop him going any further down that path.*

"What makes you so certain about all of this?" Basil asked Clarence. "I could just slash your throat and kill you so easily now."

"You could and you may, but I don't think that you will," Clarence replied. "The Ancient Ones have spoken. It is all foretold." *He is a smug bastard.* "That is why they have contacted each of us. They saw our futures. I was shown a vision of some of it." *He seems to have regained some more of his poise.* Clarence looked at Virginia and licked his lips before blowing her a mockery of a kiss. She was sitting up and listening but she almost fainted again at that.

"What about the girl over there?" Basil asked, pointing at where his wife was sitting with the rescued girl cradled in her lap and arms. *She is young and even smaller than Ia and she looks so like a small child there in Astrid's arms.*

"She is almost gone anyway. They do not last long once we scratch them with the knife. Anything that they feel seems to be multiplied and their mind goes. Pity. She was pretty and once she could sing very well and tell stories.

She would have made a lot at her trade before we hired her for the voyage.

"She used to be one of my family's servants but I broke her in a few years ago and she fled afterwards. The bitch shouldn't have run away, I wasn't finished with her. I wanted to take her again. She didn't know that I was on board when we hired her. However, she is not important and would have died anyway in the next few days. We would have given her to the men to use up the last of her like we did with the other two." *From that wail it looks like at least a couple of the sailors have just realised that they have no chance of surviving this either.*

"Once she was nearly gone then we would have cut her throat. We usually bring more sluts on a trip so that they last longer, but the good ones are getting scarce and word must be passing as it is getting harder to convince any of them to come with us. Soon we will just have to be grabbing peasant girls that we fancy. We are powerful enough to get away with that. Who will believe their families against what we may say?"

He is looking at my wives now. "I may take the one who is holding her though, I would like to latch on to her tits…" His head rocked as Basil hit him hard across the mouth. Quickly he turned and apologised to the Princesses for losing his temper in such an unprofessional way before resuming his work.

Basil continued with his questions for some time, getting names of the people on this Order of the Gryphon and other details. *Unfortunately, Clarence knows little about Arnflorst and its defences, although I have all I can get.* When he could think of no more, he asked Virginia if she wanted to know anything.

She really should not have asked about her mother, should she? She near fainted again when she heard what her mother had been up to with the whole Order. Even Clarence, her nephew, has taken her, and he is more than happy to provide details on that front.

It seems that Virginia's father was going to die soon as well. He has refused to join the Order. At least he knows nothing about what it really is. Anyone that finds out its nature and tries to back out dies straight away. He has just refused to join what he had calls "a silly secret society playing at the olden days of the last cycle and refusing to grow the Duchy as it should be."

Clarence laughed at that part. "I think that the real reason he refused to join was that he is too tied up with the girl who is now his former mistress. She ran away and he is still trying to find her before the Duchess or the Order do. We have chased after her, but she has eluded us so far. This mistress, Thorn, is another we will sacrifice when she is caught."

"Does anyone else have any other questions?" asked Basil, looking around the ship.

"How many of our people are still alive from Moorea?" asked Taine.

Clarence shrugged. "Most of the men died or were killed almost straight away. We took one hundred and fifty-three north. Six didn't last the whole trip after we gave them to the crew to bind them to us." *The other captured crew have shrunk further back into their huddle as if each is trying to hide among the others. Adding those six to the two dead on this trip, I wish we could put them in the Arena back in Ardlark.* "Some more have probably died since…I don't know."

Basil turned to the Princesses. "Kill him now or later?"

"Now," said Rani without hesitation.

"But our people will we want to question him," said Taine.

"He is a mage," replied Rani, "and I have a feeling that he is a strong one from the time it took to drain his mana into the storage magic." He turned to Clarence. "Are you a strong mage?" he asked. "Can you cause a man to die with a single spell?"

Even in the position he is in, Clarence cannot resist bragging. "It was I who killed the Abbott. I crafted my own special spell and there is no one else who can cast it. It makes a person look like they have just died in their sleep. I tried it on a few others first, and on several since then. It works very well and no one has an idea what has happened to them."

Theodora is shuddering at that. He turned back to the islanders. "See, it is far too hard to keep him secure. He can even throw off the enchantment that has been cast more easily than a normal person can.

"I am sure that your people can question these other ten. They are just as guilty as Clarence is. Don't worry, we know exactly where the island is where your people are. It is our destination. We shall call first at a few places to get food and more people to come with us, but where they are is where we are headed. We are sure that it is where the last battle of our quest will be fought."

Clarence was asked if he wanted to undertake a Confession and receive Last Rites, but after crudely rejecting the offer, he was led to the side of the ship and held over the gunwale as his veins were opened. After he had bled a bit and started to go weak, he was tipped up and his body was allowed to fall into the sea with his hands still bound.

His blood must have attracted some large predators, for as soon as the body hit the water there was an immediate tussle over it. The battle was won by a giant Oared Lizard the length of the *River Dragon*.

It has jaws longer than a man and a row of teeth like small daggers. I have not seen one so big before. It lunged through the other marine creatures and out of the water with Clarence's body already half-swallowed.

His legs were already deep inside the beast as he gave a last scream. *It seems that he is still alive, or perhaps he had a contingency in place that revived him. If so it is only for a brief time. For the first time there is a sound of despair in his voice as he cries out.* The other creatures fled away from where the giant beast fed. It gave a shake and the rest of Clarence disappeared down its throat with a wail.

Chapter XV

Theodora
30th November

Virginia has ended up sitting weeping against Ursula's ample bosom. It seems that the scales have finally fallen from her eyes. What we made her read in her cell in Mousehole has now been placed within the context of her own life. Perhaps she can now see herself as if she were a victim of one whose words were being recorded.

Having heard Clarence's boastful confession, she now has to re-evaluate everything she saw and heard amongst her own people. I really do not think she likes what has been revealed to her. Her mother, in particular, seems to be most loathsome. How do you learn to accept that?

Olympias

The Puleleiite is most excited to go over the maps Basil found with me. These are written in several different hands, but they are the most detailed we have seen. Theodora has confirmed there is nothing she has come across—and apparently she has looked hard—in the libraries of Darkreach that will equal them.

On them are marked the currents and the winds. Those are the pathways of the seas. One chart even shows how some of these change with the seasons. Some show the lands and who lives there and some even have notes in their margins about what lies there.

None of us quite believe the note attached to the map of a place called The Desert Land. *It is written in High Speech and cautions travellers to be wary of landing in its blistering heat, warning that magic works differently there and that anything known by those who land will be very nearly useless. It says to avoid it if it is possible.*

The Great Southern Land, with mysteries foretold in our books, is even more mysterious as a map. It only shows what can be seen from the sea and has a warning, again in High Speech, not to land "lest you lose your memory and your mind—that is, if you survive at all". On these maps there are lines that run up and down the page in grand curves and other lines that run from left to right. Olympias explained what she thought they might be to the Puleleiite, and they marvelled about what these lines confirmed for her about the size of Vhast.

Christopher

Now that the River Dragon *has returned to Tabuaeran, the islanders there have taken aside and examined the ten other crewmen and dispatched six. The four that know the most about the evil they have been a part of have been kept for the people from Ulithi and Tupai, when they arrive, to re-examine if they wish.*

The others have ended up bleeding their life out into a hole in the island before their bodies are dumped in the same hole. We gave them the chance to confess, but only one chose to talk to an Orthodox priest, a young lad who ended up dying while at the same time crying out contritely for his mother.

All the dead of the island are apparently placed in the pits, but only a very few, the worst criminals on the islands, get to see their destination as they are dying and the others are placed there reverentially and with ceremony, not dumped there with less reverence than a dead cat receives. Only the one who repented of his sins received a service and prayer over his body, although I will pray for the souls of the others later. Everyone deserves that much.

Christopher
34th November

*B*asil looks most concerned. "It is Jillian, the girl… So far we have only saved her body from them, not her mind… Because of the blade that was used on her, each day she gets worse and her mind slips further and further away from what is around her and towards death and extinction and perhaps towards feeding the Adversaries." *I was wondering about that.*

"You may have seen that my wives have put her in swaddling clothes now. What is more, when she cries Astrid lets her try and suckle on her while she drips drinks into her mouth. It is the only way to get her to take anything at all. She is almost gone away completely in her mind into being a baby."

He has stopped as if he is considering what to say next, or how much to say. "Ia goes sometimes to a place just like Dobun does. It is a different place and she says that she sees Jillian there. There she is to be seen as a small, hurt animal, like one of the little round hoppers, but with no mind left in her at all." *I want to hear more of this place.*

"Ia says that there Maeve and Fluff-Ball care for her as she and Astrid do in this world. I don't understand that at all, but she seems to know what she is talking about. We, my wives and I, we want to know if you can do anything for her. Ia has tried her mind trick and all it does is calm her and allow her to sleep. She says that she cannot return her to us. What can you do?"

The Bishop took a little while before replying. "I have seen your wives in their striving," said Christopher. "I have continual cause to keep calling for blessings on Astrid and on her compassion for others ever since she first saved me. I have not forgotten the girl but it is going to be…difficult." *To say the least.*

"I think," said Christopher, "that she has run away to another happier land in her mind. Perhaps it is a place where she is still herself and where she can fight back against what is happening to her, but I think that if she dies there her soul will be lost. It would be easier to call her back to her body if we were home.

"To an extent it will be like what happened to Anahita in Dwarvenholme, but there her soul was just lost and wandering. Here I will have to fight as I do it… I may have something I can do, but I do not know. Bring them all tonight for Hesperinos. Hopefully, God will smile on us. Even Ia and the animals, they are all connected to her. If she is getting even worse, then I will have to act now rather than wait."

That night in the service those present saw the girl, cradled in Astrid's arms and sucking on her breast as if she were only a few months old. *Astrid tries to dribble honeyed water into her mouth as she does so. Astrid and Ia are both looking haggard as the strain is telling on them as well. Again the hill-cat is patiently being clutched tight like a stuffed toy.*

The Bear Folk are all here looking on, as well as several of the islanders. I would say that it is not just Ia who has seen a shadow of the girl in their spirit world. They are all concerned as well. Having saved the girl's body, allowing the Adversaries to claim her mind and her soul would seem not only to be unjust, but also a major victory for our enemies. They might even be able to use it to find out what is happening here at sea. No one I talk to is sure about this.

Once again Christopher was obviously worried about what he was about to do. *My wife is obviously fighting to control her tears and Simeon and Aziz both cast concerned looks in my direction.* The service progressed. Astrid came up to Christopher and received absolution in her own name and then, after Jillian was re-baptised, her eyes staring blankly up unfocussed like a newborn child, in her name as well.

With that, Christopher moved into attempting his miracle and calling on Saint Mary Magdalene, as patron of sinners who repent, and Saint Anne, not only patron of those returning from the dead, but also of those who challenge and fight against evil by protecting others. He called on Michael for victory and Jude in forlorn hope.

Winifred was invoked for healing, and Nicholas as the patron of children, even on Astrid's patron of Kessog to aid her and finally his namesake as patron of travellers to find the girl a path back. When he finished, he was staggering and almost fell. "It is done," he said. "It is now in the lap of God, and we will see what His will is." With that he started to collapse, and Bianca and the two other priests leapt to his side and carried him away to rest.

Astrid
36ᵗʰ November

It has been a while, but I think that Jillian is beginning to show signs that she might be about to slowly return to her body. At first we thought that Christopher's intervention had only worked to stop her getting worse, but I am sure I see some very small signs of improvement in her. Her eyes are starting to focus and follow people around.

She still clung to Astrid as if she were an infant, however, and still insisted on trying to suckle. *I dried up my milk just before we left and after Anna and Thorstein stopped sucking on me, but, I am embarrassed to admit that, after a couple of days of this pretend suckling, my milk has come back in.*

At least Jillian has now stopped losing weight. Perhaps it will not be for long. "Just as well I am built for this," she said to Ia with a wan smile. "You could not produce enough for a grown woman with your little teats."

The islanders are referring to me by the name of Rongomaiwhenua *and they all look at me very differently and almost reverentially. They won't say why, but they keep bringing me food as I sit cross-legged, now almost continually feeding my woman-infant. I am getting used to these* bananas. *It seems I have several names now. I wonder if I will ever use my Inuit one again.*

Eventually Harnermêŝ revealed that he thought Rongomaiwhenua was the Kanaka's "earth mother", a special goddess for a people who did not touch land often, and so this was a term both of great respect and of endearment from them. *Earth mother indeed… It is easy to see that it is not going to be a quick return to a full life for the girl.*

Rani
1ˢᵗ December

*T*he two ships of the Nomads have returned to Tabuaeran filled with people from the other islands and, now with all of their Khitan back with us in the sky and the two other ships trailing behind with Sea Nomad crews eager to rescue what was left of Moorea or at least to avenge them, we are headed north towards, perhaps, the final conflict. We still have three weeks until the start of spring.

Chapter XVI

Olympias
6th December

We first swept northward over the placid ocean up towards the coast of the New Found Land. It did not take long for the shore to come into view. We first saw it only from the eyes of our riders, but then the green-light box showed it as well. At least the box makes it easy to keep it at a constant distance. However, the coastline changes as we move along it.

When we first saw it the coast had started off running east to west. The land there was lush and green and it even looked a little like the coast of the Swamp with no visible settlements. This is the home of Yabaribaykus's tribe. However, Human villages started to come into sight and the east-west coast soon turned a corner marked, according to their new maps and confirmed by the riders, by the bay at the entrance of the Meander River.

Just upstream of the delta our aerial scouts could see the growing town of New Ashvaria. Once the settlements started and particularly above this corner the land was more like the coast of Freehold.

As it turns out, we were not very far below the mass of the New Found Land when we finally set out from Tabuaeran and the coast has been sweeping past us rapidly. I have been happily using my instruments to shoot the sun and the stars and, on having my calculations confirmed, making satisfied notations in my journal and on the navigation charts.

Taking advantage of a current that the charts show sweeps north along the coast we added our own breeze as well as a local wind that has favoured us as well. Between them we have made a most rapid progress up along the shore.

Although no large or armed ships have been seen, several times we have seen fishing boats. These are generally inshore in shallower water near the edge of the current. They have all rapidly fled west away from our three *unfamiliar vessels, one even abandoning its nets. We have not pursued them.*

Then the settlements all died away and no more vessels were to be seen. The coast beside us is just forest. According to Yabaribaykus, this was the home of another tribe of his people, and traders journey nervously between the Counties along the coast as they hope to avoid conflict with his people.

I have been intent on going further north on this coast. I am following my newly obtained charts to where it seems likely that there is a port that will probably allow the River Dragon to re-supply and get some fresh food on board for us all.

According to what we now have, from the charts that the Meander Rose has yielded up and from what Clarence and the sailors said, we are headed for what is probably the home of those who smuggle goods and people back to The Land. We have left behind the County of New Ashvaria and our destination lies in the north of the next batch of settlements, those of the County of Sweetwater.

Simeon had just been trying to get as far from the monastery as he could. He had accidentally stumbled on the same port. It was from there that he had come back to The Land and he had been asked no questions when he found a ship headed our way and offered his unskilled labour in return for transit.

In grateful return for his passage he had asked no questions about the cargo, but he thought it was likely it was an illicit load as well, even though he had seen none of it. Although Didymoteichon is a Baronial seat, it relies on the sea for its livelihood and, being the furthest major settlement in the Newfoundland from Castle Mount, it seems to also be in the best position to be the most relaxed in its attitudes to the rules.

What is more, it certainly has the most incentive to do so as well. It is far from the main parts of the Duchy and, despite sending people to represent them at the Curia Burgess, like most isolated settlements it is likely that the people there would see more of tax collectors than they would see of the fruits of that tax.

Astrid

*F*or us, her two new mothers and her new father, we are being driven to distraction as Jillian gradually moves from being a newborn to becoming a two-year-old, with all that implies. She has very quickly regained her strength as her physical abilities begin to return, and so cannot be left alone for an instant in case she ends up in the ocean or somewhere else where she would be in danger.*

How much she will be a new person and how much the old none can even guess. If I am not there, she will take Ia's embrace, but that is all. Basil and Christopher are the only men she will let near her. Fluff-Ball, weighing near half as much as the person carrying her, is being very understanding about her new role as a stuffed toy. The cat is only reluctantly released from Jillian's embrace if she insists and then only if Maeve takes her place while the cat attends to her own needs.

At least I was able to start weaning Jillian off the breast on the way up the coast. Although she still seeks the comfort of my breasts, she is now taking solid food and experimenting with words. She is also rapidly becoming older in the way she holds her face. It no longer has the look of complete innocence of the very young. We look forward to this week passing and having her out of saying "no" to far too many things.

Between her own needs, the babies that she could feel growing inside her and the added demands that a breastfeeding adult placed upon her body, Astrid was now eating huge amounts of food, even by her own standards, but she was still losing weight and looked gaunt around the face. *Both my husband and sister-wife have expressed concern, but we hope that it is only temporary and will soon pass.*

Olympias
early morning 7th December, the Feast Day of Saint Paul

*W*e *have found our destination. The lead saddles found it from on high. Now, as we draw closer, I have brought all the saddles on board, except for two, which have been landed on the Sea Nomad ships with riders in case they are needed to carry a quick message or to look at someone who unexpectedly approaches us. They can keep watch from out at sea.*

The *River Dragon* approached the small town, with the sun rising into the sky behind them. *It is very noticeable that this is the first place we have seen where the fishing boats just stay in place fishing, or even sailing past our ships further out into the ocean. They ignore the strange brigantines headed towards land and show neither fear, nor too much unseemly curiosity.*

The two Nomad ships soon put out sea anchors and stayed in position as the smaller *River Dragon* headed in to the port. *The Nomads have their own food requirements and, despite the extra people that they have on board, do not need much in the way of supplies from the land. It is also not usual for them to seek any contact with the people from outside a very small circle of ports around the world, and this is not one of those.*

"This ship was built for someone else," Theodora explained to the Kanakas that they had on board. "For some reason they never returned to finish their purchase of it, but we knew there had to be somewhere like this, where this sort of vessel would be familiar to the people who lived there." *We never did track down who it was.*

"Why build a ship in secret," she continued, "if you do not have a secret destination in mind for it? When this is all over, Olympias will probably want to start coming here regularly. If trade is still tightly restricted to the New Found Land, it should be well worthwhile for us to break the restrictions. There must be many people here who would be glad to sell their spices and herbs to a free dealer, instead of an official one, and set their own price for a start." *This is true.*

"If we also consider adding trade to and from the Goblins, we are looking at a lot of money to be made, and Yabaribaykus tells me that the Goblins are not the only tribes in this land. There are tribes of Kharl and others even more secretive that the settlers from Freehold seem to know little about." *All we need is a way of making contact. It all sounds so easy, far too easy.*

"From the sound of it, just selling tools and metal to the Goblins will bring us in a lot of money and, if we are to end up having to fight Freehold at some time in the future, such a trade will weaken their hold on this land and so, hopefully, reduce the aid and the money that they can expect to gain from here."

Theodora shrugged. "Of course, all of this is dependent on us winning our next battle, I know, but we are starting to think about the longer term, and all of this is a little like our game of chess, where you have to think several moves ahead all of the time. I am good at chess," she concluded smugly.

Astrid
an hour later

There is another, nearly identical, vessel to our own already docked in the port and the first time that we excited any interest was as we were tying up at the dock behind it. The local idlers suddenly realised that the crew on our vessel are not familiar to them and, indeed, that the crew they now see are quite foreign in appearance.

Shilpa and Basil, one Hindi and the other with bare arms and showing his slightly scaled skin, are a shock to the locals, who are obviously not used to seeing anyone but Freeholders. They were both getting off the River Dragon *to go and find a providore when they were noticed by some of those idlers on the dockside.*

However, the best reaction was reserved for when they realised that we have several non-Human members among the crew, including a Goblin. In case there is any trouble I am on the deck near the gangplank, my weapon in hand, and Ia is the one who now has a tight grip on Jillian. People have begun to gather to look at what is going on with our vessel.

It is evident that they are motivated more out of curiosity than anything else as no one seems alarmed by us, even by Denizkartal. People stand or sit, some in groups, and pass comment on the crew of our vessel and some even point out its weapons to others. Not only is there a lack of reaction, but it seems that there are no customs officials here as no one has appeared to attempt to levy a tax on what we might have on board.

At least we no longer have to keep an eye on Virginia. Since hearing from Clarence about the Order of the Gryphon and its plans for her she is no longer so eager to see her own land again and, while she is below deck, she is there voluntarily and staying well out of sight of any people who might want to kidnap or kill her. We told Theodora about this, and she didn't believe it. She has gone below to check with the girl before she needs to attend to what is going on up here.

There is a small castle close by on a hillside just above the village and, after one of the people hanging around near the dock hastily ran up there, a man has appeared, walking quickly and with a few retainers following him. He is a tall and well-rounded man, but not fat. I would say that he just had a large frame to start with and that he is well fed.

He is not unpleasant to look at and young, not more than seventeen or eighteen, and tall, a hand taller even than I am. He is well-dressed in fine wools and carries his sword, not a rapier, with assurance. The men with him, a couple of obvious guards, one a man and the other a woman, are more out of breath than he is as he looks around without seeing an obvious person to talk to apart from me.

I am still barefoot, wearing trousers and a shirt, and do not look to be an obvious person to address. He keeps looking around for a person of authority as everyone is ignoring him. Olympias and the crew are still busy fussing around with the details of a ship docking in a port. I suppose that, as amusing as it is to watch his growing puzzlement, I should say something—if he can understand my Latin, that is.

"My name is Astrid the Cat," she said in her sing-song Latin and smiled, deliberately showing off her teeth. *The guards have recoiled and one started to draw a sword before his master gestured at him.* Astrid shook her head and waved a finger at the guard, in the manner of a mother warning a child approaching a biscuit barrel. She looked back to the young man as she continued and swept her left hand around "…and this is the *River Dragon*."

She then gestured up to the mainmast where their flag flew. "We come from the village of Mousehole in the Southern Mountains of The Land. We are on our way to Wolfneck in the north, and need to re-provision. And you are…?"

"I am Baron Elias Tobias," replied the man in a surprised tone. *He is not used to being asked questions in a tone like that in his own town.* "Are you in charge of this ship?" *He is looking at me and at the wide variety of people who can be seen on her deck. I think he is already aware that I am not, but he cannot see someone who obviously is.*

I can see that his eyes are taking in our weapons, the various small children, and a ship that certainly looks like it is, with its stone throwers openly displayed and a rack of weapons on show, a vessel on the way to war. The River Dragon *is making no pretence of looking at all like a normal trader, even if it is not sure what exactly it is.*

Astrid gave a short laugh. "I am not even in charge of my own life," she continued in staged resignation and with a wry smile before continuing in a more cheerful tone. "Would you like to see a ship's captain or a Princess? I think that now you have a choice." *I kept my face blank when I said that. If anything, the look on his face has become even more uncertain.*

"I will get you a Princess. One of them seems to be free now." *The cousins are standing nearby.* She waved Adara off in Theodora's direction as she came out of her cabin. "Nice little town you have," Astrid said, looking back around to the Baron. "How are the Goblins in your area? What do you think of the Treaty? Do you see much trade from outside here in the port? Do you have much trouble from the Ducal authorities? Are you for or against the Gryphon?" she asked the Baron, without much of a gap between questions for him to respond.

I am just watching his face to see what shows on it as each question pops out. It seems to sometimes work for Basil. The young man doesn't seem sure how to respond. Before he could do so, Astrid had changed direction again, and was now introducing him to Theodora. *I did, however, note that a flicker of disgust wiped the puzzlement off his face when I mentioned the Gryphons.*

Theodora

"We are only here briefly," Theodora stressed. "We stop only for provisions." *Perhaps if I bring him on board? I can fill him in on what is happening, and who we are, and perhaps sound him out for the future. His guards look nervous, but then Astrid is grinning at them. She does seem to have that effect when she does that. I need to be open about this; our religious differences could be important for a start.*

I heard Astrid's last question, and his answer to that is important. He is trying to do the same to me on smuggling. Rani and Olympias had sat down near them during this conversation but neither had said anything. *Already I can see that our stores are coming aboard. Time is running out for us to get anywhere in our talk. Someone will have to stop the verbal fencing.*

"I do not have time to beat around the bush," said Theodora. "We are about to leave and sail away to the north. I am going to answer directly what you have been trying to find out. We are happy to break any blockade on trade with you. The guard boats your Duke uses are nothing to us as we have already destroyed both the *Goldentide* and, most recently, the *Meander Rose.*" *He looks surprised at that.*

"The *Goldentide* attacked us first and the *Meander Rose* had already been taken over by our enemies. We have destroyed the only other powerful boat in these seas that we know about, but we are fairly sure that your people have one more galleon at least, or at least soon will have. When we have concluded what we are doing, our captain shall probably want to return and trade with you. If your Guardia Costa try and interfere, we will happily get rid of them, as so far your authorities have shown themselves to be enemies to us.

"Our supercargo has already been ashore, and I certain that she now knows exactly what you have for us to trade in and what you want, as long as your traders do not mind her being of a different religion…and here is our captain, Olympias." She waved at Olympias, who put her hand out and took the Baron's hand without being asked and shook it. "She will return. Does that answer your questions?"

The Baron nodded. *He looks a little stunned.* "Now answer mine," she continued. "Do you know of the Order of the Gryphon? How do you feel about them?" She could see him pause. "Come on, man, we don't have enough time to muck around in polite conversation. They are the ones that took over the *Meander Rose* and they are most definitely our enemies, and they should be yours as well. You do not wear one of their rings and yet you know of them." *He looks at his hand.*

"You must realise by now that if you are not one of them, you are likely to be a marked man as far as they are concerned." She stopped and looked at him. *He is looking around him as if he is making sure that there is no one in earshot who should not be here.*

"It does not pay to say too much about them," he said quietly. "They have very powerful friends and no one knows them all."

"They are about to have a lot fewer powerful friends except in Freehold and here, and we actually do know most of them now. We may not know all of their servants, but we know the people in their Order who are full members." She noticed Basil standing by and turned to him. "Basil, can you please get a copy of the list of the members of Order of the Gryphon to the Baron in the next few minutes before we go." Basil nodded and hurried away. She then turned back to the surprised Baron. "How do you feel about your Duke?"

"I don't know how he stands," the Baron said. *There is a note of surprise in his voice at the change of direction in the conversation.* "He has laws against free trade, but he does not seem to do much to enforce them and I think that they come to him from the Old World and are not ones of his own choosing." *Perhaps we should talk to him, then.*

"He is accused of being a tyrant by some rumours and to have killed the old Abbot in Castle Mount by others, but on the other hand he encourages the Magna Curia Ducatas and the Curia Burgess Ducatas to give a voice to the nobles and to people…" He trailed off. *He needs to hear this directly.* Theodora beckoned Simeon over.

"This is Father Simeon," she said. "He was born in New Ashvaria and was once one of your priests. Simeon, tell the Baron what happened at the Abbey at Sweetwater."

Simeon looked at the Baron. *He is wondering how much to say.* "I was a monk," he said. "The old Abbot, Franciscus, made me a priest just before he died. I now know that Leo, the current Abbot, who is a degenerate and a member of these Gryphons, had him killed by Clarence Garlin. However, I have left my life as a monk behind me and I am now a priest of the true and Orthodox church and am no longer a schismatic," he concluded determinedly.

"You are very definitely sure of who killed the Abbott, then?" the Baron asked. Simeon nodded. "So, despite what we keep hearing, the Duke wasn't really responsible for his death? It was others?" the Baron continued. *He really wants to make sure. He seems not to care a fig on the religious question. It is all about politics.*

"No," said Simeon. "We have questioned the man and it was definitely the mage, heir of Epibati, called Clarence Garlin who did it and he was acting for the new Abbott Leo. We have executed that man for his crimes." *He sounds disappointed that his changing his religious affiliation is ignored.* "I would hazard a guess that Leo probably sent the rumour out to undermine the position of the Duke."

"In that case I suppose that I am for the Duke," said the Baron. He thought briefly and then continued: "What do you think I should do? I am pretty much alone here and without too much counsel. My parents died recently." *He is obviously still a young man and it is clear that he needs help. Once we go, he has no one to turn to who knows what is happening.*

"Can you get Virginia?" Theodora said to Simeon. The priest nodded and headed off.

Elias Tobias

*T**his woman who calls herself a Princess is telling me what she knows about Freehold and its current politics. I am entranced. This woman, who comes from Darkreach, or at least a small village somewhere that I have never heard of, seems to know more about the court of my Queen than I do.* "While she is being brought..."—she is waving at someone—"how do you feel on the Goblin question? This is Yabaribaykus."

The Baron looked at the Goblin. *I have to look at him twice. He looks like a Goblin but he is dressed and equipped, and even armed as if he were a normal person, except for a lack of shoes. I think that I can speak my mind here and I am far more certain on this point at least.* "I, personally, am glad of the Scutari Treaty. If it holds it means we get to have trade instead of having people die." *The Goblin seems to like what I am saying, but I suppose that he would. Oh, that means that he understands Latin.*

"My people are the ones who are on the edge of all of the settlements, and they get to do a lot of the dying...a lot more than the people who are not living on this frontier do. It is not fine for them to be able to say that we should keep fighting on their behalf when they do not pay for the fighting, nor do they do the dying. We have more than enough land at the moment. It is much more than we need at present when even hamlets can still have a day or more of good walking between them...and I am sure we can come to some agreements if we need more."

This Theodora looks at the Goblin. He nods at her, so they seem to agree on something. "Yabaribaykus comes from your land, even if he is not of your local tribe, the Halkgenisovadin, but now he speaks other languages as well as his own. I am sure that he will speak to your local tribes for you as an interpreter before he returns to his own tribe, if you wish."

The Goblin is eagerly nodding, and it sounds a good idea to me. Tentatively, the Goblin held out his hand to the Human and, equally tentatively, the Baron shook it as the two sized each other up. *I think it is obvious to all that this is a new and strange experience for me.* "He will also tell you more about us and what we are doing. I am sure you will find in him an adviser you can trust." *I am to get a Goblin adviser assigned to me? Given the Treaty, I suppose that it makes a lot of sense, actually.*

Theodora now turned, and Elias' eyes followed her gaze. *Father Simeon is coming back with a young, and very attractive, girl. She sort of looks familiar. She seems reluctant to meet me.* "Virginia, come and meet Elias Tobias. He is the Baron here" *She has turned and gone to flee and is only stopped by running into the priest.*

"Girl, pay attention," said Theodora. "Elias, meet Virginia Norbery… Yes, *that* Virginia Norbery." *That is why she looks familiar. I saw her in Castle Mount a couple of years ago when I swore fealty. She is supposed to have disappeared along with the* Goldentide.

"The Order of the Gryphon want her dead—well, actually, they want to kill her in one of their bizarre rituals, so she has been hiding below decks. Close your mouth, boy, you are a Baron and have to look the part. Virginia, Elias seems to like your father and not your mother's friends in the Order of the Gryphon. Do you want to stay with him?"

She stopped talking and looked, with one eyebrow raised, from one of the young people to the other. *I am speechless and looking her up and down. She is doing the same to me. I can feel myself starting to blush. So is she. She is much prettier now than she was back then.* Elias' mouth opened and closed a couple of times. Virginia's hand had started to play with a stray lock of hair.

Astrid

We could be here for hours at this rate. These two obviously need a prod, and this is one of my roles. "I think that he is even unmarried," she said. *From the way the Baron is now definitely colouring, I am right. Now he has turned quite a bright red.* Astrid turned to the girl she had spanked as if she were a naughty child. *She is doing the same.*

"You wanted a husband, girl," she said. "Well, here you are. What is more, he is even of the right rank, and he looks to be well-favoured. I would also say that he has a chance to become quite rich if we are to keep on dealing with him as our contact here in the New Found Land"—she paused—"and if our side wins in this war, of course."

Theodora

Astrid has succeeded in making it even worse. She glared at her. *Damn her just grinning back at me. Now both of the young Newfoundland folk have gone even more completely tongue-tied. I think they realise that there is an obvious attraction that has appeared suddenly between them, but this is not how these things should go.*

"Make up your mind, girl," Theodora said sharply. "You didn't even want to get on this ship in the first place. You have been trying to leave us ever since, and now we are about to set sail into battle again."

Virginia found her voice eventually. *Her eyes are still on the young Baron.* "Can I come back here when these Adversaries are dead? Will you bring me? Will you help me deal with the Gryphon people? I don't want them to kill me."

Theodora nodded. "Yes, but you don't get your dowry back. We captured that fairly."

"I am sure that I wouldn't need a dowry," blurted Elias. *He is somehow blushing even deeper as he realises what he has just revealed. That has set Virginia off blushing again, and we are surrounded by a circle of grinning bystanders, including, it is interesting to see, Elias' two guards, who are not even attempting to hide the smiles on their faces.*

"We need to go," interjected Olympias, and the Baron was bundled off the *River Dragon* with a note in his hand from Basil that he had not yet looked at. *Indeed it is something that he might even be unaware of. His eyes are almost entirely on Virginia. He has just kept the list in his hand and waves it as if it were a scarf or token, forgetting what it actually is, as we cast off and leave.*

I noticed that Yabaribaykus was talking with the guardsmen, and now has all of his stuff with him. He stands with the guards beside him on the dock, with his weapons in hand and a pack. He should have with him copies of the Treaties that we have with various other groups, a short lexicon of Goblin to Latin words, and other things, like his smith's tools.

Theodora looked around. *In contrast to her normal behaviour, Virginia stands quietly at the stern of the* River Dragon, *looking behind the ship as we sail out. We may have only stopped for food, but at least that may have led to another problem now being solved. I will offer some prayers of thanksgiving later.*

Chapter XVII

Theodora
7th December, an hour after leaving port

We have rejoined the others, and now we all sail to the east and a little south. According to our new maps, the Human-settled parts of the New Found Land lie well to the north of most of The Land and that is the course we must follow to reach Wolfneck. The wind is coming from almost directly behind us. Again, from what Olympias has told us from the maps, it blows almost constantly from that direction and we should have a following wind and sea as we sail across.

Now Virginia is approaching, and she looks very subdued. "Perhaps," she said, "I should have mentioned this, but I was…distracted. I am fairly sure that I saw my father's mistress in the background when we were in Didymoteichon." *That is certainly something that it would have been good to know while we were there. Perhaps Yabaribaykus will find her.*

Olympias
10th December, it is Remembrance Day for Darkreach

With the addition of our own wind, the leagues have flown past for our three vessels as we speed over the sea. Occasionally the lookouts on the saddles and on the ships have reported a whale sounding on the surface ahead or beside them. Astrid says that the first harbingers of the annual spring migrations are starting to appear around us.

I wonder if I should point out to Astrid that this is the day when the Empire mourns for the loss of her people around Wolfneck over three thousand years ago. The irony of heading there now to fight against the same enemy is large. It is something we all learnt about in school, but I don't think anyone has ever pointed it out to her and her brother.

We make our first landfall for The Land at the north-west corner near Greatkin in the new confederation of Amity and, rather than stop the ships to check on what is happening, the Princesses have used the saddles to visit the northern towns of Amity to check on its progress and needs, and to bring the people there up to date. They intend to continue doing the same all the way along the coast as we head eastward. I am mainly keeping out of sight of land, but we are still keeping contact with the shore through the aid of the green-light box.

The Princesses and their escort have returned to the River Dragon *after nearly a day away. Greatkin has gradually fallen behind our ships and so, eventually, did Hobden Bay. It was then the turn of Aberbaldie to be left behind us. The land disappeared at Hobden Bay but is back visible to the starboard on the green-light box.*

Rani
14th December, the Feast Day of Saint Andronicus

I *have riders who are keeping an eye out ahead, to the port, and to our rear. The chance of our opponents doing something to try and stop us is magnified as we head further and further east and get closer to them. We can try and hide, and we do, but there are always ways to find someone if you look hard enough. We proved that when we found the craft that was apparently called the* Dragon of the Seas.

When our riders arrived at the Bulga they were told that the message of a possible last battle has gotten out—no one seems certain how—and that people, both veterans of the fight against the Brotherhood and those who did not take part, are already making their way to Wolfneck by land and by boat from all over the North.

Our riders come back from Bidvictor with the same message, and this time they bring passengers with them. They have the mage Justin Speller and his apprentice riding along. Just as they had waited for us in their village on the way to the Brotherhood, now they wait for us to go past to the battle by sea.

It seems that everyone in the north knows what is about to happen, and that at least some of the army of the north are being re-assembled by their local captains and headed east. We may need them, but will we have the ships to hold them?

If the Adversaries still have any spies in the area, ones who could report to them, or even if they are using magic to look around at what is happening, it also seems that there will be no chance of catching them unawares. Surprise was a faint enough hope for us before finding out about this gathering of an army, but now it is going to be impossible.

If everyone in the north now knows what is happening, then it is certain that our enemy is being given a chance to gather their own forces together as well. Where will they draw them from? Whether the army of the North will outweigh the forces that our enemy can gather is anyone's guess without knowing what they have behind them.

I need to plan for the idea that we will be expected. The best that we can hope for will be to have a small amount of surprise in regard to the timing of the attack. Somehow I have to work towards achieving that.

Theodora
very early on the 18th December, the Feast Day of Saint Sebastian

I have been casting spells each evening to help update my normal prediction of the weather to come and all has gone well with them. Both the spells and the predictions of the experienced sailors, those who just look at the sea and the sky and who feel the wind in their faces, speak of clear weather conditions being expected for weeks, along with an almost constant, mild westerly wind.

One thing that we have all agreed upon is that it is a gentle spring and that no storms at all are expected for our transit. News from riders on the fleet's port flank, telling of a great storm sweeping on us out of the north-east, is more than a small surprise. Astrid knows these seas well. She can wake up and explain this.

Astrid came up from below. She looked at the clouds gathering in that direction, shook her head and wrinkled her brow. "A wind from the north-east," she said, "is not common at any time of the year at this latitude, and the chance of a full storm coming from that direction, particularly at this time of year, is very low."

Astrid frowned and then waved her arms around and began pointing at the features that were visible, the following wind, and the long, smooth swells. "Look at the clouds, the waves, and the wind. It all tells only of a smooth passage."

"Do you mean that it is not natural, that the storm bearing down on us is the result of an enchantment or a summoning?" asked Theodora.

"You are the mage, not me. I don't know. It is just not what I would expect at this time of year, or indeed at any other time. It is the wrong time of year, it is coming from the wrong direction, and it doesn't fit any of the other weather signs." Her eyes suddenly went wide. "Can you even make a storm like that? One so huge?" she asked in awe. She looked up at black clouds ahead of them that presaged a storm as violent as any of the winter gales. "One of our great storms?"

There was a pause as Theodora thought for a moment. "Yes," she replied cautiously, "I think I could, but it would not be easy even for me, and I am not sure that I could do one so far out of season." She looked pensively at the clouds ahead for a while before continuing.

"Granther could do it, I suppose. I guess it is safe to say that they know we are coming. Hulagu is flying just in front of it and, from what he says of its strength, if that hits us we may lose the Nomad ships and, despite our ability to mitigate a storm, even we will be in peril. I need to think…and I only have a few hours to do it in. Keep people away from me."

Theodora went and sat in her folding chair beside the mage's hatch with a slate. Occasionally she would look up and stare into the north-east where clouds were now gathering, growing darker, and rapidly drawing closer. She kept Astrid near her, and twice she asked the northern woman questions about the directions of winds and currents, what was normal, and what would be expected.

Theodora
over an hour later, it is still night

"Astrid," she called, without even looking to see if the woman was nearby, "get every single mage on all of the ships here, and bring them fast." She looked north-east into the night. *We have nearly a full moon of Terror and now the storm is a thick black block towering over the horizon and coming quickly at us.* "We have perhaps half an hour only before it hits." Mages were woken on the *River Dragon*, and saddles quickly set off to wake others.

It did not take long to gather them all together. Once they were all assembled in front of her, Theodora looked at the gathered mages. She was holding her husband's hand tight; it did not appear to be a conscious act, just the normal unthought-of act of a person seeking reassurance.

"I cannot dispel this," she said. "From what I can work out, this is magic so powerful that all of their mages must have combined to produce it." She looked around. "A while ago I thought that I might have been able to raise such a storm, but I no longer think so. It is a powerful weapon that they have raised, but I may have an idea how to counter it. At least I hope I do."

She smiled. "I do not like performing such a spell as this without having practised something approaching it and thinking hard about how it will all fit together, so I have taken another spell I have and adapted it. Are you all willing to give me everything that you have—and I really do mean everything." She was looking at the mages around her as she spoke.

"I will need all your stored mana…and I will need you all to be overdrawn and you have to leave nothing behind. You will be drained."

There is nodding to be seen from around me, along with more than a few worried looks, especially on the face of young Gurinder, who will be taking part in her first major casting. She stands between her sister and Goditha, nervously holding a hand of each of them and seeking reassurance from both her sister and her adopted semi-parent. At least I see no dissent.

She stopped talking and turned to the captain, calling out: "Olympias… move us to being the ship closest to the storm and bring us directly into it… and let the *Ofu* know to come around to behind us and bring the *Rongo* close behind them as well. They need to be in line behind us so that the storm must hit us before it hits them… Get sweet drinks and food ready for all of us for after we cast, we will all need it." *At least I hope we have a chance to need it.*

"You will have to have people ready and waiting to look after anyone who collapses." With that she sent the ship's crew and its passengers into a flurry of activity as the pattern on the hatch, which was not usually kept in a charged condition due to the danger, was primed and heavily reinforced by the first mages to spend their power on their counter-enchantment.

Finally, and it seems like we are just in time, we are ready for the casting itself. Ahead of our small fleet the storm is growing steadily closer. I want it close, but perhaps not too close. To those watching as it came on, it seemed to be growing, even as it drew on the normal elements of unstable air and water.

Now it is close it is obvious that this is not a natural storm. The waves within the front of the enchanted area can be seen heaving within the storm. They are being lashed hard by a gale that does not exist at all only a few hands in front of the storm's edge. The saddle riders have all been brought aboard and the sails taken in just in case the spell fails and the ship has to fight for its life.

Those people who are not directly involved, or who will not be handling the River Dragon *if the spell fails, are sent below to a safer place. Behind us the two Sea Nomad vessels are making their own preparations, reefing sails tight and rigging lines. If the spell fails I hope that they will be close enough that the calming spell on the River Dragon may extend a little way to them—enough to give them some help.*

Olympias

Theodora has kissed her husband and taken her position in the pattern. A very shaky Goditha, who has already overdrawn herself in charging the pattern along with the other casters of the element of Earth, is holding the scroll with the words and motions of this new enchantment written out on it as Theodora begins to speak and move in the patterns that she is using for her counter-spell.

Sometimes the gestures and movements of a mage casting a spell almost resemble a dance. This is one of those times. Theodora's movements almost echo the rhythm of a gentle and seductive dance and she sways to and fro within the pattern. At the moment it is as if a flame is dancing in a zephyr or a flag were flapping gently in a soft breeze.

Around her stand the rest of the mages who have not yet contributed their mana to the casting. All of them are holding their charged storage devices in their hands as they wait to contribute what they have within them and what they have in storage to the enchantment. If it were not something that may fail and kill us all, it would be fascinating to watch. She turned back to her wheel.

It will be very dangerous for all of them, but it will be even more dangerous for Theodora. Not only will she be drained, but she will also be the pipe that so much raw magical power will be channelled through. I heard someone say that she will temporarily be holding more than four or five times the mana that it would be within her normal ability to cast. That has to be a desperate act and quite chancy for her.

The storm was only a few minutes away and the roar of the rain on the water, as loud and as violent as a giant predatory beast, could be easily heard growing closer when Theodora, as she chanted, stretched out her hands to one after another of the waiting helpers, turning them over languidly as if she were revealing her zils, her tiny dancing cymbals.

She gestures with her fingers and beckons the mages to give all they can to her. One after another, almost as tangible sparks, their mana passes into her and many of the donors collapse into the arms of waiting attendants. They are dragged clear and warm honey infusions, brought up from Gundardasc's galley, are poured between their lips.

I swear that I can see the skin of the Princess actually glowing with the amount of contained power within, and this time it is not just her eyes, but all of her. Her eyes glow as if they were lights shining out of the face of a statue. The rest is like a halo all around her. Jesus Christ and all the Saints, it's frightening. Theodora finished her chant and her dance when the storm was barely a chain away from the bow of the *River Dragon*.

Briefly, Theodora stood leaning forward with her arms tucked close to her and her palms towards the storm as if she were pushing against a wall. *I am sure that she can only hold that pose for a short while. Her legs are wobbling with the strain and she is striving hard just to stay upright. I think she just slid back along the deck a little.*

I can feel the River Dragon *herself shudder as if she too were alive and taking a part in the struggle.* Olympias gestured to Astrid to move close to the pattern. *She understands me. She can jump into the pattern to grab Theodora in case she collapses on top of the heavily charged lines. They might explode if she did that.*

Astrid

*T*he concentration and strain can be seen on her face. Is it just me, or does she now look as gaunt and old as her ancestor as she strives to overcome the power of the original spell? For the first time, his features are standing out in more than just her eyes. Maybe I am the only one close enough to see it. I hope so.*

The River Dragon *is shuddering like a living thing, but it is also still slowly forging ahead under the force of its magic.* Astrid glanced to her left. *The storm is getting no closer, and I think that it is in fact moving backwards ahead of the ship as she moves forward. However, it is still a little less than a chain in front of the bowsprit. It is a close thing.*

The waves are now moving ahead of the gale, and we are sailing an ocean that seems to heave in sympathy.

Gradually, as the muscles on Theodora's neck tensed, she brought her hands a bit more back towards her body and then she leant far forward at an impossible angle. *She is pushing her hands away from her as if she were pushing against a heavy wagon that is bogged to the axles in mud and she cannot move her feet from where they, too, are stuck.*

Immediately after she has done that, I can see that, yes, the storm ahead of us is now very slowly retreating. With her arms raised towards it, her fingers outstretched into the north-east, she is driving the tempest back whence it came. The storm abates slowly at first, gaining momentum with each passing moment, returning to those who sent it to us. Now they will be the ones who have to deal with it. I think Theodora said they would have exhausted themselves sending it. This could be very interesting for them, then.

The sea ahead of us, now that it is no longer lashed by the gale, is growing calm again as we ride into it. Aided by the calming spell on our ship, the waves are subsiding to a level that fits in with the now returning mild westerly wind. I can feel the stern lift up as the following swell comes past us and we surge forward on its crest.

As the storm retreated, and almost boneless in her fall, Theodora collapsed forward. *Her stance is now impossible to hold without something to push against.* Astrid jumped into the pattern, careful not to put a foot on any of the lines.

"Now they can either work out how to dispel it or else suffer from it themselves," Theodora muttered. *Yes they can. Screw them.*

She has a smile on her face, but she is now out to it. Astrid carefully lifted her Princess clear and put her down beside her husband. *Rani is almost out to it as well, but she is conscious enough and has at least the strength to clutch her wife's hand.* Astrid checked and found a strong pulse. She grabbed a passing mug of sweet, strong Kaf and starting to dribble it slowly into Theodora's mouth.

People have begun to re-emerge from below decks. They are all standing around like ninnies, looking ahead at the storm heading away from us, as if that has always been the path it was on. Olympias ordered the riders back into the sky and brought the ships back onto a course directly towards Wolfneck. The motion of the ship under their feet changed slightly.

Astrid
a few minutes later

*N*ow Basil, Ia and I are off to Wolfneck with our animals. Who knows what is happening there? At least I can leave our child-girl Jillian behind with the doll I made her. I have left her with Verily. She still shrinks from men and still cries for me if she is scared or hurt. It is a relief to be away from her; she still even tries to suckle and I have to go through drying-up again.

I am heartily sick of having to keep stuffing cloth inside my jerkin to mop up what leaks out constantly. At least, seeing that I am back to wearing my mail all of the time, it is impossible to see the almost permanent damp patches that are now a feature of my aketon.

Astrid
mid-afternoon

The entire order of dockings along the wharf will need to be re-organised to allow the Rongo *and the* Ofu *to come into the river and tie up. According to what the Nomads have told me, the water should be deep enough to allow the two ships in, but one will have to tie up outboard of the other as the dock is not long enough for the big ships otherwise.*

The local craft moored now will need to be taken further upstream, away from the wharf, and tied up against the bank or even, with the smaller ones, just pulled up out of the water. The wharf now looks far smaller than it did in the past when I was growing up here, or from when the River Dragon *was the largest craft to ever come and dock in the village. Even the much newer wharf at Didymoteichon is bigger than this.*

I wonder if such visits will become a regular occurrence once this is all over. Will Wolfneck, the first port in The Land to receive a visit from the Sea Nomads in an age, stay favoured? I suppose that it depends on whether the Nomads hunt whales. At least I am sure that they will be interested in the timber we have here. It could be so good for them for planks and masts for their ships as well as on the island villages.

They are keeping a good lookout from the river light. We could see the activity in the village begin to increase as soon as we hove into sight. As we approach, people are heading to the wharf from the tents set up outside the village in the grazing fields. Hang on… Tents? How many people are waiting for us here?

I know that people are coming here from all around the north, but will three ships be enough for all of them that I can see? Oh, that is right; Ia's dream indicated that more ships will be used from here on in as well. I guess I didn't have enough faith in what she saw. Which ones will we take? How many did she say?

The people were all headed towards the wharf, so that was where Astrid brought them. The three Humans dismounted from their saddles amid the waiting crowd and Maeve promptly hopped onto Fluff-Ball's back after having her tail nearly trodden on several times just in going from one saddle to another.

There is an area of clear space all around my cat. She is lashing her tail to and fro and radiating that frigid air of displeasure that all cats can project at will. That she is already much larger than most cats, even the local ones, helps with this projection.

Siglunda is already standing there waiting for us to land. She does not look happy. She looks annoyed. She has her hands on her hips. Stuff her. "It is your fault that we have been descended upon by all of these people," Siglunda said crossly. "We are running out of food and how are we going to fit them in if more arrive?"

"And hello to you, Captain, and I am very glad to see you as well," replied Astrid as she nodded to her brothers and ignored her father. *Siglunda does look harassed, and I suppose that she has a point. She needs some sort of appeasement.* "You can relax. It is probably nearly all over." She raised her voice a little more: "I greet you all and I think we can say we are hoping that what is coming should mark the last major battle."

There is some murmuring at this, but at least it sounds positive and I heard a couple of faint cheers. She turned around and faced away from the wharf and looked out at the crowd, raising her voice even louder. "We will need these boats moved out of the way and moored upstream against the bank," she said at the top of her voice to the waiting audience.

"If you think that our ship the *River Dragon* is big, just wait and see what we have brought with us this time. We have two big ships from the Sea Nomads. That will mean nothing to most of you, but they are each more than twice the size of our ship. Now move these, please." The local people started to get into their ships.

Before mooring ropes were untied and returned to their boats, sailors threw others to eager people on the shore so the craft could be dragged upstream, making way for anticipated vessels. None of the local men and women seemed to wait for authorisation from their own village captain, and the ships would be tied to trees further along.

Astrid grinned. *It feels odd, almost like before a thunderstorm. There is a feel of anticipation in the air, as if they are all taking part in some festival activity. It is an Up Helly Aa with the fire and destruction yet to come when we finally land on a hostile shore. People are laughing and joking with each other as they set to with a will.*

Once people were in action she turned to Siglunda again. "Now, Captain, our ships will be in before dark and our Princesses will want to see the representatives of those who are here and then they will want to get them organised for what is to come." *On that question I had better see who we have.* She turned and looked around her.

A circle has formed all around us and we stand in a clear space. I may not remember all of their names, but around the edge of the clear space I can recognise several faces from the campaign along the north coast, from the Dwarves who sailed with us to Skrice, and from the south. There are Bear People, and faces from Erave Town and Evilhalt and... What in hell are Kharl doing here?

She nodded to them all in turn and tried to speak even louder. "This time the Adversaries know that we are coming. The battle started this afternoon. They tried throwing a major piece of magic on us and we defeated it. I am not sure how they cast it, or even how we defeated it, but our Princess Theodora thinks that they will not be able to do a casting like that again for some time." *That has set up some approving murmurs as the word is passed back through the crowd.*

"What is more," she continued, "the way it was defeated may have hurt them and may have totally wrecked any ships they have. It is very possible that they are stranded on their island now and may have even lost people from it." *I need to wait again to let what I say spread out. The crowd is growing and I do not have the speaker with me.*

"They sent one of the great winter storms against us and we turned it and sent it back to them. It was far stronger than any storm I have seen. Some of you will know how strong a mage our Darkreach Princess is. She says that she would have no hope to cast the spell they cast and it took all of the mages on our ship combined to defeat it, but defeat it they did."

She looked around. *People are still just standing there as if waiting for instructions. I hope Rani won't be angry with me, but too bad. They should start to organise.* "We will take people on board our ship and on the ships of the Sea Nomads. From here we will also take the *Vindur-skefi* with us as a fourth ship. That has been seen by our seers." *More word being passed back.*

"The others will be too slow, but we will use the non-detection discs from them, and those from the wharf, to help us with the big ships we have with us. You can have them back later, after this is all over." She shook her head. *What else do I need to say? Stefan is better at this than I am. Perhaps he should have come.*

"I would like to take more vessels and it will be crowded, but any of the knorr will be far too slow for the voyage that is to come. They certainly know that we are coming to attack them, but we hope they may not know when we will leave here and exactly which way we will travel to get to them. We will want to keep some small advantage that way."

She thought for a moment. *Most of the rest should be between the leaders, but what else should I say? Oh yes... They probably would like to have some good news to sustain them.* "I think that I can safely tell you that the last of the so-called Masters is dead and the stolen Darkreach fire ship that we were once all so afraid of has been sunk with him on it." *The Dwarves look happy at that.*

"What is more, we have sunk another of their ships as well. That means all of their armsmen and mages on both ships are lost to them, and there were a lot of them. What is possibly even more important, we have already slain one of the Adversaries and defeated one more of their plots." She was about to stop when she was struck by a sudden and mischievous idea.

"… and if you are wondering who this little girl is…"—she waved at Ia—"You will already know that the men in our village are allowed by the Church to have more than one wife. This is my sister-wife, Ia. So treat her with respect… And what is more, we have yet another sister-wife still at home looking after the children. Stay clear of our animals as well. They are not the tame beasts you might hope for." She waved at Fluff-Ball and Maeve and then grinned to herself. *After all of these years of having shit put on me it is a great delight watching the expression on my father's face out of the corner of my eye.*

She decided to add a bit more: "And Basil has managed to make us all pregnant at once." Briefly she enjoyed the now completely outraged look on her father's face before she deliberately turned and kissed one after the other of the two people standing beside her. *At least our husband is looking a little proud at the way I finished.*

The rest of the time waiting for the ships was spent in organising the dock for the arrivals and answering questions on everything from whether the village of Mousehole still needed men to move there and had women looking to be brides—*the answer is obviously yes to that*—to how to kill an Insak-div—*either let me do it or else work in a large group and stay clear of their weapons.*

She managed to get a moment for herself to tell her brothers about Thorstein, his marriage, and that they now had six nephews and nieces. "Have any of you managed to find a girl yet?" *They all look embarrassed.*

"We need someone to ask for us," said Karl, the oldest of them. "We don't have a mother and we don't have you and"—he cast a sideways glance at their father—"someone is getting further and further wedded to the bottle and he doesn't seem to try very hard to do anything for us."

Astrid grunted, "I will see what I can do. You are coming with us, I presume?" All four were nodding at her grim expression. *My shaming of them on the last visit is still in effect then. I will give them a little reward.* "I am now the matchmaker for our village and, it seems, in other areas as well. I am sure that, once this is all over, if we manage to survive, we will be able to find you someone suitable."

She grinned at them. "After all, I found Hrothnog a bride and managed to find husbands for a couple of the daughters of a Caliphate sheik. You may be far more *nekulturny* and not have as much to offer, but you are strong and have some prospects. How hard can you lot be?" A thought struck her. "Do any of you want to spend your entire life out at sea?"

Chapter XVIII

Astrid
late on 18th December, the Feast Day of Saint Sebastian

It looks as if, with the way they are handling their ships as they come up the river, the captains of the Ofu *and the* Rongo *make Olympias look careless. Being used to the open seas and the large open docks of the Sea Nomad towns, they are nervous. They are taking a very long time with their approach, checking the depth constantly even when they are several bowshots out.*

Checking the throng around her, Astrid went looking for Basil and found him talking to a Kharl on the fringe of the crowd. She drew him aside. "The village is completely full of people…and a lot of them I have never seen before," she said, looking at the Kharl, a Kichic-kharl in Darkreach uniform with the marks of a Starşiyrang on it, and then began looking further afield. "It may be a good idea that you and Ayesha should guard the Princesses at all times."

He nodded and agreed. "I was already thinking the same for when she comes on the shore." Astrid looked back at the approach. *The short wooden dock is crowded as people jostle to see ships that are more than twice as tall as any that they have seen before and with not just two courses of sails but provision for up to five on masts that are taller than many of the trees in the forests around them.*

The two groups of people, on land and sea, are also looking at each other with curiosity. The colour of the crew and passengers of the large ships is strange to those on the shore while the diversity of those on the shore, including the Kharl-like features on the locals, indeed including a group that are actual Kharl, will be just as strange to those on the ships who are returning looks of wonder one for one.

Rani

I may have recovered from my casting by the time we have docked, but no caster will have the ability to throw an enchantment for at least another day. That, however, does not affect my other abilities. Leaving her wife asleep in the cabin tended by Nikephorus, Rani gathered the leaders of the groups represented in Wolfneck into the tavern, the Brodir Lind.

She took with her both the captains and the Puleleiites of the *Rongo* and the *Ofu* and several of the Bear folk as well as Christopher, Hulagu, Dobun, Stefan, Astrid and Ia as her advisors in different areas. *It is crowded and there are people from all over. Everyone wants to be here, it seems. I suppose that, in deference to where we are, I should use Darkspeech.*

I am sure that there will be enough people around who speak both that and another language to be able to translate anything I say. I will just need to pause frequently to allow for the translation. Astrid has told me what she said to the waiting people and, for once, she said the right things, and that relieves me of the most important parts that need to be said up front.

Rani waited for them all to settle down and find places to sit before she started speaking. After greeting them, she started directly on the nub of what tonight would be about. "Even before we—that is, the Mice—first started on our journey at the behest of fate, it has been our custom to not make a definite move until we have consulted the various sources that might give us direction.

"Indeed, for two of us such prophecy is what caused us to move at all in the first place. Tonight, and publicly before you all, we will be looking at the destiny that lies ahead. Others will not be able to say what they discover until tomorrow. You may tell your people this just as you may tell them the result of what we find out."

Rani looked around her at the eager faces that surrounded her. *None have moved. They seem to be still waiting for me to tell them something. They have all travelled a long way to be here now. I suppose that I really should tell them a bit more than I have so far, but there really isn't much to say yet. Perhaps if I explained our methods, at least they could take that back to their people.*

"We will use the methods that have worked for us so far. I will start by consulting the cards in the manner that we have used up until now. Bishop Christopher uses another method of prognostication and will practice his stichomancy. Ia, who has just joined us, will use her crystal ball and tell us what she sees inside that." *Ia is looking very nervous at that idea.*

"Tomorrow Dobun, Chief Shaman of the Clan of the Horse, will let us know what he is able to see in the realm that he will visit tonight." *Dobun looks even less pleased about that than Ia does, but I am not worried about that. Hulagu will make sure that he does the right thing.*

She looked around her. "That accounts for the means available to the Mice. I have to say I am not so foolish as to pretend that we have a monopoly on good prophecy. If any of you or any one of your people feels that they can add to what we find out, please let us know and we will add their understandings to what we are able to obtain." *I need to look at likely people and gauge their reaction.*

"For this leg of our quest," she continued as she looked around, "as we have gotten closer to the source and origin of the evil that seeks to affect and control us all, it took all four of us to reach a consensus that has given us a firm direction to go in and instructions on how to act. I regard it as very likely that this time it could be the same."

She paused and looked around at the crowd again. *We have one of the Bear Folk, a Dwarf, one from our last expedition who I am sure is one of their druids, and a Kharl hung with leather bags and pouches, all looking expectant. I am sure they are all nodding back at me as if they will be speaking later.*

She nodded back to each of them as she saw their interest. "I see others whose methods will require them to take the night to achieve a result, and so they will be speaking to us tomorrow as well. That is good."

She was about to close her remarks for now when she realised something. *Kharl... Yes.* "There are some here that I do not know," she said as she turned to a pale-green Kichic-kharl. *He stands beside one who, although still fully armed, will probably be their druid, from the extra things that he has hanging off him. From what I remember from Darkreach, that is a uniform that he wears and those marks on his arms are his rank... But what it is, I have no idea.*

The Kharl took her hint quickly. "I am Starşiyrang Tarakratz," was the reply, and indicating the druid, added: "and this is Primus Mardrikrat. We are from Cold Keep. We have had your ship and a ship from here visit our village. Our Governor heard about all of the trade opening up further south so she decided to find out if there was a land path that we could perhaps follow to reach you, as we have no ships of our own for trade and we are not used to these northern seas anyway." *That makes sense.*

"She sent us over here to find paths into the Lost Lands and how we would be received if we came over with some things to sell. We had to wave and call to people to be brought across the river, but they greeted us well once we arrived. When we returned home we told her about what you are going to do now and she sent us back to take part in it instead of sending us to trade.

"We do not have orders from Ardlark, so we hope that the Antikataskopeía there is not upset. Local Antikataskopeía women say this is good but we are not sure, she is only a Starşiyrang like me, not a high officer." He grinned, exposing his mouthful of straggly teeth. *We can deal with their concerns straight away if they are in doubt.*

Rani looked directly at Basil. He quickly took her meaning and spoke up. "When I am in Darkreach I am called Tribune Akritas of the Antikataskopeía and I report direct to the Emperor, and this is my wife Astrid, who knows the Emperor far better than I do, and over there is my sister Epilarch Akritina." *See, the Kharl looks happier already.*

"I will tell you now that you will not get in trouble and I ask you to thank your Governor for us when you return. We will make sure to mention you, your initiative, and what you do now to the Emperor when next we see him." The Kharl's eyes widened at these words. *He seems very pleased, particularly with the last part of what Basil has said. That must mean something good for him.*

Rani looked around again. "As Astrid told you earlier, we needed to cast a major enchantment today to defeat one of our enemy's, and my wife is still unconscious from it and I am weak and badly need sleep so that my head is clear. So unless anyone has anything that is important now…" She looked around the gathering. *Everyone is staying silent. It seems as if no one wants to speak at this stage.*

"Then, until tonight, I will leave you to talk among each other or to those of our people who will be on shore. Please let our people—Astrid and Stefan are known to most of you—know how many people you bring to the fight, how they are armed and what magics you can deploy, particularly that last part."

She waved at the Mice up front with her. *Several from the North are looking towards where Stefan stands already.* She looked around again. *Still no one is speaking up. Good, I can get some rest.* Rani rose and nodded to them all and then hurriedly went off to the *River Dragon* to snatch some much-needed sleep for a few hours herself.

Rani

I smell *Kaf*—she sniffed—*and keftethes, tiropatakia, and croissants.* She opened her eyes and sat up. *My invaluable and almost omnipresent servant, Nikephorus, is standing here with a tray for two with those and other goodies on it.*

My wife is lying face down and stirring sleepily, but she does not respond to a shake or even a gentle pinch on her naked backside, only stirring sleepily and muttering something that might have been something like "go away"—or, almost equally possible, a lewd suggestion involving getting back into bed.

Either way she is not awake and fully conscious, but at least she is not still in shock. I will leave her there until she wakes herself up and makes her own decision to rejoin the world. She will be less grumpy that way when she finally gets up. Rani was soon helping herself to her third pastry. *Oh, dear God. How far have I come in my own personal journey? My wife has changed me so much.*

I just threw aside the rug that was covering us when I sat up and then quickly replaced it over my Theodear to keep her warm once I decided to leave her. Now I sit here fully naked and eating in front of a man without a second thought. What to wear…? Ahh, Nikephorus, the perfect servant, already has things ready for me to wear out on a stand. How does he know exactly what I should wear to go to a meeting that will be planning how to run a battle?

Is there a manual of such matters of etiquette? He has laid out clean long and short underwear as well as, smelling faintly of my significant spice essence of myrrh, my padding. Beside it is laid out my harness with sheathed sword and main gauche and pouches for wands, but no helmet. There are warm, thick socks and stout and comfortable boots. The leather of everything smells of oils and dully gleams.

Beside that are a small wax tablet, a book and stick, my casting book, my cards wrapped in silk, and other important things. Then beside those are a fairly severe set of jewellery of plain mithril and ruby to show that I am a mage and what sort I am. She looked at what was there. *Yes, this collection will really set the right tone. If there is a manual on such things, then Nikephorus has studied it very well.*

"Thank you," she said as she rose to dress. "Are they already gathering?"

He smiled. "Astrid has placed herself in charge, ma'am. They are very definitely gathering now. You should be ready to make an entrance. I will be staying with the Princess, your wife, and Gundardasc has things ready to warm up as soon as she shows any sign of waking." As he spoke, he was handing her items of clothing and helping her on with them.

She finished and went to head out the door. *He has just made a tut-tutting noise.* She stopped and he started fussing with her hair and attacking it with a brush. "You are to lead them into a battle… You must project confidence," he said fussily. "It would never do for you to look as if you are dishevelled and have just risen from a bed…especially when you have." *There simply has to be a manual and he has memorised it.*

After a little more attention—a check that everything was in the right pouch, a critical survey of her appearance and an adjustment of her left earring—only then, after making sure that she had wands in the pockets of her padding, and knew which ones were in which pockets, he allowed her to leave her own cabin. *Basil and Ayesha are both outside the door. Who comes with me and who stays with Theodear?*

Astrid

I have the room set up to my satisfaction. Those who will be attempting to make a tolkovaniye, a reading, either now or tonight, are at the front facing the others. I have made very sure that Ia has not eaten as many of the hashish biscuits this time around. We brought a supply of them all the way from home wrapped up in wax paper in a box. They are sure to be stale by now, but the effect will hopefully be the same.

Already she is quiet and more than a trifle dreamy. She is sitting in a soft chair with Maeve on her lap. My chair beside her is full of Fluff-Ball at present. One glance from the growing cat is very effective at keeping away any others who might be tempted to try and sit in it. A table stands ready for the use of all three who will speak tonight.

She looked around to make sure it was right. *It is covered in a black cloth and has a chair tucked under it for whoever needs it. Bianca has brought her things and a side table stands ready with all that will be required to change the table into an altar for when it is needed in that role. She even has a proper altar cloth, folded up and brought from the church, ready there for us.*

The room is full. It is actually more than full and there is scarce room to move. Where there are seats, people have to stand to allow others to pass. We have chairs down the front, and what would otherwise be a low stage, but for most there is only space to stand. Now we are all waiting on Rani and talking as attendants try to serve them, even though they have to wriggle through the subdued press, and jugs are being passed around through the crowd.

Christopher sits with Bianca and with the others who have agreed to do some form of reading tonight or who will report in the morning before we leave. Although they all seem to be deep in conversation with each other and with their neighbours, people are getting more than a little nervous with the wait and the place is starting to smell like the crowded tavern that it is.

We have all been in here for some time now, with no indication as to when we will start. I have organised Solveig to play on her harp to keep them entertained to some degree. It has been soothing so far, but I fear it is starting to lose its effect. Should I send out to the ship to see what is happening?

Was that the door? Rani swept into the room with Basil close behind. *He must have lost the toss, because Ayesha is not here. She will still be on board the* River Dragon *standing over Theodora with Marianus prowling the deck and keeping watch there on the wharf and over the side.* "Clear a path," she called, and people struggled to allow the mage through.

Astrid moved to her chair and easily picked up her large lump of a cat, putting her ankle on her other knee to create enough lap for it to sit on. *It seems such a short time ago that she used to be an adorable little kitten, but now I am sure that Ia is lighter.* She started to scratch the cat as she liked, behind the ear and under the chin, and Fluff-Ball began to purr.

Rani stood behind the black-draped table and looked over the assembly as Basil came to stand behind his wives and in front of where Astrid's weapon was leaning. *It is not just a coincidence that I left him a space there where he is able to look out over the crowd and watch almost everyone in it.*

Rani

It is crowded, but we have space here up the front. Rani took her place, standing beside the chair behind the table, and started to draw her cards out of a pouch. She surveyed the room. *They are all looking at me in anticipation. Again I will be using Darkspeech, but Harnermês has been joined by a few of the apprentices to translate what I say into High Speech, which most of the Nomads present have at least some of. In addition, there are those who speak Dwarven, Hindi or Greek. It looks like it is all as ready as it can be. I should start by saying a few words.*

"Good evening, everyone," Rani said. "My wife is still sleeping off the effects of the spell that was cast through her today and so will not be joining us. It was a major spell, a spell as large as any that has been cast in the West for many generations, and probably larger. It could easily have killed any one of us if it had gone wrong in even the slightest part."

She looked around again. *There are a lot of people that I either don't know or at best know only in passing. Perhaps more of an explanation of tonight is in order.* "For those who have not been with us before when we have done this, I will be doing only a short reading of the cards. We have had success with that form before as it seems harder for our opponents to cloud what can be seen in such a simple reading." *Is that enough? Perhaps not.*

"I also trust that the answers we find will not be so obscure that we cannot understand them. If this is the case, though, I hope we can find meaning by gaining clarification from our other seers. After I am finished, Ia will look into her ball." She looked at Ia. *Ia seems to not be paying much attention to what I am saying, or to anything else. Her face seems very blank and her irises have again almost disappeared behind her dilated pupils.*

"…and then the Bishop will look into the older Testament to see what lies there." *At least our Bishop is nodding brightly, even if he does have a very serious expression on his face. He is still so young to be filling such an important role, but he has done everything that is needed so far. I hope that those watching do not take his youth for a failing.*

Looking around for a last time to see if anyone wanted to add anything, and seeing no response, she leant forward and picked up the cards. Rani beckoned Bianca to come and sit in the chair in front of her before she passed the cards to her.

I need to sound confident about this. Our leadership of them is based solely on their belief in our decisions and abilities. Hopefully Ia can do what she is supposed to do. She proceeded, again addressing the crowd. "I would like you all to banish any other thoughts and to concentrate on the way ahead, or at least on what lies next ahead for us as a group. Although it is hard, please try to banish any personal thoughts or desires as the Presbytera shuffles. I need you all to think only about our task ahead."

Bianca rose and again there was practised shuffling, cutting, reversing and melding of the pack as the cards flew through her fingers. *Eventually she seems to be happy with her work and she has tapped the cards on the table to square them and then placed them carefully onto the black woollen cover of the table before returning to her seat. Now it is my turn.*

Only now did Rani sit down in the chair. Carefully, she moved her sword so that it did not tangle in an undignified way with the legs of the chair or with hers. She smoothed her padding and closed her eyes, one hand flat on the cloth on each side of the pack, and then paused. *Now I need to gather my thoughts and clear my own personal feelings out of the way so they will not interfere with what I say. I reach for the clarity of the void within.*

Breathing deep, she inhaled the rich smell of the myrrh rising from her padding. Only then, and with her eyes still closed, did she reach without hesitation and picked up the cards and dealt four of them out on the cloth, laying the pack aside after she had done so.

Astrid

What with all of the build-up and preparation, I have been holding my breath. As she quietly drew some air in, she listened. *It sounds like everyone else here is doing the same as I am. The only noise in the room is a deep rumbling purr coming from my lap, and that just adds to the tension in the room.*

Rani only now opens her eyes and, moving her gaze down to the table, begins to turn the cards over. The first card shows a single hand holding an elaborate jewel-hilted broadsword up into the sky in front of the blazing ball of the sun. I am close and can see that there are two different sets of words at top and bottom. "The Ace of Swords," declared Rani.

She turned over the next. *It is upside down. On it is painted a man, seated on a throne and wearing slashed clothes in the Freehold fashion and armoured in gold-worked half-plate. I know more about their armour now. He wears a bevor around his neck and at his right side is a sallet, ready to go on his head. There is a golden Crown fixed onto his sallet. I saw one of those in a hall in the Palace in Darkreach; it may even be the helmet and Crown that this card is modelled on.*

His right hand bears an upright sword, and his left hand rests on the arm of his throne. The throne is made in the shape of a tall castle, alongside which a stream splits in two to go around it like a moat. The top left corner of the card has a blazing image of the sun in it and the right top corner has a golden-bodied and bearded depiction of one of the Hindi gods. "The King of Swords…reversed," Rani intoned.

She paused before turning the next card. *It shows the Latin number ten and a stack of ten logs joined at the top. The logs are on fire and a man lies across them, being burnt to death, as if he were subject to the extremes of the auto-da-fé that the Freehold Inquisition do to people, but his hands and legs are free and not bound. A banner lies across the top on which there is written a phrase.* "The Ten of Staves," she said.

She then turned the last card. *It has the number six in the Latin form and shows six poles stuck in the ground, staking out the corners of a hexagon that is marked on the ground. Inside this is a naked woman. I would guess she is a Hindu Goddess from the way she wrestles a much larger, naked horned demon of ghastly visage.*

She has been successful and holds him over her head while other demons wait outside the hexagon, perhaps ready to fight her in turn. Again, two words are each written at the top and the bottom. "The Six of Staves," she declared. *Almost as one we are all taking a breath. It is a very quiet room as we wait for the interpretation of what Rani sees there.*

Rani spoke again as she pointed. "Our first card, that stands in the position of the enquirer…of us…is the Ace of Swords. These words written at the top of the card, the ones that apply, read 'triumph' and 'power'. The card represents the element of Fire. It declares the triumph of passion and the dominance of the will and zealous, sometimes even fanatical conviction. Most directly it is the sword of righteousness." *And for us that means…?*

"In this case I believe that it tells us that we are the sword of righteousness that acts to strike down evil and I think that it is fair to admit that the Mice, at least, tend to a certain fanaticism or at least single-mindedness in our quest." She looked up at the audience and broke her concentration briefly by smiling slightly and saying to them in a lighter voice: "It really would not be a geas quest that we were on otherwise."

Her voice then turned back to being serious and she went straight on: "The second card stands for our history and where we have come from to reach this point. The card we see here is the King of Swords and he is reversed. Normally this card represents a man of volatile temperament who is a born fighter and ruler. He is a person who is used to command and who is accustomed to dramatic and decisive action. He is accompanied by the war God Indra." *But this is reversed.*

"Reversed, as it is"—*for once she knows what I am thinking*—"the card speaks to us of the abuse of power, of tyranny and of cruelty. We know now there is a past of this that we think stretches back at least to the end of the last Age, if not before that. We are seeing some things now that tell us that it goes back even further, perhaps to the start of life on Vhast. We know little of that yet, but the clues lie all around us." Astrid looked at the Bear Folk. *I would say that the way they looked at each other then is another clue on that front.*

"As the history of what has happened to us personally, it tells of an empty striving for control: first the failed attempt of mastery over the servants, those who first ruled the valley where the Mice now hold sway; then, as was foreseen in the cards and by prophecy, came the fall of the Masters themselves in Dwarvenholme, and now, finally, we are starting to bring the Adversaries down." *One down and five to go.*

"First we saw the destruction of the Brotherhood and the rebirth of those lands into the land of Amity. Then we saw the destruction of their outposts in the Caliphate and perhaps in other lands and on other waters, although there is still more to happen there. Lastly now, on this trip, we can start to talk about the eventual final downfall of the Adversaries themselves in their own fortress. Once that is done, the rest should flow."

She paused for a while. "Our next card is the Ten of Staves, and it tells us our way forward and what is about to happen," she said. "It shows the immolation of a person on the fire of torment. The only words written on the card lie across the top and they read 'The Last Trial before Glory'. This card speaks of a final trial before an enduring reward. The greater the trial that must be faced, then the greater the reward there is. This card does not talk of a temporary and temporal prize of money and wealth, but the far more enduring reward of honour, fame and legend." *If you have the right skalds around to tell the story, that is.*

"If it were reversed, the card would talk of the shameful avoidance of pain and of a consequent absence of pleasure. It would tell of both obscurity and domesticity for the enquirer. So in one direction this card indicates fame and glory and in the other a disappearance from the page of history. Upright, as it is, it tells us that our direction is to go ahead despite, or perhaps because of, anything that appears against us. It says that we must push hard and strive with our enemy even if it seems impossible... Perhaps it is better to say: especially if it appears impossible.

"The last card we see is the card that tells of the final result that lies ahead. This time it is the Six of Staves, marking the boundary of the field where the goddess Dhurga defeats demons. The words at the top of the card read 'triumph' and 'conquest' and those for the reverse read 'fear' and 'delay'. Upright, as it is, it means a triumph over great difficulty and a glorious victory over almost impossible odds. However, it has to be said that often this card means that persistence beyond what may be thought normal is required to push through a barrier."

Again she paused to look up and around the room, catching the eye of the leaders present as she did. "In all of our journeys and in all the time we have consulted the cards over our course of action during the last few years, we have seen none of these cards before," she said in a flat and matter-of-fact tone.

"Before, our cards have always indicated to us that there was more to come, that we were not yet to be finished with our task. There is nothing equivocal or 'perhaps' about what we see laid out before us now. These cards all speak clearly of a final resolution and of our victory. They tell us that the way ahead will be hard...very hard...but we will prevail, even though many of us may perish from this world in the striving." *I suppose that they need to hear that, so they don't lose heart halfway through a battle, but it does sound a bit bleak.*

"Those who die—and many will—will only perish in this world. They will live on in legend and will gain a reward that is not to be found on this plane. I believe that we now have guidance in a very final way. Unlike some other readings we have had over the last few years, some of which have been surprising precise in their direction, this says nothing at all about the detail of what we must do. But it says everything about the shape of what will come in its finality." She stopped and her shoulders slumped, and she began to pack away her cards.

She would still have been tired from earlier. It is evident that this reading has taken even more from her. Now we are seeing discussion and a stirring among them as people realise they clutch drinks that are going flat. There is a near simultaneous draining of mugs

Astrid turned and looked at her sister-wife. *The chair of prophecy is now vacant, but she isn't moving and she shows no sign of knowing that now it is her turn.* Astrid sighed a little before standing and putting her cat down on her chair. Basil took Maeve and Astrid led Ia over to the chair and sat her down before standing behind her with her hands on her sister-wife's shoulders.

I cannot show this, but I am worried. Ia seems to be even more affected by the drugs than she has ever been before. However, now that she is here and seated in place she is finally moving of her own accord. Slowly, so slowly, she opened the satchel that hung at her side and brought a stand out and placed it on the table.

She pulled a cloth-wrapped object out of the depths of the bag and, careful not to snag the cover, placed it on the stand. Astrid felt the whole audience lean forward, breathless in anticipation, to watch Ia as she raised the cover, revealing a large sphere of crystal. There was a collective gasp, a release as it were, and she gave the ball a wipe with the cloth, then folded the material and placed it to one side. Her hands were placed, palm down, either side of the ball. *Around me I can feel the tension building as people look at the slow preparations, as if they are themselves of magical portent.*

The whole time since she first stirred, Ia had acted as if she were moving in her sleep. *Her eyes stare almost straight down before rising briefly to look directly out, as if there were a void in front of her instead of a crowded room of people, before she closes them. It almost seemed as if she saw none of them as if she were in a world all of her own.*

As her eyes fell into a gaze that seemed to focus through the ball, her hands now reached out and cupped the crystal ahead of her without touching it, hovering and slowly moving a finger's width distance away from the surface, almost as if she were polishing it. *The whole of the time that she is doing this she does not look up or say a word. Her eyes are closed again and her hands keep moving slowly around the ball.*

She is not even acknowledging that there is anyone else here. Now the tension is really building, higher and higher. Fluff-Ball's purring sounds louder and louder in the silence. It took a long while, but finally Ia's eyes opened, her gaze focussed on something that was far, far away from her.

She now stared straight into the globe and transferred that distant gaze to what lay within it. *The room just drew a collective breath. I can see, and I presume others can as well, that the huge, clear crystal globe, which, only a short time before, had lain flickering on its stand as it reflected the candles and light globes of the tavern, is now grey and full of swirling clouds lit through with flickers and sheets of white as if from lightning.*

Ia slowly spoke then, as if she were a voice from beyond a grave or from on another plane. *I can feel the hair on my neck rising, and Fluff-Ball has gone silent.* If anyone had looked at the animals, they would have seen them both sitting up attentively with pricked ears, looking at the ball. Ia strung some words together clumsily and there were long pauses in what she said.

"I see us gathered here and I see this river," she said. "I see the three ships that have arrived become four and then in turn become five... I see three islands one after another and I see people lost and hidden... I see welcome and then caution and danger and finally I see bloody battle... I see that the last is a striving and a contest that will shake the world and a contest that will make the earth tremble and a strife that will shake the very heavens." There was a long pause. *She shudders.*

"The earth is now bathed in blood and at last I see the fall of the mighty, those who would be gods. They are cast down from on high, and I see their death and the obliteration of what they stand for and of their long-cherished and bloodstained hope and plan, but what I see is not sure...it is only one path. It is not graven in stone and the contest will be close... We still need to make the right decisions to make it true." *As always.*

"What is hidden must enter the light... I see people rejoicing as their hope of freedom is sustained and yet others both happy and sad at their victory... I know some of those others... I see them in my mind's eye and in front of me and some wear masks of blood... I see that the King who is to be has been conceived although they will not rule for many years." *Now we are getting to be obscure.*

"There are one after another of lesser battles, some large and some small, and they are taking place all over Vhast, as the shadow that has been cast for long ages is slowly stripped away piece by piece and finally light shines forth over all of the world. Win or lose, live or die, I see fame and glory for us here that lasts for an age on this world."

There was a longer pause. *Butterfly's voice now sounds in awe at her own next words*: "...and even on others...many others... I see...my daughter... She is beautiful...so beautiful, but I fear that being unborn within me as I see this, she now sees what I see. It is a lot for a child to be born into knowing and seeing."

Ia said that last very gently and a trifle sadly. She smiled softly down into the ball and then she slowly collapsed, as if she were boneless, into a heap on the table, her black hair partly covering the ball, which had now gone as dark as night itself, the colour of her hair. Astrid leapt towards her to make sure she was not hurt.

The few who could see the ball clearly could tell that it was lit by a single bright mote of light in the centre of the black and that the smoke was gone. Gradually, that light receded into a distance none could perceive and only then the globe cleared of the blackness and resumed its normal clarity. *She is unharmed, but she is also unconscious.*

Murmurs began to rise through the room. Astrid quickly looked around as she held Ia. *The watchers are clearly impressed by what they have heard and seen. It is obviously a fell reading for many but made so much more impressive by its grim words.*

Basil was quickly there and began packing up the ball, returning it to its case. Meanwhile, Astrid dumped Fluff-Ball from the seat and then gently picked up Ia as if she were a small child and carried her back to her chair, sitting with her sister-wife curled up on her lap and seemingly asleep. The two animals sat at their feet and Basil rejoined them on Ia's chair.

Christopher quickly came over, felt Ia's pulse, then laid his hand on her stomach and closed his eyes for a while. When he opened them, he looked at the concerned faces of Basil and Astrid. "She will be fine, and the baby will be as well," he said softly, the words meant for their ears only. "Both have a strong reading...but it is heavy and lethargic from the drug. I am sure they will both be in good health again after they have slept." The two nodded and smiled gratefully up at him.

Rani

I have a room full of people who need to be calmed a little after the words they have just heard. Even if the words are hopeful and spoke of victory, they are obviously dire for many of the listeners. Who here will die? People can be seen looking around them. At least only Ia could see the blood on their faces. Rani stood up again and moved to behind the table.

"I think that we need no explanation of what Ia has seen," she said, "and speculation is useless unless you are a seer. Some of what Ia said is clear... We knew that we would take a ship from here with us when we sailed—perhaps the fifth vessel is from Skrice. As for the rest... All that you can do is to do your best... Any of us may of course die, but everyone who goes into battle knows that this may be their fate and my cards spoke of the struggle being hard." *They meant the same, even if they did not sound as dire as her words.*

"At least we know now that the deeds that lie ahead of us and the legends about us will live on after our earthly bodies are left behind…and what could be better than that?" She looked up and could see many of those in front of her nodding at that thought. "Now we only await Bishop Christopher to seek an answer from the *Holy Word* and complete what we are looking for tonight."

Bianca

My husband has risen from Ia's side and is coming came over towards the table. I have nearly finished converting it into a makeshift altar. It is already laid with the altar cloth. I have set out some icons. A chalice, a cross, and candles on their sticks stand ready. I just have to light the candles, and I have Basil's little tool for that.

"I will be performing the Christian service of Hesperinos before I seek guidance," Christopher said to them all. "If any of you are offended by this, please feel free to leave now, but I will not ask you to enter any of the prayers or take any more part than you are willing to. Some of you may, in fact, be interested in what we do…from a professional point of view, of course."

He grinned and looked around at various druids and others who were already leaning forward with their gaze fixed on what Bianca was up to. *No one is moving away.* She nudged her husband and Christopher signalled that he was ready to begin his service. The many Christians present took part in it, although those who wanted to come up to receive communion at this particular service—and there were many of them, given its significance—had to wriggle their way past druids and other priests and priestesses to do so.

That went for a lot longer than it should, what with the crowding and all. Christopher had preached a service around the text of John 15, Verse 13: "Greater love hath no man than this, that a man lay down his life for his friends". *It seems to have been well received, even by the pagans. Many of the listeners are nodding in agreement as he made his points.*

My husband is a good preacher who has a habit of knowing what is in the hearts of his audience and speaking well to the issues that people face and that they fear inside themselves. He was going to use another text tonight, but then he is always willing to extemporise if he needs to and this one seemed to put heart back into the audience.

When he had said *Amen*, he then held up his hands. "If your faith allows you to pray for intervention in the affairs of men from the On High," he said "then I ask that you pray that we might receive guidance through what I am about to do." Bianca handed him her cherished volume and Christopher launched into his own prayer for guidance.

When it was done and all had said *Amen*, or their equivalent, Christopher closed his eyes and picked up the book, putting its spine on the altar table and allowing it to fall open. Feeling ahead of him, he put his finger down and moved it around until he felt paper under it. He opened his eyes and looked down at what was in front of him.

"We have found the Book of Deuteronomy in Chapter thirty-two, verse forty-three," he said. *I have no idea what that is, but he sounds very happy.* "Here it says: 'Rejoice, O ye nations, with his people; for he will avenge the blood of his servants, and will render vengeance to his adversaries, and will be merciful unto his land, and to his people.' Amen."

After a moment's silence, Christopher looked up ahead of him and he resumed speaking. *His voice is full of a mixture of awe and pleasure.* "This verse lacks any precision as to where we are going, or how we are going to go about our task, but I think it is very clear already as to what we will do when we get there." *I suppose it is indeed most clear on that.*

"It is up to us how we go about it, but we will render 'vengeance to his adversaries'. What we have just seen is very like the reading by the Princess in that it gives no detail of the action to be taken—that is up to what we decide— but it talks only of the result." He sounds very satisfied with those words and rolled them around as he repeated "vengeance to his adversaries".

"Is it coincidence that those we fight are called Adversaries and that they are named in this verse? I think not. I am more than satisfied—in fact I am delighted—that once again with this reading we have a very clear direction, that we are going to go forth to do God's work in this world." He made the sign of the cross and gave a blessing. With that he turned and sat down again, giving Bianca back her Bible.

Rani then stood up and looked out over the crowded room. "That is all for us tonight," she said briskly. "We will see you after breakfast in the morning to hear what has been added to our readings by those who will enter a different plane to see what can be seen. In the meantime, I think it would be good to go back and tell your people what has been revealed tonight."

She smiled wryly. "Try and focus on the more positive aspects of what you have heard. It will help to give our people heart." There is a murmur of quiet amusement at the last remark. The meeting broke up into general conversation. *I help Christopher and then take Astrid's weapon, while Astrid kisses Basil and leaves him to guard the Princess. Then, with Astrid carrying Ia, we head back to the ship, trying not to trip on the animals underfoot.*

Astrid

I have only just returned myself and Basil comes hard on our heels. Rani has decided to come back to the River Dragon *almost straight away herself. Basil can get all of our sleeping gear together and we will stay on deck tonight.* Together the two made a bed out of sleeping furs and cushions for Ia on the deck. She was promptly joined by two animals, while the other two decided who would sit up and keep an eye on her first.

Ia
19ᵗʰ December

I have been sleeping on the deck and I can feel one of the animals curled up in front of me and Basil cradling me from behind. She opened her eyes. *And Maeve is sleeping on top of the hill-cat. Astrid and Jillian are sitting beside us looking at me. Between their hands stretches a cat's cradle and the two are in the middle of a complex shape.*

"I made another mistake with how much of the drug I took last night, didn't I?" she asked contritely. *And my mind is still a bit of a fog as a result. I need Kaf.* She looked around. *The dawn is still breaking around us. It is still very early.*

Astrid nodded with a smile, without interrupting what she was doing with the threads. "It depends what you mean by a mistake. What happened this time?" she asked.

"I have always made them fresh before and did not know if they would lose strength, and I knew that you would make me use less and not take another biscuit, so I used a lot more hashish in each biscuit," she said. "I guess they didn't lose any virtue in that time… What did I see?"

"That is what we thought," said Astrid, and filled her in on what had been seen by her and by the others. "It is time to get up now and have breakfast. We want to be in time to hear what our various shamen and druids saw in their dreams last night." Gradually the pile of sleeping bodies began to sort itself out into separate, hungry parts and to attend to their various personal needs.

Astrid
an hour later

Once again people are beginning to gather in the Brodir Lind. I am early enough to make sure that our family have seats near the front. It seems that Shilpa has already found out who will be talking and has seats reserved for them. She must have been up early.

Now we are all assembled, and the Princesses are coming through the door. Theodora still looks drawn from casting beyond what she should have, as she stands there with hollow eyes and, despite Nikephorus' best efforts, with still-visible shadows under them. She is walking with the aid of her husband, and although she smiles at those around her as she comes in, it is a wan smile without any colour in it.

The spell took so much out of her that she looks gaunt. I think her eyes are even a duller colour than usual. They are still golden, but they are more muted. The reaction of the Kharl when they saw her eyes, staring out of her hollow face, was very interesting. They were waiting near the River Dragon when I came off the ship and, ever since, they have been following me around. I wonder, will they now start following the Princess instead?

When the Mice had taken their position at the front, Rani stood and welcomed everyone and pointed out that that they would begin loading the ships immediately after the meeting, and that they hoped to be on their way by lunch. She also quickly ran through what had been seen last night, as if they needed any reminding, and then handed over to Shilpa.

Rani

Dobun is going to be the first to speak. He looks nervous. The Khitan have the smallest representation of any of the groups here. Today, unusually, there are even more Kharl present than there are Khitan. He has risen from his chair, I see. All eyes are upon him and today there is no table to hide behind. Nervously, he cleared his throat.

"Last night I visited the real world and saw others of my people. I saw a way into the future, but the further forward and the further north I went, the harder it grew. I know that the direction we have chosen is right because of this difficulty. The last island could not be seen, nor could the battle to come that must be there.

"One thing I am sure of is that there will be a steed of the sky that must be destroyed before the Horse totem can truly claim the skies as our own. This destruction must be done with magic if it can be done at all and so"— *he is looking hard at my wife and me*—"the Princess Magi *must*"—*he really emphasised that word*—"cast nothing of offence in the battle until the need is evident to them…no matter what happens, no matter how dire all else looks." *We just sit there through the battle? Really?*

"What I saw tells me that there will be one and only one chance for a final success in what we are doing, and if it fails then the war will continue for yet another Age. Of this I am certain beyond words. Other mages may act as they need to, but as for the Princess Rani in particular, you must reserve your power until the right moment, and it will involve both the sky and a steed. More I cannot say." *I don't even think that he really means* will not *this time, either. I think that he has given us everything he has.*

Dobun finished and quickly sat down to murmurs about what he meant by his words, and the Princesses looked at each other. *Theodear is raising her eyebrow at me. She knows what I have been working on, and it is quite a spell of destruction. I guess that we will find out in time if I have been working on the right one to use. It sounds as if I might have, but you never know.*

Astrid

Shilpa has organised the druid of the Omáda of Kichic-kharl that come from Cold Keep to speak next. If anything, Mardrikrat is even more nervous than Dobun. He is a Kharl who is in lands, the loss of which is remembered on a day just past, and has been so remembered for three thousand years. He has all of these Humans, many of whom have never even seen a full-blood Kharl before, staring at him.

Mardrikrat rose and looked around. *His size means that some cannot see him easily and have to peer around others to the unusual sight. His green and scaly skin, large eyes and prominent teeth make his origin obvious. His dull green hair is showing from under his padded leather armour cap and he wears a bow, bow case and a sword as well as several other odd-shaped pouches and a small pack. He might be a priest, obviously of The Living God, but he clearly goes to war alongside his charges.*

"I made sacrifice," he said "and I prayed to the Living God. What I received from my God was to trust to what the Cat Woman told me to do. I have to go with her, and follow her closely and do exactly what she tells us to do lest we fail." *Now everyone is looking at me. I am the only Cat-woman present, I suppose. I suppose that explains why I am being followed.*

"You know," Mardrikrat continued, "that earlier we said that we were not sure if we should be here? Now I am absolutely certain that we should. I am far less certain if we will be among those who live and I know nothing of what will happen generally, but now I know we are doing exactly what our God wants us to do, I am more than content with that."

There is awe in his voice as he finishes. I have to admit Hrothnog has an impressive voice, too, when you first hear it...and every other time after that as well. "He said so to me directly. I have now heard His Voice ringing in my head in all of its terror and its wonder. I know no more of the battle beyond what we must do."

The Kharl shuddered a little before he shuffled off to sit down beside another small, green figure and next to the large, hairy bulk of the Bear People. *He is looking small and fragile next to the other southerners, and even smaller still next to the Bear Folk. I guess that Hrothnog wants me looked after, then. I am not sure if that is good or ill news.*

Astrid
after some shuf ing around

*T*he Puleleiite *rarely leave their ships, and never leave the villages. We have the Puleleiite of the Ofu here today. That must have taken some arranging by someone. From what I have been told, not only is there a long history of non-involvement with the people of the land, but the Puleleiite rarely share the detail of their insights even with their own people.*

She is a small, dark and older woman with her face completely covered in an elaborate blue ceremonial tattoo. She is wearing a plain skirt and shirt of sh hono and has necklaces of shells around her neck. "I have only looked at the sea," she said. *As few understand Olelo, she speaks in High Speech, and she has to pause as people start to translate to others all around the room.*

"I see no storms ahead and I see good winds for us. I see three islands, I see death and I see that we will find something or someone, I am not sure which, that has been lost or has stayed hidden for a long time, for a very long time, almost a time beyond time. I do not know what we will find. I know that we must be cautious, very cautious, and not travel rashly in unfamiliar waters. There is a silent danger hidden under the waves." With that, she sat down again.

Next to stand is one of the Dwarves. *I know that he is named Geir, and he comes from North Hole and is here with Baron Cnut Stonecleaver.* Astrid looked harder. *I am sure that he is either very young or else is a woman. Given what is happening, it is unlikely that there would be a young druid trusted with this task, though, so I am sure that it is a woman Dwarf who is about to speak.*

I have spent enough time with Dwarves I should be able to tell. Above the squat build, the armour, the hammer, and the shield on her back is a relatively wispy beard and smooth skin. The voice, however, gives little away as Geir speaks in a tenor register. The speaker addressed them in Dwarven, and again paused for translators to do what they needed.

"One thing that struck me from last night as I...performed my rites... was what the child-witch Ia said about a King... I will tell you what that was about." Geir turned to face Ragnilde. "I know that your husband must make it official, but I tell you now that you bear within you the next King of the Dwarves. Keep them safe..." *That causes quite a sensation around the room.*

"As for our other task—and I must admit that after finding the other, what lies ahead in battle was far less important for me to find—I have little to add except that it will be grim and fell. We face enemies even more varied than those gathered here." *We get a significant look around the room and the audience look around as well.*

"We will have a mighty fight on our hands on the ground, and although it will be essential for success that our battle on the ground is fought and won, the final, and the most important, battle will be that which happens high in the air at the end." *Geir looks at Dobun, Dobun looks at Geir, and they both nod.* "It will not be on the land, that is all I have to say." The Dwarf turned and resumed her seat. *Murmurs all around the room; they are certainly getting a lot to talk about today.*

Lastly we have Calgacus of the Bear Folk. He stood, and then stood further. *He is not only the tallest person in the room, but he is also one of the most hirsute. His black hair is bound back from his face into a thick-braided tail and his beard hangs down nearly to his waist. His bare arms, circled with golden bands, are larger than many people's legs, even mine, and are also covered in black hair.*

He is dressed in loose, tailored leather. Except for a blade sheathed along his belt—a mere knife for him but a shortsword for most—he bears no visible weapon. Of all those here, he is the only one who is not apparently armed for battle. He himself is the weapon. He looms large in the room and seems to almost fill it with his presence.

Even seated he was taller than many are when they are standing, and Mardrikrat, walking back to his seat beside him, seems puny in comparison. The room is hushed, as if his presence has brought the peace and calm of a deep forest glade into our midst. There is even a smell of honey and spring about him.

There is a reason that his people always spend so much of their life outside, and it is not just a love of that world. They really are not built for the confines to be found inside the towns and villages and buildings of other races. Even I feel lost inside one of the buildings of his people, and Ia would have to climb to get into a chair.

When he speaks, his voice strikes a deep bass sound that is felt almost as much as it is heard. It is in the same range as Hrothnog's, but one brings terror and the other brings peace. He speaks in Hindi, rather than his own tongue, and again this will be translated to others who need it when he pauses.

"I have brought my people here to follow a prophecy," he said. "It has long been known among my people that we had to stay hidden from the world and apart from it until certain signs were brought to us. This is prophesying that is far older than this cycle, far older than just this Age. It is a prophecy that dates from the very start of this world." *He looks at the Princesses, at Hulagu and then at me. Why me? The others are leaders. I am just a warrior.*

"We were told by the Mother, when she birthed us, to stay hidden until we were visited by the Mouse, the Horse and the Cat." *Holy shit! I hate prophecy that is about me.* "That has happened and been seen and witnessed, and the time that we have dreaded for two Ages has come upon us to mark the end of the Third. Up until now we have lived quietly in our woods. Now you will often see us out in the world." *So, everything is about to change?*

"The Age of Magic has come upon this world, not just in The Land, but in the rest of it as well. I tell you now that what we do marks the end of one Age and an entering into a new one, and it is partly up to us to help find the many hidden people of this world and to bring them out of that hiding. This will include not only all of Father Simeon's people that he has somehow failed to mention to anyone else…"—*there is a big pause now and everyone looks at the priest, and Simeon looks surprised and a little guilty. Does that mean he is not the only Werewolf in the New Found Land? There is a tribe of them?*—"but also several other races like them." He looked around again and paused for even longer. *He is waiting for what he says to sink in after the translators are finished.*

"What I have to add to the prophecies that you have heard today is simply this: there are a people who live on the island that you call Ovington. I do not know who they are or where they are found exactly, or how they have remained hidden from everything, but they are the first ones that I am drawn to find and bring out into the world again. They are the first of the Hidden Ones that we will help bring out to regain a place out in the world." *Who lives on a small island and yet still stays hidden from the whole world?*

"I know, both from my divination and from the tales of my people, that we need their help to succeed and that without it we are certainly doomed and may not even reach the battle. I also know, from what I saw, that our success with them is not certain." He turned and lumbered back to his seat. *He moves like a Mathan, a giant bear, even when he is in Human form, and I should know how a Mathan moves.*

Once again the room is full of murmurs and comments. Now we have Rani standing and the room fades to silence. Everyone is looking at her. Does she have more to add? Rani looked around the gathering. *She is checking whether there are any others who would speak. Soon all of the people are looking about, but no others speak up.*

"That is all, then," she finally said. "Now is the last time for you to make a decision as to whether you wish to come or to withdraw from this venture. If none have any more to say"—she paused briefly—"then let us begin to load our ships and to set out." The room rapidly filled with movement and voices and other sounds as, with a collective sigh, attendees rose from their seats and began to work their way outside to gather their people for the trip that lay ahead of them.

Chapter XIX

Hulagu
19th December

Before even dawn has fully broken over the northern coast, as others begin loading the ships with stores, and well before the rest are awake, we are leaving the coast behind and flying out to check over the huge expanse of the ocean beyond the river. We set out, our masts rising into the light of the rising sun, while the waves below us are still dark. As far as the horizon, the northern ocean bears no remembrance to the storm that was first conjured, and then repelled, only yesterday. The low, long swell runs from the west, its surface broken only by whales and marine reptiles coming up for air and the small splashes of diving birds and marine leatherwings, which hunt the fish below.

Now we are looking not just for visible craft, but also anything hiding among them that won't be revealed until the ships leave port.

So we watch these wakes, and we look for other flyers, for anything that is strange or odd.

That is, if they are visible. If they fly as Astrid and Ayesha do, they will still be indiscernible, but there is nothing that can be done about that. We stay clear of Skrice at this stage, although some of my riders can see that far. Apparently the islanders have already reported on their far-speaker that they have no problems, and that they wait for us to arrive.

We know, however, that if our enemy starts to look for the wake of vessels, instead of the ships themselves, then like the tracks of passage of a human on the grass, it is quite possible a carefully worded clairvoyance spell might still reveal the course of the ships when they set out. I now know that there are so many things to think about in trying to hide or to find a large ship.

Hulagu looked down from his place over Wolfneck. *Despite the chaos on the dock, it is taking a surprisingly short amount of time to load everyone who would be going on board the ships. All of those who had survived the attack on Skrice, and who wanted to come this time, are loaded on one ship or another, although on this trip there are far more Dwarves than we had with us before.*

He filled his time by trying to pick groups out and count them. *More than two filled hands of Dwarves are there. There are over three filled hands of the Bear Folk. Most of them are archers, and the rest carry huge axes to be used with both hands. I talked with some of them. Not all are shape shifters.*

Even those who cannot change are bigger than most people, men and women both. The archers draw giant yew staves like Astrid's as their main weapons, with shafted arrows up to an ell long that would do wicked damage with their iron heads. Their bows stand as tall as they do and, indeed, many are twice as tall as some of the Kichic-kharl.

The single Omáda of the small Kharl from North Keep tell me exactly where Astrid is. They follow her closely and nothing anyone says changes their mind. They insist they will take up little room. The Rangers from here are all coming, of course. There are people from Erave Town and Evilhalt who followed the Bear Folk as they travelled, and there are also nearly a hand of filled hands of soldiers, priests and mages from the villages of the north.

Lastly, two full files of the Basilica Anthropoi from Greensin will be leaving their horses in Wolfneck and coming along. There are only a small number of them, but they are by far the heaviest infantry among us. They are all clad in iron lamellar amour with mail-draped helms covering the faces and thick leather boots reinforced with splints of iron. Splinted leather is also on their arms. Shields are on their backs. They carry lance and bow, war darts, maces and swords. I guess they will use their lances as long spears.

They are really the only ones of our whole army who are heavily armoured. Stefan says he hopes they will provide a small but solid and disciplined rock for their opponents to face and hopefully break against. Some of the other spears will be able to form up behind and around their front rank. The discipline of the Basilica Anthropoi will help a line of less-experienced people hold against magic, and a charge and their armour would also better protect the less well-armoured behind them from the archery of the enemy.

Olympias

We set sail into the first day of spring with four very full ships. The holds are full of people and the decks are crowded. Those who can have even taken up places in the rigging. Now we do not just have our usual two animals on board: the Bear Folk have brought their own as well. I nearly trod on the tail of a very large cat earlier. It just glared at me.

All the augurs are sure that the cold gales have subsided for good. The leaden grey of the winter sky does seem to be gone, and the gentle westerly winds and pale blue skies of the new season promise that they are here to stay. I hope that they do not lie. The local ship shows very little freeboard for a start. I would be nervous sailing in her with only a few fingers of timber between air and water.

I am keeping the ships close together. I hope that by doing it this way, some of the hiding spells of the forerunners will help to disguise the wakes of others.

During this short voyage to Skrice, Rani, Stefan and Astrid are shuffling between the ships, talking to the various leaders and mages, trying to work out how to best employ such a mixed force who have little experience of working together. It seems that the Kichic-kharl get nervous when my sister is away from them and they look out for her with a glass.

At the same time, Ariadne has begun the task of re-assembling her large arbalest, which has travelled so far in the bottom of a hold. She has her husband and others to help, and a chain of people pass the bits up from where they lie in the hold. It may be needed soon, but how they are going to move it around is another question.

My crew have to work our ship around their passengers, and cries of "make way" are frequent. They grow even more frequent when some of the passengers begin to feel the effect of the long swell on the movement of the ship. This is particularly so for those travelling below decks. It is a first time to sea for most of them. Travel through the rigging is easier for my crew.

Other passengers, all of them archers, spend much of the trip standing or sitting up in the tops as they sway back and forth like trees bending in a wind. Some even cling unsteadily to the shrouds of the ladders while sitting precariously on the thinner ratlines. Many of them have not been to sea before and some of these nervously clutch ropes as they rock to and fro.

Even in the light breeze and low sea that we are blessed with, there are some among those on board who spent much of their time hanging over the rails. This often leads to much amusement and accompanying loud cries of "watch under" from those of the others who do not suffer in the same way. Will people never tire of jokes about offering greasy bacon to the ill?

Olympias

Of the four ships, only the Vindur-skefi *and the* River Dragon *are able to fit into the small bay at Skrice. Although there is room for them inside, both the* Rongo *and* Ofu *draw far too much water to enter the safe harbour. Using their far-speaker, the people of Wolfneck have kept those of Skrice appraised of events as they happened, though, and the people on the island are already set to go.*

They have suffered much from their northern neighbours and, to keep their families safe, all who are on the island need us to succeed. Three hands of them—mages, and all of those of fighting age—will be coming in one of their own craft. The ship will not be filled by this number, so it can even take on board some of the people from other craft.

It is not long before the four ships that sailed from Wolfneck are all anchored or drawn up for the night. Those without room to sleep on board are sleeping on the island in empty houses and barns. We have sentries aloft and the green-light box sweeping around. All is in place for us to leave harbour with the still air of dawn and with the fifth ship.

Although the unknown island of Ovington is only a short sail away to the north, it has been decided that it will not do to try and approach its unknown shore in the looming dark. We were told in the foreseeing to be cautious in the way we travel, so cautious we will be. I have no notes at all on the water that lies around either that island or the next and can find no one local to tell me, so I am glad of that.

Chapter XX

Olympias
20th December, the sun is just rising

Now we sail north into unknown waters. We have the five ships in our fleet, fulfilling that part of my other sister-wife's prophecy. The ship from Skrice has the Basilica Anthropoi on board, as well as the islanders. This makes a little more room on the other vessels and, as it is a craft that can beach rather than anchor, it will allow the warrior monks to quickly get into a position to help protect the landing if needed.

It, and the Vindur-skefi, *now lag behind the rest, but they will catch up at Ovington. They will be needed in the end, not now. Although they are far slower on the open ocean, laden as they are with only a hand of freeboard available to them, possible only on this smooth sea, these two will be the only larger vessels that can safely make a landing on a beach.*

It would be up to the people on them, and any people that fly in from the River Dragon, *to hold a beachhead until the others, the vast bulk of our forces, can disembark from the larger ships. Except for the* River Dragon *with its saddles, the other vessels will all have to bring their people ashore by small craft, and it will be a slow process.*

The saddles flew low and high over the sea, searching for signs that all was not as it should be. However hard they looked, the swell was only a pace high and the sea almost glassy smooth, running from the west under a light breeze. The wave tops had a length of several chains between them.

I am told that, although still falling behind, even the two well-laden vessels, sailing as they are without their own wind, are making good enough time. Water is creaming from their bows and around their leeboards as they beat up the coast of the island of Neron, following behind the rest of us.

All of their passengers sit still, as they have so little freeboard left. Anything else on the water would have shown up easily, but apart from fish, fish lizards and the occasional sighting of a migrating whale blowing on the surface or dancing in the air on its tail to land with a crash, there is nothing to be seen that will disturb their passage.

Now we are around the westernmost point of Neron, the island of Ovington comes into view. Even when we first see it in the distance its long, low shape takes up the length of an outstretched hand, fully between the tips of the little finger and thumb, on our horizon. Nothing of interest can be seen there, even as we draw closer, and many eyes are eagerly trying to see something…anything.

It is large, nearly flat. The edge of the island is only a narrow fringe of shrub-covered, rocky beach with a slight slope. The only empty ground is the area washed by the tides and a few small outcrops of black, eroded rocks leading out into the sea. There is a small rise in the centre—more a low and wide plateau, one that takes up most of the island—than it is a real hill, but apart from the heather and other low bushes on it, that is all.

Flyers have flown over, staying well in the sky, and others keep watch all around us from mastheads, but why we are supposed to be here is not apparent to anyone. All that can be seen are the flat ground and the endless short shrubs that are covering it.

Under the bushes, in burrows and in the bare spots, flyers report a seemingly unlimited number of seabird nests. The few areas of rock on the shore are the crowded home of colonies of seals of different types. Nowhere on the island is there even a sign of a creek or ponds of fresh water, let alone people.

As the allies approached the land they took the ships around to the starboard, travelling east around the island. *We have been able to see most of the shore on the western side of the island as we approached. The land runs roughly from the south-east towards the north-west. According to the people of Skrice there is an anchorage, with shelter from the west wind, low on the east coast, which they use occasionally in storms.*

Olympias
some time later

I have come back from my own flight now. The anchorage lies between the two longest of the rocky outcrops. The northern outcrop is also the tallest as it is near the height of the central plateau. I have us circling widdershins around the island, keeping only a few chains from the shore. The saddles are out and taking the depth of the water and relaying it back.

The island might only be a low-lying one, but the sea floor appears to shelve quickly down from it. I am told that, even within a couple of chains of the shore there is more than four fathoms of sheltered water to be found for us to anchor in.

Olympias brought them to a stop inside this shallow bay. *It has a real beach behind it, the only sand to be seen on the rock-crusted coast. There is little enough that can be seen, though, as strands of kelp, no doubt brought by offshore storms, litter the sand. However, there is as much shelter here as any place that I can see along the whole coast.*

The only disadvantage is the amount of kelp, which forms a forest in the sea below us but, as far as can be seen, that seems to be the case over the whole length of the coast. Not only I, but the captains of our ships, are all now hoping that the weed will not foul our anchors when it comes time for us to leave.

From the ships it could easily be seen that nothing was moving on the whole island except for the multitude of seabirds in their nests and the seals sitting on the rocks, all of them looking with curiosity at the newcomers. *The birds cover the entire island between the shrubs and, in their clouds, make the sky raucous with their cries. Now we all stand on the decks of the ships looking around and wondering what to do next.*

"We will get the smaller vessels to move all of my people to the shore," said Calgacus. "I know that we are supposed to be here, but we will be of no use and we will not find out why if we just sit here in the sea. We have been sent here for a reason and, from what has been seen by the seers, the key to that reason must be somewhere in front of us on the land."

They all stood for a moment looking at the empty island, wondering about what direction to take before Olympias nodded. She launched the *River Dragon*'s boats and began to move the Bear Folk to the land. *They are large people and it will take some time, but now that the boats can move by themselves we only need one of the Mice to crew each, and not several rowers.*

As it was, the large Bear Folk almost capsized the small craft. *The Bear Folk are really not used to being on water at all.* Alaine was sent on a saddle to get the two other ships to anchor outboard as the two smaller vessels gradually caught up. In the meantime, Olympias made preparations to keep an eye to the north.

From the end of the island of Ovington, the Shunned Isle, Arnflorst, should be readily visible. Our ships are probably invisible to magic and perhaps also to many other means of finding them. Despite this, if we can see their island, then any people or any other creature that is there should physically be able to see us as we wait motionless at anchor. After all, the bare masts of the Ofu *and the* Rongo *are far taller than the island itself.* She looked up. *Even our much smaller* River Dragon *is close to the same height as the land beside it.*

From the *River Dragon* it could be seen that, as the Bear Folk reached the shore, about half of them spread out immediately into the scrub. *There they are raising clouds of raucous birds, so it is very easy to see where a person is.* The other half stripped off their clothes and began to change immediately and, once the discarded garments and other items of the changers were gathered up the pairs began to roam around the island, one fully Human and the other a Bear.

The Bears were of all sizes and shapes. *Without surprising anyone, Calgacus has transformed into a gigantic Grizzly of the far north, and he is not the only one.* As well as looking around them in case of attack, those in the sky and those on the ships kept an eye out on the Bear folk as they began to investigate the entire island.

They are making a thorough search of the narrow coastal plain and walk only a few paces apart at most. As they move, hordes of birds rise around them, screeching in objection. Some of the birds tried to attack, diving and swooping, gyrating and wheeling, and they had to be continually beaten off.

Soon the people were regathering on the beach, and some of the bears regained Human form. *It is obvious that a spell of some sort is being cast.* Once that was done, all of the birds continued to wheel around them in their agitated flight but, when the Bears had all resumed their shape, and they had again spread out and begun moving, there was a clear space around them where no bird flew.

Carefully the walkers moved around the island, gazing apparently at their feet as they did so. *If there are people living there, surely they have to come to the sea at some time and no matter how well they hide them, with so many looking so carefully, at least some sign of their tracks will eventually be found.*

It took the searchers half the day to go around the island, moving sunwise. They were nearly back to the ships, only two hands of filled hands north, when the watchers noticed them all abandon their line and begin to converge onto a single spot. Once they were there, they all stood in a circle as one of their people picked something up and examined it before passing it around. Several of the bears appeared to be sniffing the ground as the humans scattered a little and looked more intently at what was there. Several of the Human-shaped Bear Folk pointed at bushes and others joined them.

Now they are all looking inwards to the centre of the island from where they stand near the shoreline. They talk a little more, and then reform their line. This time it is parallel with the shoreline. Slowly they begin to move towards the centre of the island. Again they stop as they go to examine the ground and pick their way between the plants and the occasional rock.

It seems to me that now and then one pair will stop and begin to turn back until the others call to them, or grab hold of them, and urge them back to their route. Only the actual animals seem not to turn back. Around them in the sky the sea birds still swirl and protest, their raucous screeches of indignation heard even from the boats.

It took a long time, but eventually the searchers reached the low plateau and began to move up the slope leading to its top. *They are now touching each other; several try to turn back and are stopped by the others. Once, over half of them turn at the same time but are urged forward. The top of the plateau stands only a few cables above the surface of the water, but it seems to take them a very long time to climb up to it.*

Reaching the head of this short slope they halted and appeared to be talking backwards and forwards among themselves. *Slowly, still touching, the Humans even holding hands, they are beginning to converge onto a single point and move forward onto the flat surface. Again, some are turning and being pushed forward by those behind them.* They had not gone very far on the low plateau when the watchers on the ships saw with wonder that the Bear Folk, pair by pair, were beginning to disappear from view as they stepped forward.

"They have entered some sort of magic field," said Theodora, in a voice loud enough that all of those on the *River Dragon* could hear. "The whole centre of the island must be an illusion..." *Now she is trying to work out how to cast a spell that large, even as she talks.*

"As a general rule you can feel a single item from only around a pace away. How far away you can feel the presence of magic increases by a complex rule as you add more items and as you become stronger in using it, but for a field as large and strong as that would have to be, you should usually be able to feel it from a distance similar to the size of the field itself." *I am sure that the apprentice mages are fascinated.*

"Any mage riding along our road would know when they were near Mousehole, even if they were blindfolded. With what we have in place there, I can now feel the valley before I can even see it. No caster, no matter how new to the craft, could walk past it without feeling the strength of what lies behind our rock walls."

She turned to the island and considered the size of the plateau. "If the field there covers the whole plateau, then we are well within that area, and yet I can feel nothing. That means there is more than one illusion, as well as various other non-detection enchantments in play, and they must all be very strong. As well, it would seem that there is a strong avoidance field of some sort and perhaps one of forgetting. Most people only put these on a small treasure box or a keyhole."

She turned to her husband. "Did you see the way that some of the people would try and turn back to the coast? I will bet that, when they come back, we will hear from those who turned that they'd completely forgotten what they were supposed to be doing there. I can cast a hex to do that for a person or two at close range, but it is a strong enchantment to perform, even for me."

Rani
a little later

I do not know what to do except sit and wait. We need to be ready for… anything, really. With their weapons ready, most of the people sat around and talked or ate. Some sharpened blades, while others prayed or just sat silent in the spring sunshine. *It seems that many on the ship are glad we have stopped moving and just lie there out of gratitude, or else refill their stomachs.*

She turned, looking to find something to occupy herself. *Ia is playing a child's game with Jillian. I have heard little of her for a while, and Astrid is no longer complaining about feeding her.* "How is she acting now?" she asked Astrid. "How old does she seem to be?"

"She acts as if she were a child of eight or so," Astrid replied. "At this stage, at least when she is awake, she has no memory of what happened to her, but she remains terrified of men and will only run to Basil or Christopher for help if Ia, Bianca or I are not nearby. Her nights are still filled with nightmares." *I suppose that is understandable.*

"She sits entranced, listening whenever Christopher speaks during a service, and seems to be able to remember almost anything that he says and can repeat it word for word. She has the same approach to any song that she hears. It is as if she were empty inside," said Astrid, "and waiting like an empty jug to be filled. She is like what your wife says about a new-cast magic matrix, hungry and wanting to fill up."

"So she is almost starting over again?" asked Rani. Astrid nodded.

"She has language and little else; although she learns so quickly that perhaps she is just remembering those parts. Clarence said that she used to sing, after all. She learns from us all of the time. When she is occupied and happy playing with her doll or with one of the animals, she often sings my song to herself."

Chapter XXI

Astrid
20th December

It only lacks an hour before sunset when Calgacus re-appears in his human form and dressed just as he is normally clad. He has a woman with him that I have not seen before. From her size and the way she is dressed she is not one of the Bear Folk. After waving at the ships from where Calgacus had first re-appeared, the two people began to move down the slope towards the water.

"Let us go", said Rani. She turned to the people in the rest of the ship. "We may be some time," she said. "Do not be concerned if we do not come back tonight. We will undoubtedly have to bring them fully up to date on all that has happened, and you all know how long that can take." She turned to Olympias. "And please let the other ships know so that they do not get concerned. Keep the saddles out in shifts all night and keep alert. Watch the sea and sky carefully and pay attention to any change in the weather."

We are acting on the idea that the people on the island are shapeshifters in some way, so those of us with the most direct connection with animals are those who will go. After listening to what had been said in Wolfneck, Rani even consulted us about who to take onto the island. Obviously our family will go.

While Jillian was left with Bianca to look after her, Ayesha and Hulagu, Basil's family with their animals, as well as Parminder, Father Simeon and his wife Danelis, all moved to their saddles and took off. They followed the Princesses, aiming towards the point where the two on the beach seemed to be headed.

When the fliers arrived, the saddles were all stacked above the beach, then covered over with canvas to prevent the countless seabirds from soiling them. They were done before Calgacus and his companion came down the slope, picking their way slowly through the vegetation.

It gave Astrid a few moments to look over the stranger.

She is tall and has a solidly built frame, and wears a loose-fitting dress of sh-hone. The scabbard on her belt is worn sideways, in the northern style; inside may be a seax, a fighting knife or a dagger. She has no other weapons and her silver-grey hair is, like Danelis', not the grey that comes from age. She is not a young-looking woman, but very attractive for all of that.

Despite not being young in appearance, she is not old-looking, either. In fact she has a look of both age and wisdom, and yet still of youth and vitality. It all means that her actual age is very difficult to determine.

Astrid grew impatient at their slow progress through the shrubs and started up towards them. *Now, why am I walking towards the group on the beach? Why am I here? Why is my sister-wife laughing at me?* "What are you… Oh," she said, as realisation dawned on her. *Damn good spell.*

Astrid spun around to face the woman who was approaching.

She turned her attention to the unknown woman: *I am right.* "But we know about your spell now," she said. "Should that not let us go up there?" She had spoken Inuit, figuring that the people here might understand another northern language.

"No," said the woman in the same tongue. "That is why I am here to bring you up to our village. We will do introductions and explanations when we arrive. You will now have to hold hands with each other, and then with me, or you will find that you get lost all over again and we will have to return for you."

They started to walk along in a chain, with several of them feeling a little ridiculous. They must have seemed like a row of small children from the school out in a foreign village with a single adult in the lead to guide them. The animals seemed to have no such problem, just as the bears and other animals among the Bear Folk had not been affected. They began to pass single file up from the beach towards the plateau.

Around them, nesting birds noisily complained at the interlopers, again diving and swooping at all but the woman who led them and Calgacus, who now brought up the rear of their group. The birds seemed to be particularly upset by the presence of the large cat. *Fluff-Ball has to walk close to me to avoid the attention of the birds as they repeatedly rise and dive down at her.*

Astrid had to juggle her bardiche around, but she had attached a strap of leather to it and so was able to sling it like a bow over her shoulders. It wasn't comfortable, but it did leave her hands free. As they reached the top of the short slope—a certain point on the slope—each looked about, perplexed, as one after another, the people before them faded and disappeared..

To their eyes, everything seemed the same on the plateau as it was below them on the shore and, when it came time to disappear there was no difference in what they could see ahead—except that the people ahead had gradually disappeared as they walked. This left the person behind them seemingly holding on to empty air. *I can feel Basil's hand as I hold it, but not a thing can be seen of Basil himself, or indeed my own hand that is holding on to his.*

The sun is still where it was, the ships are still floating and the birds still fly and nothing ahead has changed, just that Basil, and everyone ahead of him, has vanished. Yet I can sill feel the warmth of his hand in mine. Some of the birds, as they fly, go within the area where the spell must be, but they appear no different when they do so and most fly straight out again.

Ahead of us it seems that the view there is just the same as that behind us and what we could see from the saddles. There is a large area of low, scrubby bush and almost endless nests, with birds continually landing and taking off again. The cries of the birds ahead are as loud as those of the birds behind.

When the scene changed in front of her, Astrid stopped abruptly and stood briefly looking around the top of the island until Ia bumped into her. *It is very different to anything that I expected.* The woman who had brought them up the slope was waiting only a few paces away at a gate in a long dry-stone wall that seemed to stretch around the whole plateau.

Outside the fence, the ground is still covered with the same stunted shrubs, the same seabirds drop towards their nests or rise towards the sky. Inside the fence there are fields, trees and houses and there are no seabirds. Where we are is already quieter than it was on the slope. The trees that are visible now are not the stunted and wind-blown trees that we saw on the west of Skrice.

Here there are apples and other fruits and a grove of oaks and other trees can be seen that would not have looked out of place near Evilhalt. There are roses and beds of flowers and probably other herbs. Well apart from the other fruit trees there is even a small area of pines near the fence a little way away, and in the distance a small patch of what looks to be real forest.

From the look of the pines, they are being specially grown for timber as they range evenly in size with perhaps a difference of a few years of growth between each row. Once the people had started emerging into the clear area and as they were assembling, the woman cast her eyes over them. *She is looking at us all and carefully noting our weapons and the differences between us.*

She looks at who stands with whom, at the animals that came with us, and she looks at various items worn and carried by people in a way that indicates she can feel magic. She has ample time for this examination as, in return, we are mainly busy looking in wonder at the people, the village and the fields and woods that lie in front of us.

The island of Ovington is not small, and the area that must lay under the spell of hiding is as large, if not quite a bit larger, as the area taken up by any normal village with all of its fields and attached woodland. There is room for open fields, for cattle and for sheep as well. There is even a small lake and some bridges visible that must cross small streams. Through the area, birds can be seen flying, but they are not seabirds; these are the birds of field and forest such as we would expect to see far further south.

Ahead of us are around fifty large houses and some other buildings. They are built more like the houses in the far west of the land, or the ones in Didymoteichon in the New Found Land, than those that are to be seen elsewhere. They definitely do not look like our houses of the north, that lie mostly buried in the earth for protection.

Our houses are low and snug, built to survive the storms and the snows of winter. These are large houses, with two or sometimes more storeys. They are houses that have been built for extended families of several generations. More buildings can be seen scattered around the island, presumably hay sheds or shelters for animals or other farm structures.

The fields are divided up by stout, well-maintained dry-stone walls similar to those we are starting to get at Mousehole. Occasionally there is a gate of timber, and I see narrow lanes between them. Except in patches, perhaps where repairs have been made, the type of stones making up the wall just ahead of us can scarce be made out for the grey-green lichens that cover it. These fences must have been made a very long time ago.

Astrid looked around at the trees and plants again. *It might already be spring in the north, but that does not make it warm outside on the rest of the island, where we came from. It is still fairly chill outside this area of magic as the sun sinks, just as it still is in Wolfneck.*

But it is not like that here.

Here it seems more like the northern summer is already fully upon us. The sun, shining bright in the clear blue sky above us, makes the day feel drowsy and warm instead of just taking the chill off the air. In the silence, if you listen, you can even hear the sound of bees somewhere nearby, and the tweets and songs of birds trill and pipe around us.

When the attention of the Mice had all returned to her, the woman spoke up. "My name is Sìle," she said in a heavily accented form of High Speech. *It sounds a little like she is gargling as she talks, and sometimes she seems almost to swallow letters. The effect is strange when combined with the normally liquid sounds of that tongue. I wonder what she is saying.*

There was a flurry of translation among the Mice for those with none of the language. "I am the headwoman of the Shaelkie, and apart from those very few who have found us by accident after having been lost at sea in our waters, you are the only people of the Cutach Bheatha, the short-lived, to have set foot in our village of Seòlaid since we set it apart from the rest of the world over two Ages ago." *That is a very long time. Six thousand years? More?*

"We have generally stayed apart from the world outside, but we have been told that tales still linger of us, and some of you may have heard of us as the Merrow. I have to say that, in that time, many of the Cutach Bheatha have landed on No h-Eilean Samhradh, for one reason or another, but only a very few of them have ever found us before without us wanting them to do so. Most of them ended up forgetting the experience." *Yes, I can understand that.*

"Your companions, the Bear People, have made it possible for you to come this far. They have only had the chance to tell us a short but interesting tale. Now we would have you follow me to where my people are waiting, and then you will talk to us and we will listen to what else there is that you will say to us. If we are satisfied with what you have to say, then it is possible that our time of isolation may be over, just as it has ended for the Bear People." *Why do I feel that there will be a catch to this?*

"However, I must tell you that, if we are not satisfied with what you say, then you will all leave here and all of you, and those who ride in ships out on the waters of our island in waiting, will forget what you have seen. You will forget that we even exist and what led you here. Bear all of this in mind when you act and when you speak."

And there it is, the catch. She speaks with the calm assurance and certainty of a person who has never been proven wrong before on a matter like this. She obviously has grounds to feel certain that the power of her people can do what she says. They must have done this before.

Following Sìle, we all moved on into the village. As we go, the Shaelkie look curiously at us and we look back. All of the villagers I can see have the same sort of loose clothes and, although a few have hair that is blonde or black, most have the same grey hair as our guide.

Few of the people we see are working, and those that are seem to be hurrying to finish what they are doing. Generally, the people mostly seem to be moving towards the same place as we are headed, or else getting ready to do so. Almost all of the Shaelkie that I can see are adult. Most look to be of the same apparent age as Sìle, indeterminate, possibly young but also possibly very, very old.

As they slowly moved inwards, Sìle pointed at the few important buildings. There are only a very small school, a meeting hall, her house and a few others. "Unless we mix our blood with those of the Cutach Bheatha, we have always been a very long-lived race. We will often live until we die either by accident or by design." *They are older than Hrothnog? I doubt it.*

"The founder of this island refuge two ages ago was my great-grandfather, and the youngest full-blooded person here is my great-great-grandchild. Among us we have very few children, and we will do anything to cherish and protect them from harm," she said as they entered an open square where there were seats and tables. *So, they are not that old, then. Some of Theodora's family may even be that old.*

While Calgacus was still with them, the rest of his people were already seated there on benches and with mugs in their hands and food in front of them.

"Now…once you have made yourselves comfortable, and the last of us have gathered, you may introduce yourselves and begin your story." The Mice looked around them. *There are at least ten times a filled hand of people present and attentively watching us. A few stragglers are still arriving. Among these there are only two hands of persons who are not recognisably adult, ranging from infancy almost to the point where they must be approaching Sìle's apparent agelessness.*

Astrid looked from them to Theodora and back. *I wonder, knowing what we know of her family and how long they take to age, how old these "young" people actually are. Theodora still only looks a bit older than I am, and yet she has seen over one hundred and twenty years. All of the people, even the young ones, are staring hard at us as Sìle ushers us to some seats at the front of the gathering.*

The people that are already here are watching us with a flat and blank look as they study us. It is a look that is hard to put into one category, a mixture of part curiosity and, at the same time, perhaps, part hostility. It is quite possible that perhaps there is some resentment in the people of the island at our intrusion into their lives.

Like the Bear Folk were, but even more so, they are not sure if they want their lives to be overturned by the outside world. As well, while the youngest ones at least sit with a wide-eyed wonder at the appearance of strangers, the older people are obviously far more cautious. The Bear Folk have been sat down beside the villagers and apart from where we Mice are being placed; most of the Bear Folk, even Calgacus, seem to be a little nervous in the way they sit and look around them, something that I have never seen before.

Theodora

The Princesses had quietly consulted with each other as they made their way into the village and then Theodora had spoken a few words with Ayesha. *I will talk first to the villagers, but Ayesha will be doing the real storytelling when the time for that comes around.* While the other Mice seated themselves, the Princess stayed standing and looked out over the crowd as the last of the stragglers came in and made themselves comfortable.

Except for the visitors, all of the people in front of me look similar and are obviously related. In many ways it is almost like standing up and making a speech at any gathering of my family in Ardlark, but without the constant crowd of servants. Everyone I can see looks related, and all of those older than me will judge harshly anything that I say.

I should bear the comparison to my family in mind to at least try and make their gaze less intimidating. Well, there is no use delaying any longer, it looks like all of them that are coming are here. The point is to try and get these people to side with us, even if I am not sure why we must. I might as well plunge straight into the whole story and not leave any surprises. None have indicated differently, and I cannot speak that language that Astrid has, so I will speak in High Speech.

"My name is the Princess Theodora do Hrothnog," she started, "and my husband is another woman, the Princess Rani Rai"—she indicated her—"and I suppose that between us we are the people who are in charge of the ships that wait off your shore and who have come to see you and hopefully break your isolation." *There is no reaction to any of that.*

"Although my husband and I rule only a small and isolated valley in the southern mountains, the people of our valley are drawn widely from all over The Land and a few beyond. Our people, and those who we are leading, who are still on the ships, have come to us from The Land and the New Found Land to the West, from among the Kanaka of the seas, north to Skrice and down to the Southern Isle of Gil-Gand, from Warkworth to Ardlark." *Again there is nothing coming back.*

"We are on a long journey, or perhaps more accurately I should say that we have been set upon a long quest that has lasted many years. I was born in the Palace in Darkreach as a descendant of Hrothnog, and my husband was born a Battle Mage in Haven, but we ended up leaving our homelands as did many others of our people." *It is a hard audience to work.*

"You see some of them here in front of you; others are on the ships and even more of them are still in our home valley keeping most of our children safe. Ayesha"—again she indicated and Ayesha inclined her head politely—"will tell you how we got together and what has happened so far to bring us to your island." *Still nothing at all.*

"With your permission, when she has finished we will answer your questions and then I will say why we are here." She looked around her at the watchers. *No one has objected to what I proposed, and at least several of them are nodding now.* Feeling inexplicably relieved, almost as if she had passed some unknown test, Theodora went over and sat down next to Rani as Ayesha stood, moved to the centre of the gathering where she could be clearly seen and began to speak.

As time went by, people began to rise and fetch food and drink. These began to be passed around freely. The drinks were mainly ales and meads. The food had lots of cheese and pickled foods from vegetables to fish, but there were even different sorts of olives.

It soon became very evident to Theodora that Rani had been correct in what she had said on the ship. *It will be another long night ahead of us. The islanders are just like the Sea Nomads or, really, any other isolated community. However much they hold themselves aloof from the rest of us, and might like to think of themselves as self-sufficient, they are in fact starved for word of what is happening in the world outside their little enclave and they are very obviously enthralled by what they hear.*

Occasionally there are noises of approval or amusement. Ayesha is drawing the story out and giving a lot of detail in what she says. She is describing places that these folk will never have seen and populating them with the people and animals that others are used to, but to these people will just be legendary.

Theodora focussed her attention on the islander's reaction to the different parts of the tale as it unfolded. *From the shared smiles at certain times in the tale when there is speculation about the past and what had happened then, it is obvious they have some knowledge that we lack but, if they really do have only eight generations covering two whole Ages, then they each live far, far, longer than even my family do.*

My family can cover, perhaps, one Age with that many generations, but it will more likely be twice that many cohorts. I wonder how much The Granther knows and has not shared with us. If these people know so much about the past, what does he know? Astrid is sitting there on a spread cloak on the ground with her partners and playing absent-mindedly with her animal.

The annoying woman seems to have noticed the same reaction from the audience and, although she only has only a few words of High Speech, is intently watching what the islanders react to as well and is asking her sister-wife questions as the story is told. If what I heard in the Palace is correct, the last time that we were there Astrid spent a long time closeted with The Granther on her own.

I ignored it at the time as not being important. Now I am left wondering if the infuriating woman has come upon some information that she has not shared with the rest of us. If she has more knowledge about the past, what is it? I can see a hint of speculation on Astrid's face as she looks at the audience. She is obviously weighing something up in her mind. What is it?

Christopher had foreseen this long session happening again and had given them a supply of mild healing potions. Hulagu tended his wife and kept her supplied with drinks as she went on so that her voice would not fail. It was just as well that this was done as, even without the usual side tales and songs that they used in a more normal village to keep people's attention, the tale continued well into the still, mild night.

While some children went to bed and others were curled up on a cloak or a rug, most of the locals stayed awake and attentive right up to the end of the tale. It was very noticeable that they showed particular interest in what was said in the story about the sea battles. It was the only time they actually stopped Ayesha in her tale, as several of them wanted to know the precise location of all of them.

Ayesha had to ask Astrid to help her on those questions as she felt somewhat lost navigating outside the mountains, and especially in as featureless an environment as the sea. *Even Astrid seems ashamed to admit that she cannot be sure as to exact locations; while she might have the latitude right, we are still working, with our charts, on how far around the world something happens.*

"The charts that we now have and use," she said, "have neat lines drawn on them that divide the world up into set areas, but unfortunately the actual world lacks the same neat lines on it. I have to rely on what I remember of sailing times, and the way that current flows and its colour to indicate where things possibly are." *They seem to understand that.*

"Luckily, using our own wind to travel gives more constancy to our voyage and we have improved our maps as we go. I am able to be far more accurate in my guesses than I would have been only a few short years ago."

Theodora
21st December, just after midnight

Eventually Ayesha drew her tale to a close, having introduced, on Theodora's instructions, all of the Mice present and their relationships and their background as a part of the tale. *The brief part of Simeon's story that they were given has excited far more attention, and even a few quiet words of discussion between them, than almost anything else in the story.*

Otherwise the multiple marriages and other relationships among the Mice that cause much comment and questions elsewhere do not even raise an eyebrow among the onlookers. It may be the first place we have visited in all of The Land that this has been true. Eventually, Ayesha draws to a close with real applause ringing around from her audience. She seems very grateful to take her seat again.

Theodora started to stand but Sìle gestured her back down as she stood and looked around her at the other villagers, as if gauging what they wanted her to say. She exchanged looks with several before starting to speak.

"You are about to ask us to help you in this quest on which you have become engaged. We already know that from what has been said, and before you do so, we wish to discuss what has been said so far and to work out between us how much to tell you of ourselves. I would ask that the Mouse, the Horse, the Wolf, the Cat and the Bear withdraw while we decide what we are going to say from this point on."

Again she looked at the villagers, and several small nods could be seen from among them. There seemed to be no dissent and so she gestured at another woman, who must have already been prepared for this as she immediately stood and then came over to the allies, waiting for them to stand and brush themselves down before escorting them all away out of hearing range.

As the rest left, Maeve tried to stay behind, curled up on the cloak and feigning sleep, but Sìle knelt down to her and spoke gently. "And you can go along with the others as well," she said. "If you were to be invited to listen in on what we have to say, we would have done it." Haughtily Maeve stood and stretched herself in a leisurely fashion before trotting after her mistress.

Even I can see that the animal is trying to pretend that it is all a mistake and her intentions have been totally misunderstood.

Having moved the group well away from the village to a small patch of grass beside the path with a small shed, a tree and a bench, their escort produced some baskets of food and drink from inside the building and handed them around.

"You will wait here, please," she said. "We will call you when we are ready."

She now just leaves us here to wait while she returns to where the others are already having their discussion. Although we can all see that a quite animated conversation is going on in the village, even Astrid, who has the best hearing among us, no matter how much she strains her ears, and however quiet we all stay, cannot hear a single word of what is being said.

All that we can see are impassioned arguments as one person after another stands and makes short speeches or else fires questions at different people before getting brief replies back. Eventually, when they seem to have exhausted all of their arguments, Sìle again stands. She must have summed everything up, as she made a last speech and then possibly called for a vote. It is hard to tell.

Theodora
several hours later

It took some time before the Mice and the Bear Folk were all brought back into the village. Sìle was standing up waiting for them. The other villagers stood in a crescent behind her. "We have decided that the time has come for us to tell you all about ourselves," she said. *That is a start, at least.*

"This is a big decision for us, the largest we have made since we hid ourselves away. No one outside of this village has learnt any of this in the two Ages that have passed since we set ourselves aside, and we have used our spells to try and remove any knowledge of our existence from the world outside. We have always thought that we were alone in the world, in many ways, but it seems that we were wrong and this is not the case at all."

I am betting that they are no more alone than the Bear Folk, or Simeon's people, and them I want to know more about as well.

"When we hid ourselves away and first cast our spells, it was partly because the Enemies were moving to Arnflorst and partly because we believed, from what we saw to be happening around us, that we would be persecuted by the rest of the people on this world. Now we have seen two examples of others like us with you... But I get ahead of myself." She stopped and waved her hand out over the assembled villagers.

"We are all skin-changers on No h-Eilean Samhradh and we are all also, I suppose, what you would call shamen. Each of us is a priest or priestess of our element, which is either Air or Water, depending on the person. None of us cling to either Fire or Earth. Unlike what happens with the short-lived, which of these two elements we will adhere to has nothing at all to do with the time of our birth." *That is just as Christopher, or Ia, their Element is determined by their Faith, not their time of birth.*

"We have lived here on this island since long before the Enemy—those who you call the Adversaries—moved to the island beside us. For various reasons we were already hidden then, with far weaker spells that were not as...*complete*, and they still did not see us as their magic was not very strong then. They mostly used other means to look around and, as you have already realised and told us in your story, mere machines are very weak in the face of strong magic." *That is true.*

"Since then we have stayed hidden to most and, if we have been seen, it is as a seal or as a spirit. We talk openly only with the Inuit, but then their religion leads them to expect to see talking seals. We have been talking to them for so long that we are a part of their very folklore and most of what we know about the world we get from them."

"We have kept that contact so that we do not get completely cut off. We heard the story of Mathanharfead, for instance." *She is looking hard at Astrid, and the girl reacted when the words were translated. Why?* "I suppose that the Bear Folk set themselves aside in a similar fashion to us, but they lack our skill at hiding and making people forget." *Calgacus can be seen nodding at this.*

"If we can help you destroy our Enemy, we will do what little we can. It is part of our nature that we need to keep our island safe before all else. To this end we specialise in defence, distraction and controlling the weather, not in attack, and so most of us will be best staying here in case the Enemy strike out at us." *Not the help I was hoping for, then.*

"Your homes may be a very long way from where we are here near the centre of their power, and yet they still sent a Dragon against you. There are three of those that live near to us and the great wyrms, alone of all the creatures of the world that we know about, would possibly be able to find us through all of our enchantments if they were motivated to. We are not sure how they do it, but the Enemies are very capable of giving them that motivation."

Again she stopped and looked at her people. "Although we can destroy ships by various means, we have little in the way of the magic you use in land battles. Whether you know it or not, what you really need us for is to get you safely to their island. It is our role to be your guides and not to fight alongside you, which from what you have said of battles, we think we would be very poor at anyway, as we have no skill at arms, either." *Getting there safe is very good.*

"It has puzzled us for some time as to what they are, but the Enemy has for the last year been putting things to float in the water that they have anchored to the ground under the sea so that they sway around like sea-tulips in the currents. We neither know what they are, nor what they do, and our divinations tell us very little about them." *I don't even know what a sea-tulip is.*

"We have been able to find that they are not magic, and we are fairly certain they will do evil and kill somehow if they are touched. We have been worried about getting too close to them and that is hard, anyway, as anyone coming close begins to hear painful noises in their head and their joints begin to ache. We have decided that not only could getting too close to them do us harm, but it could also reveal our existence."

I will bet anything that these are more of those machines that Ariadne is so fond of. I wonder what they do. Theodora nodded to show she understood. Sìle continued after she saw this: "We will, however, send people to go with you. The Enemy have left a safe path for their friends to travel through. It will be our job to guide you past these...*things* to a safe landing on their island and, when you hopefully finish and win, to guide you back out." *That sounds excellent, really.*

"We have tried and we cannot find these things with magic, and so I doubt that you would be able to either. We can only see them with our eyes and with the feel that you get from them, and they lie just below the water so you will not see them with your eyes from above the surface. What is more, if you can keep your ships close to each other, the Enemy may not see you at all until after you have landed." *That is sounding better and better, then.*

"After having heard your story, what we will do and not do may sound like cowardice to you but remember that we have chosen to cut ourselves off from the world. We thought that this would be for all time. What we have decided to do for you now overturns our customs of two Ages. We can do no more than this until they are defeated and the threat of the Dragons is removed."

Again she looks around her people as if to see if she still has their support. "Whatever you say and however you ask, the continued existence of our people must take priority with us as it has for millennia. If you lose in the coming battle you will also lose all knowledge of us. You cannot reveal what you do not know."

Although the power of such a forgetting made them both very nervous, it took only a glance at each other before the Princesses were quick to agree to what was proposed and, after discussing the practicalities, people began to move into the building that had been put aside for them for the rest of the night. The Bear Folk slept outside. "It will not rain tonight," said Sìle, "and you need to tell us what weather you want for the attack."

I must have looked a little surprised. Sìle continued, addressing her: "We have control over the weather for this area here, and over the surrounding seas, if we choose to exert ourselves. Such control could perhaps lead to us being found, and so we only do it rarely, but this is one time when we are sure that it must be done." Theodora looked at her husband. *That is up to her.*

"We did not know anything about that unnatural storm that the Enemy raised until it was too late, but somehow you sent it back to them anyway and we then had to work hard to protect ourselves as well. Your counterstroke was a disaster for the Enemy. We went into the water when we saw what was happening and now we do not think that they have any ships at all on their island that have been left whole as a result of it." *That is good. I'd hoped it would do that, but I only hoped.*

"They may have other ships in other places, but certainly not here and now. Anyone at sea when the storm returned was almost certainly drowned. They lost many very large ships." *I will leave my husband discussing what weather is needed. We need at least some sleep. It is likely that the battle will mean a very long day for us. Tomorrow is nearly here and we will only get a few hours' sleep tonight at the very best.*

Chapter XXII

Gamil the Predestinator
2nd Moldin, the Year 546,985

Seated at her desk and looking almost straight down through the sensors on the station, ones that worked on mechanics rather than magic, Gamil sighed. *You'd think I would be able to look down through the sky and see what is happening now. There is a sensor platform nearly directly overhead to the island and quite near the main space station of the Daveen, despite their many repeated attempts to make sure that it has an accident.*

Sometimes in the past they have even succeeded in that, and the sensors, and sometimes even the platform itself, have had to be replaced, but currently I have a well-defended wide suite of sensors there. Much good they do me. I wish, with all of the equipment there, that I could see what is happening on that island, but I cannot.

My researchers are even now following as many lines of enquiry as they can but everyone seems puzzled. Despite being in a geostationary orbit, with theoretically a direct view, my sensors may as well have been looking from the far side of the next planet for what they tell me, and it is currently nearly opposed in its orbit.

My people tell me that more research is needed on how the vision has been blurred so badly, but that does not help. At least I have been able to use our satellite to block communications between those on planet and those off planet. I have used that ability sparingly, and perhaps my opponents think that their occasional lapses in communication are accidental. I hope so.

I have been blocking since the storm was sent out, and they must realise by now that it is no longer an accident. At least, with the ban on landings that is currently in place, those who are on planet are ignorant of the force that is now approaching them, unless they pick it up using their own skill with magic. She smiled.

Like my people, though, I suspect that the Daveen, despite their greater magical ability, are still so reliant on technology that this is one of the many areas where they may be worse off than either of my pieces on Vhast, or even the Renegade. His complete abandonment of the technology of his people beyond, apparently, a certain amount of biological capability, seems to have worked well in the long term as a strategy.

At least I know a tiny amount about the people who live on this island. They are only accidentally picked up sometimes as they move to the water. We follow from there and I know little more about them than what we see then. It is little enough. Despite them being located where they are, I really had not counted on their involvement.

They hold themselves aloof from the world and I have, in fact, deliberately ignored them from all of my calculations for the whole of the last Age. I know that they have acted in the past to remove knowledge of their presence from the world and I expected them to keep on doing that. It seems that I was wrong to have taken this view.

I now have to wonder how my people decided to come here. Again I wish I could see everything that is happening, particularly those last two meetings in Wolfneck. My techs have been unable to give me a single usable word of them, although we caught some side chatter outside, but it mainly concerned chances of survival. It was nothing substantive.

I wonder if the islanders can counter the explosive mines that have been laid around the island. What effect will that have on the calculations? I hope that it will be positive as the die is now cast. I will be spending the night looking at that, and wondering what else the islanders can bring to the contest. I do not like unexpected surprises.

There is now no chance of the final battle being avoided; Armageddon, Gotterdammerung, Ragnarok, there were so many names for it in the legends of this world, and on others. It is interesting that the battle has not been cast in that sort of apocalyptic light by the actors I have chosen. They know these are mortal enemies they fight but, despite their power and although they often speak of them in religious terms of good and evil, they refuse to apotheosise them. The tools of their opponents may do so, indeed often do so, but my players do not.

I will have to think a lot more on that matter. Within their view of theology they seem to be very able to distinguish a spiritual enemy from one that is merely a physical threat. It does not matter how powerful or evil they are, there is a line that is drawn. I do not think that even different conceptions of what constitutes evil seems to matter to them.

With luck, it seems to be likely that the hardest part of our long work on Vhast has a chance to be over by tomorrow night. There are still so many different ways that it can all play out and it is hard, even for me, to calculate the fine detail—and I was the one who set it all in motion and have more information about the situation and the players than anyone else!

It has long been proven that the more people involved, and the less important they are individually, the easier the calculations over a particular event or series of events are. However, the reverse also applies. It is easy to work the maths, using semi-group theory, with a large and thus more predictable mass of people.

The more people there are, the more they conform to an ideal pattern and so they became more predictable. They become like a fluid in a container and subject to a set of behavioural laws. It becomes much harder to pin down details of the effect when there are small numbers of important and non-typical people. The ones I chose, and those that they have gathered to them are, fortunately or unfortunately, quite non-typical.

By definition they are outliers and outliers...well...by definition they are odd. Just as in physics, so it is in the social sciences: while the behaviour of the mass can be described with some certainty, there is just far too much uncertainty involved for a prediction with a single person for it to be useful in any way. Thus every calculation we have ever tried that involves the Renegade has always failed.

Although they are not supposed to, many of the junior people under me have run their own computations and are placing bets on what will happen next. I have deliberately chosen to ignore the breach of protocol and the broken rules that necessarily flow from these bets. After all, given the importance of these events and how long some of these people have been working here, you have to expect this to happen, and you need run no computations to come to that conclusion.

The computer usage that has been involved has already been marked down in my budget as essential staff training. She smiled. *I have seen how the betting lies, and the odds on different outcomes for some of the individuals. I wonder if I can use an intermediary to place a bet or two for me. I think that there will be some surprises in store for those that place wagers among my staff.*

Even though they have watched events unfold to this point, I think most of them are far too conservative in what they think might happen. We all came from a culture that has long used technology to travel between the stars and to perform work and even feed us. So, despite our experience with the long experiment that we are engaged in, we, like the Daveen, are all far too wedded to the supremacy of technology. My people cling to it fervently despite the evidence directly in front of them. I think I will have a dabble.

Chapter XXIII

Theodora
21st December, the sky is just showing light in the east

Those of us who had a short sleep in the village of Seòlaid are now awake and being given breakfast. It is not a breakfast that I am used to, but it is hearty at least. For a start, there is no Kaf and I need Kaf in the morning. Buttermilk and tea are not good enough. Some Kaf had better be waiting for us on the River Dragon *when we return.*

Now that we are done with eating, five naked Shaelkie, three men and two women, are accompanying us back to the water along with Sìle and four others who are dressed. They pay even less attention to being naked than we do to bare breasts at home. Sìle is clad the same as she was the previous day.

The five naked ones walked straight into the water, where they could be seen to be changing shape as they went. Soon five very large seals were playing around in water, greeting the seals on the rocks and being greeted by them in turn. As the Mice regained their saddles, the Shaelkie played for a while with the wild seals before each headed away to the ships.

Olympias

Well, that was something to see. Now we have a seal riding in the sea near the prow of each vessel, watching the wondering onlookers and their interpreter onboard. I am told that those of the north who live and work with the sea have legends that speak of the Shaelkie, but few think they will ever see them unless they are drowning and beyond hope in a gale.

Sile and the others have been brought to the various ships on saddles. It looks like Rani has Astrid going around the other ships with instructions. There is, even with the sky beginning to grow lighter in colour, a thick spring fog lying heavy over the ocean. So thick is it that the two ships waiting farthest offshore cannot be seen as more than vague shapes, even though I know where to look for them.

If you were not expecting them, your gaze may have passed straight over them. The first indication that we are underway would be when Astrid arrived to tell them. These fogs are not uncommon in northern waters in spring and summer when there is warm air flowing over a cold sea and should be no surprise to the Adversaries. However, apparently this one has been made for us.

The enemy watchers will scan the fog with magic, and hopefully fail to find anything, and then the fog will serve to physically hide us all from the shore of the Forbidden Isle. They might even be made complacent of attack by the thickness of it. Who would attack or move around in unknown waters in such conditions? Hopefully they will trust in their traps to warn them.

Sile herself, from the deck of the River Dragon, *will find out what is happening from the Shaelkie in front of us. She communicates with her own people in an odd, barking speech. She sounds a lot like a seal to me. It carries quite a long way, though. I can faintly hear those behind us as well. They will lead our ships to Arnflorst. Where needed, the Shaelkie in front of each ship can speak to the interpreter in their ship.*

The two drakkar pulled away from the beach as the other three vessels shipped their anchors. Gradually they formed up behind the *River Dragon* with the *Rongo* and the *Ofu* each towing one of the drakkar behind them. *Apparently, where we are going the channel will be too tight for the two smaller craft to tack and beat, and they will be too slow if they just row.*

Besides, if they do row then the rowers will be exhausted as they try to keep up. We have a fair distance to travel before we have a chance to fight. Arnflorst would be in sight from here, if the mist were not about us, but it would still be several hours of hard work at the oars with very heavily-laden and deep-running craft.

They will have to be towed towards their landing site as if they are just large longboats. They have, apparently, been told to keep their oars out to stop them getting too close to the larger ships and colliding. In the deep fog the riders on the saddles have to be kept very close to the ships as well, so that they do not get lost. It all goes to make every one of us quite nervous.

As they set out into the open ocean, the fog grew ever thicker around them. Soon the lookouts in the bow of each ship could barely see the windows or the sternpost of the vessel in front. Those who were stationed in the mastheads of the ships could see nothing but greyness and, on the larger ships, not even a hint of their own deck.

It is a captain's nightmare to trust another whom they do not know to take them through waters acknowledged to be very dangerous and where a slight error would mean death. The drakkar kept their oars ready to stop them running into the ship in front and to help with turns, and the others had sweeps out for the same purpose. All through the thick and clammy fog, the voices of the Shaelkie echoed eerily.

Gradually they crept over the sea in an ominous silence, the fog acting to muffle any noise they made. Stefan and Astrid flew up and down the line, giving instructions to those who would be landing and telling the soldiers to try and rest for a few hours, but while the experienced people might be able to sleep, it was certain that many others would not.

Long queues are starting to form to see priests of various faiths as people make themselves ready in other ways. The rising sun has become a ghostly orb visible through an almost opalescent grey curtain, and above us the fog has gradually lightened, not because it has begun to dissipate but because of the brightness of the morning.

Astrid had obtained a head binding from one of the other northern ships and she now donned it. It was made of fine, scraped mica bound in leather, and was worn over the eyes. She offered one to Olympias, who cautiously put it on. *Instead of making me blind, looking out through the thin rock I can see far more than I was able to before.*

The bindings make everything darker, but I can see clearly for over twice as far. I think that I will keep it off, though. I prefer to rely on my guide and what the green-light box is telling me. I cannot see the latter through the head binding. The magic of the green-light box sees far further than my eyes do in any case, although its magical circle can say nothing about what is happening close up to the ship.

"These glasses are a secret of the north," said Astrid. "We don't know how they work either, but it is not magic."

Instructions are being passed up to the sailors from the water and Sìle is calling them, pointing out new directions when they are needed. It is soon obvious that we are coming very close to the shore, according to the circles of the green-light box. It makes me nervous. I know nothing of the depth of the water here or about these strange objects that I have been told lie in it concealed and waiting for something to touch them.

I really do not like putting my life in someone else's hands like this. It is against my nature. I have to force myself to obey this strange woman who stands on the deck of my own ship and, using her, rely on the creature ahead of us that she talks to. I can only do that by thinking of them as if they are the pilot I would have assigned to me on entering the harbour in Ardlark. I do trust their directions.

Eventually, but still well before midday, Sìle gave Rani new instructions. "Send your saddles to the other ships," she said, "and tell them not to talk at all and to otherwise be as quiet as they can be. We are nearly up to their harbour, and we do not want to enter it. They may still have a watch at its entrance and we do not want to alert them, and we will be only a few filled hands of hands away from them."

It was not long after that she ordered Olympias to put the helm down hard and the column of ships gradually turned one by one to the starboard, so that they were now going widdershins around the island. They sailed on and Sìle kept correcting their course as they went around.

From the green-light box I can see that we are following the shoreline of Arnflorst closely as it curves around. We must be circling a cliff, as the box refuses to show any more than what must be, at most, a hand of filled hands away. Finally, Sìle brought the *River Dragon* to a halt and started to bring the other vessels beside it.

"Now is the time," she said, "for us to go to the small ships and to begin taking people to the beach. Ahead of us there is a cliff to climb, but your ships cannot be seen where they are from within their city and so should be safe from most direct magical attacks. We are now anchored where we need to be. We will let the fog start to burn away. Normally it would have done so before now, and they may be getting suspicious about it."

The allied ships exploded in a flurry of activity as the saddle riders carried instructions from the *River Dragon* to the other vessels. The drakkar, let loose from the ships that had towed them, surged forward under the power of their oars, racing each other to be the first to come to a rest with a crunching sound on the shingle beach.

In the rapidly clearing fog, I can see that the eager landing party are soon pulling the craft further out of the water. Their bow ropes are secured to rocks in case of waves, and the craft empty quickly. They will stay there now until the battle is over, one way or another. Their crew and passengers are soon forming a line as they pass up the steep obstacle that they have in front of them.

The Rangers of Wolfneck are already on top of the slope and are waving an all-clear to the slower and more encumbered people behind them before starting to run out into the clearing fog to explore the area over which we will soon fight.

Those of the Mice not docking the ship are quickly following Rani's directions. The saddle riders begin to carry the others to take up places on the cliff, a few chains high, which lies in front of us. It is more of a very steep and rocky slope with grassy patches than it is a real cliff, and it is easily climbable as we are now, but it would be nearly impossible if we were opposed at all. Archers on top would massacre climbers.

Defended, it would have been as hard to take as any castle wall, harder actually as no tower could be brought against it and it could not be broken down easily by an engine or even by magic, and the slope is not firm stone but you can see that it is generally small rocks and stones that slip and roll away from the feet of the climbers.

Olympias brought the *River Dragon* as close as she could to the shore, carefully sounding the depth of the water as they went. Finding enough for her purposes, she instructed two saddles to take ropes ashore while another two took anchors out from the bow and stern of the ship and lowered them. These were then brought taut to ensure that the ship would not drift around.

Now we can use the long magical carpet to get the passengers off the ship quickly. Soon we have them filing nervously over it as they walk in the air. Some are peering over the sides down at the water even as they walk on a layer of woven cloth above it.

Although the two Sea Nomad ships started landing people in small craft immediately they were still, once we are empty of our own passengers I will get first the Rongo *and then the* Ofu *brought alongside us. They can use the* River Dragon *as if it were a pier. It will be safer and far quicker than just using small boats.*

Soon, all those who are going to be taking part in this phase of the battle, including Ariadne and her rock-thrower, are being ferried over to the clifftop by the Mice. She has also taken one of the light throwers up with her as well. Despite the risk, she will set them up beside each other so she can go from one to the other as she needs. I still have the other here to defend the ships if necessary .

Ariadne

I *have my husband with me already, and he has co-opted both Aziz and Deniz-kartal. While at least four Humans are needed for the ballista, two experienced Hobs and a Boyuk-Kharl can handle it easily. I have Krukurb starting to bring ammunition up to us as the others build more stable platforms and work on improving the position for our weapons.*

They are already filling our gabions, the wicker baskets which we carry around. When we have them filled, they will provide us with some cover from view and a little protection from more physical threats. Despite the chill morning, all four were soon sweating with the exertion. *As we work, the sun burns off the early fog, revealing all around us the land will be fighting over.*

Most of the saddles and the second carpet are bringing people up the slope to the clifftop. The saddles can only manage to carry one extra person on each trip, and generally not a large one. However, using the saddles avoids the scrapes and cuts that come from making the climb, which the priests are running around fixing with salves.

Soon we will be ready for the enemy to find us.

Chapter XXIV

Rani
21st December, it is still mid-morning

We seem to be on the edge of a sort of very large, shallow dish in the ground a couple of sea miles across. Ahead of where we are setting up, the land slopes slowly downwards. We have trudged across a pasture of grasses and some small bushes to reach this spot, but the rim is covered in those same bushes, so the pasture may have been cleared of them and the grass encouraged to grow.

Gradually, in the middle distance, several hands of hands away, some poor-looking fields are becoming visible through the damp, clearing fog. The fields would be at their best in the early spring, but it still looks to be fairly sparse growth, and certainly would not support many people.

The island is not a big one anyway, and if the few other fields that are most likely around are just like this, then huge amounts of food would need to be brought into the island if there is to be a large force garrisoned here for any length of time. Rani looked out at what was revealed. *Even I can see the paucity of the land. Perhaps we could just put everyone back on the ships and blockade our enemy until they starve.*

No, that would only destroy this one army of the Adversaries. Just as I was told happened when all of this started on the plains, when the Khitan had Dharmal supposedly trapped, the leaders would still be able to flee elsewhere and leave their minions behind to die. No, it has to be brought to a head here and now.

I have some of our mages attached to units. These casters are the ones who are most likely to be moving around during the battle. Most of them are lesser mages and apprentices and they are the ones who will be most relying on wands for offence. They will use their own mana for the defence of the soldiers they are with, something that soldiers facing magic are always glad to see.

The stronger mages are setting up patterns and making preparations behind the spears and above them. I am nervous about not casting anything offensive myself, but at least I have Justin Speller and many other competent casters with us, and Goditha and several of the other Mice are growing stronger and are now capable of bringing their own castings to the battle.

The prophecy about me holding my fire plays on me. I suppose that it is supposed to. I have thought about the spell that Astrid convinced me to develop. If my casting is to be needed, given what the prophecies said, I am becoming more and more certain that this enchantment is the one I will employ. She made sure that everything was at hand and laid out for her to use it if it did turn out to be needed.

In the meantime, I have given all of the talkers out and hopefully I will be able to co-ordinate the different parts of our force with them. They may enable us to do what we want to do. Until I am needed to cast my one spell, I will not be able to fight at all. I will be taking the role of being the general of our forces.

To think, I once had the temerity to complain to myself that Sharan had not given me enough work in this sort of role. Now I look out at the people ahead of me and those still coming up from the ships behind us, as they settle into place, cursing, joking and praying; all of them are waiting for my orders to be issued, orders which will send them out to kill and to die. Suddenly, within her soul, she yearned for the simplicity of that time that seemed so long ago.

Astrid

I have gathered my axe-wielders from the battle on Skrice and Stefan has drawn together his spears. I will, no doubt, have some more large opponents to look after and Stefan and his people will bear the brunt of their foot. Eleanor has again taken the archers, but she now has to convince the Bear Folk archers, those who cannot change their skins, that they should not just follow the rest of their people.

Astrid and Stefan, who happened to be near each other when she had one particularly loud altercation with one who spoke Hindi, smiled at each other. *It is the lead up to the battle along the coast all over again. At least we now have some of the people who were there with us again, as does Eleanor, and at least those people know what to do without having to be told too much.*

Rani

*G*raddually the fog is finally clearing and, a bit over a hand of filled hands *of paces away a partly ruined city is slowly becoming visible. It is out of range of most of our weapons, but still we will wait. Above us a fine blue sky is gradually revealing itself. I can hear some starting to complain about the sun and the heat.* Soon Rani had water-bearers moving around their forces with water bougets in yokes around their neck.

I wonder if we should take advantage of our unexpected arrival to attack them in the city. We would have surprise on our side. She mulled the idea over. *No, it is a bad idea that just sounds good. Here we can see the battlefield and we have the high ground. If we go in there we would be fighting on unfamiliar ground and without support.*

The advantage would lie entirely with our enemy, who undoubtedly would have strong-points, traps and other advantages. If we go in, not only would we be attacking in staggered bunches as people arrived up the cliff, but also each of our attacking groups could be picked off one after the other as they wander around trying to find a target to hit in unknown terrain where they could easily be trapped. It is better to wait out here, close to our ships, and to see if our enemy emerge before we commit to doing anything rash like that.

Admittedly, where we are gathered out in the open, our enemy might try to cast a single large spell that will cover all of the allies in a giant explosion or a miasma of death, but my wife is ready for that with a counter-spell and supplies of Sleepwell in case a second or even more are needed.

She has ready the original to the enchantment that she had adapted to turn the storm-casting back on the island. Any attempt to destroy us in a single spell could well be fatal to the caster and, if we failed in the storm spell, our enemy would probably be well aware of that possibility. As for lesser spells, most of our mages are tasked to defend rather than attack. Usually this is the option that places less strain on the caster and so is better suited to weaker mages.

In the meantime we all wait: resting, chatting and, in some cases among the men and women of the north, even catching up for the first time since the campaign against the Brotherhood. I see that many are taking a chance to have something to eat, even. All that is left of the fog are a few last wisps that are rapidly disappearing. We just keep up a relative silence.

Nothing has taught me what to do with the Bear Folk. The archers were easy, but those that can change will only fight in their bear form and it is hard to fit them into a conventional battle. Perhaps I can use them in a role as an ambushing force. I will send them, with many of the Mice flying low above them on saddles, to swing around to the right. It is now clear that the rim runs from their cliff in a broad sweep right around the city.

Far to the right is a long patch of broken rock, lying there as if, at some time long ago, a huge spire of rock had tumbled down the slope. It now lies as a long field of large, broken boulders interspersed with brambles that will both hide movement and at the same time hinder it. In many ways it will provide a border to the battlefield.

A wise commander takes every advantage of the terrain available. If we can attack from that concealed flank, it could be useful for surprise as much as anything else, and even a small force appearing unexpectedly could startle the enemy and cause them to panic. That is where the Bears and the Mice will lie in wait. They will take no part in the battle until they are called for. The Bears will attack on the ground and the Mice will use their archery to cover them.

As for the Sea Nomads, they rarely fight and have never done so on land or on such a large scale. They have their weapons, but they only use them against the occasional pirate, and seaboard battles tend to either involve magic, and sometimes artillery, or else are short-range and hand-to-hand affairs with no advance strategy other than boarding a vessel and overwhelming crew and militia. They are not sure what to do in this battle.

Rani assigned them to Eleanor, who kept them behind everyone else to protect the archers and to act as a reserve. In the meantime, as they waited, a large number of oversized and unarmoured men and women were waiting, patiently seated on the ground with a collection of weapons, some of which no one had ever seen before, and which varied from spears and lances to green stone axes to long and slightly curved swords more than the height of a man.

I can see that Eleanor has already pulled from their ranks their few archers and slingers and, despite their displeasure at such a move, has made them stand with her other missile troops.

Marking the left side beyond our spears are some bushes. I can conceal some others in there. I think that is the place of the Dwarves. They will have no one standing to fight in front of their crossbows with their low trajectory and, being armoured, they will serve to anchor the line at that end.

At least the slingers seem satisfied here. Probably for the first time in their lives, those from the Sea Nomads have all the rocks they could want, and are building up piles of missiles—piles that are surely larger than they could conceivably need, but that doesn't stop the slingers from adding more before the battle begins.

Chapter XXV

Theodora
21st December, it is around midday

*I*t is obvious that we have finally been noticed by those in the city. Everyone watched as a small group of Kharl came out of the city and began to cast around as if they were looking for something. *They are of a race I have never seen, or even heard of, before. They have skin so dark a green as to be almost black. Their faces most closely resemble very short-furred bears.*

They all wear broad-brimmed, flat conical straw hats as if a direct exposure to even this pale sun will hurt their eyes. They have come out casting around among the ruins on the fringe of the city as if they have lost something or are looking for the burrows of some rodent.

Suddenly, almost by accident, one of the searchers looked up and saw the army arrayed along the top of the slope only a hand of filled hands away. He did a double take and looked hard again before shouting in alarm, something that was too faint to be heard by the allies as more than a squeak. He then pointed up the slope.

The others looked up and obviously saw what he had seen as well. A variety of cries erupted and suddenly they went back a little way, and all quickly dived behind rocks. Eventually, first one and then another reappeared briefly. Among the assembled allies, an occasional laugh could be heard. *Rather than being a fearsome threat, our first encounter with the troops of the Adversary has a humorous cast with their diving for cover and then bobbing up and down.*

More than anything else, they look just like a pack of meerkats with hats, all curious to see if someone is approaching their nest and nervous that something actually is.

Eventually, one of them waved a command and two of the little Kharl ran back towards the ruined city, occasionally stumbling over obstacles or maybe over their own feet as they glanced back to confirm that the enemy troops weren't a mirage.

Each time they fall, a wave of laughter erupts among the allies. The ones that are left behind continue their bobbing up and down, even though no one shoots at them or moves towards them.

Gradually other people started to appear from the city. Some ran as small, disorganised and scattered groups, others moving as a solid block and some even marching as already-formed units. *Some of the enemy soldiers who are appearing are more familiar Isci-kharl and Kichic-kharl, and there is a pair of Insak-div. A few even appear to be Sea Nomads, while many of the others are from The Land, Freeholders or perhaps even from the New Found Land.*

Astrid tells me that there are even some tribesmen from the frozen north dressed in their hide and fur-lined garments, unlaced in the unaccustomed warmth and with hoods thrown back. She says that they may only have their usual bone-tipped spears that will be useless against any armour stronger than light leathers.

As well as the familiar, there were many races that no one had seen before. There were many who had yellowish-bronze skin and who wore lamellar armour. They moved in large blocks made up of straight lines of men.

Some had great banners attached to their backs on poles. The banners had no devices or badges, but were a solid colour: red, green, white or blue, which were covered in short lines of white or black, drawn in a way that suggested that they may have been writing. As well as the large banners, one person in each row had a smaller banner attached to their back.

Some of those who appeared were obviously officers. Their arrival was obvious, as they very quickly started to organise the army that was assembling. Looking through a telescope, Theodora examined them. *Several of those officers are very tall and thin, pale-skinned people who are wearing glistening bronze armour. It seems that some races never learn. The Eldar are back again and, as usual, have chosen the side of the Adversary*

Soon they could see, running out from in front of the assemblage as if they were scouts, a hand of strange-looking men, each wearing only a rope around his middle with a small, inadequate tassel hanging from it at the front. *These men are dark-skinned, almost black, and, through my telescope I can see that they have black woolly hair and bodies that are covered in cicatrices.*

They have stern and hard bearded faces and carry stone-headed spears and wooden clubs, some sort of flat bent sticks and long, narrow wooden shields. They are looking hard at the ground as they run and begin calling to each other. They split into two groups and run along the front of their force and up the slope, now well within range of our archers.

They hardly glance at us as they move, bravely doing what they are supposed to and ignoring the danger. Rani has ordered us to hold our fire, despite the temptation. It is obvious that these men, heedless of the threat to them, have been told to check to see if any of us arrayed on the clifftop have come down into the city or have laid any traps.

Eventually their two groups reached the ends of their army and stopped and waved at each other. They seemed to have satisfied themselves that no one had moved down into the city, and then they quickly ran back down the slope over the rocky ground and returned to the ranks.

With almost their whole army drawn up, there was a last set of arrivals. *A large group of lizard-like creatures have appeared to fill a space that seems to have been left for them in the centre of the line. They walk on two legs but lean forward, using their tails to balance themselves.*

About half of the lizards are Human-sized, but most of the rest are smaller even than Kichic-kharl and look somewhat like heavier built Pack-hunters with hands that can hold weapons. However, some of the lizards are big, bigger even than the Insak-div and looking more like Thunder Lizards, that have both shoulders and real arms.

These giants glare sidewise at the two Insak-div stationed beside them, and it is obvious that the Insak-div are looking back. It seems to me that the two small groups of colossi are paying little attention to our army and are really looking for an excuse, any excuse, to attack each other.

All of these new arrivals seem to also really be lizards, but they brandish weapons and wear armour and some hold banners as if they are people. The little ones even have bows, quivers of bolts on their backs, and some carry spears as well. The next size up have swords or axes and round shields, and the big ones have the same, but their one-handed swords are at least as big as a normal two-handed blade would be or, indeed, even bigger. There are four of the big ones.

The medium-sized ones all wear fantastical-looking helms that look like lizard grotesquerie. A group of the medium-sized lizards in the centre of the others carries a small platform on their shoulders bearing a slightly larger, and far fatter, version of the lizard shape on a bench-like stool that is almost a throne.

Beside him is one of the small ones and behind him on the platform is a large box. The seated lizard is covered in drapes of gold and jewels, including a collar much like mine. He wears a high, fan-shaped and elaborately decorated headpiece. In one hand he has a jewelled staff surmounted by a crystal ball. He will be a mage then, as well as their leader.

Banners covered in squarish pictoglyphs that look like faces, as well as swirls and strokes, rise from the rear of the platform. The first sign of their appearance had been the sound of their approach. As they moved, the lizards kept up a deep-throated, but still sibilant-sounding chant. It changed once they stopped, but now they were hitting their shields with their weapons in time with the beat in an obvious attempt to intimidate.

Suddenly, from behind the allied units of spears and bows, the Sea Nomads started to emerge into the gaps between, and once they were there they began their own chant and a war dance. *It is similar to the one that we saw when we arrived on Tabuaeran, but there is no mistaking the difference between the two. This dance is definitely one of war. It is full of challenge and menace.*

The allied forces looked at their own war dancers and at the performance from below. *There seems to be a general agreement that our people are far more impressive as they not only chant, but can dance as well. It looks like there are definitely some Sea Nomads among our opponents as they soon begin their own dance, but they lack the numbers to make it as convincing as the dance that our people are doing.*

Astrid

*W*hile the dancing is going on, I get the chance to move my axe-wielders around, Humans and Bear Folk both. My brothers trail behind me along with my Omáda of Kharl.* As she went she spread the same message as she reformed them from four into six wedges: "We are to take the big ones. Kill the others only if they come too close to you. Do not lose sight of our job. There is one wedge for each of the six. Circle and engage them and pull back one by one." *I wonder if they will actually follow my instructions.*

"Do not try and be foolishly brave. Do not close with them unless they are blinded or disabled or you are behind them, or you will die. If your giant is killed, join the next wedge. It will be my job to kill them once you hold them." Her face took on a savage smile as she turned and looked at their opponents.

"Remember that I have done this before and most of you have not. Remember also that we don't have to survive, we just have to outlast them." She turned to her Omáda of Kichic-kharl. "In particular, you will not get in my way. You are all archers, you should help the injured get clear and hold away from the rest of us and always aim for the eyes and the head of the giants." She looked hard at them.

"At all cost you are to avoid hand-to-hand combat. You are too small and frail for that. However, anything that can be done to slow those giants down and keep them off balance is good. Your arrows, or indeed any arrow except one that explodes with force, would likely do little to any of the giants if they hit them in the body, but it generally only takes one shaft in the eye to blind any creature, and that will change the odds greatly." *These lizard creatures are even larger and stronger-looking than an Insak-div, and attacking them is going to be an unknown task.*

Rani

I am getting more and more worried. Unless those ones in the bronze armour are them—there are too many of them for that to be right—there is, as yet, no sign of the Adversaries themselves, and their army shows no signs of advancing into battle. They look as if they are waiting for a spell or for something else to happen, or even for us to come against them.

I have kept a rough count and our people are not just outnumbered by those arrayed against us: there are at least twice and perhaps even three times as many of our enemy as there are on our side. If we have to attack now it will be suicidal. If it settles down to become a waiting game, then eventually we will have to advance to force an engagement and the longer we wait the more prepared the Adversaries will be.

We cannot just get back onto the ships and leave. It will be a problem for us if we have to advance as we will lose our slight advantage of elevation. Our owning the high ground is our sole apparent advantage and can act a little to counteract the numbers stacked up against us. It looks like once again the cards will be right in what they presaged. This will indeed be a hard trial for our people.

She briefly wondered why the Adversaries had not used this huge force to invade The Land and then realised a possible reason why. *They have been gathering forces from all over Vhast and they probably all have their own ships. They were only waiting for the* Meander Rose *and the* Dragon of the Seas *to return and join them.*

Once they have a supply of victims ready to sacrifice as they need, it would only take three or so trips of those larger vessels, and presumably what small craft they have, to shift this whole body of troops across to the mainland. It would be crowded on board, but Wolfneck lies only a day away to the south if they want to sail hard, and once they land safely there they could quickly gobble up the villages of the north one by one.

I realise what we have to do now. She told her wife to move beside Ariadne, with a kiss and an instruction to be ready with counter-spells. *From the look of it, apart from the slope and the hidden riders, the sole advantage we have is in having the only artillery on the battlefield. Even with as few pieces as we have, our enemy has none, and what we have can reach out and hit anything that we can now see. It is time to use it.*

What is about to happen should excite a swift response from the casters on the other side as they are forced to respond. Rani used the talker to give instructions to Ariadne. "They are not moving," she said. "They are content to just wait for us to attack them. We need for them not to think that clearly. I would like you to see what you can do to stir them up and get them to come forward, please."

Chapter XXVI

Ariadne
21st December, it is around midday

The Insakharl took a last look around the field through her telescope as she considered the problem. *I can use both of my weapons at once: the ballistae will start out aiming at one of the giants and the more precise light thrower at one of the pale ones in the bronze-looking armour. There is one I have marked as a likely Strategos from the way he gives orders and is so very quickly obeyed.*

The ballista will take longer for its shot to arrive and so it will fire on my call, and then I will use the other. Having made her decision, she quickly gave her instructions to the men and moved to her place. *If my first shots work, they will provoke a fast reaction from them. Everything is now waiting for my word.*

It is time to start. "Fire," she called... *One...two...* She pulled the trigger. *I have it correct.* She didn't wait to look at the result of the ballista shot. She had carved her target in twain and she sought the next one she had marked out. *He is already moving. I missed him.* She succeeded in carving a swathe through some of the other pale ones around him and a banner fell.

Again she fired and again and again. Each time she killed some of their opponents, but it was not until the fifth shot that she got the one she was after. Only now did she look at the general effect. *Where are the next targets to be? One of the giant lizards is down and the ballista is getting nearly ready to fire again.*

Someone on their side must have realised that the advantage has just changed over to us. Standing still will lose them all of their officers. Someone must have started giving orders on the other side. The whole line has slowly lurched into motion. The Princess is starting to cast something from where she stands ahead of and below me.

A fireball erupted from the other side and flew towards the artillery. It came within a few filled hands of them but Theodora held her hand up. The fireball stopped, hovering in the air; she flicked her wrist as if cuffing something, and the morass of flaming death reversed its trajectory to return to the enemy. *I like that. They won't.*

The first fireball had been closely followed by two others. Theodora now raised two hands, did the same, and they also flew back; the second had been only ten paces away when it halted mid-air. *That was close…and terrifying.* The first then hit back near where it had come from, and this was followed by the other two. Huge explosions marked their arrival.

If the enemy had co-ordinated better and launched them all at once, it is likely that Theodora would not have been able to handle all three, and it is most likely that we would all have died as a result. Now the enemy have some mages who are at least hurt and may already need major healing.

There is nothing I can do about spells. I will leave our magical defence up to mages. I will return to finding officers and banners…and mages. Killing mages now seems a very good idea. The second shot of the ballista slammed straight into a phalanx of those warriors in the lamellar with the big banners.

Ariadne only noticed that as she was knocking out the banners at the same time. *The soldiers seem more concerned with their banners than the loss of their people and, once they have the banners raised again, continue to advance solidly; they just close ranks over their dead. They have barely paused in their steady march up the slope and have started a chant of some sort. I will tackle easier prey.* She called out the same to the men.

Rani

*M*ore spells are coming in towards us. This time they are better cast, sent at the same time and aimed at different areas. Theodora stops one and sends it back and Justin, using a different spell, sends another spinning away in a high arc that comes to earth almost at the rear of their opponents, but the third has impacted squarely on one of Astrid's groups of axemen.

The priests, some of whom are using the carpets for mobility, are quickly there, but there are twenty men laid low in that explosion. I doubt that any will be back in the battle. I hope Astrid realises that she has lost them.

Rani looked at those spells. *I can guess how much it took to throw such powerful blasts at that range. Surely the enemy casters are now overdrawn and will be using mana from storage only. Unfortunately, they could have lots of stored mana and, while it becomes harder and harder to use it, and indeed more dangerous as you do, it can still be used.*

When your life is on the line, you take chances that you would not consider if you were in the safety of your house on a Holy Day. Of course they could be using Sleepwell, but many refuse to touch such things as they fear the madness of addiction even more than they fear dying. Our casters are working their spells at a far closer range and defence is easier than attack, but soon they will be using up stored mana as well. At least the enemy are getting closer.

Eleanor

*I*learnt things from One-Tree Hill. Our Mice, those that are on foot, and who can use them, can now start using the flight arrows of the Khitan. I have been working on this at home in the valley. Despite having to make the parts for the arrow rest, so that they can be used with the longer foot bows, we are now sending the tiny darts well beyond the range that anything else can fire except artillery.

If she had taken the time to look she would have seen the occasional annoying strike of those small shafts causing a person to fall or drop a weapon. *As a weapon, and with so few of them, they are of little value on their own but, as had been shown with the Brotherhood, they are annoying and sapping to the morale of those they are used on.*

What is worse is that they are so small they are hard for people to see and to ward off with a shield. It helps that some of the small shafts have been enchanted and their landing is marked by little puffs of fire or the crack of small bolts of lightning and the occasional scream. Those hits are more than just a little annoying, and anyone hit by one of those is usually felled or at least drops back.

Rani

*S*ome of the enemy units have battle chants and these are starting to be clearly heard, even if the words are not understandable. The enemy are moving closer, trampling over their own fields as they come. Of the allies, only the Sea Nomads have anything like a war cry, and although they have now obeyed orders and moved back to their original positions, they do at least keep up their chants.

Now, on both sides as the range comes closer, staff slings begin to come into play. We attackers on the heights have more staff slings than the defenders *below us, and we have a more stable place to fire from, not having to advance. We also have the greater elevation and so can hit further out, but still here and there a strike from a bullet or a stone means that one of us will not be going home.* One fell out of the air short of Rani. *It seems I should be glad that I am wearing my helmet with its enchantments to protect me.*

The heavy lead or stone shot of a staff sling striking from that range is almost always fatal, and at the very least it breaks a limb and, with a jagged rock, sometimes severs it. As well, firing into packed bodies of troops almost always means that a shot will hit something. It will not be long before the normal bows come into play. Still it is the case that attacking spells come from the forces of the Adversaries and none, except defensive ones, come from us.

The rows of allied spears still stand, waiting and looking nervously at those advancing towards them. Most of my people are not really soldiers. They are really only farmers or tradesmen. It is obvious from the way they are dressed and armoured, from the way they move together as units, and so quickly obey orders, that the bulk of the people coming towards us up the slope are actually permanent, trained soldiers.

My farmers will be facing professionals. As we foresaw, it would be a fell encounter indeed. At least most of them now have the experience of facing the charge of Brotherhood chariots to draw upon. It is a different type of battle they are in now, but at least it gives them some measure of confidence in themselves and, more importantly, in the people who are around them and leading them.

Ariadne

I am pleased. She had noticed where one of the spells had come from. *The casters there may have eliminated a second of Astrid's axe groups, but they won't do it again.* She had used the light- thrower and had the men follow up, and put an enchanted ball into the area as well. *From the sudden lessening of spells, it seems we may have taken out more than one mage, most likely at least three or four of them.*

We need to try and repeat that. She started actively seeking out mages with the two weapons in a combined attack. *Our targets can only heal themselves a limited number of times. From what I have heard my Princess say, trying to cast when exhausted is dodgy in the first place. Let us make it more so.*

I know that healing—from a miracle, a spell or a potion or berries—may leave you whole, but it also leaves you very exhausted for a time, and these mages are probably overdrawn on their accounts anyway. Even if we do not kill them, if we can keep them tired, anything that they try to do will make it more dangerous for them to cast.

After a few more successes it seemed the enemy mages had either run out of mana, were all dead, or had just stopped casting. *I suppose that exactly which does not matter. What is important is the fact that they have stopped casting and I can return to looking for officers. That worked at One-Tree Hill.*

Astrid

*"D*amnation. Saint Kessog. I need your aid here." *Someone on the other side must have seen me re-organise the axes and worked out why. Now I have lost another group of my axemen to a mage.* Astrid turned and called instructions to her brothers, who were standing behind her as a part of a wedge, and pointed at their target.

They now have to deal with one of the advancing Insak-div all on their own. I thought it could happen at some stage, but not necessarily this early in the battle. They did so before in the battle at Skrice; now they will have to do it again.

Eleanor

*T*heir crossbowmen have been firing, now my archers can join the slingers *in firing back.* A smallish cloud of a hundred shafts flew, she called again and a second hundred went, and then a third, and the last archers fired and the first were soon ready to pull again. *We are slightly uphill of the enemy and have, mainly, stronger bows.*

This gives us slight advantage in range over their bowmen, or whatever those lizards are. They have started to fall to our volleys, before their archers can even begin shooting. Being on the move they can fire less often, as well. An archer on foot has to stop to shoot and there are no horse archers among the enemy who can shoot while they allow their mounts to move them.

She looked around. *In fact there were very few enemy cavalry at all; what is there looks like Freeholders who are staying with the foot crossbows. That helps even more.* Eleanor's people kept up an almost continuous rain of shafts down on their opponents. Soon there were very few enemy archers left and the archers turned with impunity on the advancing foot.

Rani

Gradually, as a result of the missile fire and along with Ariadne's efforts, the forces are starting to get a bit more even in their numbers, but it is taking a long while and there are still nearly twice as many of the enemy, and many of them are far better armoured than anyone up here except the small group of Basilica Anthropoi in front of me who are currently using their bows.

Soon the forces will be engaged hand to hand and that advantage in numbers will really begin to count. Already, as the ranges close, lesser mages have now moved into action. The enemy seem to have a lot of them. They are mainly using wands at present, but some are beginning to cast spells and Ariadne again is changing her targets to account for them. A lot aim towards her, and my wife is busy.

Goditha, wearing armour and using a shield against incoming arrows, is standing near the front ranks at one end of a unit of spears. She may look like a spearman, but she is now preparing to cast and she has slipped it around on its strap so that it hangs on her back. I know what the woman wants to do, and I have been unable to convince her to do otherwise.

Our mason has insisted that she is now strong enough to take part in a battle in her own right as a mage. Parminder did not seem to be so sure of this, and now it is my turn to hope that she will be safe. The oncoming lines of those strange men with their lamellar armour and long pole weapons are getting very near Stefan's spears and have already broken into a determined charge uphill.

She would have needed to use a lot of stored power, but Goditha has finally finished her cast. I cannot see the ground in front of the charge, but I can hear screams and cries in a language I do not know, and a huge section of the enemy's front row has just disappeared from view and others follow, falling on top of the first.

The pit that Goditha wanted to open up just in front of the charge must have swallowed a line that was sixty or more men long and hopefully a few ranks deep. She has caused the earth to swallow hundreds. That would sow chaos in even the most disciplined troops as people struggle to avoid falling in and others try to escape, while still others still try to attack over the bodies of their own people.

Screams rise as barrages of allied spears continue to pelt those still standing across the pit. That section of the battle has quickly become a slaughterhouse… and luckily it is one that favours us.

At least I can now see Goditha running, or rather staggering, back around the spears to where the priests are. She has an arrow in her shoulder, which she is clutching with her right hand, but she also has a big grin on her face under her helm and she is laughing. Will she get free and clear without challenge?

No, the enemy must have identified the caster and they want revenge for what she has done to them. She is being chased by at least a filled hand of lamellar-armoured men. They chase her with weapons like halberds. Both Goditha's wife and her adopted daughter are waiting. Parminder soon released her first battle spell, a fireball. *Her casting has enveloped over half the group and left most of those who are hit on the ground. She will only have one of those for the battle.*

Gurinder then cast a lesser blast. It hit a man with a small standard on his back squarely in the chest. *He has fallen, his banner in flames. Even from here I can hear his screams above the general din.* The two women then began firing wands at the rest of the pursuers. The men didn't catch Goditha as her family helped her move back to safety behind the spears.

Soon none of the pursuers were left on their feet and no more came around the line to attempt to catch the mage who had destroyed their lines. *Those spells have nearly broken that whole unit of attackers.*

Astrid

*T*hey have broken into a charge—well, really only an uphill jog.*Astrid finished her prayers, kissed her icon of Saint Kessog, tucked it away between her breasts under her armour and stood up from where she knelt. *At least the Wolfneck men near me have been heartened by the sight of my icon, and more so when my Saint was named. Even though I have never tested it facing a monster of the land before, this is obviously the right occasion to do so.*

Now it is time for us to move. I will get rid of a known enemy first. Much as it hurts to say it, killing the Insak-div will be easy and the lizards will be much harder. For a start, they are larger. Oh, well, I told them that we don't have to survive. She grinned and loudly cried out her final orders to her axes, and they slowly began their own charge, spreading out as they ran to try and encircle their targets.

We are the only Allied troops moving forward. It is up to others to keep the rest of the enemy forces off our backs while we deal with the Insak-div and the giant lizard men that are the front rank of the enemy advance. The archers are supposed to concentrate on anyone who comes close to us. I prayed hard that the whole tactic works.

She leapt ahead of her men. She took the one on the right and could sense, out of the corner of her eye, her brothers leaping towards the other. Her half-grown cat bounced alongside her with its tail standing out like a stiff brush and most of its fur standing straight out and making her seem to be twice her real size. The yowling attack cry that echoed around their part of the field could have come from either of them.

The Insak-div that was in front of Astrid roared and swung low at her to cut her in half and, to its surprise, she leapt up in the air in one of the moves of the Insak-div of the Imperial Guard and came down with her feet briefly impacting on his bardiche as it swung through the air. She used the brief impact to bounce off it and rise up into the air again.

Her opponent didn't have long to be surprised at his weapon being torn from his grasp. Her bardiche came down on his head and split his helmet, and the head beneath, into two halves. Blood fountained out of the cloven skull and the huge creature fell supine and twitching as the shocked Kharl behind it halted mid-charge.

Seeing their giant ally so quickly dispatched by a mere Human must have made them shit themselves. What is more, they cannot easily get past it to attack me with the giant thrashing about wildly as it dies. She landed on the ground in a roll that took her clear of her fallen foe and was already heading towards her next target at a run.

My brothers can deal with theirs on their own. She turned to the right. *The lizards move slower but the Bear Folk in that wedge were overconfident. Despite my orders they have gone too close to a giant lizard and two are already down. There is a two-handed axe stuck fast deep into its shield and it seems to have struck deep enough to be lodged in the arm as well.*

Two of the Bear Folk have managed to get behind it, but they are forced to give their attention to holding off the numerous smaller lizards there and cannot manage to do anything to attack the giant at all. They were hard pressed at what they were trying to do as it was and are now back almost level with the giant lizard. Its tail is thrashing from side to side between them but luckily it has not noticed their presence as it slowly lumbers forward.

Without a pause, she launched herself at the beast. *It might be a lizard, but it stands on two legs and so it has a knee just like any other biped.* As she ran she could see that the thigh sloped out from the body, giving it an odd sprawling stance, rather than being fully upright like most bipeds—well, most of the bipeds she knew, anyhow. She took advantage of this slope to bring the bardiche down hard with both hands, just as if she were chopping wood, and just above the armour that protected the actual joint.

As she pulled the blade out, from the corner of her eye she noticed her cat. *Fluff-Ball is wrapped around the head of a human-sized lizard next to me, with a hissing and yowling noise coming from the cat and a similar one from her victim. Behind me, my sister-wife and husband will be protecting my back.*

In front of me the giant beast now roars like one of the forest giants that it must be related to. It opens a mouth that is very full of sharp teeth and turns its head to glare at me. Its sword is on my side of its body and it draws it back and tries to turn to make for a better strike at me. As it did, she hit out again and this time the bone gave way and, with a spray of blood from the leg, it toppled towards her.

She had to dance to the side as its roar turned to a curious whistling scream that kept on and on. *Its head lies near my foot with gnashing jaws trying to reach me. It struggles to bring its arm and sword free to strike at me even as it lies dying.* Its curiously small eyes glared malevolently at her so, with a grin on her face she raised her arms high and plunged the point of the bardiche into an eye socket, and then pushed hard so that it went deep into the skull.

The whistling scream stopped and the body began to thrash around like a headless snake on an ant's nest as the mouth opened and closed futilely. A wailing hiss came from the lizards behind it. *It is as if some sort of demented kettle has been left for too long on the hob and is now fast boiling away its water and screaming its life out into an empty room.* Astrid had to struggle to keep hold of her weapon as the head thrashed around violently and the creature died under her feet.

Hulagu

"It is time to come out of hiding." *Finally Rani gets us to do something.* He called out and waved the Bear Folk into motion from among the rocks along the side of the fields. Lumbering heavily on four legs like the Bears they now were, they came out from the flanking rocks. *So far the enemy have ignored the rocks, except to send a couple of filled hands of flanking men, archers who also carry light spears and with swords at their belts, running through them.*

All of the archers are dressed in a way I have never seen before. They are all Human men with square cut beards and leather caps and loose, colourful trousers and shirts with elaborate designs woven into the cotton or silk. Whoever sent them into the broken ground has apparently forgotten them, or else has not expected them to be in a position to attack yet.

Whatever offensive they were supposed to launch will not happen now as they all lie dead around us. We saw them and they emerged between the rocks into an ambush. They fought hard, bravely and well, firing their bows, using spears or drawing slightly curved swords to do so, but not for very long.

Most of these men had brought magic to the battle, quite a lot of magic, more even than we have on us, and several of the Bear Folk and the Mice have needed a lot of healing. One of the smaller Bear Folk is probably going to take no more part in the fray ahead. They are very lucky to still be alive.

I will wait until the Bear Folk engage before bringing the saddles out of cover. With luck our attack onto the rear of the block of Freeholders nearby will come even more as a surprise that way. The riders in the sky would otherwise stand out to their targets more than the ground-based attack will.

Once the lumbering Bear Folk are about to engage I will bring the saddles out to fire into the enemy rear and to sow confusion. Although there are getting to be less of them, we have marked out every surviving person who even remotely looks like a mage or a priest that they can see from our hiding place. They will get special attention as our main targets.

Chapter XXVII

Stefan
21st December

I have taken my people, who are each armed with either a long spear or a pike, and formed them up into three blocks. The front row of all three is for those who have some armour or at least a shield. I wish more had one or both of those. I have taken the one in the centre for myself and have made sure that it contains the least experienced people.

I have given my most practised people to my wives, who are on either side of me and who have strict instructions regarding what to do. Some of their men and women I have been training on and off ever since we left Greensin for the north coast over a year ago. I trust them to look after my wives. There is no one else everyone will look to. I just have to hope that my wives can inherit my authority to command and that their people will obey what they say.

They have not really been in a battle before as captains. I can only hope that my women will not do something rash. I have confidence in their practicality, but until it is tested in a place like this, you never know. He looked right and left nervously, while still seeming to project confidence. *At present they seem to be holding their people in place nicely. That is all that they have to do at this stage.*

The inexperience of my chosen group is now showing. Several of the men about me are so nervous that already weapons have fallen from their sweaty palms. They might have trained with them in their home village, but the fact that these are really just ploughmen or tradesmen or apprentices or herders really does show now that they are in an actual battle.

He dismissed the fact that only a few years ago he had been exactly the same, confident enough in his skills to think of training others, until it came time to actually use them to keep himself and his warriors alive. *Arrows have been coming from above and behind us and heading out for some time. Now around me our people are starting to be wounded and even die as the enemy archers open up.*

The priests are already busy with prayers and potions. Further back and to the side he could hear the occasional solid *thunk* noise that Ariadne's rock-thrower made when it released. The reassuring noise was soon followed by an explosion out in front as the blast tore a hole in another enemy group. *I just wish that it would tear some holes in the lines of these people I've never seen before who are now advancing on my unit.*

The artillery are totally leaving them alone. I must remember to thank Ariadne later for that. These men wear bronze lamellar, such as a wealthy Khitan might and some of my front row have, but there the resemblance ends. I have never seen helmets like theirs before, with crescents and horns of metal on them.

Their banners have a series of lines on them that must mean something, and most bear pole weapons. Studying them earlier using my glass, I noticed these combine axe with pike and have a spike on the rear as well. They look very efficient. If the spear doesn't work they can pull a shield out of the way or chop away at range. At least our pikes are longer. I wish we had more pikes, a lot more pikes.

I hope that, whatever Goditha is planning to do to them, it works. We will need all the help we can get. They are not only better armoured and armed and more professional, but they even outnumber my men. He looked at Astrid at the far left. *She looks to be shuffling her axes around for the last time. All of the giant creatures, and the lizards and the Kharl that are behind them, are aimed squarely at Adara's spears on my left.*

I hope that Astrid stops them somehow. The Kharl and the smaller lizards alone would be a more than fair fight for my wife and her men. Those giant beasts are an entirely different thing. I can see she is yelling at her men, who are looking nervously at the giants ahead of them. If they drop their weapons and flee there is nowhere for them to go, but I know that fear has a way of forgetting little details like that. There is no choice to the matter. We now have to win this battle or we all die.

He looked to his right. *Bryony and her men face a block of mainly Freeholder types. They have heavier armour than her people do, although their crossbows cannot keep up with the rest. As had happened for the Brotherhood, the soldiers who are in front of them are blocking their lower trajectory weapons from being used effectively.*

She is well outnumbered, but she has the advantage of position. The advantage in missile fire is at least starting to show for her there. I can see that, behind the advancing troops, scattered over the ground are bodies that lie still or try to recover from being shot. The armour may help protect them but is also making their advance slower.

He heard Astrid, even at the other end of her men, calling out her last orders and the little groups of men started running forward and spreading out, their two-handed axes in their hands. He wished them luck in his head before turning to call out to his troops. "Now ahold steady," he said. "Pray to Saint Maurice for aid, if'n you need, but just ahold." He crossed himself.

"We need to let t'em arun onto our points. As t'ey arun you hast a chance to aim. T'ey will ha' difficulty aholding a shield steady an' you can brace your spear butt as if ahunting a boar. Front row, aim low an' t' man behind aim high when t'ey come in. T'ey can only use a shield agin one of you… Godit'a," he called towards the other end of his men, hoping that he was being heard, "any time anow would be good."

The woman nodded and started her chanting. "Steady… T'ose who hast martobulli, prepare to cast… T'row." Several of the enemy could be seen to fall or at least clutch wounds. "Now take your positions… Rear akeep t'rowing… Brace for impact."

Suddenly it became apparent that Goditha had finished her casting as a roar went up from his men and nearly half of the enemy's front rank disappeared into a pit that had suddenly appeared at their feet and just in front of his people. *S'blood, it worked.*

He was soon too busy fighting with the unhindered ranks on the enemy right to assess the situation. *I can hear a lot of screaming coming from that direction. Hopefully it is all coming from the other side.* There were a few explosions as of spells being cast, but they were hard to hear through the roar and the cries.

After the first impact it had settled into a pushing contest with his front rank shields locked together and spears from the rear stabbing forward and the people there trying to keep themselves and the line intact as their enemy tried to tear holes in their ranks.

I have given instructions to the men who make up my other flank as to what should happen next if Goditha's spell worked, and I have left a trusted man to oversee them. Hopefully we get to find out soon.

Eventually he could see more men appearing on his left as troops moved there from the one side, where they were little needed, to this side where they were. *The men we fight are small, but they are tough and they are disciplined and stubborn and they die hard. I have wounds and no time to tend them, and my men are falling as well, falling in numbers.*

We are hard pressed. Some are being pushed back, but at least the enemy seem to be doing a lot of the dying as well. Now he could see that his men, reinforced by a charge from the flank by the men of the Basilica Anthropoi had an overlap now. *I can see the enemy unit being wrapped up and made into a ball. A ball of metal that will get harder and harder as it is made smaller and smaller.*

Here they will stand and die and take as many of us with them if they can. Seeing that they have both the discipline and the advantage of better armour and skill than most of my people, they can still easily win. Stefan had one more trick up his sleeve, just for this eventuality. *I have no intention of playing fair with my foes.*

Once the enemy were nearly surrounded by his men and women, he called back to a man he had kept aside, one who had said that he could throw well. *I really hope that he can do what he says and was not just boasting.* The man threw a single molotail high through the air into the middle of the enemy unit where the largest banners, and hopefully the officers, were.

Someone there realised the menace of the object in the sky, whatever it was, and tried to strike it away with their pole arm, but that made the effect worse as the molotail exploded above the ground and released dripping flame to spread out further. *Now, instead of my people fighting a compact and disciplined body of troops, we face men forced forward by the panicked mob behind as the flame eats into their flesh.*

His man threw another molotail and yet another. Each of these caused more devastation where it impacted and terror where it did not. Screams and pleas, or possibly prayers, were tearing out of people's throats and, except for a very few who fled back towards the city before his people managed to join their ranks behind the unit, it became a massacre as the other side lost the cohesion and the discipline that was their strength, and the units of men broke apart and so died.

Astrid

*N*ow *for the next one. My men around the lizard are trying to dance in and out, but this lizard is fast, and it has a very long reach. However, they all seem to have a weakness. It looks like they cannot bend or turn as well as a person can.* The man directly in front of her staggered back. *He is alive, but he has dropped his axe and is holding himself together with both hands.*

She moved forward and grinned. *Let's see how good my balance is.* The smaller lizard men had forced their way up to the tail of the great beast so, casually striking a couple of them down, she had to jump. *It felt my landing on its back.* She stood with a foot on each hip and with her blade across her body, and now struck out at what looked the junction of two bones in its back between a couple of flat plates of natural armour with a short, blunt spike on them.

The beast had been trying to shake her off, even before she wounded it. After she struck it, it became frantic. She leapt, rather than fell, to land to its shield side. *Again there is that strange whistling scream and it tries went to move around and strike out. Fluff-Ball has ended up on the lizard beast's head, biting and scratching at the creature.*

It doesn't know what to do about the two attacks. Its knees seem to be giving way but, due to the stable tripod formed by legs and tail, it still stays upright. The arms went up towards Fluff-Ball, and it swatted towards its head with its sword to drive the cat away. *That exposes its ribs as the shield on the left arm lifts away.*

I wonder if the heart is in the same place. She planted the point of her weapon deep between its ribs and then nearly lost it as the beast roared and brought the shield back down onto the blade. *My strength lets me hold on to the shaft, but I heard it creak.* She was able to pull the blade out. *The beast looks at me under its hat of enraged hill-cat and tries to reach across its body. One of the eyes on the giant head has been torn out and is hanging loose from its socket.*

Astrid danced back towards the creature's rear, nonchalantly dispatching another two of the smaller lizard men as they tried to interfere with her as she went. *The beast is trying to follow me. I was right. Its legs don't work properly.* As it twisted it fell into a heap. Fluff-Ball leapt clear.

The axemen that follow me can finish it without needing me here. Astrid was now facing back the way she had come. *All of my people are coming up the line behind me and starting to keep the man-sized lizards at bay while I deal with the others. I am halfway through the giant lizards and the next one has several arrows in it already.*

Damn their archers! She'd taken a shaft in the arm. *It has gone through my armour as if it wasn't there. It must have been enchanted to do that.* Impatiently, she pulled it out and paused to take a swig of a healing potion. She prayed as she did so. *That has to help. I really do not need the weakness that healing wounds will bring and I cannot afford to delay in killing these beasts as the remaining two are nearly at the spearmen, and they would eat them, perhaps literally.*

Rushing through the following, smaller man-sized lizards, bowling over one and killing several, she realised that it would be too hard to get to the monster itself as it neared the spears in front of it, and headed for the tail. As she dispatched the last interference she leapt, bringing the bardiche around and down onto the tail.

That got its attention. The last two paces of tail started flopping around on the ground, nearly completely severed from the rest of the beast. Roaring, the creature shuffled around to face her, tearing the tail-tip free, the blood flowing from the severed end flicked around the fight.

Several of its smaller cousins, charging towards her, were bowled over. Astrid didn't wait for it to complete its turn, and ran around following the stump of the tail. *Next I will try for…there.* She swung out and attacked the rear of its leg, ducking as the massive sword plunged through the space where her body had been.

She slashed at a tendon and then braced herself as she brought her blade up in a block. She felt her feet go deep into the rocky soil as she took the impact on the blade of her bardiche. The hand pulled back from her and she followed up, aiming at the wrist. *It is not very bright.* It pulled the hand out of the way and exposed her real target.

Quickly, she slashed across the stomach of the beast, leaving a gaping wound. *Its guts are beginning to cascade out onto the ground. It cannot stop its ponderous turn, and it has trodden on its own organs as it moves. Again there is that whistling, hissing noise. It must be a cry of pain.* She didn't stop, although it was reaching for a pouch that she had not seen before on its chest. *That must be a potion of its own.*

It is intelligent enough to use magic, then. She slashed again and severed the guts on the ground from those still inside. *Its mouth gapes open above me with that noise coming out in a continuous scream like a giant, demented kettle in agony. It makes me want to clutch at my ears to cover them.*

It has to be in great pain… Good… Now a thrust to the chest, and again as it paws feebly at the pouch. That is it. Its eyes are glazing over. The giant lizard-beast is dead, even if it has not yet started to topple.

Hulagu

*T*he Bear Folk have started their task by taking on and killing the crossbows and archers behind the Freeholders. One after the other, the missile troops there are run down and killed, for most of their weapons are near useless against them. A few must have had enchanted heads on their missiles as some of the Bear Folk come back out for healing, but most of the enemy have died in vain and without affecting the result.

The noise of the battle ahead, and the distraction of the explosions among their ranks from the ballista, must have made too much noise for their dying screams and cries for help to be heard by the troops ahead of them. *That is even better. Now we take advantage of it. They have nothing now to reach us up in the sky.*

As soon as the missile troops started dying, the Mice came out and started to head towards the only cluster of mounted men. *From their shields, these are nobles of some sort and their retainers, riding on the far left of the advancing unit, and now coming to help their crossbows, but they are too late.* Just as their first arrows were striking their targets, the light thrower and the ballista began to hit the same troops.

Between the three sets of fire, the Mice just had to take on one man who had escaped the first carnage, had turned his horse, and was about to flee. He must have seen what was behind them as he raised his arm and, turning his head towards the ones in front, was obviously going to shout a warning. The man was hit by a hand of shafts from the Mice and disappeared in his own private explosion. Now they turned towards the remaining mages still advancing at the rear of the foot.

Bryony verch Dafydd

I am nervous. Our husband insisted that Adara and I have to take charge of a unit each. We are both even wearing some armour for the occasion. We walk around in steel legs and Stefan has found breastplates suitable for women; with the shape of the armour around our breasts, there can be no doubt of our gender.

For once we have helms on, with our hair curled up in braids just as Astrid wears hers. We even have red crests on the top like a horse's mane so our men know us. "Almost all of t'e spearmen we hast come from the north or from around Lake Erave or Wolfneck," Stefan told us when we objected. "Some hast already fought under me an' all of t'em know of me as a captain an' t'ey will atrust me an' afollow me. T'ere is no one else t'at we hast t'at t'ey will do t'at for."

Adara was going to object but he held up his hand. "No...you're not me, but t'ese men do not t'ink it like t'at. I don't mean it like t'at. You're my wives. T'ey know about t'eir captain's wives an' you hast met most of t'em and t'ey will afollow what you tell t'em to do because you hast my authority." He looked hard at us then.

"T'ey may just be farmers, but most of t'em will be too proud to retreat if'n one of my women is agoing forward or even is just aholding ground...I ha' found good an' experienced lieutenants for you. Listen to t'em if you are in doubt, but basic our job with t' spears is to hold still and let t'em die against us. All you ha' to do is keep the men an' women under you in place."

Now I have to put that into practice, and all of these men are looking to me for direction and leadership. Inside myself I am not sure of whether I can do that. I am not really a soldier. I am just dressed like one. I only have the training that our husband gives to everyone in the village on Krondag. I am a hunter and I am meant to be facing boar or lizards or something that does not carry a weapon.

The battle will start soon. The last confessions are done and the priests have finished praying and talking now and the last people are shuffling back into their places. I suppose I should say something. Stefan hadn't said anything about that, but I know he always does, and I heard one of Astrid's little chats to her men at Skrice and it seemed to work to whip them up. Now, what do I say to them?

"Right", she started. *I am meant to sound confident. That was not too confident as the first thing to say. I need to speak louder now.* "At least all we have to face are Humans. There are a lot of them ahead of us, but most of them seem to be just Freeholders and they didn't even have the balls to attack the Brotherhood, and we have already destroyed that. How hard is this going to be?"

I got a cheer out of that. It might have been a bit forced, but at least it was a cheer. My block of spears are well and truly outnumbered by the men ahead of us and our opponents are far more fully armoured. At least they are starting to fall to the archers and to Ariadne's weapons. What else can I say?

"I want us—those who have darts and javelins—to throw them once they are in range and to keep throwing them until you have to use your hand weapons. Our job is to be the rock that they break on, and we have help coming out from among the real rocks. The Bear Folk and our riders are in there to be the wave that washes the enemy ship onto the rocks. Whatever else happens, we hold our place. It is our honour to do this."

What I said may have been confused—actually, it does not even make sense to me when I think about it—but this time the cheers are louder and less forced. I am not sure I said anything important at all. We have already given them those orders, but her people seem to have liked it, and I suppose that is all that counts.

From among their ranks she could hear shouts that were the names of villages or of patron Saints as people made their last preparations and tried to find the courage for what was about to happen. *Some, mainly women, are even calling my name.* She glanced at a woman near her. *Why is Aphra Jenkin calling my name? She is my second. She must be confused.* She looked ahead. *The enemy are now breaking into a jog as they come up the slope.* "Get ready and brace… On my word…"—she judged the distance—"throw!"

Hulagu

The front ranks of the Freeholders are engaging the spears under Bryony just as our group of Bear Folk and Mice hit them from behind. The lumbering charge of the Bears carries them deep into the ranks of the Freeholders and those who stand with them. Just as Rani has done up top on the edge, they have put their more lightly armed and armoured troops at the rear as well.

In the case of the Adversaries' forces, these are the renegade Sea Nomads, the near naked black men and some others from who knows where. They have no hope of standing against the impact of the Bear Folk, or our arrows. All that they can do is spread disorder up through the ranks as they try to escape from the death behind them.

This worsened for them as Hulagu sent his wives high to begin dropping molotails into the centre of the body. Once this had been done, the Bear Folk, and the spears on the slope above them, served merely to contain their opponents as they tried to break out. *Bryony's spearmen are being forced back a few paces in their centre, but they are managing to keep their line unbroken. That is the important thing. If we can keep our enemy in and contained, they will all eventually die.* None offered to surrender, nor was it suggested.

Rani must have seen what is happening here. Our reserves, as lightly armoured as they are, have begun to arrive in the battle from the rear of the spears. They must have been told to help contain the flanks of our enemy and they have joined in circling around the killing ground. It will be over soon.

Theodora

To me it looks like all of our opponent's major mages are down, or at least they are not casting any more, and this is all that we need anyway. Wands are still being used and a few lesser casters are being picked off as they try something. I am out of all of my stored reserves and out of mana again, and I am not sure how many doses of Sleepwell I have taken. She looked ahead of her.

Stefan's men are being hard-pressed on his left flank. His spears face opponents who are far more skilled than they are. Both sides are dying, but the allies' line is looking dangerously thin. Goditha managed to kill a lot of the enemy, but they started with far more men in the first place. She looked around.

The Basilica Anthropoi have been pulled out of the line to be a reserve for times like this. My husband is busy. She drew her sword and called out to Michael, the Praetor in charge of them, and pointed with her blade. *He is nodding at me.* Even over the battle sounds, she could hear his orders. "Two rounds of martobulli..." she joined in. "Walk... Jog... Charge." *Why not? I cannot really cast again.*

Just in time we hit our opponents, just as a gap appears in the spears. We are fully armoured in iron, far more heavily than the men we face. We are all with enchantments and blessings on armour, on weapons, or both. Our opponents are dying...not easily—there went part of my shield—but they die... The gap has been filled and more than filled. The last spearmen on our left have died, but the church troops are now in a single rank.

Theodora was in the centre of the line. *The Praetor on my left is now ahead of me. His file is wrapping around the enemy right. Instead of the flank of the spears being turned, the enemy are now the ones who are being wrapped around and bottled up... Their rear are starting to have to turn around to avoid being attacked on their unguarded backs.*

From what I can remember from classes, this is the beginning of the end for most units. I can see spearmen, and even Goditha, fighting with sword and shield as they close the gap from the other side. From behind her, her wife and daughter are hurling blasts of fire and air from their wands, but she is fighting like I am and protecting them from anyone rushing to try and stop them. The gap is closing...closing...my God...

Stefan has used molotails. The enemy unit ahead of her became a frantic mob... More flame. *A few of the enemy have managed to run before the two sides joined up... The rest just fight harder, but they are dying...from flame, sword, mace, martobulli, or wand... They are all dying and we don't even know who they are.*

She was not sure that she would ever forget the screaming as men burnt alive in their armour and yet were still trying to kill her and take her with them into hell. *I am covered in blood and dirt and smoke. I need a new shield, this one is missing pieces. My armour is dented... Why do I feel so...exhilarated, so alive?*

Astrid

I now face the last of the giant lizard men. It saw me coming and must have seen what I did to the others. It is now ignoring the allied spearmen ahead of it, people who really are only a few paces away, to turn to face me. My own people are forming a line around us to keep the other lizards at bay so it is *now one to one. One single Human woman and one giant lizard man who is at least five times my height. It is really not fair to the lizard, but who cares?* She thought for a moment as the two moved around.

I have speed and agility while the lizard has both mass and reach. With the enchantments that I wear now added to my own strength, which of us is stronger is about to be revealed. At least my body has recovered from its healing. We have already tested our strength against each other a few times. In the long term, I would lose in this contest as the lizard can easily use its weight to bear me down. She broke free from the tussle and moved clear.

The lizard lacks finesse in its blows as it mainly likes to chop straight down against a single opponent and, although they can sweep from side to side, its inability to swivel well in its hips restrict its blows. On the other hand, I cannot get a blow past its shield. It isn't particularly good at using it, but it doesn't have to be. From where I am the shield seems to be so large that it could be used as a raft for an elephant...a big elephant.

To add to my problem, the lower legs on this particular beast are also clad in massive metal greaves. I have tested that metal and it is very thick. I have no chance to do more than leave a faint dent in it. The huge shield makes the left side, the side that is facing our archers, nearly invulnerable. Cautiously, the two ill-matched opponents fenced at each other with outsized weapons for some time as the battle formed an open circle around them.

Fluff-Ball broke the impasse by pouncing onto the lizard's head. Neither Astrid nor its victim saw its leap, but suddenly it was attacking the beast, aiming at the eyes. The lizard gave way to the impulse to bat the hill-cat away, and it raised its arms. This gave Astrid the opening that she had been looking for, and she danced in to once again slash across its middle to disembowel her opponent.

The giant lizard now ignored the hill-cat and advanced on Astrid as she skipped out of its range, but it was too late. *Now it is just a matter of time before it dies. It could, however, still take a lot of others with it. Once again a lizard's guts are spilling onto the ground ahead of it. As Fluff-Ball springs clear of the beast's head, my own Kichic-kharl archers must have caught up to where I am as they are now feathering the area of the eyes and the open mouth of the monster from close behind me.*

It will not take me long to finish the beast off as it screams its long, high, whistling scream. I hate that noise. Then it was just a matter of withdrawing the survivors among her axemen and archers from between the two lines of troops. They finally broke clear, but they had lost over half their number in the battle.

Setting the fittest to keeping the enemy at bay, she had priests and healers attend to the wounds of the others before turning to go back to the fray. *Why is Ia stopping me? She wants me to drink some potions.* She looked down. *Damn. I need another set of armour.* Suddenly the pain of her wounds became real. *Why do I never seem to notice these things at the time in a battle? It really is just as well that I have a wife to care for me. Everyone needs a wife to do that for them.*

Thord

*T*hord hefted his long hammer in one hand and reflected on his experiences since he left the mountains. It seemed as though a lifetime had passed. *I have come so far and seen my dreams come true time after time. I have seen plains and forests, the ocean and far-flung lands. I have been a part of finding Dwarvenholme and killing the enemies of my people. I now fly around instead of riding my poor neglected sheep.*

Perhaps I should find a new rider for him.

Now I am a legend. It is usually a sarcastic joke to say about a Dwarf that he was a legend in his own lifetime. It means that he thinks far too much about himself and his own importance. However, in this case I know that I really am a legend. I have even sat quietly and somewhat embarrassed in the back of a tavern, my cloak hood shielding my face, and heard skalds sing songs about me and my deeds, and they were nearly mostly even true.

I am even wealthy beyond the dreams of avarice, and that means a lot to a Dwarf. We have a keen sense of avarice and to us it is not a vice. What is more, I have a noble and handsome wife whom I am coming to adore and who I think feels the same about me. Shyly, Thord looked sidewise at his bride and, in the quiet before the battle, thought about what they had heard in Wolfneck. *My child is to be the King? Who would have thought that when I left home? Mother will be pleased.*

Of course, prophecy will only come to pass if we survive this battle, and that is not certain. My people are on the extreme left flank of the allied line. Luckily the enemy are advancing on us, so this time the Dwarves will not be left behind by those with longer legs. We get to face these hordes of lizard things.

I have been told it will be the job of the Dwarves to ensure the enemy cannot surround and neutralise our spearsmen. I think my people's main task will be to destroy the enemy line and help Astrid's people escape after they kill the giants.

I have under my command only a bit over twice a filled hand of troops, but from what I can determine that might still be the largest force of Dwarves to go into a battle for, well, at least since the Burning. I suppose that another song will be coming soon to add to the list. One of my shield walls is also a skald, so the song will not take long to surface if the woman survives.

Rani wants my people to stay concealed in the bushes until we are needed, but that would means we cannot see much. *Even standing behind the others to gain some extra height, it is hard to see more than what is immediately ahead of us. The battle has started and Ariadne and the mages of both sides are exchanging spells and missiles.*

Our people are well outnumbered. We need to do more than just protect a flank. Quickly he ordered his people with bows and crossbows to take as high a position as they could. *The others can stand ready at the end to rush out, but most of us have crossbows or bows and are going to be needed here to chip away at their numbers.*

Thord gave his orders, numbering people off and getting them into their places. *Volley fire. One… Two… Three… I know how Eleanor would have arranged it.* When she had her people start shooting, his people joined in from the side.

Every extra shaft that comes from the allied side will be useful, especially seeing that every single one of those cursed little lizards seems to have a bow. Even as he was firing he realised that the enemy seemed to have far more arrows in the sky than his people did. *They look to be using weaker bows than most of the allied ones, but those can kill just as well as a strong one can.*

The sound of explosions, the screams of the wounded and dying, were now rolling around the battlefield and the giant lizards were getting very close. *I saw one fall, I don't know why, but it still leaves two of them in view. What is that noise? The enemy are getting close, too close. Soon the front lines will be engaged.*

In front of him he could see spearmen being hit by arrows. *Some are swearing and trying to pull them out before eating berries or drinking a potion or calling for a priest, some aren't as lucky.* A youngster he had seen once in Evilhalt fell dead, an arrow in his face. *Not the first, and not the last,* he thought, shaking his head. Looking ahead to the battle, he saw another of the giant lizards fall. *I can no longer see the front of the enemy forces. All of them are in a line away from us, and we have pretty much been ignored. The time has come to get the Dwarves ready to attack.*

He carefully put his bow aside and called out for the others to do the same as he dropped the belt with his quiver on it. *It will be needed no more in this battle.* With their druids saying last minute prayers, Dwarves got their shields off their backs, drew their weapons and took a stand beside each other. Just then there was a huge cheer from the spears in front of them, and the Dwarves could feel the ground briefly shake.

I will bet that is the last of the giants. I wonder if my drinking partner is still alive. With that question in his mind, he started his people walking around the flank of the battle in a double column. He saw what was happening and realised what he had to do as he called the Dwarves to come to a jog.

We will head straight out of the bushes to the vacant space ahead, and charge into the flank of the lizards. It looks like their attention is solely on trying to kill Astrid and her people, and I think it likely that the lizard troops will not even notice we are there until we start ploughing through the small lizard archers. They won't like it when we arrive.

Chapter XXVIII

Rani
21st December, it is still early afternoon

Looking out, in each area it seems we are winning. One mage tried to flee by flying but Ariadne finally hit him with the beam as he dodged and weaved. She must have taken off whatever part of him had the flying device attached to it, and his high-pitched scream could be heard faintly over the other sounds of battle as he plummeted from the sky and hit the ground. Either he had no repair spell ready or he had already used it; he didn't get up again.

Astrid effectively destroyed the morale of one of the enemy blocks by killing the Insak-div and the giant lizard men that made up its front rank; now the others of that unit are trying desperately to break free, and instead are dying, as the Dwarves coming out of the bushes plough into their side.

I spotted a fat lizard being carried away on a litter, others covering his rear as he attempted to retreat. I got my wife away from the actual fighting and had her and a few others get on saddles and engage in a duel as they used their wands to attack. They had to keep dodging the almost endless supply of bolts of lightning from that crystal-tipped staff of his. One caster against many will never win in the end, though, and he eventually died.

Killing that one seemed to completely demoralise the rest of the lizards and, with his death, their resistance fragmented. He seemed to be what was holding them together as a unit, and the moment he died they immediately all tried to flee the field. They are even trampling on each other as they run and as they die.

It seems that our enemy either must not have had access to any molotails, not been able to use them, or else they had used their supply of the terrible weapons elsewhere. Perhaps each group that came to the battle jealously hoarded their special weapons and, along with most of the others of the

Darkreach rebels, they had all been gathered on their stolen dromond, the Dragon of the Seas.

Now, on the battlefield, there are three pyres of coiling and reeking black smoke filled with fire. Screams erupt from within them. They are all on the side of the Adversaries' forces. The burning bombs are indeed cruel weapons, but they can save a lot of lives on the side of whoever has a monopoly on using them.

Rani considered what was happening. *It seems that we have finally won in the field. If there is ever going to be a need for my spell it will be now. The prophecies said that it would be needed, and it has not been so far. Unless our enemy are holding something back and have been slow to reveal some great spell or secret weapon, the cause of the Adversaries looks to be hopeless.*

Now is the time to begin the long and complex enchantment, just in case it is needed. It is not a spell that can be cast quickly. I can see that a few other people have broken free of the other fights and are fleeing back towards the city, but I need to ignore whatever else is happening. I have to resist the urge to give orders. I need to let someone else take care of them.

Rani moved her assistants into place and began her chant. She was reading from the prepared words that Bilqis held up in front of her and wondering what would happen next. It did not take long for her to find out. Suddenly something started to rise silently out of the far side of the partly-ruined city. *It must be nearly at the other end of the island. Was I too late in starting to cast the enchantment?* The thoughts went through her head, even though there was no pause in her words.

It is too far away for Ariadne to hit it with the light thrower, although she has tried. Several times, the thing lit up red with a beam that was weakened by distance. *At that range, several sea miles, it seems that this is all she can do. It has a shape that is a bit like a sling bullet, and it shines in the sunlight as if it were made entirely of metal, a silver teardrop in the sky.*

A band around its middle glowed with a cold, white light. Slowly it started rising straight up into the air. Rani continued with her preparations and persisted with her chanting. *I hope that it will not all be wasted, and that the Adversaries are actually inside this odd flying object. It is behaving as no carpet, as no saddle, ever has, and it is like nothing that I have ever seen or heard of before.*

We surmised that the Adversaries like to use machines, instead of honest magic, and I am sure that this is another of them. Slowly it rose and, when it had reached a certain height it stopped, seeming to hover, and it looked as though it started to turn, although it was difficult to be certain.

Rani was only a bit over halfway through casting her spell, grasping the storage devices that she would drain for this casting as they were passed to her. Suddenly the object darted up into the sky and, still climbing rapidly, headed over them towards the south-west. By the time it went overhead it had accelerated phenomenally and had sent one loud noise like thunder after another echoing down from the sky. *It is already far too high to hit with the light thrower.*

The thunder was so loud that it even caused the battle to briefly pause each time it happened. *It is so loud that I can feel it on my skin. It flees so fast…* By the time Rani was ready to cast, it was merely a distant dot in the sky. *It is, however, still visible, and that is all that I need for this casting. I have worded it carefully.*

She cast and a beam struck out from her hand. It was a beam of pure magic, and she had specified in the spell that it was a line-of-sight attack. *At least in theory, if my target can be seen, it can be hit. I feel that the cast has been a good one, a very good one. I can see the beam clearly. Now I get to see how good my accuracy is in making the cast. Will it hit the fleeing object?* She held her breath. *Yes, it has intersected the path of the enemy's machine.*

The dot staggered and corkscrewed through the air. *Now a thin trail of smoke has appeared and seems to be following it in its twisting and turning.* Even those using telescopes could not see if it fell to the ground, even though some claimed to see flame, and it was no longer climbing when it and its smoke disappeared into the distance.

As Dobun suggested, I have used everything that I have inside me and then far more than that to make that one cast. Hopefully it did count. Hopefully it is over. I am very tired. Exhausted by the drain on her body from using so much mana in a single casting, Rani now collapsed as others leapt to stop her breaking the charged lines of her pattern.

Theodora

Now the rest of the battle becomes simply a matter of clearing up and holding the enemy forces at bay while they are killed by archers. On entering this battle everyone involved appears to have known exactly what it was all about. None seeks quarter and no one offers it. I think everyone on the field understood that only one side in this contest will leave Arnflorst alive. I am very glad it is us who are to be the lucky ones.

From the time that the first shot had been fired, the battle in the open had taken only a little over an hour, and soon it was all over save for the screams of the wounded and dying as the priests, druids and witches continued their task of saving as many of their people as they could and helping those who would not make it to pass on to the other side in a state of grace.

Chapter XXIX

Xú Zílì Lóng
Èrshíy Ti n zh Dì Shí Yuè, in The Land, it is 22nd December

Have we not had enough disruption and disorder arrive here in our exile outpost of Dàhé Zhèn? Was not the recent and first visit of some of the Imperial family and the loss and recovery of an Imperial Grandson enough, at least for a Cycle? Now it seems that Sūn Wùkōng is still not finished with us even for the one year.

This is supposed to be a quiet posting away from the machinations of Court that those close to the Dragon Throne experience. It makes up for its isolation with its peace, at least for those who are not sent here as punishment. Why is it not that way for me? My experience here as the Zhōuzhăng of this place, so distant from the Ancestors, has been anything but calm.

Now, after last night, everything is again in turmoil. Even I was woken up as that burning ball of fire flew through the sky. We all had time to look outside as it careered from side to side across the heavens like a firework without a guiding tail. It was not a normal yŭnshí, a meteorite. It moved differently and it was brighter and louder. It burned and it roared as it crossed the heavens above us.

Was it perhaps a portent of some sort? I am not an astrologer, so I cannot say. I have asked those who know such things. So far I have heard several say that one of the Gods fell from the heavens. Others have sworn that they saw an actually burning object. Some allege that visions have told them it was a Demon falling and burning after a battle in the heavens.

My spies have even indicated that some have had the temerity to say out loud that it is a sign that the Mandate of Heaven has passed from the Luó and a new Dynasty is called for. The names of those rash persons have been noted and a watch will be kept on them. Given what I hear from home, I will not act on what they have said just yet, in case they are right.

We do know that there was the noise that could be heard here, and then there was the fire in the night as if there had been a sudden explosion. It appears to have come to the ground not too far to the south-west of us. At least that is if the flash and the mighty wind that came from that direction as it fell are any indication.

This could be trivial, or it could be an important event. I think that I need to send word back to Shénshèng Bìhù, but first I will need to send people to find out more about it to put the details in my report. I need to put together a group who will not be missed if they do not return, but who are competent enough to make it there and back.

If I send soldiers, it will give too much importance to the event. I may even need my soldiers here if turmoil arises as a result of this. I have one person in mind who has already been useful to me. I will then look at those who arrived south on the last vessel from home and see who is suitable among them. There are always persons who seek their chance at fortune. Let this be it for them.

As The Master said, "Thus it is that the superior man is quiet and calm, waiting for the appointments of Heaven, while the mean man walks in dangerous paths, looking for lucky occurrences." I will sit quietly and wait and see and allow those who want more try their luck on the dangerous paths.

Chapter XXX

Christopher
21st December, late in the day

I need some time to reflect. The exhausted Bishop sat on a rock to collect his thoughts. *The last battle against the Adversaries in the fields outside the ruined city of Arnflorst has finished. We are tired but victorious. But there is so much still to be done. For now, the survivors of the fight are recovering. They are checking on their friends, hailing and hugging those that have survived and grieving for those who have not.*

Our priests, not just the Christian ones, have had to console far too many people. Our folk have lost friends and neighbours, brothers, fathers and sons, even some sisters and daughters. We have won the day, but it was a hard-fought victory. For a start, nearly a third of our people, largely the farmers and tradesmen of the north, those who made up our blocks of spears, will not be going home. There will be mourning all along the coast for many years.

My priests and the other healers are still busy saving those who can be saved, but for too many it is not possible and we are giving the Last Rites or an equivalent, depending on the faith of the dead. There will be many people grieving in the north and among the people of the sea. Even some among the Bear Folk will never see their quiet woods again.

Quickly, after a brief reorganisation, those of our allied armies who are more experienced as soldiers, or at least armsmen for caravans, have begun to descend upon the half-ruined city. With troops on the ground and in the sky it has been searched and, to the dismay of the Sea Nomads, the site of the last massacre of the people of Moorea has already been found.

There was one lone survivor, a girl. She is badly injured and traumatised, but she is still alive. She will recover, at least in her body. Whether she will ever recover in her mind is another matter.

Once her physical wounds were made stable and had been bound up, the Nomads brought the girl to Astrid. They openly named Astrid as Rongom-aiwhenua and handed the girl over to her as if they now had a right to demand she heal the spirit of the child. Astrid just sighed and looked at me. I have Confessed Astrid enough to know what she was thinking. Was this girl going to prove to be another Jillian, or could more normal methods of calming and reassurance work? I could only shrug in reply to her look. I am sure that she will work it out somehow. I have no idea what to do.

Rani

As the soldiers have searched the city, the occasional enemy soldier has been found. Most have been more intent on hiding than anything else, but some are attacking the searchers in a frenzied manner. Others have been discovered trying to mingle with the allies or even to get down the slope to our boats.

Even with all of the main combat finished, people are still dying in traps and from these little ambushes as they search the mostly ruined city before us. There is no way that all of the allies can just stand down and rest. Those who are sleeping and those who are recovering need to have a vigilant guard set over them.

There are no other boats at the island. A few small craft and many large ones lie wrecked in the harbour to the west, but none of them seem to be readily repairable without tools and timber that the island seems to lack. This makes the ships now anchored off the south-eastern shore the only means for anyone to escape this bleak and barren island, and it gives the enemy survivors a strong incentive to head that way if they wish to escape the charnel house that their fortress has become.

Magic and valuables were collected and all of the allied survivors would leave the battle with pouches full of treasure as some form of cold comfort. The bodies of their enemies that lay in the field were collected, stripped and put into a pile. There was, however, not enough timber anywhere on the whole island to even start to burn them.

They would have to be left to rot away in a vast funeral pile, or else be eaten by the horde of circling seabirds. It seemed that this process was well underway. The pile of dead had already become hard to see under the squabbling and heaving mass of gulls and other birds making their way to the feast. The bodies of the allied dead would at least be weighted with rocks and reverentially buried in the sea.

Bryony

During the cleanup at least one mystery, at long last, has been resolved. We were leading our spears for what may be the last time. None are experienced enough for the task of clearing the city. We are just depressingly collecting the bodies. Now I see one clump of dead, amongst the very mixed forces over near the rocks. They are clothed in a very familiar way.

Not only have I found a group of men, dressed more warmly than usual, from the Confederation, but I even recognise some faces. There lies the body of Figel, who has enough of him intact to be recognised and, presumably, some of those others who had fled the Swamp from Caer Gwyliwr Ddwyrain. Bryony pointed him out to the others.

"At least we don't have to pay out on the reward," Astrid quipped bleakly when she was finally told of this.

Astrid

I have very little humour left in me. I am exhausted in my body and my mind is just plain numb. She had gathered her people, the live and the dead together, and thanked them all. Her eyes were full of tears as she embraced them one by one, even the dead. *These people trusted me to lead them into the battle and I lost well over half of them in it.*

We lost a higher share of our people than any of the other groups on the field, but then, I suppose, we did take on the hardest task of them all. Out of the three filled hands of people who followed me into the hand-to-hand battle, only one filled hand will be going home. Karl, my eldest brother, is one of those who will not be returning. I will not have to find him a bride after all, Astrid thought bitterly.

I have even lost fully half of my Omáda of Kichic-kharl, mainly to enemy archers. At least they tried to keep clear even of the small lizards and not close with anyone if they could avoid it. Tarakratz and Mardrikrat will only return with four of their people to Cold Keep, and all of them are heavily bandaged. Hrothnog trusted them to me and I have lost a hand of them.

She looked to her side. *Mardrikrat will have a scar across his face that crosses his left eye and he will be lucky to still have its use when it is all over. Even as he worked he was peering out of his other eye and around a large pad and bandage that covered his stitches. We lack the healers to make sure that his eye is intact. I wish I could do more for him.*

Everyone in my group is carrying wounds and has rent armour. Even the two animals have been injured, and we all sit exhausted and quiet, letting our healing draughts take effect on us. Mardrikrat and Ia, our only two healers, are lying side by side. They have drained themselves and taken more doses of Sleepwell than they should and yet they are both still drained.

Now they have been fed sweet things and Kaf by Basil. They have both been wrapped up in cloaks and are sound asleep in the most protected part of a spot that is sheltered by some brush we have lashed into a windbreak for us all. Our dead have all been gathered by now and they lie in a row waiting for attention. At least our Kharl have been easy to tell apart from the others.

The Sea Nomads had delivered the last survivor of Moorea to Astrid where she sat exhausted and near weeping beside the cliff with her people gathered around her. *The Nomads seem to expect me to be able to care for the girl and restore her mind to health. I looked at Christopher and even he had nothing for me, at least today.*

As she sat holding the girl tight to her, she wondered. *The mind-control of Butterfly helped the old Caliph—before he died, that is. I looked all over the girl and could not find any of the festering scratches that Jillian had on her before she was healed. The girl has just—just!—been abused, and she is underfed and terrified. Perhaps there is at least some hope for her after all.*

Astrid gathered the girl back into her arms and started the familiar, soothing song that she was growing to no longer love but to hate, even loath, for its new associations with pain and suffering. The girl's body shook with her memories and she wept on her shoulder. Astrid's eyes looked bleakly out over the battlefield and the people gathering the bodies and crying over lost friends. *Now, each time I sing this song it represents another tormented soul I have to somehow console.*

Can I now even sing it to my children as my long-lost mother once sang it to me? As she sang and mused, over the whole field the cries of the wounded could be heard. *Once the girl has calmed down a little, and Butterfly wakes rested, I will get Ia to work her type of not-magic on her and then we will see if that is enough or whether more will be needed.*

She looked to the south-east. *I need to talk to Hrothnog, and I need to do it now. This has to be the end. I have to hear him tell me there is no more that has to be done. I cannot take much more of this. I may enjoy it when it is just me who is doing the fighting, but how can I be expected to care for all of these people?*

How can I answer to my children? How can I even protect my children if there is much more to come? Each time it gets worse. He hinted that this may be the end, but I need to be sure. What was that thing that Rani destroyed? Was it the sky-chariot of the Adversaries that she brought down in flames? Are they now dead? Astrid hoped so, and she felt that it was the case, but she had to be sure. *Perhaps we will have to chase them up into the sky where they were headed to bring everything to an end. Who knows?*

Rani

I feel drained and guilty. Apart from that one spell, I consider that I took no real part in the battle apart from sending people to die. As Rani wandered wearily around the battlefield, she realised that she must seem spotless and untouched by what had happened. *I may be the only clean person here on the field. Why are people thanking me as I go to talk to the wounded? Why are they all bowing to me?*

I have really done so little. My wife has just returned to me from helping in mopping up the last of the enemy forces from the city. She was not just directing others. Once again she had to use her own sword, and she ended up here amongst the wounded because she took charge on the field near the end of the battle, while I slept.

Somehow my Theodear has found herself again in hand-to-hand fighting beside the Basilica Anthropoi in the main battle, despite being a mage. I can see her below. The shield on her back is only half there, and what remains of its painted mouse is covered in mud and blood. I did not even see her rush into that fight.

I have not seen Basil's reaction—he has been busy—but Ayesha is aghast. She was on a saddle using her bow, but she bears several wounds herself. Her normal leather clothing—for she felt restricted wearing any better armour— was never meant to protect anyone in a battle like this.

I can feel people looking at me as I move around. I need to project calm and confidence as I thank them for their efforts and try to reassure them. It all seems too little in return for what they have given, but it really is all I can do. I feel so unworthy. We may have won, but I failed so many of our people. Was there a way I could have kept more alive?

She took a sip of Iszig. *It seems that I somehow have had Virginia and her nurse somewhere nearby all through the battle, and now they are bringing me things to eat and drink as if they are both servants, but I need my wife. She, not me, is the one who knows what to say to others to soothe them. I am not the one who has been through it all, she is the one who looks after them as their mother figure.*

How can I be strong when I can look to my left and see that even Astrid, as she sits forlornly clutching a girl of the Sea Nomads to her bosom like a small child, has tears that leave trails in the dust and blood on her face? Once again, she will need to replace her mail completely, and she will have several more scars to add to her collection.

She is empty-eyed but for the weeping, and she is staring blindly at her own people. I can see a row of bodies near Astrid, laid out side by side without regard for their race. Some are so tiny—the little Kichic-kharl—but most of the dead are from Wolfneck and Skrice, and even from among the Bear Folk. Rani was appalled. *So many people lie there, never to rise again.*

Down the slope and out on the battlefield, Rani could see that Stefan and his wives had gathered all that remained of their spears and were collecting the dead of both sides. *Before the battle I heard Bryony complaining to her husband that she was not a captain, a battle leader. Whether she likes the title or not, she is now.*

I can see a village elder, David, the Mayor from Outville. He is running around after the former slave trying to get her to drink something while a woman in mail, with a sword at her side and a shield on her back—also from Outville, if I remember her rightly—is at her other side trying to get her to eat something. She is followed by a man who is trying to do the same for her.

Goditha, her wife and their sister-daughter are coming back up from the city. Gurinder, in padded leather, a child-like helm pushed back on her head, seems to be skipping around them as the other two walk hand on hand. She is only just thirteen and yet she has just been through a day on this bloody field as a combat mage.

I saw the girl firing wands almost into the faces of some of the enemy as they pushed forward on Stefan's flank. Parminder was beside her and doing exactly the same. Dressed the same as her sister, but with her helm off, she looks just like a mage; she is too small to be anything else. If she were still in Sharan, she would be the lowest of the low; instead, here and today, she is a hero.

Her husband may also be a mage, but she looks more like an armsman in her rent mail, her helm held under her unengaged left arm and her short hair clear in the fading sun as she shakes it out. Her shield, like my wife's, has a large chip missing from its edge, its mouse bloody and scarred, and is slung at her back over her shoulder and her sword is on her left hip.

All that says she is a mage are the long pouches at her belt. However, the single spell that I saw her cast labelled her clearly as a mage of power. It may have led to the death of more of the enemy than any other single casting that came from our side. I must congratulate the girl. She was right in insisting on using it. She then followed that casting with her blade, putting her body in the way to protect her wife and daughter, who really had only wands.

Eleanor's archers are now following the mages up from the city, while others move around helping the soldiers of the spear units with the dead and wounded. Now the battle is over and helms are off heads and their voices are not muted, I can see and hear that far more of the people of our force are women than I had thought. Many are weeping over the bodies of the dead spearmen: husbands, or brothers, or even sisters lost forever. Others hold tight to people they love, men and women both.

Rani searched with her telescope and finally found Eleanor herself. *She looks very tired. She is one of the older Mice and today it shows in her body and her face. Her husband Robin is beside her and, from the hard look on his face, it will be a long time before she is allowed to even leave the valley again. From the way their hands are moving, I am even willing to bet that our Captain of Archers is pregnant again as well.*

In the air the saddle riders hovered and kept up their search for enemy survivors trying to get away. *They seem to be the only ones on the allied side who are still fully active, with bows in hand and arrows nocked. Hulagu and the others of the Horse have them well in hand and it seems that at least some of the watch tonight will be kept from the sky.*

Rani handed her wooden goblet to Virginia and again started to move around to talk to people. *I am left wondering about a long series of questions. Whether I succeeded in my casting is possibly the least of these. I know that I cast truly, and within myself I could feel it strike home. I still do not know what it was, but the shining thing was damaged enough that it appeared to be falling from the sky, and I think it must have contained at least some of the Adversaries.*

The questions that I have are more to do with our opponents. Who were those bronze-armoured beings acting as generals for their enemy? Who were the Lizards that fought us, and where did they come from? In fact, where did most of our opponents come from? My wife has talked of various races from the history of Darkreach. Perhaps she knows them. We have not had a real chance to talk yet about what happened here.

Apart from the obvious Freeholders, most of the people we fought came from lands that we might have clues about from our various maps and books, but it is time we sat down and started to seriously look at the whole of our world. Olympias may have some long voyages ahead of her once we have looked in detail at the maps.

She had one more thought that she was keeping to herself until they were back in Mousehole. *My wife might usually be the one to have ideas for new spells, but I am hugging this one tight as my own. If our enemy could use a spell to fly so high in their metal box, why couldn't the Mice do the same?*

I have seen my wife and Ruth talking about that book by Dar Lagrange that tells of other worlds. Once we have no more battles to fight, could we make something with our spells to visit them? Ariadne wants to make something that flies as well. I have heard her talk of making a metal shell to keep us safe from arrows.

When Astrid takes us up very high on the saddles, it is very cold, and it becomes harder and harder to get enough to breathe. What would be needed in the way of a spell to overcome these problems? Perhaps that is what the thing of metal was: a way of holding air. Making something like that move and keeping us warm will surely be my responsibility, but my wife will be helping us breathe. Goditha will be the one to work on the metal shell. Surely she can do that now.

Christopher
after sunset

*A*s the night starts to fall, people begin to start fires and to cook. Our few prisoners are secured for questioning later. Like it or not, most of the survivors of the battle will be spending the night on the island under the growing clouds of scavenging birds. From somewhere unknown the ravens have even started to gather on this island, one that is so far out to sea, and to tear at the growing pile of bodies, their loud cries, as always, speaking of death and a hard fate.*

I gathered my priests for Hesperinos. Our other priests have done the same for the evening prayers of each of our various religions. It was not long before heart-felt thanks for survival, in many languages, were being addressed to various deities and the Requiem began to be sung for those who would not return home. Its massed, melancholy tones even caused the scavenger birds to be silent. Tomorrow we have yet more to deal with, and tonight we priests will be taking turns to sit beside those we are trying to help to survive.

Chapter XXXI

Gamil
3ʳᵈ Moldin

*S*o, now it is over and the Daveen have failed. No longer will they be able to contest control of our project, which they tried to subvert using their guile. We can complete our goals without interference. My name will live long in the history of my people, and unlike that of my predecessor it will be associated with success. My choices, and the decisions that I made to implement them, have been shown to be right.

What is more, the Renegade did not act. He seems to have deliberately made himself one with the subjects of our experiment and removed himself from being an active participant. We are safe up here and can continue on our path of research without having to interact any more with the subjects. The Tribunal cannot accuse us of interference in any way.

I think that I can permit a party and a small celebration in our home in the sky. From our position far above it all we have watched the whole battle on a series of large screens. The spells that normally stop us from watching everything, strangely weaker here than in many other places on the planet, were early casualties of the battle. For once my people were free to hear and see everything.

Those on the ground, those who destroyed it, may not know what happened to the Daveen orbital craft, but we certainly do. The Daveen, who are referred to as the Adversaries by those below, did not make it up into orbit. My subject's spell sliced deep into their craft and it lost integrity, the ability to properly navigate, and its pilot, all at almost the same time.

Their pilot must not have had time to properly strap himself in and, although the spell itself may not have harmed him, the fall out of the craft to the ocean that lay far below would have been terminal for him. He flailed and screamed *the whole way down to the ground, and that is an image that will haunt my dreams for some time. You would expect someone with such a lifespan to be able to cultivate a certain gravitas in such a situation. He lacked any sense of composure towards his fate.*

What is more, he even seemed to lack the presence of mind to cast some sort of spell to save himself, if indeed he had that power. I am sure that I will eventually face questions as to why I did nothing to try to preserve him, but I, like most of my people, always expect people to fly just as we do, and I realised his issue too late. At least, that is what I will say. Besides, surely that could have been construed as a physical interference with the events happening below.

The others on board tried to compensate for the damage, and they all somehow managed to suit up to withstand the pressure drop. One of them nearly wrestled the craft up into an orbit before the damage it had taken finally proved fatal to the craft, and an engine erupted in flame and showered the insides with hot metal.

With a sudden loss of most of their power, the two that were left alive by then had switched to trying to bring it safely back to the surface using its design as an aerofoil. Even this had been too much for them. We watched, with mixed emotions I will admit, as the craft finally plunged into another part of Vhast in a fireball that tore across the sky like a roaring, raging comet to explode in partly melted shards on the ground, laying waste to a vast tract of the equatorial jungle of the Long Realm as it did so.

There could be no survivors of such a crash, and few will mark its fall in that nearly uninhabited place. Now it can be seen that the last throw of the dice for the Daveen, our Adversaries, has come up against them. It is likely that they have no more adepts of any power left to them, or they would have already been in place on the planet. I am certain there is no way they will be allowed to return to Vhast in any case.

Now their plots and tactics and all of their breaches: the beam weapons, the radar, the mines and the others that went down into the sea with their ships will all come up before the Tribunal when it convenes, and their punishment will be fitting and could even spread to their own worlds that lie far beyond this one.

My people, the Shing-Zu, have won. Our experiment can now continue uninterrupted to its conclusion. Although my superiors feel otherwise, I think this is not going to be very far off. The inability of my techs to interfere with any determined use of magic means those on the surface seem to be able to block anything my people want to do. The Renegade seems to have fully determined that he is no longer one of his people, but a part of Vhast. I must include that in my next report.

Where this will lead I am not sure. I have not mentioned it to anyone, but I am fairly certain we will all find out a lot more about this in the not very distant future. She started drafting a note that would cover any likely eventuality without getting her removed from this post for being alarmist.

I may have succeeded in my choice of proxies in this fight, but that does not make me immune to being pulled down, now that my insight into the minds of these people is no longer so urgently needed. I have no desire to be sitting on Shing in a comfortable and boring retirement reading the latest news from Vhast, with the interesting parts redacted, on a screen. I wish to be here watching it all unfold and seeing where it leads.

Chapter XXXII

Rani
22nd December

The first thing that we have to do today is to find out what we can from our few prisoners. Who knows who or what else there is out there in other places? Perhaps someone we have captive will be able to tell us. Are they all devoted servants of the Adversaries? Where do they even come from? Of course, this leaves a problem in that few among the Allies speak a tongue that can be used with the captives.

Luckily, one of the Sea Nomads has a little of what the Lizard Folk speak. He called it Sslan'slin, and the nation of lizards the Sslan'ssisswani. It is a very hissy and sibilant language, it seems. The single surviving lizard, one who had been found unconscious in a pile of bodies and who now sports a bandage wrapped around most of his head, is one of the smallest ones.

Most of the lizards went berserk when the one on the litter was felled. It was as if it had somehow controlled them, and when the control was taken away they had just attacked anything near them in a senseless rage until they died. They even attacked others of their own kind who stood in their way. The rest had just tried to flee.

To our Khitan and others, those who are used to seeing them up close— now that the being can itself be seen closely—it really does look a bit like a slightly shorter and stockier Pack-hunter. Like the Pack-hunters we saw at One-Tree Hill, when it is considering you it even holds its head to the side and hisses in the same way.

There are some significant differences, however. It has a larger head, and it has real hands with thumbs, for a start. What is more, instead of the brown skin of a Pack-hunter, this creature has green skin. Its feathers are different to the ones that I saw as well. In addition, its middle toe claw is far smaller than that of a Pack-hunter and it rests on the ground when it walks.

After obtaining permission, and with people standing close by holding weapons and wands on him, the lizard found out where the magic taken from his people was being held. He then went over, still under close guard, and began looking through it. *He has found something, a sort of leather helmet with iron ovals and adamantine rhomboids attached to it and mounted with topaz and opal.*

He held it up, and others identified it as having been taken off the one who was likely to be their leader, the very fat mage on the litter whose death had triggered the frenzy. The small lizard put it on, looking almost comical in it as it was meant for a very much larger head. *Only the bandages it wears kept it from falling straight off.* Suddenly, everyone heard what he was saying in their own language when it spoke. *The leather helm is imbued with a very strong translation enchantment. Nice.*

The lizard is being very co-operative and hardly needs to have Ia work her spell upon him to answer everything that is asked. He does have difficulty in understanding some of what the questions are about, however, as he—actually, it seems, a she—often cannot understand what is being asked of her. The questions make little sense to her and sometimes the answers that she gives make no sense at all to us. I don't think that our two languages always share the same words or even similar thoughts.

Whatever she says her name is, it comes out as Little Seeker *in the translation. That much we are sure of. She is one of the Sslan'ssossi, the* Least Folk, *and this is where we start to lack the right words. This is where it becomes a problem. Whatever we say here she agrees with, but when she says it back, it changes in what we hear.*

She was the slave, or the servant, or just property, or sometimes a soldier, of the fat one on the litter. The word never comes out the same and is different almost every time it is said. All of the lizards at the battle, indeed most lizards, are such slaves, or whatever the word is, and they do as they are told by the Sslan'osslii, the Great Thinking Folk.

The last order they were given was to avenge their owner's death, but that moment has now passed, and Little Seeker seemed very distressed that she was unable to do this. She did not know who killed her master, so she has already decided that she needs to attach herself to Astrid as her new owner. She—Astrid—was the one who destroyed their giant lizards, their Sslan'ssilissi, the Great Folk, and so allowed their force to be destroyed.

No matter what we ask, or how we ask it, we have no crime to execute her for. She fought as a soldier because that is what she did. She has had no hand in any of the crimes that others may be guilty of, and her owner was. It seems that sacrifice is a normal part of their culture and Little Seeker is almost expecting that to happen to her.

Astrid's face was quite comical when she found out she would be Little Seeker's new leader, or owner, or captain. Apparently this is how one of the ruling lizards gains power among the Sslan'ssisswani, the Several Folk, *by killing other leaders and so taking over their people and sacrificing the ones that they do not need.*

Rani

*N*ow that we have the translating cap at hand, Astrid will have to cope without being able to talk to her new charge for a while. At least now it *becomes easier to ask questions from the others. One by one we can put them under control with Ia's skill or with the services of a mage. We will take a short break and then they can begin to reveal their stories.*

The first one that is questioned after Little Seeker, one of those men from among the rocks with the square-cut beards, said that he was of the Persians. He says that his name is Azarzushnes *and he calls his land* Ērānshahr. *It is in the Long Realm east of the Chin and has been in nearly constant conflict with them since the beginning of time. This is the first time he has fought on the same side as them.*

He admits that he is one who worshipped the Adversaries, whom he calls the Servants of Ahriman. *It seems that, like the Wiccans, his people make a direct choice whether to worship good or evil. If they choose good it is through Ahura Mazda, and to worship evil it is through Ahriman as a personification of their chosen ideals.*

It depends on how you feel within yourself. At present his land is under the control of the worshippers of Ahura Mazda and so the worshippers of Ahriman continue to flee to refuge in other lands. He, and those with him, fled to the land of the lizards, the Sslan'ssisswani, *where they had their own leaders set up and had carved a place in their society.*

Many of them ended up on the battlefield here. Once they won here they were supposed to be going back with others to seize control of his homeland. To him, the only one of those questioned to place the matter in direct religious terms, this battle was the start of the final confrontation. To those of his people who were here, this was the beginning of the end. Now that it is over, the world as we know it will gradually, well, stop.

Now that the material forces of Ahriman have been so completely defeated in the start of the final battles, there is nothing left for his side of the struggle and his soul, and the souls of all of the others who fought for Ahriman or who have adhered to that side over the cycles, will now be extinguished. Fatalistically, he has accepted this fate. He knows that he will now die and is only sad that he made the wrong choice in the direction of his life.

His philosophy may be puzzling, but at least we are able to get a great deal of other information from him, which is being eagerly written down to add to what little we have. His people and the Chin are implacable enemies who have been locked in combat for all time across a peninsula that is cut off from the rest of the Long Realm by a great triple wall built by his people.

He bitterly regrets that more of his people were not strong enough in their faith and had not been at the battle to help their God, although many were apparently lost in several ships in the storm we sent back. He particularly regrets that none of those who came had been able to bring flame weapons with them. They had used up all of the weapons they had been able to escape their land with to carve their place out among the lizards.

Rani

*A*nother break and now it is the turn of one of those with a yellowish cast to their skins and eyes that are even more almond-shaped than those of the Khitan. They fought under the tall banners and lost many of their people to Goditha's opening pit. He said he and his people were from among the Chin, those who live in perfection in the Zhōngyáng Tiānsháng Wángguó.

He is the one who has had to be constantly restrained, for he glares at the interrogators and continues to try to break free even while being questioned. He is implacable in his contempt of any who are not just like him. He does not have a high rank, though, and he only knows what he has overheard.

"I am *Defiant Shark* of the family Xié and I am the *Shànji de Jùnshi* and standard-bearer of the fourth Tuán of the Expeditionary Lù," he said. *It has taken a lot of backwards and forwards to even find out what that means. My wife thinks he is the senior Starşiyrang of his unit. It is why he had a banner. We faced over five thousand of his fellows, and that is a Tuán. His Lù had six Tuán in it, but the other five were on board their ships when the storm hit; he calls it the* Tai'fun.

His Lù seems to be at least twice as big as a Darkreach Tagma. There may be many people in Sharan, but the actual Army—mages, elephants, chariots, cavalry, and foot soldiers—would probably only make up one of these Lù. From what he says, there are many more of them in the Armies of this Zhōngyáng Tiānsháng Wángguó than even Darkreach has under arms. Darkreach, from what I can make out, has around ten Tagma. The Chin have twenty Lù—well, nineteen now.

We would have had no chance to succeed if they had all been on the shore, but they had already been embarked in order to go on to attack Wolfneck tomorrow. His General, or Strategos—he calls him a Jiānjūn—kept them on the island as a counter to the forces of the other races that fought for the Adversaries. In particular, he did not trust the Sslan'ssisswani and those from Ērānshahr. Such a lovely lot of people they all are.

He regards it as only natural that, when called on to do so by the Gods, the soldiers of the Chin had been sent by their Emperor Luó Tiānshàng Měidé to aid the Gods in their struggle against the Demons. Apparently that is us. We are shape-shifting Demons and other lesser beings who are in their thrall. We offend against the Will of Heaven by resisting the Gods as they attempt to regain their power and their land from the winged Demons that control us.

"I cannot judge the Zǔxiān Shén. They are the Ancestor Spirits and servants of the Gods. They do as the Gods wish. My duty is to simply obey the Gods through the Emperor." *Many people have used obedience to their rulers as an excuse to do evil in the past.* "If I am set free it is my duty to keep doing what I was told to do." *So, you need to die, it seems. We were lucky to capture him, unconscious and wounded as he was, probably from one of Ariadne's rocks.*

He called his Empire a mighty people and, although they needed to keep forces at home to defend against Ērānshahr, they send forces wherever the Gods will it. He was reluctant to admit it, but apparently there is a second of these Lù somewhere at sea at present and heading here. It is due in a week or so. We will need to look into this.

Rani listened hard to the words of the banner-bearer of the Chin. She shuddered at the idea that there was a whole Empire out there who fought as the yellow men had fought and who are instantly ready to obey the Adversaries even if they do not condone their atrocities. *I cannot say so in front of Ayesha, but his people and some of hers have the same attitude to obedience. Mind you, I suspect that the thugs of Kali are of the same mindset as well. Fanatics, all of them.*

Try as I might, I cannot discern any way in which my people would be acceptable to this man's Emperor except as slaves. He keeps urging us to obey and set everything right by going now to his land and submitting to the judgement of the Emperor for our misdeeds. Personally, I am wondering how we can avoid meeting these people at all.

We have the Chin, the Persians of Ērānshahr, the Sslan'ssisswani and even the unknown races of Kharl, none of whom are still alive, all coming from the Long Realm. It had taken several trips by the Dragon of the Seas *to bring all of the others here. Each time it came some of the Chin craft had sailed along with it to take advantage of its winds.*

Luckily most of these giant vessels—from the look of the wrecks that we saw, each far bigger than the galleons of Freehold—carried more food than they had soldiers. What is more, it seems that none of the Chin vessels have their own wind, so at least we will have that on our side when we meet. They have rockets; they do not mount them on their giant vessels but only on special craft that are kept close to their shore.

Theodora

So, once again the Eldar came back. It was not enough that they were defeated at Nameless over three thousand years ago; once again they help to foment trouble on behalf of the Adversaries. It is probably just as well that Ariadne killed their leader with the light thrower. He was probably a formidable mage, as well.

Apparently even the Strategos of these Chin deferred to him. Does this mean that they will keep coming back like a plague every few thousand years? I need to make sure that the Granther knows my speculation. I am sure that I can get a letter to him. Perhaps I should even send a copy of all of these interrogations.

My husband has heard of the Eldar, but she knows little about them. The short-lived have them almost as legends, but then the entire history of the West paints them differently to the way we know them in Darkreach. It took a while, but Ariadne realised who they were eventually. Astrid still has not. Despite the Wolfneck area once being a part of Darkreach, they have the same legends to draw on as the rest of the West, and they are wrong in almost every way.

Rani

The last of the naked black men left alive said that he came from the Desert Land where the world is hottest. He said that the tall, pale mage-officers are from the Great Southern Land and my wife has told me she will tell me more of the real Eldar later. This black man, who even under magic would not tell us his name, seemed to know them best. He said that some of them were male and some were female. According to him, few went to their land and none left with their mind the same.

None of the pale mages have survived the battle. "All of us were very scared of them." *Theodear nodded when he said that.* "They regarded themselves as being above the rest of those on the island," he said, "and they were cruel, deliberately or even just casually, as no others were. They would kill a person as easily as a person would kill an ant. It was as if they did not think of anyone else as being a person." *My wife seems to agree with him.*

He spoke of the Adversaries as being creatures of the Dreamtime, as spirits who could assume sacred forms and meet you in the world of dreams. They could point a bone and a man would die, but it was an honour to serve the Dreamtime spirits as their hunters and trackers, even if he did not understand why they got him and his friends to do what they did.

Neither did he know why the magic of his kaditja men had failed as soon as they left their home. Only Dobun and the Bear Folk seem to understand what that is about and somehow I am sure they will not share their understanding with me. However, he regarded the rain, the failure of magic and many other things, such as our skin-changers, as proof that this was a spirit place.

They had been told that if they died they would go back to their bodies in their own land and no longer see the spirits. Thus he was sad to die here, but convinced that he would soon wake up in the place of his Dreaming, once again warm and with his clan around him. If he were let go free he would not return home and so he would try and kill others until he himself was slain. He is sure that he needs to die in order to properly return home.

Rani
it is several hours later

*O**nly the little lizard can be regarded as being both innocent and safe to allow to keep living, and so I instructed she be released. Astrid gave me a look at that and I had to give her the translation helmet as a sort of compensation. Now she has the lizard following her around along with the Kichic-kharl, and with Jillian and the Kanaka girl as well. She is trying to get the last lizard and the two girls to play together. It isn't working.*

We learned things about their lands, but none could tell us a thing about whether the Adversaries were all on that craft I hit, or whether there are other groups of them elsewhere in the world. I think that I need to get our various seers to look into this, and also see what they can find out about this Chin fleet. I think I will do that quietly.

None of this has stopped Basil from following his custom and noting everything down, particularly about their lands. Sometimes what they had to say, such as the black man saying that their magic had stopped working the moment they left the land of their Dreaming, made no sense, but Basil still wrote everything down. Theodear wants to send a copy of all of it to Hrothnog, and I suppose that would be polite. He might be able to add to it for us.

Hulagu

E ven while the questioning was still going on, Hulagu had discovered a new game for the riders to play. Sìle had asked him to take her out over the water on his saddle. She asked the rest of the Horse to carry rocks and to fetch more as they used them up. Curiously, they did as they were bid and went out with the Shaelkie to find out about the strange orbs in the ocean.

Once the location of the first had been pointed out by the swimmers, who then withdrew a very long way from it, the riders in the sky began to drop rocks from high up, trying to strike one of these balls until something happened. It was very obvious when they managed it, because it resulted in a very satisfactory explosion.

Alaine had to quickly dodge her saddle through the sky as a tower of water rose high from the sea and waves went out in expanding circles from the eruption. It was an explosion so loud and so violent that everyone stopped what they were doing on the island and on the ships to rush and see what had happened. Mind you, it is a fun game to see who can set the most of them off.

The Shaelkie were kept busy in locating the devices and then getting well clear of them. They knew that they had to be clear as each explosion left fish floating around in the sea and they felt its effects in their very bones, even when they were many filled hands of paces away from the explosion.

It did not take them long to discover that the safest place to be is out of the water on the rocks. We need to be nearly a bowshot above them to be safe. Still, by the end of the day, everyone involved had pains in their ears and heads and several had difficulty standing for some days. *At least the devices will no longer prevent the Shaelkie from swimming where they wish.* The explosions were a background noise all day to the people working on the island.

Rani

T he next day, after the rest of the prisoners had been duly executed, they began the process of boarding their ships to return to their homes. *The Sea Nomads will be eventually rejoining their villages, all of which should now be below Gil-Gand, but first they can take the people from the north of*

The Land home to their villages as they sail along the coast.

The River Dragon *will deliver most of us to Wolfneck and we can fly home from there. It will then go home through Darkreach. I was not given much choice on this. I was going to have it travel around in the opposite way to how we came here, but when I said a few words on this out loud I noticed Astrid take Olympias aside.*

They exchanged more than a few quiet but urgent words, and then came to me as a united front. Once the conversation was over the two both insisted on travelling that way. The sisters had received a puzzled expression from Rani, when they confronted her. *I really wanted everyone to come back together to the village as soon as was possible, but the two are determined.*

The two women had received a more calculating look from Theodora. Just as Rani was looking set to argue for having a quicker return, Theodora drew her husband aside and, after a short conversation, Rani came back to announce that it was a very good idea to travel that way around The Land and with a fuller crew than was needed just to sail the vessel.

My wife says they can keep a watch for that other Army of the Chin and we can send letters to Hrothnog with them and return the soldiers that he loaned us, but I think she sees something else that she is not sharing with me. It seems that Virginia will have to wait quite a while longer to get back to Didymoteichon and perhaps to the young Baron Elias.

Chapter XXXIII

Olympias
28th December, it is around midday

Using a telescope, Olympias examined the coast to her starboard as the *River Dragon* sailed alongside it. *Ever since we left Wolfneck, from the moment the forest rose into the mountains, as far as I can see at any rate, steep-sided valleys dive into rock-bound cliffs that are topped with barren ridges or, even if lower and sheltered, dense stands of conifers and other plants. From where I am there is no sign of a path along the top.*

Some of the valleys are only short and I can see their heads; many start with a waterfall. For others, their waters disappear around corners and seem to go back a long way, perhaps even deep into the mountains. This land will never provide a ready path for land-bound trade and only someone as lightly equipped as my sister's Kharl would ever be able to tread it easily. Like it or not, the way along this coast will be largely confined to the sea.

Offshore, isolated rocks stand tall as small islands, and even out where we are shoals lurk beneath the waves. The saddles are busy even in this relative calm. In a storm, any ship sailing these waters without knowing them risks being driven onto the tall cliffs with tumbled heaps of boulders lashed by waves along their base.

I have never seen good charts of this area. Perhaps some exist from when Wolfneck was ours, but I have not seen them. I think I will suggest that people be sent up here to map this coast. In a storm, a craft would have to seek shelter and brave one of these unknown valleys, which seem to offer as little shelter as the cliffs beyond them.

The lowest cliffs visible to the saddles as they fly down the valleys are as tall as the ship's masts. Nowhere can they find a place to put a settlement. Perhaps a dock or a wharf could be carved out of the cliffs themselves by magic, expanding on a few tiny, flat places. I wonder if one of our Earth mages could do that. I suppose that they could. If Goditha can open up a pit the size of the one she had supposedly used in the battle, how hard could it be to create a tunnel in the rock or to form a ledge?

She drew a few lines on her chart as the latest findings were called back to her on the far-speakers and then sat back and looked at what was in front of her. *Even though I have some rough charts now, they are not good ones. I am glad that I have the saddles available to me to show the way. Outside the Empire these maps are nearly useless, and they are rapidly getting covered in notes that show what we have found.*

The wind filled the *River Dragon's* sails and gave the opportunity for the crew to practice their skills as sailors rather than relying on magic.

It was hard enough getting them started towards becoming competent in the first place, and I do not want them to lose their skills. We might not always have this ship as our only one; we could buy another, or even take one as a prize in a battle, and you never know what you will be forced to do in an emergency.

The current and the waves are travelling in the same direction we are with the wind, and we ride in a leisurely way across the sea, up and down on the low swell, with crests catching us and slowly rolling under the craft and then, equally slowly, drawing ahead, creaming along the base of the cliffs when they reach them and disappearing when they go into the long valleys.

Despite being kept busy making notes on my charts, it is a pleasant day's sail. Only the shoals break the smooth waters and disturb the waves. Some of the shoals come out a long way from headlands as traps for unwary passing ships. Luckily, most of these betray their presence with islands and visible outcrops.

Astrid
30th December, early morning

*W*hen we left Wolfneck, at the start of this leg, I made sure that the crew would be keeping a good watch on the skies. It is a nervous watch for *them. It is already the time for the migration of the whales, and it will not only be my old neighbours from Wolfneck in their low boats who will be coming out seeking to catch them. I made sure they knew the three Dragons of the North would soon be out feeding as well.*

Here we are three days later, and we are starting to leave the main line of the mountains behind, when one of them can be seen in the sky far behind us, plunging into the water and coming up with one of the huge fish struggling in its claws. Everyone is looking to the rear to watch as the giant flying beast rises slowly from the ocean, water streaming off it like a mighty waterfall all around.

I have seen it all before, but if they have a glass they can watch the sea boil in turbulence at such a passage through it. Even from here you can watch lesser lizard fish and dolphins plunge back into the water from the dragon's flanks and wings where they had been picked up by accident. It is an awesome sight, and, thankfully, they ignore the boats for prey that is just the right size for them.

This was the only such hunt they saw close enough to pick out such detail. It was as close as any wanted to be. They saw another in the distance soon after, but it was too far away to see clearly. *Rani does not want to allow any of the saddle riders to go closer to find out more. She really does not understand that we are like gnats to them. They ignore us unless we annoy them or, of course, they are made to want to hunt us.*

Olympias
30th December, toward dusk

*N*o other sails were visible along the entire coast until we came in sight of our first port of call here at Cold Keep. I have never been posted here, but I assume that the few craft that can be seen heading out are going to fish. A couple are headed along the rocky shore. I assume they will be after lobster or diving for abalone, for they hug the coastline.

We have been here once before, but we are still unfamiliar to the people. The boats headed towards the sea are prudently steering well clear of us on long reaches that take them well out from the shore. They are in our lee, but if we were relying on sail we would have to tack hard to get out to them.

Praetor Perissótero Memrin do Levtidy
Froúrarchos (garrison commander) at Cold Keep

"*F*roúrarchos, Froúrarchos, come quickly," called a voice. *It sounds like one of the sentries from the tower calling down. What is ever urgent here?* Nonetheless, she pulled herself away from her warm mug of beef tea and headed out the door. *It may be spring, but the evenings are still chill here* *at this long-forgotten northern outpost of Empire.*

"What is so important?" she said as she emerged. *The woman is pointing west and out towards the sea.*

"Flyers," the watcher replied. "There are flyers coming towards us." Memrin looked north-west from the wall walkway she was on. *I can see nothing from here, just the sky gradually growing pink behind the mountains as the Kron sinks.*

"Are you sure they are not just large Leatherwings, or birds?" she asked. *She does not reply, but merely looks hurt. I had to ask, though.* The Praetor began to climb the stairs up to the watch point.

"Hurry, ma'am," the sentry called down through the doorway. "They move quickly." Memrin came to the top and looked in the direction that the malc pointed. *Those are not birds. There have been rumours of people flying into Ardlark, but there is quite a difference between rumour and actually seeing them approaching your walls.*

"Strike the gong," she ordered. The sentry reached beside her for the leather-covered wooden mallet. "Two strikes." *That will get people to their posts, but not alarm them.* Soon the area within the walls was a hive of activity. The malc were taking posts and the civilian population were seeking shelter in case it was needed. *Three strikes would have meant imminent attack; we will soon find out if I am not being cautious enough.*

Even though it was a far larger base than the tiny garrisons on mountain peaks up and down the Great Range, Cold Tower served more as a point from which to issue warnings than as a serious military force. Memrin's fingers fumbled over the chain that never left her neck and found the amulet that she wore always. *If I break this, then Ardlark and Antdrudge will know we are under attack. It will not help us, but it may help them.*

I sent Tarakratz and his Omáda west to the old Northern Reaches and Wolfneck. Did I do the right thing? Are these flyers from the people they were sent to aid or are they from the other side? We saw the flaming thing weaving through the sky over a week ago. What did that presage? If the side I have precipitated us into has lost, I am ill-equipped to stop it. We don't even have anyone up here on a training rotation at present.

"Froúrarchos, look, there is a ship out there as well. It has sails like the one that was here, the one that got us to look for a trade route. Does that mean that they are friends?" Memrin looked at the horizon. *She is right about the sails. That is all I can see. I could not recognise one sail from another, and her guess is as good as mine on the last question. I should, however, take precautions on that count.*

She thought a moment. *The river on our west is more protection for us than our walls, that is why all of our small fields are on this side of it. However, this is obviously not something from the Wild Tribes. It will be connected one way of another with whatever I sent malc towards.* She looked down and saw that her Omáda of scouts already had their wolves saddled and were waiting in the square for orders.

"Starşiyrang," she called. "Take your Omáda out and watch what happens. We will signal with a green flag if you are to return. If you see any other colour, withdraw further and be prepared to report to whoever comes up from the south. Avoid combat if you can. You are to find things out." She brought her fist to her chest and the salute was returned.

They are quickly out of the gate. She turned back to the flyers. *They are slowing down and dropping in height. There are three of them, two women and a man, and it looks as if they are headed down to the gate to our wharf. I suspect that they are friendly, then. I cannot think that flyers who meant us ill would bother coming to the door and knocking.*

She turned to the sentry. "I am headed down to the gate," she said. "What colour flag will you raise if I call out the all clear?"

"Green, Praetor," was the reply. Memrin nodded and grabbed hold of the drop pole and quickly slid down to ground level through the hole in the tower. She hurried over to the gate. *Everyone is in places along the wall. The forest gate has been closed tight as soon as the riders left from it.*

Basil
soon after

"Are you sure that you do not want to just wait until we get into port?" Basil asked Astrid as they flew with Ia towards Cold Keep. "That way a Princess would have to deal with customs and other matters instead of us doing it. Surely you need the rest."

"Rest?" his wife replied. "I may have been able to return the Kanaka girl to the *Ofu*, but I still have Jillian, a hand of Kichic-Kharl and a Lizard following me everywhere. Dealing with your port officials will be a pleasant relief, and anyway, that is for you to do. Ia and I are just here to keep you company. Besides, it is not obvious if our ship is friend or foe. It is best to establish that before it comes inside the range of a rocket or something."

Basil looked back at the ship they had left. *Its sail is visible, and it would be only just so to anyone on a watch tower. There would be no details of the craft. From the ground you would not even be able to see its green hull. I guess that she is right.*

They came in high and then, once the sounding of an alarm bell signalled they had been seen, dropped much lower, down to the height of a normal person, and slowed to a fast walking speed. They came to a stop politely outside the river gate, waiting to be identified by the nervous guards.

Praetor Perissótero Memrin do Levtidy, garrison commander at Cold Keep

"They are outside," came a voice from above her. *Everyone is looking at me.* Memrin nodded at the malc beside her.

"Open up," she said. The bar was lifted and the gate swung open by a person on each side.

"Greetings, Praetor." *He is not in uniform, but he is saluting, and his other hand is holding an Antikataskopeía sigil up for me to see. That is a nice start.* "I am Tribune Akritas and these are my wives Astrid"—*I can see that she is Insakharl, but that is an Insak-div bardiche she has strapped beside her*—"and Ia." *She is…I am not sure what she is.*

"You will see a ship in view. It is commanded by my sister, Epilarch Akritina"—*it is the ship that visited us earlier, then*—"and this time it has as a passenger, Archis Theodora do Hrothnog."

"She likes to see everything when she comes to a new place," interjected the Insakharl. *Astrid? Her accent is strange. Why is her husband giving her a look like that and why is she smiling at him in such a way?* "I am sure you can oblige her in that." *We are having an Imperial family visit? We have not seen one of them up here in the snows for many years. Of course we will show her everything.*

"We are also returning your malc to you," the woman continued. *She has lost her smile.* "Half of them, at least. They fought well and they fought bravely. The rest will be remembered on Sixth Tagma Day. I thank you for sending them to us. I will also pass my thanks to the Emperor when I see him soon." *Why is this wife seeing the Emperor and not the Tribune? She says it so casually, as well.* Memrin looked harder at the woman's eyes. *No, she is not Imperial family.*

*T*hat ship is coming in under full sail and, although I may not be much of a sailor, the direction of the sails has no relation at all to the direction the wind is coming from. There is scarce any breeze at all, and what is there is square to the way the sails face. The ship must be enchanted to do that. The sails stayed up, apparently filled with wind, until it was beside the wharf, when suddenly they dropped limply and the ship drifted to a stop.

When our fishers return to port tonight and hear about this, they are going to be pestering our local mage about it until we can get something like it for them. She, I am sure, is not strong enough to do what they will want her to do for them.

I have to admit, though, that working with our rocky shores as our fisher-men do, it would be good to have the wind at your call. We sometimes lose craft. I wonder if I can write something in a report about it being a matter of public safety, and get a stronger mage or two sent up here to enchant our fishing boats—for the public good, of course.

Astrid
later that evening

Theodora has been enjoying herself too much as a war leader, or even just as a mage and passenger enjoying a cruise. It was perhaps cruel of me to set their Governor, or whatever she is, onto her, but she needs to get back to her role as a Princess. The woman is excited by the idea of being more than just an outpost of Empire. She is more eager to talk about trade than the battle we just went through.

Now she is dragging the pair of Princesses all over the settlement. Having a member of the Imperial family talking trade to the Governor has the woman even more excited. Opening up to the lands to the west might attract more people to settle and could even create more possibilities for the people that live here now. I can imagine they would like that. This place has so little to offer now. Trapping and furs would be most of it.

It will never fully lose its military function, because of both the Dragons of the north and the Wild Tribes of the mountains. At Wolfneck we were well aware of both of those issues as well; the tribes are why we have the Rangers, after all. Apparently Wolfneck used to be a part of the Empire. Surely there had to have been a land route running through the mountains once. Maybe it can be found again.

"From the looks she is giving you," Ia said, "I think Theodora knows who is responsible for her having to inspect absolutely everything that there is to see, even the toilets."

Astrid smiled back at the glare directed at her. "I am sure that she does," she replied, "but that is her job. Hopefully we will be having little in the way of fighting to face now. She will just have to go back to being a mage and a ruler, and this sort of thing is what rulers are supposed to do, I think. She may not like it, but she likes being a Princess, so she gets the whole job or none. I thought she needed a reminder. Notice that she made Rani join in on it as well."

She pointed across the square. "See, our husband is also doing his job." Basil was talking to the Primus, who was the senior half of the local Antikataskopeía.

She looked across at Tarkratz and his hand of survivors. "Just as I suppose that I am doing mine." *They seem determined to both give me an honour guard and to also garner as much prestige for themselves as they can from their adventure. I should indulge that. Like my axes, they paid a lot.*

She went over to the group of Kichic-Kharl. "Do any of you have family here?" All of them are nodding back. "Why," she continued, "don't you go and bring them, and the families of those who were lost, to me so that I can tell them what heroes you all are." *I am not sure I have ever seen smiles appear that quickly.* With scarce a pause, they were starting to head off.

"Yes, Lyubimyy iz Hrothnog," Mardrikrat said as he moved quickly away. *"Favoured by Hrothnog". I thought I'd heard that said earlier. I was not sure it was directed at me. It seems that it is. I am not sure if that is a good or a bad addition to my growing list of names. I have a feeling that it will stick, though, at least if I ever come back here.*

To her sister-wife's amusement, Astrid soon found herself seated on a veranda in the dark with several children, wives and even widows and a widower around her. *Oh Saint Kessog, the widows, they are the ones that need me here most. The others can wait for a while. These ones had partners who lost their lives trying to protect me. They need to be made to feel that their lives were not wasted.*

One has a new-born baby. She is being presented to me. I think that I am supposed to bless her or something. She is a tiny, wrinkled green person and she has to have been born even while the battle was taking place. Her father was one of those who died and so he will now never see his daughter, nor will she know him.

"With your permission, Kyria, may I call her Astrid?" the mother nervously asked. *I swear that I will kill my sister-wife if she makes a laugh to go with that grin.*

Not sure what to say, Astrid beckoned Ia over and whispered a few words to her. Her sister-wife left towards the gateway to the wharf and Astrid looked at the woman, who was now holding the swaddled infant even more nervously awaiting a response. Astrid reached out and took the infant and waved her hand over her. "Astrid gir, Little Astrid, may you grow to be as mighty a warrior as your father was before you," she said before looking at the mother. *I hope that Christopher does not mind me sort of giving a Blessing, but I think it was expected.*

The mother is much paler than a Kichic-Kharl should be. Not only is she grieving, but it must have been a hard birth for her before that. "It is little comfort, but what he"—*damn, I do not even know his name*—"did was important for the whole of Vhast." She cradled the baby in her arms before looking at her audience.

"What all of your people did was so very important. Your Omáda from here fought alongside people like me and from among the Bear Folk. We fought archers like Little Seeker there," she pointed at the Lizard, "and we fought monsters five times my height, beasts that could kill hundreds, we fought them out in the open before the armies met, and we killed them."

Ah, good, Ia was quick. She put out her hand, quickly looking at what she was given. "This bracelet is for Astrid gir. She will grow into it." Astrid slipped it onto the arm of the baby. *It may be a long time before she does, though.* "If she comes to visit us at Mousehole when she grows, I will make sure that she is made welcome.

"My husband tells me that you will have a pension from the Emperor, but that will not make up for a lonely bed. Use this wisely when you need it." She handed over a small, but heavy, purse. *Now I need to say words to all of the others as well. They were hanging off everything I said to that mother, and she is now crying when before she was dry-eyed. I hope I am doing the right thing.*

Basil warned me this sort of thing might happen as we flew in. At least Mardrikrat, "my" druid, the one who seemed to be presiding over this presentation of people, has whispered that I need give out no more presents. Apparently only those named after me deserve the honour of a personal gift. But there is still one other thing I need to do.

"I know," she said, "that, as well as the pension, those who survived will share the gleanings from the battlefield with the families of those who did not." She looked around before digging into her pouch and looking at what came out as she emptied it. *At least one large golden coin each. Only one local one, but gold is gold.*

"Allow me to add to that as their leader in battle." She handed the money to Mardrikrat to disperse. "All of your people were in the thickest of combat instead of acting as scouts as they should have. Hrothnog entrusted them to me, but he should not have risked them like that. I deeply wish that I could have returned with more of your people. Remember them on Sixth Tagma Day. I will wear a poppy for them."

Now let us wrap this obligation up. She noticed two others mingling with the Kichic-Kharl. *Jillian stands out, but she is playing with a young green girl. As for my Lizard, although she cannot speak to the Kharl, they sort of fit together. She has her green leathery skin, and the crest of feathers on her head that rise up like a cockatoo's when she is surprised or is expressing emotions is not too different to the often crested hair of the others.*

However, her lashing tail is different, as is her forward-sloped stance and clawed feet. Despite their scaly skin, the Kharl could never be mistaken in their face and body and manner as anything but mammals. On the other hand, despite her ability to speak and use her hands, Little Seeker can only ever be seen as coming from reptilian stock.

Olympias
31st December, soon after dawn

I wish they had better charts here, but none exist even in Ardlark. It is time that was fixed, if the Emperor does want to set up trade with the northern towns. Olympias had steered her vessel well out to sea before setting the course that would lead her towards Ardlark. *I should not have to head so far out to be clear of any potential shoals. Mind you, we still need to look out for this other fleet of the Chin.*

She looked back at the shore. *That should be sufficient.* "Wheel to the starboard," she called. "Head due east-southeast until we sight Putevaya Tochka Kamen. Keep our wind strong." She moved forward to make her notes in the log, staying clear of the girl on the wheel as she did so.

Without stopping at Antdrudge we have four days of fast sailing until we see the light and make another correction to bring us around to Ardlark in a bit under a day. With the saddles and the green-light box we need not even set a constant and precise bearing. We can correct once we get closer to the light. How have we sailed these coasts for so long without having these things to aid us?

Chapter XXXIV

Astrid
1ˢᵗ Undecim, it is the Feast Day of Saint Michael and just after dawn

The Princesses are still sound asleep, and I am sure will be until we come very near to the port. Ia has greeted the dawn and gone back to her hammock. There is really just the crew and me, and Little Seeker, of course. Unless I fly, I cannot even go to the jakes without her being nearby. I am just lucky that Jillian is asleep as well.

She looked west. *The navigation lights of Ardlark are not lined up yet. We still steer south-east and have yet to come around. The very top of the Palace is lit brightly, but most of it is still shaded.* Around her was the gentle sound of the water creaming away beneath the bow of the *River Dragon* and the soft creak of the rigging. She could sense, more than hear, the watch moving around and getting ready to bring the ship to port.

Now I need to make a choice. My saddle is right there. I can climb on it and go and see Hrothnog before anyone is aware that I have left, and by anyone I mean my family and the Princesses, not the crew, who will most likely just assume I am off doing something that I am supposed to. My sister is not even on deck yet. She will come up with the change, of course.

She looked at the Palace and the navigation lights. *They are nearly lined up. Soon Olympias will be called and she will try and stop me. I...I know what I am going to do.* She called out to the helm. "I am going to the Palace to make sure they have rooms ready. I will probably be back before you dock."

She looked at Little Seeker. "I will return soon." *Or not.* "Do not wake anyone."

Astrid moved quickly to her saddle and took off. Fluff-Ball leapt and joined her as she rose. *No word about telling anyone at the helm, so it even sounds like I am supposed to be doing this. Little Seeker will stay quiet because I told her to and because I have the speaking hat.*

Astrid
soon after

You would think they would be used to us. How many times have we been here now? Every time we are flying in and out. She looked at the turmoil at the doors. *This is beyond a joke.* "The Emperor said I was to be given access to him as if I were Strategos Panterius. I know that my husband the Tribune is not with me yet, but he soon will be." *As soon as he wakes up and finds me gone, most likely.*

A girl has appeared. "Welcome Kyria Lyubimyy iz Hrothnog, to the Palace, I am Zampea Gounara," she said, and inclined her head respectfully. Someone was paying attention, it seemed. That name did not take long to find its way into use. *The looks on the faces of the guards are most interesting as they hear that greeting.* "I am light. You will take me to the balcony of the Xenodokheion, and then I will show you the way to the Emperor."

She is dressed as one of the messengers that Hrothnog has in his office, rather than a normal servant. The girl climbed behind Astrid, trying not to touch her. "Girl…Zampea…unless you are used to flying," Astrid said, "you had better put your arms around me. I won't bite." The messenger complied and they rose through the sky.

Astrid looked east. *And we are just in time. I see that a few more saddles are already heading this way from the ship.*

Astrid
a few minutes later

*"It is done," Hrothnog told Astrid. *What does he mean by that?* "The ones that used to be my brothers…that you call the Adversaries…have no one left on this world. The ones that were here on Vhast were sent for a purpose. They…or, indeed, originally, *we*…were the only ones of a number so large that you would have difficulty believing it, that could use any magic at all, and so we were the only ones who could act here to reach that goal.

"We have taken several ages to advance to where we are—and you saw how little my former brothers and one sister could do without aid. We had to use people of weak will to act for us." *There seems to be many of them.* "There are," Hrothnog replied to the thought. "It is by taking advantage of their weaknesses that our race, the Daveen, gains control of a world.

"Often we…and then they…had to use machines because we were so weak. It was only when they started making the Masters that they gained much magic power at all and the Masters, who were made identical and all at the same time—which is why they were all Air mages—were actually more powerful as enchanters than my sibs."

"By then I had rejected that path as being wrong and had abandoned all that it stood for, including the machines, so…well…it is the end. I am certain that no more can come from our home world—and it is far from the one we stand on now and call Vhast—who can act as we used to. The machines we had require something to work with, and no others have shown that talent in very many thousands of years."

"So that is it?" Astrid asked. "There can be no others? It is all at an end?"

"There are others." Hrothnog waved vaguely upwards "Another people—though you have called them the Eldest, they are really called the *Shing-Zu*—but they will not interfere in the same sort of way. They are the ones who gave you so much, but they are also weaker…far weaker and, what is more, they want you to succeed, in their own way. I am almost certain they are the ones who set the people of your valley in motion, but they cannot easily, or often, do that. You can now go back to your place in the mountains and do what you want without compulsion."

"But Freehold and these other places…the Long Realm?" asked Astrid.

"The people in those places are no more or less evil than others. Some are good and some are bad. What your people choose to do with them is up to you. I will tell you now: I do not think there will be any more grand prophecy. From now on there will be only the lives that you choose for yourselves, much as I have chosen this life for myself."

Chapter XXXV

Mangana
the time is hard to determine, it could even be today

Mangana looked around him. *I do not know where I am, but I am no longer at the Place of Death, the battleground where I saw those whom I had thought to be the Sky Spirits from the Dreamtime. That is an improvement.* He had pleaded with the spirits, with his totem animals, with his connection to the land, to come and take him home… *But this is not the land of my Dreaming. Nor is it the land of my clan, and yet… Why do I feel something for it? I feel that it is my home on a very deep level.*

The pale spirit men of the sky had said they were those who brought my people out of the Dreamtime and into the parched heat of the land I belong to. Although I can read the minds of men, when I concentrate, I cannot read theirs, and so that means they have power. They had said to follow, and I and two hands of men left our families behind and did as we were told.

We have travelled all over since then, following tracks that were invisible to others. As a Spirit Man I have used my skills until they faded… No one knows why. At least I am still a tracker, even if my wooden and stone weapons were useless in the fight that has just unfolded. I was just starting to feel the different way of this land, the land of someone else's Dreaming, and once again was starting to craft words of Power.

The Sky Spirits, in their sky boat, had ascended into the realm of the sky only to fall to the fire of the people who had landed at the Place of Death. I watched from my place of hiding the dark-skinned woman, still with skin lighter than mine, cast a rod of fire that in an instant caused the boat to break into flames when it was almost out of sight.

She may be a Spirit Woman, but she is very strong in Fire instead of Earth or Water. I am of the sign of the Puraloo and when I was in my homeland I cast Fire too, but not as well as I saw her do. Her Fire reached out to the sky beyond the sight of most people. Perhaps this was the land of her Dreaming and that is why she has so much power. I saw many Spirit Women casting strongly on the other side.

He looked around. *This is a land of Water.* Looking out from where he stood, high on a mountain, he could see a city spread out below him. *I had never seen a city before I left my home. Now I have seen several. This is different to any other that I have seen, and it is far larger than most, but it is still a city…and it is a city built around water.*

I can see a big river winding its way between hills. I can see ships, huge ships… That one heading up the river has no sails and it is as big as a city itself. Above and behind me looms the bulk of a mountain. He shivered in the cold. *Is that snow on it that I can see through the swirling cloud? I had never seen that before I left my home, either.*

Before me lies a path leading across under this looming cliff. It has been used recently, and it looks like, if I turn left, I will head downhill. I need to find out where I am. I need to know if I am still in danger…and even more, I need to find out why I feel that my ability to work in the Spirit World is coming back. This is not the land of my Dreaming…Why does my Spirit tell me that it is and that I, alone so far from all of my people, have truly come home?

Glossary

Aberbaldie: a village of Amity

Adversaries: one of the names that the major protagonists in these stories are known by

Ahriman: the 'evil' God of Ērānshahr, presumed to be behind the Adversaries

Ahura Mazda: the 'good' God of Ērānshahr

Aldhelm, Saint: a Christian Saint, his Feast Day is 25th Quinque, he is the patron of scholars

All Souls: a Christian Feast day on the 24th of October, it is a day of prayer and remembrance for the departed of the Faith

Amity: the name taken for their area by the villages of the Brotherhood once it falls, it is also the name of the forest where most of its settlements are located

Anastasi, the Feast Day of: celebrating the resurrection of Christ, it is an important part of the celebration of Easter for the Christians, particularly the Orthodox

Ancient Ones: one of the many names that the Adversaries are known by their followers

Andronicus, Saint: a Christian Saint, his Feast Day 14th December, he is invoked against demons and insanity

Anne, Saint: Christian Saint, her Feast Day is 25th October and she is the patron both of those who slay the undead and those who return from the dead

Anta Dvīpa: Hindi for 'End Island', it is in Pavitra Phāṭaka and the home of Harijani and foreigners

Antdrudge: A large town in the north of Darkreach where molotails, explosives, and other flammables are made

Antikataskopeía: the Darkreach 'secret police', an arm of the military who are concerned both with criminal investigation and with treason

Archis: a word in Darkreach Greek, 'Princess'

Ardlark: a major city and capital of Darkreach

Arnflorst: see Shunned Isle

Ashvaria: the major city and capital of Freehold

Azrael: a female gargoyle (despite its name) brought to Mousehole from Dwarvenholme

Āyāt: the Arabic word for verses from the Qur'an

Bardiche: a pole weapon with a very long blade that is joined, at one end, to the shaft and at the other forms a spear-like point

Basilica Anthropoi: a Holy Order of warrior monks of the Orthodox Church west of the mountains, they are heavily armed and ride as kataphractoi or kynigoi depending on their role

Bear Folk: a group of Humans who have a high number of bear-based lycanthropes among their number. They live just north of the Swamp

Bidvictor: an independent village of the North, Human and Orthodox

Birchdingle: one of the main Bear-folk settlements

Bonaventura: a Christian Saint, Feast Day is 14th Quinque, he is the patron of negotiators

Boyuk-kharl: the largest and most intelligent of the Kharl races, they are often found in independent units and at sea

Brahmin: the Hindu priestly caste, also found as bankers and moneylenders with others handling the actual money to avoid touching anything a Harijan may have touched

Bridget, Saint: a Christian Saint, her Feast Day is 10th Sixtus, she is the patron of dairymaids, but also compassion to the poor, blacksmiths and poets

Brodir Lind (Brother Shield): a large tavern in Wolfneck

Brotherhood, The: The Brotherhood of All Believers were militant semi-Christians of an extreme Puritan type with a focus on literal truth and rigid obedience, they have been wiped out.

Bulga: an independent village on the north coast of The Land

Burning, the: a disease that causes people to go mad and destroy things, less than one person in twenty survived the years that it raged

Caer Gwyliwr Ddwyrain: known outside The Swamp as Eastguard Tower, this is a well-fortified large village in the north-east of the Swamp

Caliphate: a Muslim Kingdom nestled high in the south of the Great Range

Castle Mount: a town in the New Found Land that is, at the same time, a Barony and the usual home of its Duke

Catherine, Saint: Christian Saint, her Feast Day 24th Duodecimus, she is the patron of any trade involving a wheel, and of chaste women.

Chhand: Hindi for a verse of poetry or in a religious text

Cecilia, Saint: a Christian Saint, Feast Day 23rd Undecim, patron of bards and entertainers

Cenubarkincilari: a small Hobgoblin tribe in the southern mountains. the name roughly means 'Southern Raiders', they are friends with the Mice

Chain: a unit of measurement, 100 links (each 2 hands long), or 20.4m

Chamuel: a male gargoyle that takes up residence in Mousehole

Chin: a Human tribe of the Long Realm, they call their Kingdom Zhōngyāng Tiānshàng Wángguó (the Central Heavenly Realm)

Cold Keep: the most northerly town in Darkreach

Confederation of the Free: a very loose alliance of villages and towns spread through the jungles and bogs that lie between Haven and the mountains

Covington: an island to the north of Skrice, the second of three islands north of The Land, known to those who live on it as No h-Eilean Samhradh

Curia Burgess (Ducatas): a feature of the Newfoundland is that it has a sort of parliament, this is the lower house

Cutach Bheatha: the short-lived, what the Shaelkie call all other races

Darkreach: this is a multi-racial Empire that takes up the eastern third of The Land east of the Great Range. It is ruled (and has been since known time began) by Hrothnog

Dating: Years run over a 48-year cycle; with the twelve zodiacal signs that are used on Vhast along with the elements of Earth, Air, Fire and Water. There are twelve months of equal length, each having six weeks of six days. The first parts of this story take part in the Year of the Water Dog. A year thus has 432 days so a year on Vhast is nearly a fifth longer than a Terran year. A person who is fifteen on Vhast will be eighteen on Earth.

Daveen: a very long-lived space-faring race, usually referred to as the Adversaries on The Land, but known by many other names around Vhast

Days: the six days of the week are Firstday, Deutera, Pali, Tetarti, Dithlau, and Krondag

Dàhé Zhèn (Big River Town): a Chin settlement in the south of the Long Realm, it first appears in the novella *Dàhé Zhèn, a beginning*

Desert Land, The: a blisteringly hot continent on the equator where magic works differently

Dhargev (Our Home): a Hobgoblin village in the Southern Mountains, the main settlement of the Cenubarkincilari tribe

Didymoteichon: a small town and Baronial seat in the New Found land, it is much used by smugglers

Dochra: an oasis town on the Great Road of Darkreach

Dragon of the Seas: a dromond stolen from Darkreach, it uses flame weapons

Drakkar: a low build, clinker-hulled craft of the northern seas, they are fast and very seaworthy, but with no shelter on board and little in the way of cargo space

Dromond: the large warships of Darkreach that use a combination of sail and oar or, rarely, are propelled by their own magic, they are the most powerful warcraft around The Land

Duvaryuz: 'flat-face', what the Goblins call Humans.

Dwarvenholme: the long-lost main city of the Dwarves, recently found and being re-built

Dwarf: a race of Humanoids that tend to live below ground. All Dwarves are bearded and without breasts, they always use masculine or neutral pronouns

Dymphna, Saint: a Christian Saint: Feast Day is 15 Quinque, she is the patron of runaways, victims of incest, and nervous disorders

East Zarah: the tallest mountain on Neron Island, collectively the mountains are the Zarahs and they form a north-south spine to the island

Ell: a unit of measure, a clothyard or 115cm

Epibarti: a Barony in the New Found Land

Epilarch: a Darkreach naval rank with no real equivalent, they can take control of a small flotilla of ships

Erave Town: a town on the southern shore of Lake Erave

Evilhalt: a town at the very northern tip of Lake Erave

Ērānshahr: a land in the Long Realm, the people there are Zoroastrian and worship either Ahura Mazda (good) or Ahriman (evil)

Factor: a person who is in charge of a factory, an older term usually meaning a place of business set up in a foreign land

Filled hand: a hand is six; a pair of hands is twelve, a hand filled is thirty-six, a pair of hands filled is the square of twelve

Foreskin, the: the street name for the northern tip of Anta Dvīpa near the funeral ghāts where there are small temples.

Francis, Saint: Christian Saint, Feast Day 4th October, his patronage is to animals

Freehold: a Kingdom that takes up much of the west of The Land, 'sharing' some of the land uneasily with the Khitan, its Queen is Daphne IV Acer, there are many novellas set there concurrently

Froljarn: a herb that makes a salve useful for burns of all sorts

Froúrarchos: a Garrison Commander in Darkreach (can be any rank)

Frozkintz: a shrub from the arid parts which protects from and heals burns and, in particular, sunburn

Garthang Keep: the most northerly settlement of Haven, it is a strong and ancient fortification

Gasparin: a very hot spice found on the mountain slopes

George, Saint: a Christian Saint, and also highly regarded by Muslims, his Feast Day is 23rd Quartos, and his patronage is to cavalry and to those who fight dragons and demons

Ghāt: a general Hindi term for a wharf, a landing or a set of steps leading to the water.

Ghazi: a holy warrior of the Caliphate, what we might call an assassin

Gil-Gand-Rask: a large island in the Southern Seas, Gil-Gand is the city on it

Glengate: a town to the west of Lake Erave on the path to Freehold

Goblin: a small and lightly built Humanoid with a skin that looks more like a snake than a Human, they call themselves the Gulyabani, the Goblin language is unique on Vhast in that there are Goblins on several continents, the words used are spelt very much the same, but the spoken dialects are mutually incomprehensible

Goldentide, The: a Freehold galleon taken and sunk by the *River Dragon*

Great Southern Land: the home of the surviving Eldar and others, it is situated in the southern hemisphere of Vhast

Greatkin: a town of Amity and its capital, it lies on Cangi Creek

Greensin: a town north-west of Evilhalt, it is the home of the senior of the western Metropolitans of the Orthodox Church

Gryphon, Order of: servants of the Adversaries in Freehold

Gulyabani: the Goblin name for themselves

Guneydeolan halksulutoprak: also just Halksulutoprak, a Goblin tribal name, it means 'The Southern People of the Watery Earth', they are located to the west of New Trekvarna, Yabaribaykus comes from there

Halkgenisovadin: A Goblin tribe near Sweetwater. Their name means 'The People of the Wide Valley'. They have signed the Scutari Treaty and may now be part of the Duchy of the New Found Land.

Hand: a basic unit of measure that is made up of six fingers (1.7cm each) and so is 10.2cm long, six of them make a cubit, a hand is six, a hand of hands (or a filled hand) is thirty-six

Harijan: the lowest Hindu caste; often referred to as Untouchables, those who deal with the dead and with liminal products, they are often beggars, thieves, and criminals

Hāthī Dvīpa: Elephant Island in Pavitra Phāṭaka, it houses the Royal Elephants, among other things

Haven or Sharan: a Hindu nation at the mouth of the Rhastaputra River

Hesperinos: performed at sundown, this is the beginning of the liturgical day for the Orthodox

High Speech: a language, descended from Old Speech, which is used extensively by mages

Hillstrider: a large Dwarven sheep used for riding rather than fleece, belongs to Thord

Hob or Hobgoblin: one of the larger humanoid races of Vhast, they have hard grey skin and are very strong and are, to Humans, quite ugly

Hobden Bay: a wide bay in the north of Amity, at the head of it Hobden Creek enters the sea

Homobonus, Saint: a Christian Saint, his Feast Day is 13th November, his patronage is to cloth workers

Hopper: general term for any of the marsupial macropods

Horse, Clan of the: or Mori, a revived Khitan clan based in Mousehole

Hugron pir: a chemical mix that we would call Greek Fire, or perhaps napalm, it is used in flame-throwers and in molotails

Humans: the most common intelligent race on Vhast, they have a wide variety of original origins but, despite when they come from, seem to have all been on Vhast for about the same amount of time

Ibrik: a small bi-conical pot of tin-coated copper used to make kaf

Immobile Stars: the name given to a variety of objects in orbit around Vhast in a geostationary orbit.

Insakharl: this is not a distinct race, but a name given to those who have part-Human and part-Kharl ancestry

Insak-div: the largest of the Darkreach races, and often referred to in the West as Dark Trolls (although they are largely dark green in colour), they are over twice as tall as a Human and a lot broader

Isci-kharl: one of the Kharl tribes of Darkreach, they are large, strong and not overly bright

Iszig: a drink taken hot, it has a taste somewhere between mint and an orange (with a touch of chocolate as well)

Jewvanda: a village on the south coast of The Land on Piali Creek

Jianjūn: a Chin general in charge of a Lù

John Chrysostum, Saint: an Orthodox Saint, Feast Day is 13th November, he is the patron of priests, peacemakers, and those who seek a simple life

John the Baptist: a Christian Saint, Feast Day is 29th Sixtus, he is the patron of pilgrims and those who travel for the faith

Jude, Saint: a Christian Saint, Feast Day is 16th Undecim, he is patron of those with forlorn hopes

Ludos: a combined prison and training area where the criminals of Darkreach are confined between bouts

Kama Sutra: a Hindu religious text that is much concerned with making love

Kanaka: see Sea Nomads

Kemet-Kush: a large continent to the south-west with two civilisations on it.

Kessog, Saint: a Christian Saint, Feast Day is 10th Tertius, he is patron of those who fight monsters on land, taken as a Patron Saint by Astrid

Kharl: some of the races of Vhast, they are the most common form of Humanoid after Humans, they are in several tribes and vary greatly in appearance, but often have some animalistic features

Khitan: a group of mounted tribes who claim and occupy most of the plains

Kichic-kharl: the smallest of the Darkreach Kharl, they are around the same size as a Goblin, in Darkreach they are the scouts and, often, the sailors

Knorr: a clinker-built ship of the northern seas, they have a very low aspect ratio and so are slow and capacious, they are also very sea-worthy

Köle: a Khitan word meaning something between 'prisoner' and 'temporary slave'

Kshatya: the Hindu caste of the warriors, it includes most mages and rulers

Kyria: a Darkreach Greek word meaning 'Lady'

Kyriakí tou Páscha: Greek name for 'Easter Krondag', red-dyed eggs are made for children to find symbolising the blood of Christ

Lake Erave: the major inland body of water in The Land, it is drained by the Rhastaputra River

League: a unit of measurement equal to 3 miles, 9,000 cubits, or 5.49km

Lingam: the male reproductive parts or their representation

Long Realm: a continent that spans most of Vhast from north to south

Luke, Saint: a Christian Saint, Feast Day is 18th October, he is a patron of physicians

Lù: a Chin division, with a variable number of Tuán, but at least three

Magna Curia Ducatas: a feature of the Newfoundland is that it has a sort of parliament, this is the upper house or house of nobles

Magnus, Saint: an Orthodox Saint, Feast Day 36th Sixtus, he is patron of the North and icy wastes

Malc: a Darkreach word for a soldier of any rank

Mark, Saint: a Christian Saint, Feast Day is 23rd September, his patronage is to ferrymen as well as to thieves and robbers

Mary Magdalene, Saint: a Christian Saint, her Feast Day is the 4th of Quinque and her patronage is to sinners and those hoping for redemption

Masters, the: a group of undead druids and mages who once had control over Dwarvenholme

Mathan: an Inuit name for a form of giant bear, one appears in the story *Astrid in the White World*

Maurice, Saint: a Christian Saint, Feast Day is 9th September, his patronage is to infantry and dyers and he is always depicted with dark skin

Meander River: a major river in the Newfoundland

Meander Rose: a Freehold galleon destroyed by the Mice

Metropolitan: the title of an Orthodox arch-bishop, unless a Patriarch is created, it is the highest rank in the Orthodox faith and a Metropolitan, although still subject to a Synod of the whole Faith, is theologically supreme in their area

Michael, Saint: a Christian Saint, his Feast Day is 1st Undecim, he is patron of both graveyards and victory

Misr al-Mār: a monastery and school in the Caliphate, it is the training base for the Ghazi

Molotails: deadly jars of hugron pir meant to be thrown

Moorea: a missing Sea-Nomad island-village

Mori: see Clan of the Horse

Mousehole: a free village in the Southern Mountains ruled by the Princesses Rani and Theodora, its inhabitants are referred to as Mice

Nameless Keep: a major town, fortification and army base in Darkreach on the eastern end of the Darkreach Gap, once known as Nahmess and before that as Nam-Ang

Nekulturny: a word in the Darkspeech of Wolfneck that roughly means uncultured

Neron Island: the last inhabited island to the north of The Land, the village of Skrice is there

New Ashvaria: the major town of the Newfoundland on the Meander River, it also gives its name to the County that surrounds it

Newfoundland or New Found Land: a continent to the north-west of Freehold and a colony of theirs, known to the Goblins as 'ugrakden çok kabilu'

Nicholas, Saint: a Christian Saint, Feast Day 3rd Tertius, patron of perfumers and of children

No h-Eilean Samhradh: see Covington

Oared Lizard: a mosasaurus

Ofu: a Sea-Nomad ship

Old Speech: the oldest known Humanoid language, it is the root language for both High Speech and Ogre at least

Oldike: a large Dwarven settlement in the South-West Mountains of The Land

Omáda: a Darkreach unit, usually of two hands or twelve soldiers

One-Tree Hill: the battleground near Bulga where the Brotherhood were broken

Orthros: the first Orthodox service of the morning usually starting before sunrise

Our Lady: Mary, Mother of God, Feast Day 12th November, patron of motherhood

Outville: an independent village of the north, the people there are Human and mainly Orthodox

Ovoo: a Khitan rock shrine, usually with blue objects around it

Pack-hunter: a genus of velociraptors that is found through most of Vhast

Panic: the smaller moon of Vhast, less than half the size of Terror

Paradēśī: a Hindi word for a foreigner

Paul, Saint: a Christian Saint, Feast Day 7th December, his patronage is to evangelism

Pavitra Phāṭaka: also known as Sacred Gate and Chulün arlüd, it is the capital of Sharan or Haven

Perissótero: a suffix to a Darkreach military rank, it means 'senior'

Ploi_gós: a term used in Darkreach as the job title for a harbour pilot

Praetor: a Darkreach junior officer, there are several grades

Presbytera: the title of a wife of an Orthodox priest or Metropolitan

Primus: a Darkreach rank, roughly a corporal

Puleleiite: an Olelo word which means 'ruler who can tell the future', they are the navigators of the ships and villages

Purroloo: a small flying reptile that can breathe fire, elsewhere known as a Fire Lizard

Putevaya Tochka Kamen: Waypoint Rock, the most north-easterly point of Darkreach, a long reef of several small islands, the furthest out has a lighthouse on it

Rainjig: a very small village in the south-east of the Swamp

Rangers: what passes for a military in the village of Wolfneck, they are scouts and hunters more than anything else and they fight from cover with bows if forced to fight

Remembrance Day: a solemn Darkreach day when the loss of the parts of the Empire that are west of the mountains is mourned, this includes Wolfneck

Requiem: the Mass for the Dead

Rhastaputra River: the main river draining the mountains and area just to the west of them in the south

River Dragon: a much-enchanted brigantine owned by the Mice, it has Olympias as a Captain

Rongo: a Sea-Nomad ship

Rongomaiwhenua: the Kanaka mother Goddess

Sacred Gate: see Pavitra Phāṭaka

Sea Nomad (Kanaka): a race of people who live on floating pelagic villages and rarely see land

Sea mile: 1,000 fathoms or 1,830m

Seax: a knife or sometimes short sword with a straight blade and a strong back that reaches a point and then slopes quickly to a point

Sebastian, Saint: a Christian Saint, Feast Day is 18th December, he is the patron of archers

Seòlaid: the village of the Shaelkie on Covington

Sh-hone: a silky and sturdy cloth made from retted seaweed

Shaelkie: one of the Hidden races, also known as the Merrow, skin-changers who change into the form of a sea-lion

Shànji de Jùnshi: a Chin rank, roughly that of a sergeant-major

Sharan: see Haven

Shénshèng Bìhù (Divine Refuge): capital of the Chin realm

Shing-Zu: a race of extremely long-lived off-worlders who built Vhast as an experiment

Shunned Isle: also called Durham Rock or Arnflorst (its original name as a city), it is the furthest north of the chain of three islands running up from the Northern Mountains

Simon, Saint: an Orthodox Saint, Feast Day is 15th Quinque, he is the patron of mages

Sixth Tagma Day: a general remembrance day in Darkreach for those who have died in battle for the Empire, it is a solemn day of contemplation

Skrice: the only large village on Neron Island

Sleepwell: a forest tree that can be made into a potion that acts as if the drinker has had a night's sleep, it is quite addictive

South-West Mountains: the only real hills in the west of The Land and home to Dwarven villages

Southpoint: the southernmost town in Darkreach

Spilk: a silk-like cloth made from the webs of certain spiders

Spirit Man: in the Desert Realm the use of magic is divided by gender with men using Fire and Air and women using Earth and Water

Sslan'osslii (Great Thinking Folk): the ruling race of the Sslan'ssisswani

Sslan'slin (Folk talk): the language of the Sslan'ssisswani

Sslan'ssilissi (Great Folk): the largest of the Sslan'ssisswani races

Sslan'ssisswani (Several Folk): a Kingdom of lizard folk from the Long Realm

Sslan'ssossi (Least Folk): the smallest race of the Sslan'ssisswani

Starşiyrang: roughly a Sergeant or Warrant Officer in Darkspeech, there are several grades in Darkreach

Sthānēy Ghāt (Local Wharf): this is where much of the internal Havenite trade docks (including vessels delivering goods to Merchant's Island)

Strategos: a Darkreach military rank, it roughly equates to a General or an Admiral

Sudra: the Hindu caste of labourers and workers, which includes merchants and most of the profitable crafts

Sūn Wùkōng: otherwise known as the Monkey King, celestial messenger and God of mischief, his birthday is celebrated on 16th October

Swamp, The: the common name for the Confederation of the Free

Sweetwater: both the name of a town and the County around it in the New Found Land

Śikşaka: a teacher, particularly of weapons

Tabuaeran: a Sea-Nomad island-village

Tagma: a Darkreach Army unit, roughly equivalent to a division

Tai'fun: the Chin name for a great storm

Tarot: the Tarot of Vhast is different to that of Terra, it should be available soon in a printed set

Teresa of the Roses, Saint: Orthodox Saint, Feast Day 1st October, she is the patron of the Lake Erave area and of rose growers

Terror: the larger moon of Vhast, it provides far more light than Panic

Tolkovaniye: a Darkspeech word meaning a prognostication or a reading of the future

Tor Karoso: a very tall mountain on the island of Gil-Gand-Rask

Trekvarna: the second largest city in Freehold

Tribune: a Darkreach military rank, In the normal Army they would be in charge of several thousand soldiers

Tuán: can be thought of as a Chin Regiment of 5,320 footsoldiers

Tuman: a large grouping of Khitan, usually ten of them make up a Clan

Tupai: a Sea-Nomad village-island

Uaumi: a marine lizard, a plesiosaur

Ugrakden çok kabilu: (frequented place of many tribes) see Newfoundland

Ulithi: a Sea-Nomad village-island

Up Helly Aa: a Wolfneck festival held at mid-Winter featuring a burning boat

Varvady: a Darkspeech word that roughly means barbarians, it applies to all of those who live west of the Great Range

Vēśyā: one Hindi word for a prostitute

Vindur-skefi: a Darkspeech phrase, 'Wind-strider' and the name of a Drakkar

Vyāpārī Dvīpa: "Merchant's Island", where much of the commerce of Pavitra Phāṭaka happens and home to many tradesmen and shops as well as permanent markets

Week: each week on Vhast has six days. Generally, across The Land, these are given the names: Firstday, Deutera, Pali, Tetarti, Dithlau and Krondag. Kron is the name given to the sun. The definitions and roots of some of these names are unknown.

Winifred, Saint: a Christian Saint, Feast Day 19th Primus, one of the patrons of healing

Wolfneck: a village of Insakharl in the north of The Land, to Darkreach it used to be Northern Darkreach and is now the Lost Lands, it is the original home to Astrid

Xenodokheion: Darkreach Greek for guest quarters

Yōnī: female genitals or their representation

Yǔnshí: a Chin word that means a meteorite

Zhōuzhǎng: a Chin word that approximately means Governor

Zim Island: an island in the south that is completely covered in an unnamed ruined city, it has dense jungle between its buildings and Kraken Weed around it

Zim-Gand: the name of a city of the Eldar destroyed in a war nearly 9,000 years ago, all that is left of it are the twisted ruins of Zim Island

Zǔxiān Shén: the Ancestor Gods, what the Chin refer to as the Adversaries

Cast

Adara verch Glynis: junior wife of Stefan and lover of her co-wife Bryony, they are both from Rising Mud

Aella Sgoura: a married woman from Ardlark who belongs to the Antikataskopeía and wants to settle down and start a family, she and her husband Elias come to work in Haven

Aigiarn (Chamaku Aigiarn Mori): originally of the Lion Clan, marries Hulagu, sister-wife of Ayesha and Alaine

Aikaterine: daughter of Theodora and Rani (courtesy of Rani's unknowing brother)

Alaine (Batbayar Alaine Mori): late of the Eagle clan, marries Hulagu, sister-wife of Ayesha and Aigairn

Anahita (or Vachir Anahita Mori): Hulagu's former köle, she is the mother of Būrãn and Baul, becomes one of the Clan of the Horse and marries Dobun along with Kãhina

Anastasia: adopted daughter of Guy and Maximilian, an abandoned orphan from Sacred Gate, sister of Lazarus

Anne: the new name of one of the prostitutes rescued from Warkworth, now a sailor on the River Dragon, one of the Saints and eventually wife of Marianus

Aphra Jenkin: an experienced militia cadre from Outville and leader of a company of spears and bows in the Army of the North, there is more about her in the story *Rousing*

Ariadne Nepina: an Insakharl (part Alat-kharl) from Antdrudge. She is partly trained as an engineer but wanted a quieter life as a brick and tile maker and layer after her parents are killed in an accident. She moves to Mousehole and marries the Hob Krukurb. Their daughter is Nikê.

Arthur Garden: farmer and youngest son (of four) from Evilhalt, he comes to Mousehole seeking land and a wife and ends up marrying Make

Asticus Tzimisces: one of three kataphractoi (heavy cavalry) from Darkreach who comes to join Mousehole and marries Zoë

Astrid the Cat: an Insakharl girl from Wolfneck, she is married to Basil and co-wife to Ia and eventually Sin, as well, her youngest brother is Father Thorstein, she is known as Mathanharfead to the Inuit and becomes Rongomaiwhenua (the earth mother) to the Kanaka, in Darkreach she becomes known as Lyubimyy iz Hrothnog

Atã ibn Rãfi: a widower from Mistledross, a timber-feller, becomes the husband of Umm and Zafirah

Ayesha bint Hãritha: an ghazi of the Caliphate assigned by a Princess to guard Theodora. She is a minor daughter of Hãritha, the Sheik of Yãqũsa. She eventually marries Hulagu as his senior wife.

Azarzushnes: a soldier of Ērãnshahr and a follower of Ahriman

Aziz (Azizsevgili or Brave Lover): a Hobgoblin captured during an attack on Mousehole, he falls in love with Verily and converts to the Orthodox faith and marries her, and then becomes a priest

Balashankar VI Choudrey: Maharajah of Sharan 3,234 years ago, he was one of the rulers who invaded Darkreach and died there. See *The Stand of the Eighth Etraria*

Basil Akritas or Kutsulbalik: an Insakharl and Tribune of the Antikataskopeía, he is married to Astrid, Ia and (eventually) Sin and assigned to guard Theodora by Hrothnog, as well his sister is Olympia

Bebin: a witch and shape-shifter of the Bear Folk, wife of Calgacus

Berenike: daughter of Father Thorstein and Kalliope, sister of Iris

Bianca Palama: a foundling from Trekvarna now living in Mousehole and married to Bishop Christopher

Bilqĩs: a former slave and apprentice mage with some ability as a glassblower, marries Tãriq

Bridget: the new name of one of the prostitutes rescued from Warkworth, now a sailor on the River Dragon, one of the Saints and eventually a wife of Marianus

Bryony verch Dafydd: senior wife of Stefan and lover of her co-wife and cousin Adara, they are both from Rising Mud

Calgacus: Chief Magister (leader) of the Bear Folk, a shaman and shape-shifter, his wife is Bebin

Candidas: an animal handler for Carausiu, he is also a member of the Antikataskopeía and husband of Theodora Lígo

Carausius Holobolus: a Darkreach trader in fabric, spices or anything else, his guards are Karas and Festus, his animal handler is Candidas, his wife is Theodora and his daughter is Theodora Lígo

Cathal: the Magister (leader) of the Bear-folk village of Birchdingle, he is a shaman and shape-shifter

Catherine: the new name of one of the prostitutes rescued from Warkworth, now a sailor on the River Dragon, one of the Saints and eventually a wife of Marianus

Cecilia: the new name of one of the prostitutes rescued from Warkworth, now a sailor on the River Dragon, one of the Saints and eventually a wife of Marianus

Christopher Palamas, Bishop: suffragan Bishop of the Mountains and husband of Bianca, he is a very holy but diplomatic man and a dedicated healer

Clarence Garlin: a mage on the *Meander Rose*, a Freehold galleon, heir of the Barony of Epibarti, and a Gryphon, he appears in several novellas starting with *A Tenuous Grasp*

Cnut Stonecleaver: Dwarven Baron of town of North Keep

Cosmas Camaterus: the Metropolitan of the Orthodox Church for the south-east of The Land west of the mountains (from Evilhalt and including Haven and the Swamp), he is based in Erave Town

Danelis Alvarez: a former slave with grey hair from Warkworth, she now lives in Mousehole and marries Father Simeon

Dar Lagrange: a very ancient writer who wrote a book entitled *Speculations on the Nature of the Physical and Non-Physical Worlds*, discussing astronomy and Newtonian physics, among other things

David Granger: a wealthy farmer and Mayor of Outville

Defiant Shark of the family Xié: his name is Xié Tiǎoxìn Shāyú, but the device mistranslated this, he is a Shànji de Jùnshi and banner bearer of the Chin

Denizkartal (Sea Eagle): a Boyuk-kharl and Olympias's bosun on the River Dragon and her husband

Denny Pollard: a young shearer from Ooshz who travels to Mousehole and marries both Lamentations and Pass

Dharmal: a Dwarf and leader of the brigands who attack Bianca's caravan in *Intimations of Evil*, he ruled Mousehole and acted as a major servant of the Masters

Dionysios Kydones: a farmer from Darkreach who moves to Mousehole

Dobun (Tömörbaatar Dobun Mori): late of the Axe-beaks, becomes shaman of the Horse and marries Anahita and Kāhina

Ele'ele: a young apprentice bard of the Sea Nomads, originally from Moorea, now on Tabuaeran

Eleanor Fournier: caravan guard from Topwin in Freehold, then a slave in Mousehole, and works as a jeweller, married to Robin Fletcher

Elias Sgouros: married man from Ardlark who belongs to the Antikataskopeía and wants to settle down and start a family, he and his wife Aella come to work in Haven

Elias Tobias: the Baron of Didymoteichon in the Newfoundland

Erika Whittaker: girl from Warkworth. She marries Nadia and becomes an assistant to Kaliope.

Eshwardutt (Gift of God) Rai: Rani's father

Eustathius Manousakis, Father: a priest from Erave Town assigned to the new church in Pavitra Phāṭaka

Faatina (Captivating): the wife of Mullah Sharĩk ibn Ishãq and a bookkeeper

Fear (more fully Fear the Lord Your God Thatcher): she is the adopted daughter of Rani and Theodora and can communicate with the unborn

Festus: an Insakharl guard for Carausius

Figel ap Machute: former guard captain in Caer Gwyliwr Ddwyrain (Eastguard Tower), he flees rather than face Astrid in combat

Fluff-Ball: a hill cat and "familiar" for Astrid

Fortunata: a former slave and a dressmaker, becomes an apprentice mage and co-wife to Norbert with Sajāh

Franciscus: murdered Benedictine Abbot from Sweetwater

Galla Narchina: an Insakharl sailor and sailmaker/carpenter on the crew of the River Dragon, she is married to Gundardasc

Gamil: one of the Shing-Zu and Chief Predestinator on the Vhast project, she sets in motion the events described here

Geir: a Dwarven druid from North Hole

Giles Ploughman: former slave and farmer at Mousehole, married to Naeve

Glad: name by which We Declare Unto You Glad Tidings is known. She is a former Brotherhood slave girl who becomes Christopher's clerk.

Goditha Mason: former slave from Jewvanda, she is sister to Robin Fletcher and married to Parminder, the mason of Mousehole, and an Earth mage.

Granther: a term used in the Darkreach Imperial family to describe an older relative, "The Granther" is always Hrothnog

Guk or Gukludaashiyicisi (strong carrier): a mature hobgoblin of the Cenubar-kincilari and a carter around their tribe, he becomes their first trader to the Dwarves and decides to call himself Guk outside of Dhargev

Gundardasc Narches: a Kichic-kharl cook and sailor on the River Dragon in Southpoint, his wife is Galla

Gurinder: 13 year old girl, sister of Parminder, and apprentice Fire mage

Guy Rossignol: a refugee from Freehold and partner of Maximilian, he is the third son of the Duke of Trekvarna

Hand: in full I Lift Up My Hand to Heaven, a Brotherhood slave freed at One Tree Hill. She becomes an apprentice Earth mage and an assistant to Naeve and Goditha.

Harald Pitt: former slave at Mousehole, raised among Dwarves, he is a miner and marries Lakshmi

Harnermêŝ: (Har-ner-meess): a young man from Gil-Gand-Rask, who becomes Jennifer's lover and joins the River Dragon, their daughter is named Goditha Atalante

Haytor: a Hob who has campaigned with the Mice and now works for Guk

Hilarion Chalintzes, Father: a priest from Erave Town who goes to Sacred Gate as a priest.

Hopo: a Sea Nomad on Tabuaeran, second wife of Taine and sister-wife of Wiki

Hrolfr Strongarm: Dwarven Baron of Oldike and father of Ragnilde

Hrothnog: the immortal God-King of Darkreach and great-great-grandfather of Theodora who is now married to Fātima, he is, or was, a Daveen, known to some as the Renegade, he was once known as Hraathnaag

Hulagu (Togotak Hulagu Mori): A young Khitan, part of Mousehole and Tar-Khan of the re-born Clan of the Horse (Mori), married to Ayesha, Aigiarn, and Alaine

Ia verch Brica: a young and very beautiful Wiccan priestess from Rising Mud, she has a familiar raccoon called Maeve, marries Basil and is sister-wife to Astrid who calls her Butterfly

Iris: daughter of Father Thorstein and Kalliope, sister of Berenike

Jennifer Wagg: young woman, guard and sailor, from Deeryas, rescued from the Pavitra Phāṭaka where she was brought as a sacrifice, marries Harnermêŝ

Jillian: a prostitute from the New Found Land rescued from the Meander Rose but whose soul is nearly lost to the Adversaries

Justin Speller: mage of Bidvictor, he is nearly as powerful as Rani and a Water mage

Kãhina (or Bodonchar Kãhina Mori): Hulagu's köle and mother of Khãtun & Yesugai, becomes one of the Clan of the Horse and marries Dobun along with Anahita

Kalliope (Beautiful Voice): the name taken by In Flaming Fire Take Vengeance On Them That Know Not God when she is baptised, the young widow of a Brotherhood priest taken captive at Peace Tower and brought back to Mousehole who marries Father Thorstein, their twin children are Berenike and Iris

Karas: an Insakharl guard for Carausius

Karl Tostison: Astrid and Thorstein's oldest brother

Kassiopeia, Empress: founder of the Imperial Midwifery Service, she appears in the story *The Stand of the Eighth Etraria*

Krukurb (Strong Frog): one of the Hobs who join the Mice for the campaign in the North, marries Ariadne

Kundan (Purified Gold) Rai: Rani's brother and the biological father of Aikaterine

Lakshmi Pitt: a former Havenite, she has converted and is now Orthodox and married to Harald, she is the apothecary and midwife for Mousehole

Lamentations: a slave girl from the Brotherhood and sister-wife to Pass, she was originally known as There Shall Be Lamentations

Lazarus: adopted son of Guy and Maximilian, an abandoned orphan from Sacred Gate, brother of Anastasia

Lãdi al Yarmũk: Former slave from the Caliphate, she is the chief cook at Mousehole and very skilled. She marries Nathanael

Leo Stacey, Abbot: a Benedictine Abbot, uncle of the Count of Sweetwater, and a Gryphon

Libanius Monomakhos: a farmer from Darkreach who moves to Mousehole

Little Seeker: the only one of the Sslan'ssisswani to survive the Battle of Arnflost

Luó Tiãnshàng Mĕidé (Heavenly Virtue of the Luó Dynsasty): Emperor of the Chin

Maarshtrin: one of the Adversaries, he is killed at Ta'if

Maeve: a raccoon and familiar of Ia

Mangana: a Spirit Man from the Desert World who was tricked into working for the Adversaries

Mardrikrat: a Kichic-kharl Primus and druid of the Church of the Living God from Cold Keep

Maria Beman: a kidnapped woman from Greensin, brought to Mousehole by slavers after it was freed. She is now learning to be a Fire mage and marries Menas

Marianus Gerontas (Marianus the Old): a forty-year-old Starşiyrang of the Antikataskopeía who retires and comes to Mousehole, he joins the River Dragon and marries the Saints (Anne, Bridgit, Catherine, Cecilia, Mary and Winifred)

Mary: the new name of one of the prostitutes rescued from Warkworth, now a sailor on the River Dragon, one of the Saints and eventually a wife of Marianus

Mathanharfead: see Astrid

Maximilian Keep: a refugee from Rubi in Freehold and partner of Guy

Mele: a Water mage of the island-village of Tabuaeran

Memrin do Levtidy: Froúrarchos (garrison commander) at Cold Keep, she is a Praetor Perissótero

Menas Philokales: one of three kataphractoi (heavy cavalry) from Darkreach who comes to join Mousehole, he marries Maria

Michael: a Praetor or leader in the Basilica Anthropoi

Nacibdamiir: the young and unexpected Hobgoblin chief of the Cenubarkincilari

Nadia Everett: a girl from Warkworth, she marries Erika and becomes a mason.

Naeve Milker: former slave who now runs the herds of Mousehole, becomes an apprentice mage and marries Giles

Nathanael Ktenas: an Orthodox pastrycook from Ardlark who comes to Mousehole for Lãdi

Neon Chrysoloras: one of three kataphractoi (heavy cavalry) from Darkreach who comes to join Mousehole and marries Tabitha

Nikephorus Cheilas: a senior Palace servant from Ardlark, he is now married to Valeria

Norbert Black: a skilled blacksmith, weapons smith and armourer kept as a slave in Mousehole, he marries both Fortunata and Sajãh

Olympias Akritina: Basil's sister who becomes Captain of the River Dragon and a Darkreach Epilarch (small-unit commander) in charge of all Darkreach vessels beyond the Great Range, she marries Denizkartal

Panterius Lydas: the Strategos or General of Darkreach Intelligence (the Antikataskopeía)

Parminder: assistant cook and sometimes dressmaker at Mousehole, she marries Goditha and is sister to Gurinder, becomes an apprentice mage, and is a xeno-telepath.

Pass: a slave girl from the Brotherhood and sister-wife of Lamentations, in full It Shall Come To Pass

Procopia Ampelina: a Praetor of the Antikataskopeía in Ardlark and former commander of Basil

Puleleiite (ruler who can tell the future): name-title of the navigator of a Sea Nomad island-village or ship, several are mentioned in the story, they will often be named as the island-village or ship they are from

Ragnilde Hrolfrssen: the eldest child of Baron Hrolfr Strongarm of Oldike and betrothed of Thord

Rahki Johar: a Harijani servant from Haven, she was rescued from the Master's servants in Pavitra Phāṭaka and joins the Mice. She becomes a factor in their settlement back in her home

Rani Rai: a former Havenite Battle Mage and now co-Princess of Mousehole, she has broken caste and is married to Theodora, has adopted Fear, and is regarded as the father of Aikaterine

Rāfi: a ghazi captured when Adara was captured

Renegade: see Hrothnog

Robin Fletcher: former slave, fletcher and bowyer for Mousehole, married to Eleanor and they have adopted several children, he is the brother of Goditha

Rongomaiwhenua: see Astrid

Roxanna Black: adopted daughter of Norbert, Sajāh, and Fortunata, probable full sister of Ruhayma

Ruhayma Black: adopted daughter of Norbert, Sajāh, and Fortunata, probable full sister of Roxanna

Ruth Hawker: a former Freehold merchant, slave, and now teacher of the village children in Mousehole, she is married to Father Theodule

Sajāh bint Javed: former slave and now Seneschal of Mousehole under the Princesses, wife of Norbert with Fortunata

Sayf abd Allah: a ghazi sent to investigate Mousehole

Sharîk ibn Ishāq: Mullah who comes from Darkreach for Sacred Gate and husband of Faatina

Shilpa Sodaagar: Former Havenite trader and slave and now supercargo on the *River Dragon* for Mousehole. She takes Vishal as her partner.

Siglunda the Wise: a mage and midwife, Captain (village leader) of Wolfneck

Simeon, Father: Catholic cleric and werewolf who is born in Xanthia in the New Found Land, he ends up in Mousehole, passing through the Bear Folk, converts to being Orthodox and marries Danelis

Sin: more fully They Shall Confess Their Sin, a former Brotherhood slave girl, she becomes the domestic and child minder for Astrid and Basil and later marries into the family

Sìle: the leader of the Shaelkie in Seòlaid on Covington

Solveig Dagnesdottir: an entertainer from Wolfneck

Stefan: originally from Evilhalt, he is now in charge of the militia of Mousehole and is married to Bryony and her cousin Adara, he is also a leatherworker and has gained a reputation as a General in the north

Stefano of Erave: a student at the Mousehole school from Erave Town

Tabitha Chrysolora: born in a farming hamlet near Erave Town and a former slave, she now lives in Mousehole as an assistant carpenter and cook, she has one green eye and one blue one. She marries Neon

Taine: a Sea Nomad and leader of the men on Tabuaeran, husband of Wiki and Hopo

Tanushri (Beautiful) Rai: Rani's mother

Tarakratz: a Kichic-kharl Starşiyrang from Cold Keep

Tãriq ibn Kasîla: a quarryman from Silentochre, becomes husband of Bilqîs and Yumn

Theodora do Hrothnog: a great-great-granddaughter of Hrothnog, she is not entirely human, a mage and, at 120 years, is far older than the late teens that she appears to have, she is now Princess of Mousehole with her husband, Rani, their adopted daughter Fear, and daughter Aikaterine

Theodora Lígo: daughter of Carausius and wife of Candidas

Theodule Panaretos, Father: a former monk and now assistant to Bishop Christopher at Mousehole, he is married to Ruth

Thord Arnorson: a short and broad humanoid of the species locally known as a Dwarf, he comes from Kharlsbane in the Northern Mountains, but is now Mousehole's Ambassador to the Dwarves, he is known as the Crown-finder to the Dwarves, and is engaged to Ragnilde.

Thorn: mistress of the Duke of the New Found Land, she is first seen in the novella *Octavius Ruge's Ride*

Thorstein Tostisson, Father: priest and youngest brother of Astrid, he marries Kalliope and their twin daughters are Berenike and Iris

Tiffany Darilec: a student at the Mousehole school from Evilhalt

Toppuddle: A major town in Freehold near the South-West Mountains, its Count was killed by the Mice

Ubãda: a ghazi captured during the attempt to capture Adara

Umm bint Wã'il: Slave of the bandits from a poor farming family in the Caliphate, she is now a spinner and weaver in Mousehole and helps in the kitchen. She is now the senior wife of Atã

Ursula: the nurse of Virginia Norbery, she was also taken captive from the *Goldentide*

Usha (the dawn) Rai: Rani's grandmother, a powerful seer

Valeria: former slave, now the servant of Rani and Theodora, has married Nikephorus

Verily (Verily I Rejoice In The Lord Tiller): a former Brotherhood slave and a slave in Mousehole, now an apprentice mage in Mousehole, she can 'smell' magic and has married Aziz

Virginia Norbery: the second daughter of the Duke of the New Found Land, taken captive with the sinking of the *Goldentide*

Vishal Kapur: a young armsman from Haven, he is captured, joins the Mice, and is then taken as a partner by Shilpa

Wiki: a Sea Nomad and leader of the women on Tabuaeran, wife of Taine and sister-wife of Hopo

Winifred: the new name of one of the prostitutes rescued from Warkworth, now a sailor on the *River Dragon*, one of the Saints and eventually a wife of Marianus

Xú Zílì Lóng (Upright Dragon of the family Xú): Zhōuzhăng or Governor of Dàhé Zhèn in the Long Realm

Yabaribaykus ogulin Tatlikayisia: a Goblin freed from the Goldentide, his name means 'Wild Owl, son of Tasty Apricot' (his mother's name), he is from the Guneydeolan Halksulutoprak tribe in the south of the area

Yumn: an orphan carpet maker from Ardlark who became a prostitute, becomes junior wife to Tãriq

Zafirah: a poor spinner and weaver from Ardlark who sells herself into slavery to pay the family debts, she marries Atã as his junior wife

Zampea Gounara: an Imperial messenger

Zeenat Koirala: a Harijani and former prostitute from Haven, rescued and brought to Mousehole, she becomes a factor in their settlement back in her home

Zoë Anicia: an Orthodox baker from Mistledross. She loses her family in an earthquake and ends up in Mousehole married to Asticus

Zumruud: more fully Zumruudejedehar (Emerald Dragon), a Hobgoblin and third daughter of Guk, she is a a student at the school